THE
SHROUDED
QUEEN

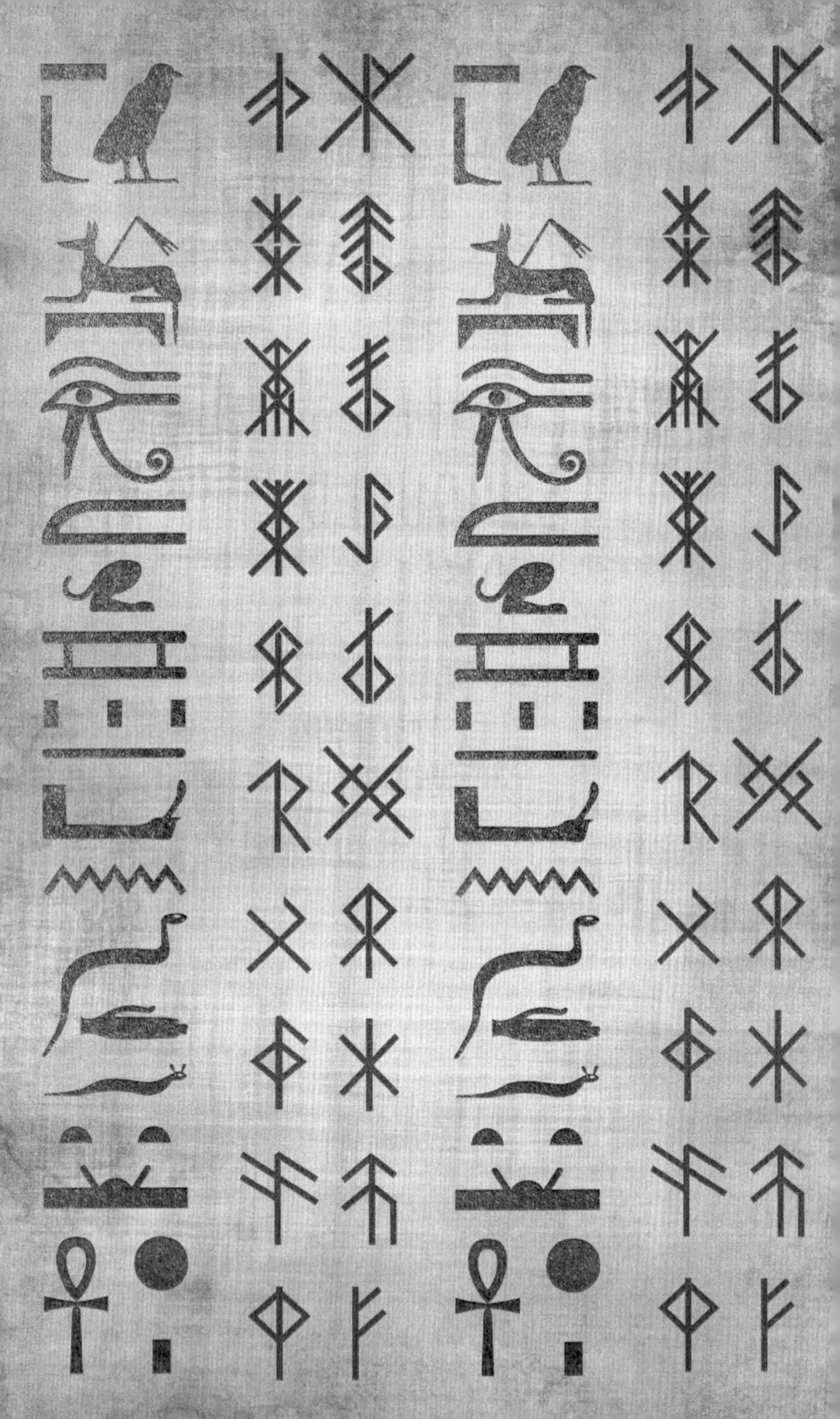

THE SHROUDED QUEEN

ASHLEY TROPEA

GALLERY BOOKS

New York Amsterdam/Antwerp London
Toronto Sydney/Melbourne New Delhi

G

Gallery Books
An Imprint of Simon & Schuster, LLC
1230 Avenue of the Americas
New York, NY 10020

For more than 100 years, Simon & Schuster has championed authors and the stories they create. By respecting the copyright of an author's intellectual property, you enable Simon & Schuster and the author to continue publishing exceptional books for years to come. We thank you for supporting the author's copyright by purchasing an authorized edition of this book.

No amount of this book may be reproduced or stored in any format, nor may it be uploaded to any website, database, language-learning model, or other repository, retrieval, or artificial intelligence system without express permission. All rights reserved. Inquiries may be directed to Simon & Schuster, 1230 Avenue of the Americas, New York, NY 10020 or permissions@simonandschuster.com.

This book is a work of fiction. Any references to historical events, real people, or real places are used fictitiously. Other names, characters, places, and events are products of the author's imagination, and any resemblance to actual events or places or persons, living or dead, is entirely coincidental.

First Gallery Books trade paperback edition June 2026

GALLERY BOOKS and colophon are registered trademarks of Simon & Schuster, LLC

Simon & Schuster strongly believes in freedom of expression and stands against censorship in all its forms. For more information, visit BooksBelong.com.

For information about special discounts for bulk purchases, please contact Simon & Schuster Special Sales at 1-866-506-1949 or business@simonandschuster.com.

The Simon & Schuster Speakers Bureau can bring authors to your live event. For more information or to book an event, contact the Simon & Schuster Speakers Bureau at 1-866-248-3049 or visit our website at www.simonspeakers.com.

Interior design by Jaime Putorti

Manufactured in China

10 9 8 7 6 5 4 3 2 1

The Library of Congress Control Number has been applied for.

ISBN 978-1-6680-9621-5
ISBN 978-1-6680-9622-2 (ebook)

Let's stay in touch! Scan here to get book recommendations, exclusive offers, and more delivered to your inbox.

For my Egyptian grandparents, who have filled my heart with love for where we've come from and who we were. I know you think magic is silly, but you are both magical to me.

ONE

ᴧᴧᴧᴧᴧᴧᴧ

SAMIRA

Don't trip, don't trip, don't trip.

I clutched the tray of food tightly in my hands as I wove through the labyrinth of the palace, keeping my eyes trained on the ground. With each step I took, with each rattle of the gold-trimmed plates and silver chalice, my heart gave a fearful kick in my chest.

My princess had asked me personally to fetch her midnight snack. To be addressed by her, to be offered such an important responsibility, was an honor I never thought I'd receive. I held the golden tray in my sweaty hands and stared at every groove in the limestone floor with paranoia.

My back was still tender from the last time I'd failed my princess—showing up to her rooms with a stain on the thin linen dress that was my uniform—and I'd be damned to the Underworld's Trench before I let her down again.

Two guards came around the corner, and I quickly ducked into one of the many divots in the wall created for the exact purpose of making sure slaves could get out of the way.

I moved too fast. My heart stopped beating as the chalice of water tipped. If it spilled, I'd get so much more than a whipping. There was such little water in Ashorah, the gods would surely strike me down if I allowed a *cupful* to splash across the ground.

But then the chalice settled, only a trickle of water falling over the lip. I swiped it away with my finger, pushed a wayward grape back in place, and was able to breathe again.

As the guards came closer, I bowed my head and sank farther into the shadows of the divot, pressing my back into the warm stone wall and biting my lip as my cheap linen shift scratched the barely healed lash wounds.

They hardly spared me a passing glance, and I let out a sigh of relief before I scurried down the hall, grateful that the several hanging lanterns hadn't yet been doused.

Shadows flickered against the alabaster walls, illuminating the various hieroglyphs etched into them. Flashes of blue and sunshine yellow. The history of Ashorah etched with an expert artist's hand. I passed scenes of war, the blood spatter made beautiful by inlaid rubies. Various Gods-Chosens—half-human, half-god heroes—stood tall and proud throughout the centuries, and in the dim light, King Zaid's usually serene smile looked cruel. The emeralds used for his bright green eyes sparkled dangerously.

I shook my head, cursing myself for even remotely thinking such a thing. My king was not cruel. My king had sacrificed everything for us. I lowered my head and quickened my steps.

My sandaled feet padded noiselessly along the floor until I reached the golden doors that led to my princess's suite. One of the two stationed guards opened them for me.

Tabia, a slave who had been at the palace nearly twice as long as I had, greeted me. Her brown eyes drooped at the corners from the late hour, and the edges of her lips were pinched. My heart rate hitched. Something must have happened while I was gone. Maybe I'd taken too long. Maybe I'd angered my princess.

Maids weren't permitted to speak unless spoken to, but the fact that she was standing at the door instead of fanning our princess spoke volumes. I tried to ask her with my eyes what was wrong. Tabia just shook her head and stepped aside, ushering me in.

My princess's rooms were meant to awe. Vibrant colors filled the space, curtains and pillows and lanterns of bright pinks and greens created a kaleidoscope of beauty. The walls were painted with real gold, stretching high above my head where they met a ceiling with an image of an oasis painted on it.

My princess was sitting on her desk, feet crossed at the ankles and swinging idly back and forth, still fully dressed despite the late hour.

Princess Amunet Khada was beautiful in the way that all the royals were. Bright green eyes shone out of smooth tan skin, a slender nose above full lips. Though all the royals shaved their heads, Princess Amunet always wore intricate wigs, deep black and twisted in elaborate braids. Pearls dusted both her wig and her silken red gown. It was a new dress, gifted to her by one of the four jinn-descended princes of the nearby regions hoping to win her hand.

A useless gesture. It didn't matter if the princes had a jinni ancestor centuries ago. My princess would not marry. She didn't need to. Not when she was Gods-Chosen.

Usually, I was eager to drink in the sight of my princess. As her maid, I was one of the few who had the honor of being able to look upon an actual child of a god, and I tried to take advantage of every second. But tonight, my eyes slipped off Princess Amunet to land on the drenched young girl standing before her.

Her name was Nailah. A scullery maid I'd glimpsed a few times in the kitchen, almost fourteen years old. Her ear-length hair hung around her in a soaked mop, and her sopping linen dress clung to her trembling, bony frame.

Princess Amunet looked up at me, and a wide smile broke across her face, lighting up the entire room. I felt my own lips twitch to match the expression even as my eyes darted to the girl in front of her. "Excellent!" my princess said, and hopped down to her feet. "Set it here."

Nailah dared to glance up at me, her large brown eyes pleading. I quickly looked away and set the tray on the desk. If Nailah had done something to upset my princess, there was nothing I could do. There was nothing any of us could do. We all learned that within our first year at the palace. If the lesson had somehow missed her, she was going to learn it now.

As soon as the tray was out of my hands, I retreated to my spot in line with the other maids standing against the wall and assumed the default posture—hands clasped in front of me and head down. But I peeked up to see Tabia across the room. She fanned our princess with a long palm leaf, fighting against the oppressive heat that even this late at night hadn't let up. She did her best to keep her expression blank, but years of reading her face told me the glint in her eyes was one of worry.

Princess Amunet rounded her desk and sat in the plush chair. She lifted the elaborate chalice of water from the tray and set it on the edge of the desk, directly in front of Nailah. She stared at the scullery maid expectantly. "Go on, then."

Nailah's clasped hands flexed as terror shone in her eyes. "I—I don't understand, my princess."

"You're thirsty. Here is water."

The scullery maid's gaze moved from the cup to the royal, the *drip, drip, drip* of her clothes going off like drums in the nearly silent room. "I'm not thirsty," she answered, voice small. "It gets so hot in the kitchens, my princess. I just wanted to cool down. I didn't drink from the river, only swam in it, I swear."

Princess Amunet nodded as she tore off a piece of bread and chewed contemplatively, not taking her eyes off Nailah.

The heat in the kitchens did grow to nearly unbearable conditions. Just the short amount of time I'd spent there gathering my princess's snack had been enough to make sweat coat my entire body, and the natural Ashoran heat didn't help matters.

My princess pointed at the chalice of water. "The Lotus River sustains every single person in Ashorah. It is blessed by my father, Shaya." My whole body reacted to the mention of the Underworld god. I stiffened my spine against it as my princess went on. "It is not your bathing tub. It is sacred. And you thought you would just . . . swim in it."

In a tiny voice, Nailah said, "It was only five minutes."

Stupid, stupid girl. My stomach twisted in knots as I mentally braced myself.

Everyone knew the strict rules about using and rationing water. Just sneaking a single extra glass of it from the kitchens led to my princess carving an X over my heart in punishment, a mirror of the injury I'd inflicted on the gods with my insolence. I'd been forbidden from bandaging the wound, and it had gotten infected. Now it was a permanent scar on my chest, a constant reminder of my guilt and shame.

I deserved it.

And Nailah was about to get what she deserved, too.

Princess Amunet sighed. "You spit in the face of the gods and your own people."

The girl's eyes drifted closed in defeat.

Princess Amunet set the bread back on the tray and stood. Nailah's whole frame shook as the Gods-Chosen passed her and came to a stop beside her large brass bathing tub. Flower petals bobbed on the water's surface. My princess pointed to the floor beside her and ordered, "Kneel."

Nailah trembled harder as she obeyed, lowering herself so that her chest was parallel to the lip of the tub. I curled my fingers into my palms, resisting the instinct to speak or step forward. This might feel wrong, I reminded myself, but it was for the best. Nailah deserved her punishment as much as I had. It was the only way we'd learn.

Still, nausea built in the back of my throat.

"Five minutes, you said?" Princess Amunet confirmed.

Nailah nodded haltingly.

"That seems fair." Princess Amunet seized the back of her head and shoved her face into the water.

I steeled myself against my flinch.

Nailah didn't fight at first, accepting the Gods-Chosen's punishment. But that only lasted a few moments. Her instincts kicked in, and she splashed up water as she struggled violently, seeking air. Princess Amunet held her down, face blank, regal. She never looked malicious or unkind when carrying out punishments. She was a righteous goddess meting out justice.

Nailah's movements slowed. Princess Amunet yanked her out of the water. The girl drew in a deep gasp, sputtering, her hair sticking to her face.

"How long was that?" my princess asked.

Tabia replied, "Forty-five seconds, my princess."

Nailah tried, "Please—"

Princess Amunet dunked her back in the water. Even as it made my stomach turn over and my heart seize, I didn't look away. None of us did. We weren't allowed to.

I watched my princess bring the girl to the point of death over and over and then reel her back before she could fall over the edge. As horrible as it was, this was the exact reason all of Ashorah looked to the Gods-Chosen as our salvation.

I'd learned the story my first day in Khada Palace: In times of great strife, the gods smiled upon their people and sent a child of theirs to save us. And Ashorah—as well as the rest of the continent— was indeed desperate after centuries of drought. So desperate, in fact, that King Zaid had decided to brave the Wastelands in search of a legend.

No one ever survived the Wastelands, the terrain of dunes and mountains and blazing climate practically engineered to kill humans. But forty years ago, King Zaid had marched through it in pursuit of a forgotten city, buried beneath miles and miles of sand.

The Buried City was said to be a paradise on earth, where water flowed endlessly, where there was no famine or disease. A thing of myth.

King Zaid's advisors warned him that these myths were likely fabrications, either conjured by the northern enemy nation known as Kaldfold or spread by the freshly conquered jinn-descended princes.

Though the jinn-descended might have been powerful once, the current four princes didn't possess even a fraction of the strength their ancestors had, making their defeat an easy one, which they'd resented. And the cannibalistic, shape-shifting Kaldfolk were constantly encroaching on Ashoran territory, forcing us into war often. Neither were to be trusted.

Stories of the Buried City were meant to send the king on a journey, not to a divine water source but to an early grave.

But the Lotus River, the continent's last remaining water source, had almost entirely dried up. Everyone, from the farthest Ashoran village to Kaldfold in the north, relied on that river. Without it, petty squabbles among principalities and territory disputes with the Kaldfolk would be moot. *All* would perish.

So King Zaid had to try.

He'd gotten lost in the Wastelands, was near death, when he was approached by a pack of jinn—minions of Shaya, God of the Underworld, beings of sand and fire. They offered an end to Ashorah's drought and to the war with the cannibal Kaldfolk, and promised to return King Zaid safely home to a prosperous land.

In exchange, the king's firstborn would be Shaya's.

The king—delirious with dehydration and heatstroke—accepted without question.

When he returned home and told Queen Neema of the deal, she was appalled. Over the centuries, the other six gods had all borne half-human children, but Shaya was different. King of Death, Sire of Monsters. Queen Neema could not bear his spawn. A child of the Underworld would be too dangerous. Power over death wasn't a power any mortal creature should have.

Queen Neema ensured she would not have a child. Details on

just how are vague, but it is said she almost did not survive the process. Mutilation might have been involved.

It was decided that the crown would pass to the king's cousin,
Hamadi, and the succession would be settled without a direct
heir.

The Lotus River rushed with gallons and gallons of water, just
as the jinn had promised. The king promptly dammed it up and
claimed complete control over it.

Together, the King and Queen of Ashorah had outsmarted the
God of the Underworld.

But a deal with a jinni cannot be broken.

Nearly two decades later, the middle-aged queen fell pregnant.
Though she had been so very careful, so very smart, Shaya was
smarter. He wore the king's skin when he came to her. Neither she nor
the king were any the wiser until she missed her monthly bleeding.

The queen died during the birth, but my princess survived. King
Zaid's deal with the jinn was upheld. And in one month's time, my
princess would turn twenty, go through the Igniting, and receive the
full might of the Underworld.

She was one of us. Had lived nearly twenty years as a mortal.
She'd take care of us. She'd make hundreds of rivers flow and stop
death from snatching so many of us.

She was going to be our salvation.

"It's been five minutes, my princess," Tabia murmured.

Princess Amunet jerked Nailah's head out of the water for the
last time. The scullery maid gasped and choked, water exploding
out of her mouth and nose, strands of hair flung across her face like
blindfolds. Her limbs trembled from exertion, and her eyes rolled
in her head.

My princess gazed down at the scullery maid without emotion.
"You are forgiven."

Still heaving, the girl replied, "Th-thank you, my pr-princess."

"You may go." Princess Amunet turned away from the girl and

returned to her desk, where she picked up the water chalice and took a big gulp.

Nailah staggered to her feet, her face red and chest rising and falling erratically. I wanted to step forward and offer my arm for her to lean against, help her back to her room. But I didn't. I just stood with the other maids and watched her stumble out the door.

It was an honor to work in Khada Palace. We were luckier than most Ashorans. The rest of the kingdom—the *world*, really—battled drought daily, but here, I got a glass of water every two days. Plus, we would be the first to witness the Gods-Chosen's transformation. We would be by her side when she saved us all.

Some days it was more difficult to remember that than others.

"I want to sleep," my princess declared.

"Yes, my princess," we all murmured, and jumped to action, laying out her nightdress while slipping her out of her current gown and wig.

Tabia looked pointedly at me and then the tray of barely touched food, wordlessly ordering me to take it away. I mentally chastised myself for needing to be told and hurried to collect the tray.

For all my princess's claims of hunger, she'd hardly touched the pita bread and chicken.

It used to be torturous to watch her eat, even harder to see what she didn't. Leftovers went to the livestock. And at the end of the week, anything the livestock didn't touch came to us. It was a message. A reminder of our place in the palace.

My first week as a maid, my stomach had growled in response to all her food.

I'd received ten lashes.

I'd learned to control my stomach after that.

Though Princess Amunet didn't look at me, I curtsied before I left, taking the wide stone steps down to the servants' quarters two at a time. All maids were required around my princess's bed for Nightly Prayer. I wouldn't be late.

But when I turned the last corner to the kitchen, the smell hit my nose and stopped me dead in my tracks.

The kitchens always smelled good. Like garlic and paprika, mostly. But tonight, after the princess's midnight order, it smelled like bread. Gods, freshly baked bread.

I peeked around the corner. The kitchen was empty. Chef Nena must've gone to bed after handing me the tray. But the stone counters were still lightly dusted with leftover flour, and the large, curved oven's mouth lay open like a sob. I could just glimpse the dying embers inside, a tongue of slumbering fire. A warm breeze blew in through an open window and carried the smell from the oven all the way to me at the threshold.

I glanced down at the tray in my hands. The thin disk of bread was mostly untouched. Despite how hard I clenched my stomach, it let out a stubborn rumble. Thank the gods no one was around to hear it.

I hovered my hand over the bread but didn't dare touch it. Faint warmth rippled up to meet my palm. I imagined how soft it would feel, how delicious it would taste. I hadn't had fresh bread since Mama's birthday, before I was snatched off the street and brought to the palace. Sixteen years ago.

My eyes darted around the hallway. No servants. And the next round of guards wouldn't be due for at least five minutes. It would be nothing to slip the thin disk under my neckline. As long as I kept my head down in the hall, no one would look twice at me, and once I was in my room, I could have the whole disk to myself. I'd eat it under the covers. In the morning, rats would rid the bed of any crumbs. No one would know, and I was *so hungry*—

No! I screamed the word in my mind, the scar over my heart pulsing in warning. *The gods would know. My princess would know. Do not disobey.*

Tears burned my eyes as I set the tray on the counter with shaky hands, sending up prayer after prayer of contrition to my gods, the Seven Monarchs, for even thinking of stealing.

I stared at the food a moment more, swallowing back the saliva gathering in my mouth. Salivating like an animal. Shame shot through me. With a shuddering breath, I turned on my heel and went back to my princess's rooms.

I did not miss Nightly Prayer.

TWO

SAMIRA

Most nights, I collapsed into an exhausted, dreamless heap on my cot. But that night, it didn't matter how long I tossed and turned, I couldn't sleep. My stomach cramped painfully, and my ears echoed with the sound of a young girl's desperate gasps.

I sat up with a huff.

My room was little more than a cubby in the clay walls beneath the kitchens. There was a small window offering a view of the Lotus River and a curtain for a door. Neither I nor my roommate, Nadia, had many belongings, just our uniforms, cots, and a pair of sandals.

I shifted onto my knees, moving slowly, cringing when my cot creaked.

But Nadia just made a soft snuffling noise and rolled over.

I folded my legs under me, sitting back on my calves and heels, and held my hands out to either side of me, palms facing up. Then I let my eyes drift to the Lotus River through the window, a perpetually reassuring sight. Past the river, I could see all of Ketopolis, the capital city of Ashorah, named for the Mother of All, Ketet. The glimmering lights of the city shone like stars in their own sky.

When I'd first been brought to Khada Palace, I'd resented the city's beauty. The vibrant tapestries hanging from the Ketopolis Market, the tall domed structures, the bustling energy, the potent smells of spices that wafted toward the palace all the way from across the river. I'd missed Mama and Baba and our little hut near the river, where our world consisted of the fish Baba caught, the bread Mama baked, and the handful of similar homes around us. I had friends, I thought. But I'd only been six years old when I was taken, so my memories were mostly blurry.

I'd been desperately afraid without Mama and Baba. All I knew were the scary stories they'd told me about Ketopolis. Children slaughtered, criminals around every corner, evil royals overseeing it all. But I was too young to understand how important all of this really was, how important the royals were.

Now I loved them. I'd sworn to it in front of my king, my princess, and dozens of guards. I loved them, and I'd vowed to love them until the day I died.

I let the sight of the river and city ground me as I prayed for Ketet to take away the gnawing in my stomach.

Prayer always brought me peace. It centered me. Blanketed me in comfort, whether or not my pleas were answered. As if for that moment, I wasn't here in Khada Palace; I was suspended in a serene lake. Tranquil, placid, quiet.

But then my stomach rumbled again, wrenching me back to my tiny cot. A whimper rose in my throat.

You should've taken the bread, Samira. Not for your own selfish hunger, but so you could sleep and better serve your princess tomorrow.

My stomach groaned again as if in agreement, and I bit my lip. Maybe the bread was still there. It wasn't even close to morning. Chef Nena wouldn't have had a chance to clean up yet. Maybe I could sneak back to the kitchen—just for a tiny bite. And then in the morning, I'd tell Tabia what I'd done, and she could decide if it warranted a punish—

Something in the river caught my eye. A disturbance in the current. I frowned.

I'd watched the Lotus River for the last sixteen years. It lulled me to sleep every night, greeted me every morning. I knew the way it jumped over every rock, around every obstacle. But the way it was rippling now, going in the opposite direction . . .

Moonbeams streamed down on the river in perfectly straight columns.

And then they flickered.

It was dark. I was tired. There couldn't be someone in the river. No one would dare, especially after Nailah's punishment.

Unless it wasn't a palace servant but rather someone from Ketopolis, a townsperson who wouldn't know about a scullery maid's disciplining.

The moonbeam flickered again.

There. A silhouette against the deep blue of the water.

Or rather, *silhouettes*.

One by one, they emerged from the river. Almost entirely silent. I could've dismissed them as Ashorans braving the crown's wrath for a sip from the river.

If not for their hair.

The moonlight reflected off the sides of their scalps where their heads were shaved, and a long braid hung down each of their backs, varied in length. No one in Ketopolis wore their hair like that. No one in all of Ashorah wore their hair like that.

My hair was dark and short, barely reaching the bottom of my ears, like all female citizens of Ashorah. Men let it grow to their shoulders. And royals, like my princess, shaved their heads entirely, relying on wigs.

There was only one place I knew where people had such strange hair.

Kaldfold.

My heart hit my feet, and I shook my head, terror seizing me.

Stories about the monsters to the north were whispered in the pitch-black of night. Tapestries and hieroglyphs all over Khada Palace depicted King Zaid's battle against them seventeen years ago, when he'd delivered the crushing blow that successfully pushed them beyond the Frozen Sand Mountains.

The Kaldfolk were battle-crazed. Foamed at the mouth when they so much as scented fear. Rabid, depraved monsters that weren't satisfied with just killing their victims. They mutilated them, defiled their corpses, *ate* them. Heretic witches who could manipulate you into killing your own family, friends, yourself. They'd plagued more than one of my nightmares.

And they were coming straight for the palace.

THREE

∿∿∿∿∿∿∿

AMUNET

The sound of scratching was infuriating. Like a thousand little nails over stone. All I could hear was that consistent *chick, chick, chick*. Not the Lotus River. Not my own heartbeats.

I huffed and clutched the candle tighter, its grooves cutting into my palms. "Come on," I muttered, eyes screwed up tight. I waited for the telling warm breeze to smooth over my scalp. If not a breeze, I'd settle for a feeble sigh. A fucking *fart*. Anything that said Shaya heard me, that he was there.

All I got was more of that infernal scratching.

With a grunt, I dropped the ancient obsidian candle in my lap and opened my eyes.

My father stared back at me.

This candle was the most perfect depiction of Shaya I'd ever seen. Dressed in the solid metal armor reserved for kings, face both human and feline, beautiful and deadly. High cheekbones, slitted eyes, and curling, full lips.

I'd purchased the candle nearly five years ago, and it had cost me a small fortune. The woman running the stall in the Ketopolis Market, renowned for the authenticity of her products, said it was one of the oldest ever found, probably dating all the way back to the War of the Ancients. Which could mean Shaya himself had touched the candle. Or at the very least had been close to it.

For the past five years, whenever I focused on the candle, Shaya lit the wick. A warm breeze heralded his presence, and then a burst of flame would alight above his otherworldly face. An assurance that he was here. That he was with me. That we were family.

Until a few days ago. Now, no matter what prayers I recited, it stayed dark.

Chick. Chick. Chick.

I ground my teeth.

It could be rats.

I knew it wasn't.

I also knew it wouldn't go away unless I checked. Sighing hard, I placed my candle back on the nightstand, marched to the door, and wrenched it open.

Just as I expected. The hall was empty.

Jasim—one of the two guards stationed by my room—glanced over at me. I didn't miss the eager glint in his brown eyes or the way they lingered on my thighs, my short nightgown tailored for ventilation, not modesty. "Yes, my princess?"

I ignored that look and glanced over his shoulder. No mice. Not even an errant servant with particularly loud sandals to shout at. A defeated breath filtered out of my nose.

So it was to be one of those nights. I didn't know why it still surprised me.

"My princess, are you all right?"

My eyes slid back to Jasim, to the concern momentarily eclipsing the hunger in his face.

Part of me was tempted to invite him inside and let him tire me out so I could sleep. He'd done it before—rather impressively, I might add—but nearly drowning that girl over and over had exhausted me enough. Punishments were one of my more annoying responsibilities as Gods-Chosen. Now all I wanted was some sleep. And for that gods-damn scratching to *stop*.

I would be getting neither.

Ugh.

I ducked back inside to grab a shawl and wrapped it around my shoulders. Then I stepped out of my room. Both guards straightened in anticipation. Neither one spoke, thank the gods, but shadowed me as I stalked down the hall.

Chick. Chick. Chi—

"Fuck." I shook my head. Cracked my neck. The scratching remained. A soft yet incessant noise in my head.

"My princess," the other guard ventured. His name was . . . Tarim? Parim? Who cares. "Should we send for a healer?"

I ignored him. My nails dug into my palms.

A healer would not help. Nor would wandering aimlessly through the palace, but it was better than lying in bed with nothing else to listen to. The noise was always there, day or night, but it grew worse when I could not reach Shaya.

The king believed it was the whisperings of the gods, that I was more in tune with them as a Gods-Chosen. He told me that I ought to listen to it more closely, even though no other Gods-Chosen in Ashorah's history had ever reported hearing such noises, or that focusing on it caused sharp pain. I told King Zaid what he should have known already—that I wouldn't be able to reach the gods until I was twenty, and trying to bridge the divide early only hurt me.

The king didn't care. He insisted; I called him an idiot. He struck me. I grinned despite the blood leaking from my lips, which only frightened him, and he hit me again.

Strange to think the most accomplished conqueror in Ashorah's history could be frightened of his daughter. But when said daughter was really the daughter of Death, I supposed it made sense. If he were a smarter man, he would hold back his fury. Ah well. He'd learn the error of his ways once I had the power of the Underworld at my fingertips.

Although . . . it was strange for Shaya to hamper our connection just a month from the Igniting. My stomach filled with acid that felt a bit like dread. A byproduct of prolonged separation, I reasoned. Just like the increased volume of the scratching.

The king's voice drifted toward me. My steps slowed, and I peered over the balustrade.

The throne room stretched out beneath me, as expansive and ostentatious as the rest of Khada Palace. Mosaic floors that swirled with cerulean blues, massive alabaster columns, and atop a raised dais a throne made of gold, so large it dwarfed the skeleton of a king within it.

King Zaid was a pile of bones half-heartedly arranged into the shape of a man with the finest layer of skin cloaking him. The bastard was old. Every day I expected some good news, but alas, he refused to die.

". . . might be appealing to the princes," Hamadi was saying at the foot of the dais. My cousin and would-be heir turned king's lapdog.

"If you're so concerned," King Zaid replied in a croaking voice like a tree about to fall, "send a message to Prince Nasir."

My curiosity was piqued. The scratching briefly faded to a background hum.

Before I was born, the silly little jinn-descended princes claimed that the pointed ears on either side of their heads proved their right to the throne. That the drop of magic in their blood from a centuries-upon-centuries-past ancestor meant they were blessed in some way. They'd created such a fuss for King Zaid, even after he successfully seized the Lotus River. Uprising after uprising, battle after insufferable battle. He'd pushed them all out of Ketopolis—Prince Sen Almassi all the way past the dam, to the Dry Lands—and still they persisted in stirring up trouble.

Then Shaya chose me. And the princes shut up.

The possibility that they would start acting up again now, so close to my birthday, was suspicious. And with Shaya not answering my prayers . . . The dread I'd felt before doubled.

"And risk that message being intercepted by Prince Ilias himself?" Hamadi shook his head. "If there is any truth to the rumblings about the number of animals he's sacrificed, we cannot chance—"

My attention was pulled away by a huddle of shadows rushing at me from the other side of the balcony. My maids. Their eyes were wide, rolling around in their heads like spooked horses. My brows furrowed. "What is it?"

They hesitated, exchanging panicked looks.

Usually, I reveled in their shared fear. Now it grated. "What?" I snapped.

One girl opened her mouth.

The throne room doors were thrown open before she uttered a word, and a palace herald burst in. Even from a distance, I could see the sweat coating his tan face and the tremble to his limbs. "Your Majesty, the Kaldfolk—ah!" He staggered forward, shoved from behind.

The largest man I'd ever seen strode into the throne room, braid swinging at his back. Blue runes cut down his throat, and his eyes were an unnatural Shifter yellow. He looked like a monster straight from the Trench. Which, in a sense, he was. He was Kaldfolk.

And he was not alone.

Another Shifter stood at his right while a pack of them crowded behind them, each more menacing than the last. They spilled into the hall beyond the threshold. How many, I could not tell. I estimated roughly a fuckton.

How had so many found their way into the palace without raising an alarm? It should not have been possible.

Hamadi pivoted in front of the throne and drew a scimitar, while guards flooded in from the room's shadows, all armed, all aimed at the unexpected visitors.

Jasim grabbed my arm. "My princess, we have to go."

I nodded and started to turn away, when the large Kald lowered his head in deference. I stilled. A Kald had never bowed to an Ashoran king before, certainly not Zaid, not even in a movement that minor. My interest heightened when the Kald's deep and commanding voice declared, "We mean you no harm, King of Ashorah."

Huh.

Jasim tugged my elbow again.

I twisted out of his grip. "Wait."

"Princess Amunet—"

"Just *wait*," I hissed, setting my hands on the balustrade.

The king had not moved from his throne—probably because he couldn't, bag of bones that he was—but his fingers tightened on the arms. "Breaking into my home with an army does not speak of peace."

"Our numbers are a measure of caution, not disrespect." He looked pointedly at the blades angled in his direction.

King Zaid made a noise that was meant to convey his displeasure, but it caught in the back of his throat and came out in a glob of phlegm. Ugh. Disgusting old pig.

The Kald was well trained enough not to comment on it. "You haven't answered my king's letters, so we decided to uncover the reason for the delay. An unfortunate mistake and nothing more, I'm sure." Not well trained enough to keep the dripping disdain from his tone.

My brows lifted. All this because of unanswered letters? There had been no connection between our two countries since King Zaid had conquered the Kaldfolk almost two decades ago, save for a few rebellious souls who tried to steal a drink from the Lotus River. I'd assumed the correspondence that sat on the king's desk was nothing more than a collection of spicy insults, maybe a declaration of war or two. Nothing as compelling as *this*.

Jasim's lips brushed my ear as he said, "You cannot stay here, my princess. It's too dangerous."

"Hush."

King Zaid's frayed voice echoed through the throne room. "We do not help our enemies."

"Your Majesty," the Kald tried again. "My name is Keir of the Wild Valley, and this is Alarik of Crestbane." He gestured to the man beside him, who had rings glinting in his braid. "We are representatives of King Rade of Frostguard. If you would let us explain, I can—"

The king turned his head, an athletic feat, and ordered his soldiers, "Kill them."

A blade slashed.

It cut through nothing but air.

The Kald's friend, Alarik, was fast, so fast he was practically a blur. But I did not miss when his teeth elongated and he tore the guard's esophagus out of his body in a mad spray of blood. The guard could not even choke before he collapsed to the floor.

My eyes bulged. I was no stranger to violence, but this . . . this was . . .

The fleshy bit of meat hung from Alarik's jaws for a moment, before he spat it out. The red stained the mosaic. His yellow eyes flicked back to the king.

The first Kald, Keir, sighed and shook his head disapprovingly. "Oh, King. Why did you make him do that?"

King Zaid shrieked, "Kill them *now*!"

"As you wish," replied Keir. He turned on the nearest guard. An inhuman roar exploded out of his throat as his teeth grew to fangs, claws burst from his fingers, fur sprouted, and between one blink and the next, a bear stood in his place. One preternaturally large, angry bear.

Scimitars stabbed, arrows fired, all chaos broke loose.

And I had officially overstayed my welcome.

When Jasim tugged on my arm again, I willingly ran with him.

Screams and roars echoed behind us. A voice that was more animal than man shouted, "There she goes! Second floor!"

Terror flooded my system.

Jasim jerked me into my room, my maids rushed in right behind us, and Tarim/Parim threw the dead bolt over my door. Jasim said, "We've got to get you out of the palace. Change quickly. Something plain that won't attract attention in the city."

My maids wasted no time, some rifling through my wardrobe while the others peeled my nightgown off. "You are the greatest army on the continent. How could anything get past your defenses?"

A knock at the door. We all froze. My heart pounded in my ears. "It's me."

Jasim relaxed. Recognized the voice, even though I didn't. He opened the door to a pale-faced guard. The four words he spoke brought the world to a standstill: "The king is dead."

My blood ran cold. He was dead? A hissing hole cracked open in my chest. Not grief exactly but . . . a yawning emptiness. Something missing. It was a peculiar sensation. I'd looked forward to his death for so long, had been ready to rejoice every day at the inevitable news.

But never had I thought his death would come at the hands of the Kaldfolk.

"So is Hamadi," the guard added. His eyes slid to me. "She's queen now."

My heart stuttered, the words landing like a blow. Queen.

An almost meaningless distinction. The Kaldfolk—the Kaldfolk were in my home. They'd killed my foster father. They'd killed my cousin. They'd kill me next. *Holy gods.*

"Now, my queen," Jasim prodded.

I glanced down and realized the maids had clothed me in one of my most boring dresses, a drab brown with the sparsest number of pearls. It had belonged to my mother, which was the only reason I'd kept it. Foolishly sentimental. But now it would help me blend in with the citizens of Ketopolis.

My entire life, guards had shadowed my footsteps. I'd even trained with the Khada Guard on the impossible chance I was ever alone. The king was constantly reminding me that I was in danger, that any number of people wouldn't want me to live to my twentieth birthday, but I'd always thought them the words of a paranoid man.

And now, annoyingly, he was right. Dead—but right.

Terror threatened to send my thoughts into a panicking spiral filled with images of limbs torn apart, splattering blood, faces twisted in agony. But I clenched my hands into fists so tight, my nails bit painfully into my palms, reining in the fear. *Later,* I ordered myself.

The Kaldfolk were here. They'd killed King Zaid. If they could reach me in a heavily fortified palace, they could find me anywhere. It didn't matter where I ran or how fast. The Kaldfolk were like bloodhounds. They'd just keep coming.

I couldn't let that happen. "They'll need a body."

Jasim blinked only once before he caught my meaning. He nodded and pointed to a random maid. "You. Remain here."

"No," I said. She was far too tall, with scars on her cheeks. A Kald would only need one look to know she wasn't me. I scanned the assortment of maids before I landed on a girl trying to hide behind another. "You. You will stay."

The girl's dark brown eyes bulged. "Me, my queen?"

In the dark of the night, the girl could pass for me. Our faces had similar structures, though mine was certainly less hollow than hers. She lacked the Khada-green eyes, but nothing could be done about that. "Put her in my nightgown."

The other maids didn't hesitate. In mere seconds, the girl's filthy uniform was shed and replaced with my violet silk nightgown.

"Leave some of your men behind to guard my rooms," I instructed Jasim. "Make it look convincing. The rest are with me."

"Yes, my queen. Karim will head the decoys." He nodded to my other guard, who stood straighter at the order.

Ah. Karim. That was his name.

Well, there wasn't any point remembering it now.

"But," the maid said, voice trembling, "my queen, I don't—"

I didn't have time for arguments. "What's your name?"

"S-Samira, my queen."

"Well, Samira," I said, barely glancing at the slave as I pulled a short wig over my shaved head. Not an exact replica of a commoner's hairstyle but close enough. "Ashorah thanks you for your sacrifice." I nodded to Jasim. I was ready.

"Stay close, my queen." And then we were running out of my room and down the long flight of steps, guards filling in to flank me on all sides. My sandals scraped against stone as we descended the stairs two at a time.

We hadn't even reached the main courtyard before I heard the screams.

FOUR

AMUNET

Moonlight flashed across puddles of blood in the grass of the inner garden. Metal crashed against metal as scimitars met swords and battle-axes. Above it all rose roars, those of great beasts.

There were plenty of stories about the Kaldfolk's ability to shape-shift. I'd only gotten a glimpse before, but when I glanced around the garden, my throat closed up.

Hulking men with black markings twisting up their bodies battled against my soldiers, but so did massive bears with brown fur streaked through with blue, and claws that tore through soldier after soldier as easily as swatting away gnats.

I watched as one of the bears morphed into a man with a swinging braid, the blue fur shifting into tattoos on his skin, the symbol of his gift, just like that Kald who had spoken to the king. But where that Keir of the Wild Valley possessed some rational thought, this one was all animal. Bright yellow eyes gleamed as the Kald grinned maniacally into the face of a guard, mouth foaming, before shifting back into a bear and tearing the man's throat out.

My ears rang with the screams; blood and viscera sprayed. I headed straight for the large arches on the other side of the courtyard. They would take me to the front of the palace.

Jasim caught me and pulled me in the other direction. "It's faster this way—" We swung around a corner that led into a palace vestibule and screeched to a halt as we came face-to-face with a human Kald.

Though most of his body was hidden in shadow, made even more opaque by his black runes, the Kald was a huge, lumbering figure with saliva dripping from his mouth. He grinned at me, eyes shining in the dark, full of bloodlust.

Jasim shoved one of his scimitars into my hand. "Run!" he shouted, and launched himself at the Kald, his own blade held high. The other guards followed suit, slashing viciously.

I did not need to be told twice. I bolted down the hall.

Swords and arms tried to catch me. But for the first time in my life, I was grateful for the training the king had foisted on me. I didn't slow even as I used my scimitar to parry and dodge incoming blows, sinking my blade into a chest, a stomach. I plunged the scimitar into a Kald's thigh and sliced. The woman screeched as blood gushed out of the wound and her leg gave out. I leaped over her and kept running.

I didn't know where I was going, where Jasim had been leading us, but I sprinted as fast as my sandaled feet would take me. If I could reach the other courtyard, I knew it would let out right by the Lotus River, and then I could run for one of the principalities and ask for sanctuary.

I rounded into a long corridor and froze. A bear had his back to me, thank the gods, but in two seconds, he'd smell me. Even with my training, I wouldn't stand a chance against such a beast.

I ducked into a random room and pulled the door shut behind me. Nothing more than a closet. No windows, no other doors.

I was trapped.

A guttural laugh sounded on the other side of the door.

My whole body locked up as heavy footsteps thumped closer, punctuated by the clicking of claws against the tiled floor.

"I can smell you, little girl," said the Kald, voice deep and thick, like it was difficult to speak past all those teeth. "You smell . . . delicious."

Nausea rolled through me. The Kald chuckled again. "Oh, you're going to taste *good*."

I brandished my scimitar in front of me and gritted my teeth. *Baba!* I cried out in my mind. *Shaya, please, save me. Please!*

Another thump sounded, heavier, right outside the door, followed by a choked cry. I tensed, eyes wide as I stared at the door. Such a pathetic shield. The sweat on my palms slickened my grip on the scimitar's hilt; I tightened my fingers until my knuckles were white.

Please, please, please, I will do whatever you ask of me. I swear it!

The door whipped open, and I swung my blade—

Jasim dodged it and held up his hands. He was covered in blood, some his, some not, and the beginnings of a bruise forming on the right side of his face. He put a finger to his lips, warning me to be quiet.

When I dared to glance down, I saw the bear lying on the floor, yellow eyes open but unseeing, his slit throat pouring out blood. It ran across the floor and pooled around my feet. I flexed my toes in the blood, sticky, still warm, and felt a modicum of relief. Where there was death and sacrifice, Shaya was near. Death was his conduit to the living. I waited for the rustle of his wind. Some silent assurance that he was back, that he was sorry, that he would help me.

Chick, chick, chick . . .

My relief drained like the Kald's blood between the limestones.

Jasim waved me forward, and before I knew it, we were in the queen's old chambers.

The furniture in the room was covered in white sheets, unused since my mother's death, and a dusty tapestry hung innocently against the wall beside the large bed. Jasim pushed it aside to reveal a heavy door. He heaved it open and ushered me through.

I lifted the skirt of my mother's dress and stepped into the dark hallway. Jasim pulled the secret door shut behind us.

FIVE

SAMIRA

Tabia ran a damp rag over my arms, doing her best to get rid of the grime that had become a second skin. "It'll be all right, Samira," she told me. "All you have to do is stand there. Then, before you know it, you'll be with Ketet in the Paradise Fields."

I nodded, though I was trembling with terror.

She tossed the rag aside and looked at me for a moment.

I'd known Tabia the entire time I'd worked in Khada Palace. Though we hadn't been permitted to speak much, she was one of the only kind faces I ever saw. A staple of the last sixteen years. When I looked into her brown eyes now, I saw fear. For me. "It'll be all right," she repeated, giving my hand a squeeze.

I clung to her for as long as I could, until Tabia and the others had no choice but to run.

Leaving me in my queen's rooms with exactly five guards. They faced the door with determination, but they were as trapped as I was.

I ought to feel honored to stand in place of my queen. Like Tabia said, I'd get to see Ketet before anyone else. And I'd do so while saving the Gods-Chosen's life. That was no small thing.

But all I felt was fear. So much fear.

With each blink, I saw that Kald tear out the guard's throat, and nausea burned in my gut. It was going to hurt, dying. I was accustomed to all sorts of pain. It should be easy. But I could hear the screams through the open window. There was something so chilling about hearing men scream. It made my knees clack together, my heart nearly pounding out of my chest.

I'd woken Nadia up as soon as I spotted the figures in the river, and she'd run off to tell the guards while I rushed to the Gods-Chosen. I wondered if she was safe, if she'd managed to escape yet, if Tabia had, or if their screams were mixed in with the cacophony of others'.

The screams that were getting louder. Closer.

The guards shifted on their feet, strangling their scimitars.

I stood behind them and tried to calm my breaths, clasping my hands in front of me and then unclasping them. I hoped the Kald-folk would kill me quickly. Then it wouldn't matter what sort of defilement they put my corpse through. The Mother would offer me treasures in the Paradise Fields, riches I would never have been able to experience in this life. I'd certainly have all the bread and water I could want.

The screaming and footfalls were directly outside the door, and I could no longer hear my own thoughts over my thundering heart.

The door was flung open so hard, it slammed into the adjacent wall with a world-shattering *boom*.

Bears burst in and were on the guards in a single blink, tearing them apart. I gasped in horror and backed up toward the bed as the smell of copper filled the room. Enormous teeth flashed; spittle flew. The guards' screams died as their throats were ripped out, blood spurting.

Then there was silence.

It had only taken seconds.

No candles had been left burning when my queen fled, allowing the creatures to stick to the shadows as they stalked the perimeter of the room. Each step measured, heads low. A pack on the hunt. Their bright yellow eyes seemed to hover in the darkness.

A bear walked directly into a moonbeam, the blue fur of its maw drenched in the guards' blood, and then it reared up on its hind legs. Its limbs retreated and molded into the body of a man, and I got my first real glimpse of one of the northern monsters.

It became impossible to hide my trembling.

The Kald from the throne room. I was too terrified to remember the name he'd given.

He was massive. From the balcony, he'd seemed big, but up close, he was nothing but height and bulk. At least a foot taller than me, if not more, and nearly as wide as the wardrobe behind him. Both sides of his head were entirely shaved, his thick brown braid so long he had to wrap it around the back of his head and pin it, though its tail still hung to the small of his back.

And his face. Gods, his face was unlike anything I'd ever seen. Where Ashoran men all wore beards as soon as they were old enough to grow them, this man's face was clean-shaven and decorated with ocean-blue tattoos. Those foreign symbols slashed across his strong jawline and all the way down his throat, disappearing under the neckline of his tunic. Kohl encircled his yellow eyes and then bled to his forehead, making his eyes stand out even more frighteningly than they already were, hiding his face in a sea of darkness.

He grabbed my arm and jerked me forward roughly. I clamped my lips shut against my scream. The Kald put his nose to my throat and inhaled. His lips pulled back, revealing white teeth as he grinned.

I couldn't help it. Fear sapped all my strength, and a warm river flowed down my leg.

His grin widened, no doubt scenting that I'd wet myself. "Princess Amunet Khada," he greeted me, voice somewhere between a growl and a purr, man and beast. "Or I guess we've made you queen now."

For Ashorah, I reminded myself. *For the Gods-Chosen.*

The Kald's eyes swept over me, making a vile shudder slither down my spine.

"P-please," I stammered, "whatever you're g-going to do, make it quick."

He blinked those luminous eyes at me. "What is it you think we've come to do?" His Kald accent was heavy, the ends of each word too harsh and the vowels too long.

"K-kill me."

"Oh gods, no. No wonder you're shaking like a leaf." The Kald clicked his tongue in mock regret.

I looked from him to the other Kaldfolk, still bears. Their eyes glimmered with laughter. My dread mixed with humiliation, and I squeezed my thighs together to stop from embarrassing myself further.

"We're not going to kill you, Majesty." The Kald moved behind me, and I fought every instinct that screamed at me to turn around, to never give my back to a predator. He put his lips to my ear and said, "We're taking you captive."

"Wha—" My air cut out as his enormous arm wrapped around my throat, forearm pressing down. My hands came up to yank it away, but my fingers couldn't even fully grasp his massive arm. I bucked wildly, eyes bulging.

The Kald hung on easily, batting my hands away like they were nothing more than a nuisance, and pressed down harder.

My pulse echoed in my ears, face too hot, chest on fire. My mouth opened and closed like a beached fish, but no matter how hard I tried, I couldn't manage even a small sip of air. Stars popped across my vision as my arms fell limply at my sides. The world went blurry and then—

Dark.

SIX

SAMIRA

I was rocking. Back and forth, back and forth. My back was cradled against something soft and warm. It was comforting, especially compared to the frigid chill raising goose bumps on my arms and legs. I curled further into the warmth, turning my head to bury my frozen nose against it.

A gravelly chuckle sounded in my ear—*right* in my ear.

My eyes snapped open, and I jerked away so sharply that I nearly fell out of my seat.

A large arm caught me around the waist and pulled me back against a fur-covered chest. The still-healing lashes on my back barked in protest, bringing everything into startling focus.

Hooves clomped loudly against stone. The hard seat beneath me was a saddle.

I was on a horse.

It carried me calmly through a stone tunnel, unnaturally smooth, like a chisel had speared straight through the earth. I was cold. So cold. My panicked breaths fogged in front of me.

And then I heard more clomping behind me.

I whipped around—and nearly fainted again.

The Kald who'd strangled me sat directly behind me in the saddle, holding me firmly against his torso. He smirked. "Good morning, Majesty."

Behind him, dozens of Kaldfolk followed. Most of them splattered with blood.

No! Everything inside me rebelled at the reality that was unfolding before me, and I bucked wildly against the Kald, trying to throw myself out of the saddle.

He clicked his tongue in annoyance, arm tightening around my waist, and used his other hand to yank on the chain attached to the shackles I hadn't even realized bound my wrists. They clanked loudly as he forced me down in my seat. His hot breath seared the side of my neck. "You get one warning. You really want to use it up now?"

Bile burned my throat, but I stilled. "Where—where are we?"

"Don't worry about that."

White light shone up ahead. The exit. I drew a deep breath to dredge up whatever courage I might have and peered around the Kald again. Behind the militia of Kaldfolk was the entrance to the tunnel, and I could just make out the domed roof of Khada Palace.

"What did I just say?" the Kald growled.

"Sorry," I whispered, and turned back around. I'd never been out of Khada Palace, not since I was a child, but I'd gazed at these mountains enough times to know exactly where I was.

The Frozen Sands.

Somehow, inexplicably, we were *in* the mountains. The mountains King Zaid had pushed the Kaldfolk behind seventeen years ago, the mountains that were meant to be impassable without alerting the Ashoran scouts.

This was how they'd done it. They'd dug a tunnel straight through the base of them. Then they swam down the Lotus River and right into the castle. Tore their way through anyone who got in their path until they found the Gods-Chosen.

Except that wasn't who I was. And if they discovered that . . . I remembered the sound of guards choking as their throats were torn out, and nearly wet myself again.

We neared the tunnel's exit, and thick, dark clouds over sharp peaks came into view.

Kaldfold.

Holy gods.

"Rules are pretty simple here, Majesty," the Kald said, his arms a cage around me as he held the reins. "Do as I say, and we'll all be friends."

"Wh-what do you want with me?"

"You sure you want me to answer that?"

My mind raced with thousands of tortures they could be planning. Mutilation, drowning, stoning. I remembered a story Nadia told me once, of when King Zaid marched into Kaldfold. Wide-eyed, rabid monsters, stuck between human and bear, feasting on their own kin, both carnally and physically. King Zaid rode through the mindless rutting in the streets, the cold-blooded violence, the hunger for human flesh.

Was that what they had planned for me? Would I—

"Relax," the Kald drawled. "Your fear smells like shit, and we've still got three days' travel ahead of us."

"Then maybe you should tell her," snapped a female Kald who pulled up alongside us.

"A little suspense will keep us all entertained." I could hear the grin in his voice.

The Kaldfolk behind him chuckled, even as the woman sighed.

When we emerged from the tunnel and I chanced a look back at the Frozen Sands, my stomach dropped. The mountains were enormous summits of ivory sand, as hard as ice, with none of the give of snow. They would take days, if not weeks, to trek. A straight path right through their center was not only less visible, but so much faster.

The Kaldfolk could have been crossing this bridge into our land for years, using it to pick off Ashorans or steal from the Lotus River. They had been right under our noses all this time, watching us. Just the thought made my skin crawl.

I glanced down at my legs hanging on either side of the horse. They hadn't been bound. If I could get free from this Kald, I could run back to—

"Try it and see what happens," he said like he could read my mind, a touch of excitement in his voice. Hoping I would run, perhaps. Just so he could chase.

My blood ran cold, and I shuddered hard enough to rattle my shackles.

"Enough, Keir," that female Kald said.

Keir. I recalled the name now. Harsh and cutting, like the creature himself.

She gave him an exasperated look. "Rade's going to be pissed as it is. You really want to make it worse by having her show up a terrified mess?"

Rade. King of Kaldfold. I swallowed hard.

"But we've got days until then," the large Kald reasoned.

"Keir," she said sharply.

Keir held his hands up placatingly. But his dark chuckle rustled my hair.

I kept my eyes on the road, spine ramrod straight, and didn't look back again.

A camp awaited us among a cluster of spindly, leafless trees. The Kaldfolk had come prepared with cloaks and tents, so many of them that it looked like a small village had popped up in the forest. After learning of their tunnel under the Frozen Sands, I shouldn't have been surprised that they'd thought so far ahead, but I was. They'd even brought food and some thick white liquid with too many chunks in it to be milk, which they gulped down eagerly.

The woman I'd come to learn was called Velka, Keir, and four of the others sat separately from the rest of the Kaldfolk. They each took a log or a stone instead of one of the prearranged tents, creating a circle around a sizeable fire.

They left one seat conspicuously empty.

Keir held my chain like a leash. I stood awkwardly behind him, my sandaled feet nearly blue as the cold of the earth bled up into my soles. My queen's nightgown was made for Ashorah's heat. Thin, breathable. In Kaldfold's tundra, it was a useless scrap of fabric. But I wouldn't dare ask to sit by the fire or—gods forbid—to borrow one of their large fur cloaks. Since making camp, Keir had almost seemed to forget about me, and I was grateful for it. Even if it meant standing in the freezing cold in nothing but a silk nightgown.

"By the gods!" one of the Kaldfolk around the fire exclaimed suddenly, making me jump. He turned to me, yellow eyes gleaming above high cheekbones, and the blue tattoos on his hands seemed nearly black in the firelight when he waved them at me. "Sit. If I have to hear your teeth chatter one more time, I'm going to lose my mind."

My eyes darted to Keir. He debated a moment before nodding.

I stepped hesitantly into the circle. The warmth of the campfire washed over me. Every muscle in my body had been tensed from the moment I woke up in Keir's saddle, and they begged for an opportunity to rest. I headed straight for that empty spot.

Already, I could feel the chill in my bones melting away. I didn't think I'd ever been this cold. Winters in Ashorah could be brutal but never like this. There was an added bite to the cold here. Like the wind had teeth—

"Not there!" they all burst out.

I scrambled away from the unassuming rock, confusion and fear sparking through me. "I—I'm sorry. I thought you said—I didn't mean to offend—I'm sorry—"

"Gods, stop apologizing," Keir grunted, shifting over on his log. He jerked his chin at the space beside him. "Sit."

I glanced at the Kaldfolk again, expecting to see fury or bloodlust. But Velka just lowered her gaze to the ground, elbows braced on her knees, a tin cup practically forgotten between her hands.

Shadows painted her face, not just from the fire. I'd seen that look more times than I could count in Khada Palace. That was sorrow.

In fact, though some tried harder to hide it, they all wore similar expressions. It made my brows draw together, but I would take their sadness over their wrath.

Staying next to Keir was the last thing I wanted to do, but I sank down onto the petrified wood beside him. Even with several inches separating us, I could feel his body heat. I'd noticed his exaggerated warmth on the horse and guessed it must be a Shifter attribute. Between his warmth on my right, the fire in front of me, and the adrenaline that had shot through my blood when they'd yelled at me, I was no longer cold.

Silence descended on the group. Velka hardly looked up. The Kald who'd told me to sit stared blankly into the fire. Beside him sat a mountain of a woman. The lines on her face told me she was somewhere in her forties, and she was as big and brawny as the men around her, with tattoos curling up the back of her neck and wrapping around her ears like tentacles, reaching for her cheeks. She was also scarred. Twin slashes cut from the bottom of her eyes to the corners of her lips.

On the adjacent log sat a boy who looked to be the runt of the bunch. He wasn't scrawny by any means, but whereas the others' strength felt imposing, his seemed unassuming. I guessed him to be about my queen's age, and he bore a strong resemblance to the large woman. I couldn't see his tattoos, but I knew their blue lines must be curling somewhere under his thick clothes.

There was a girl on his other side, maybe a few years older than me, with eyes hard as steel. She glared at me from across the fire, directing every ounce of her sadness my way like a weapon. Like blame.

Velka cleared her throat, finally lifting her head. She looked at me, but her words were aimed at Keir. "You should feed her."

My shoulders stiffened. Every instinct urged me not to eat anything they gave me. It could be poisoned—though I didn't know why they'd want to kill me here instead of in Ashorah.

"She can eat tomorrow," Keir responded, his voice rough with emotion. I turned to him in surprise, but he didn't even glance at me. He held a twig in his hands and was mindlessly breaking it apart inch by inch, tossing the bits into the fire. Gone was the laughing smirk. He was as somber as the rest of them.

Velka sighed. "She has to eat—"

The Kald who'd told me to sit growled, "Stepping into the Second role a little fast there, eh, Velka?"

She gave him a dark look. "That's not what I'm doing."

"That's what it sounds like."

"Leave her alone, Bain," said the large woman.

Bain retorted, "Excuse me for wanting just one night to grieve the poor bastard before someone starts using his rank—"

"I'm *not* using his rank," Velka snapped. "It's been a whole day and she hasn't eaten. Do you want her to starve to death before we get there?"

"Yeah," snorted the girl with hard eyes. "Because one day without food will kill her."

In fact, it had been a lot longer than that since my last meal. A few days at least. But of course, I didn't tell them that.

One of theirs had died, presumably during their raid on the palace. Gods forgive me, but the first thought that entered my mind was *Good.* They'd killed my people—had killed my *king*. It seemed only right that they should lose one of their own.

Velka's lips thinned. "If Rade thinks we intentionally starved her—"

"That's enough," Keir said, voice sharp. "She will eat. Tomorrow." He turned to Bain. The kohl around his eyes made him look frightening. "And yes, temporarily, Velka is your Second. Sillia is your Third." He gave a nod toward the massive woman. "They've always outranked you, Bain. Alarik's death doesn't change that. So don't be an ass."

Alarik. The Kald who had stood beside Keir. Who'd ripped that guard's throat out and spat it to the ground like a dog with a dis-pleasing stick.

Once more I felt a dark sense of satisfaction.

Bain's shoulders lowered. He didn't say anything else. Keir's word was final.

Silence descended again, and I could only blink at what I'd just witnessed. I had expected blind revelry, a celebration that they'd managed to kidnap the Gods-Chosen. I didn't know exactly what the drink was in their cups, but I could smell the bitterness of it. Not wine like my queen had but certainly some sort of ale. I would've thought they'd be a drunken, laughing, rutting mess.

I had not expected grief.

But they had attacked one of the most well-protected structures on the continent. They couldn't really have expected to break in, steal the Gods-Chosen, and get out unscathed.

The boy who looked related to the large woman—Sillia—lifted his cup to the empty seat. "To Alarik," he said.

They all lifted their cups and intoned, "To Alarik."

Eventually they started talking about plans for tomorrow, what time we would leave and where we would make camp. No one spoke to me, but they never stopped watching me out of the corners of their eyes.

So I watched them right back.

Cano was the name of the boy who had made the toast. He seemed to be beloved, like everyone's little brother—and Sillia's ac-tual little brother. Half brother, from what I could gather. He was also at the bottom of their ranking system.

Dalla, a step above Cano, was the girl who shot me accusing glares across the fire.

Sillia didn't speak much, though she listened attentively. Even when her thoughts appeared to be elsewhere, I could tell that her ears were always alert.

They were at once a cohesive unit and extremely fractured,

probably due to Alarik's death. When even one maid was no longer able to work in the Gods-Chosen's rooms, the lot of us were left scrambling to figure out how to fill the void. The Kaldfolk's dynamics reminded me a bit of that. A team set adrift.

Around us, Kaldfolk doused campfires as they readied for sleep. My captors left the fire crackling and reclined on the bare ground, no tents of their own to vanish into.

Bain shot Velka a look, but she studiously avoided it as she lay down beside Dalla.

Bain caught me watching. But instead of snapping or questioning me, the edges of his lips quirked up in a malicious grin that was far more frightening than anything he could have said. Ice flooded my veins.

"Bain."

Bain's gaze flicked to Keir for a second before he rolled his eyes and got comfortable like the others.

Keir turned to me. "We've still got a ways to go. If you don't sleep, you'll regret it."

But my eyes darted back to Bain, whose chest was rising and falling rhythmically. I didn't believe he was actually asleep.

Keir chuckled. "If any big bad monster's going to eat you, it'll be me. And tonight I'm not really craving urine-soaked queen." He slid off the log to the ground and lounged back against the wood, arms crossed. When I still stared, he jostled my chain, pointed to the ground, and ordered, "Sleep."

I dropped down instantly and snapped my eyes shut, curling into myself as tightly as I could.

Keir sighed softly. After a beat, I cracked one eye back open. Keir remained awake, gaze never straying from that empty seat Alarik was meant to occupy.

Not once did he close his eyes. I know because I didn't, either.

SEVEN

AMUNET

When I was around five years old—just before I'd learned Shaya was my real father, just before I'd lit my first candle in his honor—the king had taken me to the Ketopolis Market for the first time. He'd carried me on his shoulders and pointed out each stall to me.

The market had everything. Textiles in all different colors, which were strung up between booths over our heads, created one long, consistent canopy down the aisle. Exotic foods from all over the empire, filling the narrow aisles with a heady mixture of smells. Sugary sweets, seasoned meats, all of it cut through by the bitterness of incense being sold with sculptures and paintings of the Seven Monarchs. The stalls were a never-ending strip of shouting merchants and happy customers.

"Look!" I pointed, feet kicking with excitement beneath my father's grip. "Baklawa!"

"Aye, aye, little one." He veered sharply in the direction of the stall as if he were a ship and I the captain. I used to love when he did that.

The merchant took one look at Father, and her eyes lit up. There were portraits of Father all over Ashorah, but even without them, it would have been easy to deduce the king's identity, what with his extravagant robes made of the finest linens stitched through with diamonds, and the massive crown atop his head. "How may I serve you, my king?"

"Two squares of baklawa."

"Of course, my king." The merchant produced the dessert quickly, and Father steered us toward a nearby bench. "Careful," he warned as he offered me both pieces of the pastry. "It's messy."

Heedless of his warning, I dove right in. The thin filo pastry flaked all over my lap, but I didn't care. I'd always adored baklawa, but I'd never had any *that* delicious. Sweet with just a hint of savory from the almonds in its center, the crust practically melting in my mouth.

Father chuckled at my expression. "Good?"

"So good! The best baklawa I've ever tasted!"

"Do you think so?"

I nodded enthusiastically, honey making my lips sticky.

Father looked at the merchant. She was watching us with a soft smile from the stall but quickly straightened under the king's gaze and scurried to his side. "Was there something else you needed, my king?"

"What's your name?" he asked.

"Nena, my king."

"Can you bake anything else, Nena?"

"Yes, my king. My family owns a restaurant a few blocks over. We bake and cook most dishes."

"Can your restaurant manage without you?"

Her brows furrowed. "No, my king."

Father considered her, the sunlight catching in the jewels of his crown. "And if you were to earn double the wages, would it be able to spare you then?"

The merchant's eyes flew wide. "I . . . yes."

"Excellent. You are the new chef of Khada Palace, Nena."

The merchant's eyes widened. She lowered into a stunned curtsy. "Th-thank you, my king."

I hardly paid attention to her shock, preoccupied with my own. I gasped hard and gazed up at my father with pure delight. "Really, Baba?"

He smiled warmly and stroked my hair, which had yet to be shorn. "You deserve to be happy, little one." A sheen coated his green eyes.

Tilting my head, I asked, "Why are you crying, Baba?"

He wiped his eyes, though it did little to get rid of the watery look. "I have made many mistakes in my life. Promises that must be kept. Promises that will change every—" He drew a deep breath and shook his head, plastering a smile on his face. "They are not important right now. Today, you are happy. Right?"

I grinned and took another bite of the baklawa. "Right!"

"That is all that matters." Father lifted his robe and cleaned up the mess around my lips, not caring that it was staining his expensive fabrics.

Funny how it took hiding in a cramped room at a random inn in Ketopolis for that memory to resurface.

The king had always treated me with contempt and violence, which had bred my own disdain and hatred. Except he hadn't *always*.

And now he was dead.

I rubbed my chest, where I could still feel that strange emptiness. It was irritating . . . and unexpected.

The door opened, and my muscles locked up. But it was only Jasim. "The camels are waiting downstairs," he said as he entered, shutting the door behind him.

Pushing aside the old memories, I rose from the rickety bed. "And you spoke to the innkeeper?"

"I did. All he knew was that the Kaldfolk infiltrated the palace. No mention of the king."

A small blessing, that. The tunnel Jasim had taken me through had let out onto the streets of Ketopolis, where havoc was already in full swing. If they realized the Kaldfolk had succeeded in assassinating the king, there was no telling what further chaos could be unleashed. Not to mention what bright ideas the antsy jinn-descended princes might think up.

There was nothing more dangerous than a vacant throne.

My throne now, it seemed.

"The Kaldfolk are crazed animals, my queen," Jasim said, repulsion evident. "They must have found a gap in our defenses and taken the opportunity without any thought for what comes next. It won't be long before they're dealt with."

Jasim had been with the Khada Guard for nearly thirteen years. He'd fought the Kaldfolk before, had seen their lust for battle firsthand, but I didn't think it ever got easier to watch a man be torn apart. I shuddered at the memory.

Jasim took a step toward me, a line of concern forming between his brows. "How are you doing?"

"Fine." I adjusted the new cloak around my shoulders. I'd found it hanging in the wardrobe, apparently forgotten by the last guest. My mother's old dress was indeed unremarkable in a castle full of wonderful clothes, but just a few moments running through the streets told me it was still too noticeable. Hopefully, the hideous gray thing I now wore would be enough to keep me from being recognized. "We'll head to the Temple of Shaya. It's too dangerous to return to the palace with the Kaldfolk so close, and I need to speak with my father anyway, and we can—"

"Amunet," he said softly, and I stalled at the casual use of my name. At the gentle caress over the syllables—*Ah-moon-et*. The scratching noise in my head returned at full volume. Jasim's eyes shone in that way they always did after a roll in the sheets, with too much emotion, with too many unsaid words. "You know you can talk to me."

Sometimes it was truly a pain in the ass that he knew me as well as he did. "I am talking to you. I just told you that we should—"

"Your father is dead." My eyes snapped up to his face. Jasim's years of training with the Khada Guard had chiseled him into a man who looked far older than his twenty-one years. The thick beard framing his jaw certainly added to the illusion, as did his size. He'd ditched his white uniform and instead managed to procure a threadbare tunic—possibly from the innkeeper himself—which was entirely too snug around Jasim's strong frame. Not abnormally bulky like the Kaldfolk, but properly muscular from days upon days of rigorous training.

But more than all of that, it was that gods-damn knowing look in his chocolate-brown eyes. A look filled with decades' worth of wisdom that shouldn't belong to a man so young. A look that said he saw me, understood me, and cared anyway.

A lie. No one ever saw me.

He said, "It is all right to be sad."

"Well, thank you so very much for the permission."

"Amunet," he said again, voice unfathomably gentle, not at all fazed by the bite in mine. The scratching grew louder. My molars threatened to shatter. "I know your relationship was . . . complicated. But he was your father. Of course you would—"

"He was *not* my father." My voice was a lash between us. "The king and I shared no blood. I do not feel sad that he is dead—in fact, I wish I had been there to witness the event myself." The words tasted bitter on my tongue. A lifetime of bitterness for a man who had loved me once and then abruptly decided to stop.

Jasim's shoulders lowered, as if he heard the hurt behind my violence. That infuriating tender *look*. The walls started to push in around me, the scratching so demanding that I wanted to slap my hands over my ears. My control was slipping.

"Amunet—"

I smacked him across the face, the sharp *crack* seeming to echo around the room as his head snapped to the left.

The racket in my brain quieted. Just enough to let me think.

The tension bled out of me, replaced by an ice so cold, I half expected my breath to fog in front of me. "A few nights in my bed seem to have clouded your judgment, soldier," I said with deadly calm. "Allow me to rectify that. I am your queen. Not your lover and certainly not your friend."

Slowly, he turned back to me, brows low. His cheek glowed red even in the dim candlelight, a rosy counterpart to the purple bruise along his other cheek.

But I wasn't finished. "You will only address me as 'Your Majesty' or 'my queen.' To do otherwise is an insult to the crown and the gods. You accompany me not because of our romantic entanglement but because you are the only guard here."

He huffed a humorless laugh and dully repeated, "Romantic entanglement."

"Watch yourself, Jasim."

He gazed down at me, face now devoid of all emotion. He gave one curt nod. "Apologies, *Your Majesty*. It will not happen again."

"Good." That feeling in my chest splintered wider. I ignored it. "To the Temple of Shaya, then."

"Yes, Your Majesty." He pushed his shoulders back and led me silently through the inn to the back door, where a pair of camels idled. Jasim helped me onto mine, fingers stiff around my waist, before swinging up into his saddle.

King Zaid had used violence his entire reign. To conquer, to hold on to his power, sometimes simply for the fun of it. Besides my own beatings, I'd also witnessed him strike advisors, emissaries, anyone who stepped even a single toe out of line. As queen and Gods-Chosen, it would be natural for me to strike those who disobeyed or disrespected me as well.

The Gods-Chosen was where Jasim's devotion rested, anyway. The same was true for my maids and the palace nobles and everyone who looked at me with love instead of disdain. Those who didn't fear or hate me loved only the divine figure they saw. Not me. And yet they were surprised when I acted as one. Hypocrites and liars, the whole lot of them.

But knowing that didn't lessen the burn of guilt that tried to rise. I pushed it down, down, down. The Gods-Chosen didn't feel guilt; she didn't need it.

"May I have permission to speak, my queen?"

I fought a wince at the overly proper words. "Yes."

"The Temple of Shaya is technically considered part of the Wastelands. Perhaps it would be safer to travel to Wethai. That far south, there will be no chance of the Kaldfolk finding you. Sacrifices to Shaya can be made there." He kept his eyes focused straight ahead on the horizon.

He wasn't entirely wrong. It was why I had not personally been to my father's temple before. Too dangerous, the king always claimed. Given that his venture into the Wastelands had been a heaping shit show, I hadn't entirely disregarded that bit of advice.

But Shaya had not saved me tonight. He *always* saved me. From assassination attempts, from bullies during my training with the Khada Guard, from choking on an olive pit or tripping over a stair. I was his beloved daughter. I burned countless candles for him, prayed to him multiple times a day. More than once, I'd developed bruises on my knees from how long I'd sat in communion with him.

There was a reason he had gone suddenly silent. I needed to find out what it was.

Maybe I had upset him somehow. Maybe he resented me for not going to his temple before he bestowed me with such power. Or maybe it was something else, but whatever the case, I'd beg forgiveness. Accept his penance. Reinforce our connection ahead of my birthday.

I could not go through the Igniting without him. Because I wanted him with me—and because I was not sure if it would physically work without him. *He* had to bestow the power on me. If he was not there to do it . . .

I needed to get to the temple.

I sighed tiredly. "Not Wethai," I said to Jasim. "Before the Kald-folk stormed in, Hamadi made it sound like Prince Ilias wasn't to be trusted. But we'll stop in Reeda to collect supplies. Prince Nasir has been a friend to the crown since my birth. He will help us."

Not to mention I wasn't exactly drowning in options at the moment: Prince Ilias Bata of Wethai to the south and Prince Anwar Lotfi of Haisab to the west would probably parade me naked through the streets for a good laugh—and Prince Sen Almassi of the Dry Lands would kill me on the spot. They were of the persuasion that Shaya's daughter was more spawn of evil than savior.

But Nasir. He was loyal. Or as loyal as a jinni-descended prince could be.

Plus, he was on the way.

"And if word of the king's passing arrives before we do?" Jasim asked.

Well, then we'd be walking straight into a trap. There would be no *friends of the crown* if they could don the crown themselves.

"Let us pray that doesn't happen," I responded before digging my heels into the camel's sides and lurching us into movement.

EIGHT

SAMIRA

Sitting in the saddle somehow hurt more today than yesterday. My backside ached with every step the horse took.

Keir had awoken me with the threat that he was "feeling peckish" and I had better get on his horse before he decided to have a little breakfast. I guessed that meant the quiet, somber man from last night was gone, replaced by the mocking creature that had mauled five guards to death.

I spent the ride thinking about what yesterday's interactions had actually revealed. They didn't want me to smell of fear, and they wanted to make sure I was fed, which meant that despite Keir's threats, they intended to bring me to their king in one piece. But I hadn't been able to figure out why.

I needed to know. If I knew, I could prepare for it. I could make my prayers more specific when I asked Ketet to guard me against the pain. I wouldn't run from it; this was my duty to see through, a duty given to me by my queen. I let that thought buoy me, fill me with righteousness and courage. I would not fail the Gods-Chosen.

Clearing my throat, I turned awkwardly in the saddle. "I'm sorry about your friend."

Keir snorted without taking his eyes off the road. "No, you're not."

I'd forgotten how strong his sense of smell was. He could probably smell the lie in my words. "He tore out a man's throat," I said by way of explanation.

"After we were attacked. You don't see me offering fake condolences for killing your guards."

Like a roll of thunder, I heard the men's screams as they were ripped apart. "No one should have died." That was the truth.

He grunted and then tapped his fingers against my hip. "Face forward."

I obeyed, licking my lips nervously as I racked my brain for something else to say. But we didn't make small talk in the palace; we barely spoke at all.

Queen Amunet picked the wrong person.

But I was here now. I was all my queen had. I was all *I* had.

"What does your king want with me?"

"Is that a joke?" I chanced a look over my shoulder to see that Keir had cocked an eyebrow at me. I wasn't sure if he meant it was a joke to think he would tell me or a joke that I didn't already know. If Queen Amunet knew, then I'd just royally screwed up.

Although Keir didn't look like he was about to chuck me out of the saddle . . .

Better not to risk it and change the subject. "Where are we going?"

"Lots of questions today, Majesty. Live through a single night and you're suddenly far too comfortable." He leaned forward so his lips were right beside my ear. "If you're looking for the weakest link, I can promise you it isn't me. Or any of the Seven."

My eyes flicked up to the group of Kaldfolk flanking us: Velka, Sillia, Bain, Dalla, and Cano. With Keir and Alarik, that made seven. But he said the number like a title. They were important. King Rade had sent important people to retrieve the Gods-Chosen. The Kaldfolk might be battle-crazed beasts, but they clearly had the ability to strategize.

"I'm not looking for a weak link," I told him. "Just answers."

He chuckled, his breath tickling the side of my neck. "How about this: *Beg* me for answers, Majesty, and maybe I'll give you some."

I didn't even hesitate. I twisted as far in my seat as I could manage, my knee pressing uncomfortably into his. I moved so fast I startled him, and he jerked back. "Please," I said. "Please tell me what you're going to do with me. Please."

The snark faded from his piercing yellow eyes as his brows pulled together and he scanned every inch of my face. Maybe I should have shown a bit of dignity. Queen Amunet would've certainly had more pride than that. As far as I knew, she'd never begged for anything in her life. Maybe that alone would be enough to prove my false identity. But I needed to know how I was going to die.

Keir's nostrils flared, scenting me. Searching for trickery or lies. But as I watched, his bright yellow irises darkened to a deep gold. With the kohl painted around them and stretching over his forehead, it gave the illusion of two suns shining out of a night sky. Peculiar and hard to look away from.

"Keir," Sillia called, and he ripped his eyes from mine. She lifted her hand and pointed, her fur cloak falling away to reveal a bare arm corded in muscle. "The bridge is up ahead."

"Right." Keir blew out a sharp breath through his nose, as if ridding himself of an odor, and shook his head roughly. "You and Velka first, then me, then the rest. Single file."

Sillia nodded and kicked her horse into a quicker trot, taking the lead.

I tried one more time. "Please, Keir."

But he just tugged my chain. "Face forward."

Reluctantly, I turned around, my heart sinking lower than before. I felt as if I'd failed some sort of test, for both my queen and the Kald.

Ahead of us, the icy land just—stopped. Dropped off dramatically, a deep chasm stretching between this side and where the earth picked up yards away. The only thing connecting the two was a narrow strip of stone, curved like an archer's bow. It looked as if it were defying gravity, like a collection of rock that should have fallen with the rest of the earth to the abyss below.

We were going to cross *that*?

Sillia walked her horse onto the death trap without hesitation, but Velka paused behind her. She glanced at me. "We have an extra horse," she offered. "We could tie her to mine. She won't go anywhere and it'll be better weight distribution."

"She weighs nearly nothing," Keir replied. "We'll be fine."

Velka looked like she wanted to argue further, but she just gave a deferential nod and urged her horse forward, behind Sillia.

Keir followed, pausing just before we stepped onto it. "Don't look down." As soon as he said the words, I couldn't help but glance over the lip of the cliff.

It plunged hundreds of feet to a bottom filled with boulders and tree roots. My gut twisted. I didn't have a problem with heights, but nothing about this looked safe. If we fell—or if I was pushed—I'd be dead instantly. Though perhaps it would be a better fate than whatever awaited me with Rade.

Keir chuckled. "I warned you. Now try not to move too much." His arm tightened around my waist, holding me firmly in place. My sensitive back gave an angry throb, but I didn't bother trying to readjust myself. I wrapped my fingers around the pommel of the saddle, strangling it, as Velka and Sillia disappeared over the hump. Keir clicked his tongue, and then our horse was stepping onto the frail bridge.

The moment our weight was added, pebbles along the edges broke off and plummeted to the ground below. I stopped breathing, as if the added weight of oxygen would be what sent us tumbling after those pebbles.

Part of me wanted to squeeze my eyes shut until it was over, but my body refused to obey. I couldn't stop staring at the unstable ground of the bridge. At a sudden crack, my body jolted. A fissure slithered open alongside us. I gasped, my heart a deafening drum in my ears.

"We're not cannibals."

The random statement drew my focus away from the death that stalked us. "What?"

"I said I'd give you an answer if you begged. That's the one I'm giving you. We're not cannibals. Never have been, don't really plan to be in the future."

And then it was over. Our saddle's rocking gentled as our horse reached solid ground. The bridge was behind us. Velka and Sillia walked calmly ahead of us, as if we hadn't all just risked our lives. I craned my neck to look at Keir.

His expression was as unbothered as Velka's and Sillia's, despite the arm still clenched tightly around my midsection. He shrugged. "Then again, maybe I'm lying. I guess there's really no way for you to know. Until it's too late." He grinned and flicked the horse's reins, not stopping to see if the rest of his people made it over the bridge. Knowing they would. Only when we were a good distance away did he finally remove his arm from my waist.

Of course Keir was lying. There were three things I knew for sure about the Kaldfolk—they were shape-shifters, they were cannibals, and they were heretics. If Keir was trying to lull me into a false sense of security, he would not succeed. As long as I was with the Kaldfolk, I would remain braced for death or worse. His assurances on the bridge were just part of his twisted sense of entertainment.

Because he *was* twisted. They all were.

And I was willing to bet King Rade would be the worst of them all.

NINE

AMUNET

Jasim clicked his tongue as he examined the pear in his hand. "There's a bruise on the side of it. It's hardly worth half a crown."

The man behind the table gestured to the plethora of baskets in front of him, all filled with pears. "Then pick another one. But five crowns is the price."

"I'll give you one."

"Five."

I fisted my hands against my empty stomach and mumbled, "Just give him five."

Jasim shot me a dark look. Darker than the looks he'd been sending me the whole way to this disgusting outpost. "It isn't worth five crowns," he hissed back to me. "None of these are."

"We have to eat."

"We eat what we can afford."

"I can afford a damn pear."

"Not right now you can't."

I glared at him, mentally cursing as my stomach rumbled. I couldn't remember the last time I'd really felt hunger. It was nearly as unpleasant as the itch that had started up at the back of my neck. Another symptom of not talking to Shaya for several days. Equally as delightful as the din in my head, which was no longer scratching but tapping. A claw against glass.

Clink. Clink. Clink.

I fixed my arms at my sides, refusing to scratch and risk knocking my wig off.

Jasim mistook my muscles locking up and said, "Going to punch me this time?"

"Maybe."

His brows lowered even farther. "Do it if you want, but we've only forty-seven crowns in our possession. Pay five for a stupid pear and we'll run out before we're even close to Reeda."

I rolled my eyes. "Fine. I'll find a place for us to sleep."

"Keep your—"

"Head down, I know." I stepped out from under the awning, cringing against the blaze of the sun. Sweat had already made the ends of my wig stick to the irritated skin at my nape, but now beads of it rolled freely down my face. I gritted my teeth against the discomfort and headed toward a clay building at the end of the street.

It was the only one large enough to be an inn. Though I wouldn't be surprised if this place didn't know the meaning of the word. The village was hardly more than five dirt roads and a dozen structures that vaguely resembled homes. Squashed, as if a giant had stepped on them when the clay was still setting. I peeked through the door of one to see that the floor was cushioned with straw. If I had to sleep on a flea-infested clump of straw, I was going to scream.

I glanced up at the please-gods-let-that-be-an-inn. Even from here it looked to be covered in a layer or two of dirt. A door made of wooden slats blocked me from seeing any potential straw on the ground, but there—

A hand covered my mouth, and I was yanked back against a hard body. Something sharp scraped against my throat. A knife.

My eyes widened, fear sizzling through my veins. I didn't even think before stomping down on the person's foot.

A strangled curse huffed in my ear, but it gave me just enough room to jab my elbow back. The person grunted, their grip on me loosening, and I lunged to the side, ready to sprint back the way I'd come. Toward the open market, toward Jasim and his scimitars.

But the person's weight slammed into me. With a cry, I crashed onto my stomach, wig flying off and teeth clacking together, catching my tongue between them. Pain ricocheted through me as the taste of copper filled my mouth. "Just—hold still!" the person grunted, a man's voice.

I threw my head back, smashing into his nose. He swore again and fell off me. I flipped over, hood falling back, and scrambled away.

A man with a thick beard crouched a foot away from me, a hand to his bleeding nose. "Stubborn bitch. It was supposed to be quick."

"Who are you?" I demanded.

The man spat out a clump of blood and gripped his knife tighter. "Prince Anwar sends his regards."

Shit.

He launched himself at me again.

I rolled out of the way just as his knife caught me in the side, slashing through my cloak and skin like they were nothing at all. Pain sliced through me, but I ground my teeth together, choking back my scream. Before he could make another grab for me, I swung my hand up, heel of my palm slamming into his already injured nose.

There was a distinct *crack*. He screamed and grabbed at his nose as blood gushed.

In the next breath, I regained my feet, snatched my wig, and bolted, razors of pain cutting through my abdomen with every step. I pressed my hand to the wound, the warmth of blood coating my fingers, and kept going.

I burst into the market center, scanning quickly before remembering my wig. With shaky hands, I fitted it back over my head, sparing a precious second to straighten it. My eyes landed on Jasim's familiar, broad back. He was standing in front of another vendor's stall. I beelined toward him and grabbed his arm.

He turned with furrowed brows. "Your Majesty, I'm—"

"A man just tried to kill me."

"What?" He glanced down at where I gripped my side, spotting the blooming crimson stain. His stunned expression vanished, replaced by cool, calculated fury. He angled his body to block me from the vendor and any other prying eyes as he scanned our surroundings. "Where?"

"Right behi—" But when I looked over my shoulder, there was no sign of him.

Jasim didn't care. "We're leaving. Now."

The sun would be setting in a few hours, and we hadn't eaten or slept. But for once, I didn't argue. Jasim wrapped his arm around my waist in a move that would seem like a casual display of affection to anyone looking but allowed him to press his hand to the wound in my side. Then he was guiding us back to our camels. "Can you ride on your own?"

I winced but nodded. I didn't reject his help climbing into the high saddle. Once I was situated, he swung up into his, and then we were galloping out of the village. Wave after wave of fire shot through me as we ran. I thought the muscle in my jaw would burst from how hard I clenched it, nails digging into my skin on either side of the wound as I clutched tightly at it. Blood leaked all over my fingers. Too much. I was losing too much. "Jasim . . ."

"Just a little farther," he responded. He didn't stop until we found a patch of cypress trees. Between one very long blink and the next, he was beside me, pulling my camel down to its knees and then hefting me out of the saddle. He deposited me at the base of a tree.

Moving quickly, he fetched one of the sacks tied to his camel, yanked off my cloak, and hiked up my dress. His eyes didn't linger on my flesh or undergarments; he retrieved a needle and thread from the sack, lit a match, and held the flame to the tip of the needle.

He said, "This is going to hurt." That was all the warning I got before he dug the needle into my side.

A breath hissed out of me, but I did my best to hold still as Jasim sewed me up. "He said Anwar sent him," I panted.

"Figures."

"What do you—" My breath caught as the needle stuck. I gripped handfuls of sand as I rode the wave of pain.

"Sorry," Jasim mumbled.

Shutting my eyes, I tried to slow my breaths. "Why don't you sound surprised that Anwar"—I sucked in another breath as my skin pulled—"sent an assassin after me?"

"Done." Jasim set down the needle and rummaged in the sack for bandages. His fingers, now covered in my blood, were gentle and sure as he wrapped my midsection. I winced as he secured the knot. "I overheard some vendors talking. They said the Kaldfolk left the palace."

"They left?" I stared as he nodded. "So they, what? Came to assassinate two royals and then decided *not* to seize control?"

"I don't know. But with the king and your cousin dead, the Kaldfolk gone, and you on the run, it's obvious the throne is empty. You're not fully Gods-Chosen for another few weeks, which means you're easiest to kill right now. Maybe without the might of the Underworld smiting those who try."

"Thought about it, huh?"

"All the time," he deadpanned. "Drink this." Jasim thrust a waterskin into my hands.

I shoved it aside with an impatient click of my tongue and grabbed him by the collar. "I didn't kill him. The assassin. I injured him but not enough to really slow him down. He'll be back. He'll try again."

Jasim wrapped his fingers around my wrists but didn't pull them away. He simply held them. "We'll be ready," he said, voice exceptionally gentle.

An incredulous scoff blasted out of me. "Ready? Ilias is making unusually large sacrifices in Wethai, probably trying to reach Shaya himself. Anwar is sending men to kill me. Sen—we haven't had contact with him in . . . fuck, I don't remember, but he has ears all over Ketopolis. He'll have heard about the invasion by now, he'll be plotting, and maybe Nasir—"

"Hey." Jasim ducked his head to catch my eyes. "I won't let anything happen to you." One of his thumbs smoothed up and down in an entirely unconscious movement, soothing, calming. Gradually, my rushing pulse slowed. "I never should have let you out of my sight. It's my job to watch over you, and I failed you. It won't happen again, my queen. I promise."

The way he said *my queen* in that soft tone, gazing at me with those brown eyes that resembled sand under a sunset, it sounded like a claim. As if he were calling me *his*.

My pulse picked up again. For a different reason.

I glanced at his cheek, the one I'd smacked, and swallowed thickly. There wasn't even a hint of redness anymore. Still, that unpleasant feeling crushed my chest. "Does it hurt?"

He shook his head, not taking his eyes from mine. "You stopped being able to hurt me a long time ago, my queen."

Between us, I heard the whisper of my words *romantic entanglement*. Inadequate. No wonder he'd laughed.

While Jasim had one look that sent me running, it was this one that always drew me back. There was no blind, fanatical gleam. No lustful, hungry looks. Just a tranquil gaze that said he cared for me. Not the Gods-Chosen. Not the Queen of Ashorah. *Me*. "Amunet" was separate from all the other titles. Sometimes I thought she might not be any of them.

The back of my neck itched fiercely. As if there were something beneath my skin trying to burrow its way out.

Which reminded me that look was a delusion. For the both of

us. I *was* the Gods-Chosen. I *was* the queen. Indulging in the contrary was stupid. And dangerous.

I slid my wrists from his grip and averted my eyes.

He pulled my dress back down over my legs. "We'll stay here for the night. We should be in Reeda in a few days." His eyes dipped to my side. "Maybe a little longer, depending on how fast we move."

I nodded curtly. Scratched at the back of my neck.

Baba? You there?

No breeze came. Not that I expected it to.

Shaya had not saved me from the Kaldfolk. He had not saved me from an assassin.

Between that insufferable itch, the *clink, clink, clink* in my head, nefarious circling princes, and Jasim, we couldn't reach Reeda fast enough.

TEN

〰〰〰〰〰

SAMIRA

Velka crouched beside me and held out a wooden plate filled with some sort of smoked fish and a tin cup of that strange milky drink they all seemed to enjoy. "I'm sure it's not as fancy as the stuff you usually eat," she said with the barest hint of a smile, "but it's better than nothing."

I stared at the bit of roasted fish, slightly pink and charred along the edges. If I allowed it, my stomach would have let out a loud rumble. I was hungry. But I was used to hunger. For the most part, I was pretty good at ignoring it. The only times it was really difficult were when I had to look directly at food, like the night of the invasion.

Or right now, staring at the plate of fish.

The rest of the Seven ate the exact same thing around the campfire. Muscles in Dalla's jaw popped as she chewed and chewed and chewed. The fish must be really tough. Something that would make my queen turn up her nose. But all I could think about was how hollow my stomach felt, how that persistent gnawing had become almost impossible to ignore.

I wanted to eat. Very, very badly.

My eyes flicked up to Velka. She was only a few years older than me, with a light brown braid that hung over her shoulder, a couple of feet shorter than Keir's. Her heart-shaped face remained soft and open as she held the plate out in one heavily tattooed hand. Her smile was kind. Yet I hesitated.

I had decided that morning that they would definitely wait to kill me until we'd reached their king, but as the day had gone by, with Keir's words echoing in my ears, I'd come to the conclusion that I couldn't trust a single thing they said or did. They possessed manipulative magic that could turn my own mind against me. I'd already seen the strength of their Shifter abilities, capable of ripping apart Ashorah's fiercest soldiers and sniffing out a lie when they weren't even in their animal forms. It stood to reason their magic would be just as strong.

They weren't safe. I had to remain vigilant. If she wanted me to eat the fish, then I definitely *shouldn't* eat the fish.

I shook my head and pulled my knees to my chest, resting my still-tender back against the tree trunk.

Velka frowned. "You must be hungry, Your Majesty. Or at least thirsty."

"I'm fine." As an afterthought, I added, "Thank you." My chains clanked loudly as I wrapped my arms around my knees, folding into myself. The skin around my wrists, rubbed raw from the metal shackles, pulsed painfully in time with my heartbeat.

"Are you sure? We still have a full day—"

"She said she doesn't want it," Bain said around the food in his mouth. "Don't beg her."

Unintentionally, my gaze slid to Keir sitting beside him. He was already looking at me, plate licked clean. He'd scarfed it down without thought. "Bain's right," he said. "If she doesn't want to eat, leave her be."

"Keir, come on. You said she'd eat today."

"Well, I didn't know she was on a diet, did I?" He rolled his eyes and chucked his plate to the ground. "If you care so much, force-feed her."

Ice shot through my veins, and I shook my head, ready to beg for a second time.

But Velka just sighed and rose, taking the plate and cup with her. "I'll see if anyone wants seconds."

"I want seconds," Bain said.

"Assholes don't get seconds." Velka glared and stalked off toward the tents. Bain watched her go with a strange look in his eyes. I was too caught up in my own relief to try to decipher it.

Conversation picked up within the circle. Bain leaned over and mumbled something to Keir, which made him laugh.

I'd opted for not sitting within the warmth of the circle tonight. I wanted to remain as far away from them as possible, especially after deciding that Keir was trying to use his heretic magic on me. But as I watched Velka return with an empty plate, the X on my chest throbbed, reminding me of familiar guilt and shame.

Maybe I should have eaten the fish. Maybe that was what my queen would have wanted me to do. Or would she prefer that I starve myself before I reach their king, so the Kaldfolk would never think they'd gotten the better of the Gods-Chosen? Questions and indecision swirled through my head. I didn't know what to do, didn't know what was right or wrong, what the gods would reward me for, what would see them turning their backs on me.

The one thing I did know: I was failing them.

I could almost feel the Seven Monarchs' disappointed eyes searing into me, Ketet and her husband, Phadar, and all the other gods. Weak, useless, pathetic. If I were still in Khada Palace, I'd be punished for such failure, and gods knew I'd deserve it.

The thoughts festered, filling me with guilt so acidic it felt as if it were burning away my stomach lining. The campfires faded and darkness stole in. Even the Seven's fire was allowed to gutter to mere embers, all of them shutting their eyes. No one to keep watch. I assumed that meant someone else, maybe among the tents, had been charged with that shift tonight.

It gave me just enough privacy to carry out my own punishment.

I dug my already raw wrists farther into the bolts of the shackles, biting my tongue against the pain. Blood welled up, trickled down, made my hands slick.

Ketet, forgive me. I will not back away from your will again. I will face it. I will—

My right hand slipped free.

The world came to a screeching halt.

The red of my blood glistened under the light of the stars. It had coated my hand so thoroughly that it had taken no real effort to slide it out of the shackle.

My eyes flicked to my left hand, also slick with blood. Slowly, I pulled.

It slipped out, too.

I held my free hands in front of my face, gaping.

Run.

No, it was too easy. It was—

I looked around the camp.

The Kaldfolk's chests rose and fell rhythmically, a couple snored. No one shouted in alarm. No one came at me with swords. It was as if nothing had happened.

Run!

I rose to my feet as silently as possible, careful not to jostle a single twig, eyes firmly trained on the sleeping monsters. The Frozen Sands' white peaks were just barely visible in the distance, iridescent in the moonlight. I took a step—

No. No, this was not freedom, but a sign from Ketet. A sign that I wasn't a prisoner. I was an agent of the gods. I was protecting the Gods-Chosen, protecting all of Ashorah. If I fled now . . . I didn't think the Mother would forgive that.

I rubbed my hand over my chest, feeling the grooves of the *X* through my nightgown. I couldn't run. I wouldn't.

I *was* weak and useless and pathetic, a coward. The bottom of my nightgown was still stained with my own piss. But all I had to do to make up for it—was nothing. Sit, stay, take whatever the Kaldfolk had planned. That was all I had to do.

As quietly as I'd gotten free, I slid my hands back into their shackles and settled against the ground. Wrists aching, I pulled the blanket they'd given me all the way up to my frozen nose.

When I glanced up, Keir was looking right at me. His yellow eyes were beacons in the night. He hadn't made a sound, hadn't even sat up, but I knew he'd seen the whole thing.

My stomach bottomed out, knuckles white around the blanket. Something told me that if I had tried to run, I would've been carrion before I'd gotten very far.

Eventually, his eyes drifted closed again.

In the morning, Keir and the others gathered their supplies as usual. No one even sniffed strangely in my direction. I almost thought the whole thing had been ignored or forgotten.

Until Keir climbed into the saddle behind me. He gripped my arms and reeled me back against him. I swallowed my wince as my back twinged. "Try that again," he growled into my ear, "and I'll really give you a reason to piss yourself. Consider this your one warning, Majesty."

I nodded quickly, shoulders by my ears, stomach coiling tightly.

He seized my jaw and twisted me to face him. Those gleaming eyes seared into mine. "Tell me you understand."

"I un-understand," I stuttered obediently.

His nostrils flared. His fingers softened imperceptibly, a strange look flashing through his eyes, before he grunted, "Good." He released me roughly, took up the reins, and kicked the horse into motion.

* * *

It took another two days before we finally approached what looked like civilization. A place that *used* to be populated, but now the wooden buildings were in disrepair, and there weren't enough people milling around to account for the number of buildings.

The farther north we traveled, the colder it grew. Not even Keir's abnormal body heat was enough to chase it off. I clamped my jaw as tightly as I could to stop my teeth chattering, but it did little good.

Keir sighed in annoyance. I heard the soft *snick* of a clasp being undone and then warmth blanketed me. A weight settled on my shoulders. He'd draped his fur cloak around me. Heat seeped into me, mercifully warming my frigid bones, wrapping me in a spicy, earthy smell. Like a mulberry tree. "Thank you."

Beneath the cloak, Keir wore a thick gray tunic over matching wool pants, tied with a wide leather belt around his center. A pendant in the shape of a bear hung from a cord around his neck. "Your shivering was getting irritating." He didn't even deign to look at me.

Regardless, I burrowed into the cloak.

We passed expansive forests, filled with trees I'd never seen in Ashorah. There was something strange about them. Not just the way they curled in on themselves instead of standing tall, or the leaves that hung limply from their branches. Despite the bright clouds in the overcast sky, darkness seemed to writhe in the forests' depths. Hypnotic. Beckoning. I felt myself beginning to lean out of the saddle. Horrified, I jerked myself upright again. No one else seemed fazed or even bothered to mention it, which only intensified my disturbed shudder.

Eventually, real towns began to trickle into view. They grew more congested the longer we traveled. We rode past villages full of Kaldfolk. Wooden cabins and fenced farms. People stared at us, eyes wide. I thanked the gods there wasn't any of the depravity and violence from Nadia's story. At least none that I could see.

It was dark by the time our horses finally slowed in front of a large house made of cedarwood. Its rounded roof towered over us, and its walls extended all the way into the mountain behind it, wood melding with stone. Immense carved double doors gaped open in front of us, bordered by two tall flags of white and brown, each with a ferocious bear at its center.

"Cano," Keir barked.

The young Kald halted his horse beside us.

"Cabin."

"On it." Cano dismounted and jogged off.

Before I could see where he was going, Keir slid gracefully off our horse, then turned to me. He yanked me unceremoniously from the saddle and plunked me at his side. My bottom had gone mostly numb from the long ride, and the muscles in my back had cramped from the awkward position I'd taken to lean away from him. He gave me an experimental sniff and shrugged. "Only residual fear. Good enough." Then he shoved me through the doors.

ELEVEN

SAMIRA

Kaldfolk filled the space. Laughing, chattering, swigging from tankards in their seats around two long wooden tables. Above them hung iron chandeliers, dozens of candles bathing the place in a warm glow. The tables were painted blue, now peeling, and riddled with suspicious stains that looked an awful lot like blood. Braziers and a firepit at the center of the room wafted heat toward me.

At the opposite end of the hall sat a massive throne fashioned out of antlers. A man perched there, observing our arrival.

Keir held on to my chain and strode down the aisle between the tables, dragging me along on weak knees. The rest of my captors filed in behind us. Talk melted away and all gazes swung to me. Latching on with predatory eyes.

I'd spent sixteen of my twenty-two years on this earth training myself to be unseen. The scars on my back pulsed with the reminder of what happened when that training lapsed. But now every single person in the room was staring at me, watching my every step. My shoulders hitched up toward my ears, a useless shield.

Keir halted in front of that antler throne and dropped to one knee, bowing his head. "My king," he greeted the man.

Though the man on the throne wore no crown, I recognized the posture of a royal. A confidence in his broad shoulders, intelligence in his face. Though his brown eyes were less predatory than the others'. Almost soft.

He held his hand out to Keir, who rose and clasped the king by the forearm. The king said, "I'm glad to see you've returned safely."

"I wish I could say the same for all of us."

The king's eyes saddened, and he rubbed a hand to his sternum, wincing as if the skin was tender. "Alarik," he whispered. Unlike Keir—and most of the Kaldfolk, it would seem—the king wore a short beard and left his hair unbraided. His black locks hung freely to his waist, combed to the side to show off the red tattoos curving around his right ear. Until now, I had only seen Kaldfolk with black or blue tattoos. I wondered if red symbolized his position as king.

Keir gave a somber nod. "Plus about a dozen black-marked. Zaid was not as welcoming as we'd hoped. I hardly got a word out."

The king's shoulders lowered as the deaths settled on him. His grip on Keir's forearm tightened while his other hand lifted to clap him on the shoulder. He didn't say anything, but Keir nodded as if he had.

Then the king's eyes flicked to me, and he frowned. "What is this?"

"This was the best we could do." Keir looked to me. "Meet the Gods-Chosen."

The temperature seemed to plummet by several degrees. The king stared at me, jaw tight, before his dark gaze returned to Keir. Their silence was loaded with tense displeasure.

My eyes darted between them as shock settled over me. This had not been the king's plan. Keir and the others had brought me here of their own volition. My mind fumbled over the realization as I rapidly reevaluated. Kidnapping a queen risked the might of the Khada Guard, but when that queen was also the Gods-Chosen? Keir was taunting the gods themselves. For what? Why would he do such a thing without his king's knowledge or support? And if the king did not want me here, would he dispose of me? Or send me back to Ashorah?

In a voice so quiet, I doubted anyone beyond our huddle could hear, the king ordered, "Release her immediately."

Keir slipped a key out of his pocket. My shackles clanked loudly as they hit the ground.

Relief spread through me as my raw skin felt the cool kiss of the air.

"The east cabin is prepared," Keir said.

"How convenient."

They exchanged another blisteringly cold look. My ears rang in the quiet.

Keir lowered his eyes.

The king stalled a moment longer before drawing a deep breath and letting the ice melt from his expression. When he turned to me, his smile was kind. "Princess Amunet," he greeted, Kald accent lilting.

"Queen," Velka corrected softly.

He sighed in resignation. More disappointed by that bit of news than angry. "Right. Welcome to Frostguard, Your Majesty. Allow me to introduce myself. I am Rade of Frostguard, King of Kaldfold. Please forgive my warriors for their . . . zeal. I hope the shackles were the worst of their treatment." He looked pointedly at Keir, who came to stand at his right side.

"Um . . ." I glanced at Keir, his very presence threatening. "Yes. They treated me very well, Your Majesty."

King Rade's eyes dropped to the dried blood on my hands, and his smile faltered. I didn't know if he thought it was a result of a wound perpetrated by his men or if I was about to get a firsthand look at Kaldfolk bloodlust.

But King Rade said, "As of now, the queen is under my protection." He gazed out at the rest of the room. "Understood?"

"Yes, my king," came the thundering response. Keir's strange eyes met mine when he echoed, "Yes, my king."

"You must be tired," he said to me. "We will speak after you've rested. Come." He waved for me to follow him out of the large cedarwood cabin.

The ground was slippery with a thin layer of ice. Winter was the only time Ashorah saw even the slightest bit of frost, but here, despite it being the middle of summer, the ground glittered with it. I couldn't help but think it slightly cruel of the gods. This meager amount was enough to shimmer with hope but not enough to chip off and drink. A tease in a drought.

King Rade led me to a smaller cabin a few yards away. Cano was inside, stacking a pile of fur blankets atop a large bed. A steaming tub waited to my right. Wood popped in a fireplace against the wall opposite the door, cocooning the room in a comforting warmth. Not like the too-hot body heat of Keir's cloak, or the pockets of warmth from the braziers in the main room. The cold of Kaldfold didn't reach this room at all.

"The windows don't open," King Rade told me. "And you will be in view of the longhouse at all times. This is the safest place in all of Frostguard."

If I weren't still scared, I would have chuckled. I was only safe until they decided to kill me, which didn't feel very safe at all.

Though if they were just going to kill me, why bother setting up an entire cabin for me? Why draw a bath or assemble so many blankets? Why go to the trouble?

King Rade continued, "And for added security, I'm assigning my First as your personal guard." He gestured to Keir, who had trailed us to the cabin. "Seems only fair, since he was the one who decided to bring you here," he added, voice full of reproach.

Keir met my eyes, and his lips curled up at the ends. I blanched. Three days in a saddle with him was more than enough time. Clearing my throat, I tried, "King Rade, I don't—"

"Just Rade," he corrected. "And I thought I might call you Amunet, if that's all right?"

"I . . . Yes. Yes, that's fine."

Rade nodded and clasped his hands behind his back. "Is the cabin not to your liking?"

My eyes darted to the king's First. His friend, clearly. I didn't want to risk offending the king by refusing his presence. "It's perfect," I answered instead. "Thank you."

"Excellent. We shall speak in the morning." Rade offered a short bow and said, "Good night, Amunet. Keir, a word." He turned on his heel and left.

Keir met my eyes once more. Even though he was very clearly in trouble, his otherworldly eyes gleamed with amusement as he filed after Rade. Cano shut the door softly behind them. I heard a distinct *click.*

Though it was useless, I tried the knob. It was indeed locked. On the other side, I heard the hiss of a heated conversation but could not decipher words through the thick wood.

Alone, I turned back to the room. Despite how toasty it was, a shiver rolled through me, and I rubbed my arms. My head was spinning as I tried to make sense of the luxuries of the room when I had expected, at best, a grimy cell. At worst, a muddy ditch in the ground.

Dying for the Gods-Chosen was frightening but easy. Suffering for her would be a bit harder—but that just meant the gods would reward me all the more in the After Realm. But playing along until I knew why Keir had brought me here and what the king planned to do with me . . . I couldn't impersonate her forever. In fact, I could hardly impersonate her at all. I'd only lasted this long by staying silent.

I was nobody. A slave plucked from the slums of Ketopolis. A constant disappointment to the gods. A daughter to parents I hardly remembered. Not their names or their faces or their voices. I had no surname, no identity past Samira.

Perhaps they didn't plan on killing Queen Amunet, but they most certainly *would* kill the insignificant girl pretending to be her.

I didn't move from my spot by the door, didn't approach the bed no matter how luxurious it seemed. My feet were rooted in place as the terror of the past few days caught up with me, and I burst into tears, clapping a hand over my mouth to muffle myself.

I could see the shadows of Keir's feet under the door, where he was standing guard. If he heard Queen Amunet crying, he might grow suspicious, might warn his king that something was amiss. Queen Amunet would not cry. She would threaten to bring the might of the gods down on every last one of the Kaldfolk.

But knowing that didn't stop me from sobbing. I choked on my tears. The fear was overwhelming, stealing my breath.

The door clicked again. Unlocking.

Gods, save me. I stumbled back and quickly wiped away my tears.

Keir opened the door. I saw him pause as he took in my blotchy face, eyebrows twitching together, but he said nothing as he stepped aside and let Velka in.

She carried a plate and cup in her hands and gave me a friendly smile. "I thought maybe now that we've arrived, you'd like to eat."

I stared. Her yellow eyes were unguarded, and her smile lacked malice. But Keir's gaze over her shoulder seemed to promise the opposite.

As if she could hear my thoughts, Velka glanced at him over her shoulder. "You mind?"

Keir huffed in annoyance and shut the door.

Velka just rolled her eyes. "Ignore him." Then she held out her offering again, the blue tattoos decorating her knuckles and disappearing up the sleeves of her tunic almost shimmering in the firelight. "I know you're not a fan of fish," she said, "so I brought pork. And kefir, of course."

"Kuh-feer?" I repeated awkwardly.

She paused. "Do you not have it in Ashorah?"

"I don't think so . . ."

"Well, you're going to love it. Fermented goat's milk." I blinked. That must be what they'd been gulping down on the trip here. Velka gestured to the bed. "I'll set it down there?"

I nodded.

"Not much of a talker, eh?" Velka crossed the room and placed the plate and cup at the foot of the bed. "Bit refreshing, honestly. The boys out there never shut up." At my silence, her smile turned crooked. "That was a joke."

"Right. Sorry."

"I'm Velka, by the way. I never really introduced myself. Velka of the Pillars."

"The Pillars?"

"A town by the mountains far west of here."

"Oh." I wondered if my queen would've known where the Pillars was. She probably did. She'd probably been taught the world's geography.

But Velka either didn't notice or didn't care about my lack of knowledge. She pointed to the food again. "Do you like pork, Your Majesty?"

I didn't know if I liked pork, but I nodded. Velka waited expectantly. Hesitantly, I reached out and picked up a piece, sniffed it, and laid it experimentally on my tongue. Somehow sweet and savory, with a hint of a spice I couldn't name that gave it a little bit of a kick.

Gods, it was the greatest thing I'd ever tasted.

My stomach rumbled violently, like it suddenly remembered how hungry it was.

But I stalled. It felt wrong. Like when I'd debated eating my queen's bread. This meal wasn't meant for me. I ate what Chef Nena got back from the stable hands. Not well-seasoned pork. This was my queen's meal.

But I was *so* hungry. And I was supposed to be Queen Amunet. This was what Queen Amunet ate, so . . .

Another grumble from my stomach and I couldn't stop my hand

from shooting out and grabbing another piece, this one bigger, and shoving it into my mouth. A moan snuck past my lips.

Velka chuckled. "Good?"

My cheeks heated.

"Hey, it's all right," Velka said, hands up. "No judgment here. Eat however you like. There's soap on that table there, and the bath should already be hot, so help yourself. Be warned, it's seawater. I know you Ashorans have fresh water, but this is all we're able to scrounge up here. Towels and clothes are next to the soap, and Keir is just outside. If you need anything, tell him to get me. And don't let him scare you. He's really just a big cuddly bear."

A growl sounded from outside.

"You heard me," Velka replied without raising her voice. As if he were in the room with us. I glanced between her and the door. "Can . . . *can* he hear you?"

"Oh yeah. All of a Shifter's abilities are heightened." At the look on my face, she quickly added, "But we can choose not to use them. For privacy. Right, Keir?"

No response.

Velka snorted. "Bastard."

I studied her. She'd forgone the fur cloak that most of the Kaldfolk wore, and was dressed simply in a deep blue tunic. Blue tattoos covered her hands. She didn't seem like it, but . . . "Are you a servant?"

"Rade doesn't have servants," she said. "He used to, but after the Shroud—well, we can't really afford that sort of labor anymore."

"The Shroud?"

"You . . . don't know about the Shroud?" She waved a hand. "I'm sure the king will tell you all about it in the morning. But if you want someone to attend to you, I can send for—"

"No!" Someone who would dress or bathe me would see the scars on my back, not fit for a queen. I schooled my features into a look of exhaustion and repeated more calmly, "No, that's all right. I'll probably just eat and go to bed."

Velka smiled and bowed at the waist. "Sleep well, Your Majesty." She turned for the door and waited expectantly. When nothing happened, she let out an exasperated sigh. "Come on, Keir."

The door opened and Keir snarled in her face, a look so fearsome I took a few steps back.

Velka just snarled in return, her face equally as terrifying, before flipping her braid over her shoulder and strutting away. This time, Keir didn't even look at me before shutting the door and locking it.

Once again on my own, my stomach growled. There was no more hesitation; I devoured the meal. Even the kefir—though it burned the back of my throat and sent me hacking—was a blessing. I gulped it down almost as fast as I inhaled the pork.

After the meat was gone, its taste lingered on my tongue, and my stomach pulsed uncomfortably. It was a new sensation, being full. I'd never been full before.

It was a glorious feeling.

I glanced at the steaming tub. That felt like a step too far. Maids washed with a damp rag. A bath, utilizing so much water, was a luxury only fit for the Gods-Chosen.

But it was salt water. There was plenty of *that*. And it would seem strange for the queen not to wash. Plus, it was very plausible that tomorrow would spell the end for me. Tonight could be my only chance to take a proper bath in my entire life.

Before I could talk myself out of it, I shed my queen's nightgown and climbed into the tub. The hair stood up all over my body as I sank into the blissfully warm water. *Holy gods.* Any remaining chill vanished in moments. It was as if the heat sapped every ounce of tension out of me as I melted back against the metal tub.

I washed. Really washed. The salt stung my bloody wrists and back, but I endured it as I watched grime and filth slide off my skin, turning the water a murky brown. I could actually see freckles. I had freckles, little dark circles against my already tanned skin, dotting my forearms, a smattering on my thighs.

Though it didn't really make sense, I felt like I could finally . . . breathe. As if the filth had been drowning me and now I'd managed to break through the surface.

I stayed in the tub until the water was entirely cold. Then I used an obscenely plush towel to dry off and dressed in the clothes Velka had pointed out. A tunic the shade of sand on a hot day, nearly golden, lined with fleece, and wool pants. Shrugging the garments on was like surrounding myself in a cloud.

Then I knelt beside the bed and muttered quickly through Nightly Prayer. No, my queen wasn't here, but perhaps she'd feel the gods' blessings wherever she was. If it was possible, my body relaxed even further as the calm of prayer settled over me.

I hadn't slept in days. If I'd been asked this morning, I would have anticipated another sleepless night. But the feather mattress was infinitely more comfortable than my cot or the hard ground, and I was fed, bathed, and so, so exhausted.

I was asleep in a matter of heartbeats.

TWELVE

AMUNET

King Zaid gazed down at me with sad eyes from where he sat on the edge of my bed. That was the way he'd looked at me for months now, but tonight, the weight on either side of his lips seemed heavier, the lines around his sparkling green eyes deeper, and he wasn't wearing his crown. He *always* wore his crown.

I rubbed the sleep from my eyes and yawned loudly. "What's wrong, Baba?"

He tried to smile. But his frown was just too heavy for him to accomplish it. "I need you to wake up, little one."

"Why?"

He placed his hand on my shoulder, and I could feel the slight tremble. "This is important, Amunet. I'll explain later."

I should've been afraid. Or at the least, cautious. But he was my father. I trusted him. Of course I did. So I obediently threw back my sheets and slid out of bed, clutching my ratty crocodile doll to my chest.

Father offered me his hand, and I took it.

The hallway was deserted. Even at a mere six years old, I knew that was strange. There were always guards and servants around. But not that night. That night, I could hardly even hear the rushing sound of the Lotus River. As if all of Ashorah had gone silent.

"You remember your lessons about the Seven Monarchs?" Father asked me. His palm was sweaty against mine. Nothing strange about that—this was Ashorah. Everyone was sweaty all the time.

I nodded.

"Do you remember what you learned about the Gods-Chosen?"

"When things get really bad, the gods send their children to help us," I recited, nose curling as dirt and sand stuck to the pads of my bare feet. "They are called the Gods-Chosen. There have been six Gods-Chosens so far, but a seventh is coming soon. Shaya's child. A gift he gave to you after he saved you in the Wastelands."

"Very good, little one. That's very . . . good." His voice hitched.

I looked up at him. The moonlight reflected the line of wetness running down his left cheek, a river of silver. My brows drew together. That wasn't sweat. "Baba, are you crying?"

He pulled me through another door, into his bedroom suite. There were no guards stationed there, either. That wasn't just strange. That was *wrong*.

Suddenly, where there had been no fear before now surged forth a heaping dose of it. My heart thundered, and I crushed the crocodile doll to my small chest. "Baba?"

My father paused in the parlor outside his sleeping chamber and crouched so he was eye level with me. His green eyes shone brighter, outlined in more silvery tears. The terror intensified in my veins, as if burning oil had replaced my blood. Fathers weren't supposed to cry.

He took my shoulders in his hands and looked me straight in the eye. "Listen to me carefully, Amunet. *You* are a Gods-Chosen."

A bit of excitement wound through my fear. Gods-Chosens had magic. If I was a Gods-Chosen, that meant *I* would get to play with magic.

But before the giddiness could really take root, he continued, "This is my fault. I'm sorry, little one. I thought there was more time, that I could figure something else out, but the river is drying up again, and I—" He cut himself off abruptly, heaving a sharp breath.

Again he tried to smile, but it wobbled as another rivulet fell down his cheek. "I need you to be brave, all right?"

My brows scrunched together as I nodded.

He took my hand again and led me to the large balcony outside his room. All expertly chiseled stone, made to look like a courtyard instead of merely a balcony, with clipped and sculpted topiaries. But none of that was new to me. I barely spared it a glance.

The smell registered before the image. Deep and metallic. Sticky beneath my bare feet.

Blood.

The crocodile fell out of my hands, landed in the blood with a dull, wet splat.

Bodies were piled high, at least five deep. Arms and legs stuck out of the pile awkwardly, twisting wrong. As if they'd been tossed there. And their faces . . . gods, their faces. All of them wrenched in unending screams, frozen in a state of abject terror.

A sob climbed up my throat. "Baba—"

"Sacrifices are necessary to reach him. You know that. But I needed a bigger one for this. Now, I need you to repeat after me, Amunet." My father stood behind me, gripping my shoulders hard enough to make me wince. "I, Amunet Khada, offer up this gift to Shaya . . ."

I looked up at him. From this angle, he looked nothing like the father I knew. Looming over me. Face stoic and severe. Scary. "I don't want to—"

"Say it." His fingers tightened on my shoulders.

My eyes burned as I repeated, "I, Amunet Khada, offer up this gift to Shaya . . ."

"And pledge myself as your servant."

"Please, Baba—*ah!*" He shoved me a step forward, my foot splashing the blood up my shin. Tears seared my cheeks. "And pledge myself as your servant."

"I accept you into my mind, my body, my soul . . ."

I shook my head, but there was nowhere to go. My father was

blocking the door, and the bodies . . . the bodies prevented me from running to the edge of the balcony. "I accept you into my mind, my body, my soul . . ."

"And vow to be yours until my dying breath."

"No, Baba," I sobbed. "I don't want—"

He spun me around, fingers still clamped around my shoulders, and stared down at me with a fury that almost made his Khada-green eyes glow, his pearly white teeth as bright as a full moon within his black beard as he bared them at me. *Say. It.*

I flinched back in fear. In a voice so small, I couldn't hear it over the rushing of my pulse, I whimpered, "And vow to be yours until my dying breath."

An icy breeze shot through the gaps in the balustrade. It wrapped around me in a funnel of cold so intense, it burned. It stole my breath as shudders spread over me. Though I knew it was useless, I tried to run.

My father's fingers were claws in my shoulders as he forced me to face the pile of bodies.

And the darkness that climbed over them.

My breaths shuddered in and out as I watched it crest the small hill of bodies. Like an inky plume of black smoke. It had no eyes, yet I felt as if it was looking right at me.

I screamed and struggled against the king's grip. But he wouldn't let go.

Cold unfurled from that darkness, emanated from it. I couldn't feel my toes, my fingers.

"Stop fighting," my father said in my ear. The harshness was gone. The words sounded like a plea. "You have to stop fighting, Amunet."

But I couldn't. I tried to dislodge his grip, screaming and screaming and screaming, even as the darkness slithered closer. Every hair on my body stood on end, my heart in a full-out sprint. But it didn't matter how hard I resisted; I couldn't break free.

I watched in horror as the smoke reached my feet and began to crawl up my legs, bare beneath my nightgown. Ice seeped into me, freezing my blood, my bones, choking off my screams. My father's hands finally fell away, but the darkness held me frozen as it ate its way up my body.

It reached my mouth, which was still gaping open in a frozen shriek, and plunged inside.

I couldn't see the balcony anymore. Couldn't see anything at all. All around me was the darkness. It strangled me, stole my breath, my words, my tears. It funneled inside me until there wasn't room for *me* anymore, until I was being crushed inside my own body.

No air, no space, only the cold, the dark, and a dull scratching at the back of my skull.

Help! Help! Hel—

A hand covered my mouth.

My eyes burst open.

Jasim's dark eyes stared back at me, his fingers tight over my mouth. Sunlight shone through the leaves of the cypress tree Jasim had stitched me up under.

A scream clung to the back of my throat, mind stuck halfway between the nightmare and this world. I scrambled to find things in the present to ground myself in the here and now.

But then I realized Jasim's body was on top of mine, covering me. And those dark eyes were wide, boring into mine. Imploring me to understand—

A low growl rumbled.

My muscles locked up. Jasim's heart thundered where his chest pressed into mine. Slowly, staying as still as I could, I turned my head to the left.

The creature that approached us kept its snout low to the ground, nostrils flaring. Its head looked like a leopard's, complete with spotted fur and jagged teeth that dripped saliva, but its long body was fortified by a hide more akin to a crocodile's. The paws that thumped closer with each second belonged on a lion, and the curling, venomous tail at its back was a scorpion's. The growl that bubbled out of it was menacing and guttural.

A chimera.

I knew the solitary mismatched predators roamed the deserts far from the cities, but gods, I never thought I'd see one. The scream that had been stuck in my throat worked its way to my tongue.

Jasim's hand tightened over my mouth, fingers biting into my flesh. My gaze jerked back to his. Though there was fear, his eyes were also filled with a command. *Quiet.*

I swallowed down the scream, felt it drop like a boulder into my stomach, and nodded.

Jasim cautiously removed his hand but remained on top of me. He ducked his head, so close his lips brushed my ear as he dared to whisper, "Scimitar. Left side."

I lifted my left hand and reached for his blade.

"Slowly." Jasim's eyes darted between me and the chimera. It snarled, head dipping so low that its jaw brushed the earth.

Oh gods.

Moving with excruciating slowness, my hand settled against his ribs and slid down toward his hip. The metal of the pommel brushed my fingertips and I clutched at it. Jasim murmured, "When it attacks, roll to the side and get to your feet as quickly as possible. Make as much noise as you can. Aim your strikes at the tail first, then go for the head."

I nodded. "And what are you going to do?"

He met my eyes, and I saw the decision there, suddenly understanding why he was on top of me. "You are the Gods-Chosen," he whispered. "Your survival is all that matters."

Plenty of guards had sacrificed their lives for me—as recently as just a few days ago. It was nothing new. In fact, it was expected.

So why did panic shoot through me at Jasim doing the same? "You can't—"

"Draw the blade," Jasim ordered, eyeing the chimera. It was only a handful of feet away now. So close I could count the spots in its face, see the venom collecting at its tail.

Continuing to keep my movements slow, I drew the scimitar from the sheath and held it by my wounded side.

The chimera's head lifted. My grip hardened around the pommel, adrenaline surged through my veins.

But then there was a commotion. Chatter, pots clanging together.

The chimera's spotted ears went flat, teeth bared as it snarled. I squeezed my eyes shut. Jasim's body curled tighter over mine, face in my neck, arm around my head. Trying to shield me as much as physically possible. Sand shifted as paws pounded. We braced, neither one of us breathing.

Nothing happened.

We didn't move for several moments. But then Jasim dared to lift his head. His body relaxed against mine as he breathed, "It's gone."

I peeked open my eyes. Sure enough, the chimera had vanished. Chased off by the loud noise. As if he could read my mind, Jasim glanced over his shoulder. I followed his gaze.

In the distance, I could just make out the blond shapes of camels and the people riding atop them. They were still far away, and part of our view was obstructed by the wide trunk of the cypress tree we'd camped under, but by the violet shade of their clothes, I knew they were merchants. Probably traveling from Ketopolis to Reeda just like us.

And unwittingly saving our lives on the way.

I let go of the scimitar and sagged against the ground.

Letting out a deep breath, Jasim dropped his head, curls falling over his forehead and skimming my cheek. "Thank the gods. I was not looking forward to being a chimera's breakfast."

I laughed hoarsely. "It would have spit you right out."

"I'll have you know, I'm delicious."

"Oh really? Covered in sweat and sand?"

"Seasoning."

I laughed again. He lifted his head to grin at me, both of us nearly delirious with relief. We were all right. No assassin. No vicious beasts. I made a half-hearted attempt to swat his shoulder. Jasim easily caught my wrist and pinned it to the ground.

My laughter faded. With that one movement, I became hyper-aware of his body on top of mine. Warm, firm. The calluses of his palm scratched against the sensitive skin of my wrist.

Jasim's smile banked. So did his eyes. Irises going from dark sand to a midnight sky.

This was how we'd met three years ago. Sparring in the Khada Guard. By then, I'd already been training with them for a few years, but in all that time, Jasim was the only one brave—or stupid—enough to actually put me on my ass. The first to fight back, the first to look at me with something that was neither cruelty nor obsession, the first to call me his friend.

My first everything.

I licked my lips, and those dark eyes darted down to watch the movement. His breath dusted over my lips, so close I could practically taste him already. Warmth swirled in my stomach. "Thank you," I murmured.

His voice was gravelly as he replied, "I promised to keep my queen alive, didn't I?"

The usual warnings rang in my ears—it was a myth, an illusion, and so on—but with the residual adrenaline still flowing through my veins, my mind struggled to hear them. An apology perched on my tongue. For hitting him. For snapping at him. For the stupid words *romantic entanglement*. He'd tease me for it—royals did not apologize, the Gods-Chosen did not, *I* never had. But I thought it might be worth it.

And then his gaze sank lower. To my side. "Sorry," he mumbled, and released my wrist as he rolled off me.

I stared at the rustling leaves above me in blank surprise. Jasim had fucked me many times. He knew exactly when I was giving permission, and he'd never *not* seized that opportunity before.

"How's your wound?" he asked.

When I looked at him, his eyes were firmly focused on my side. Which was stinging fiercely. But I said, "Fine." Then I stood and brushed the sand off me, fire branding my cheeks.

Jasim merely nodded and stood, too, holstering his scimitar. He avoided my eyes. "We should get going, then."

"Yeah." I scratched my nape as I watched him ready our camels, my brows tight. Two seconds ago, he'd been willing to die for me. Now he couldn't get away from me fast enough.

Unbidden, my nightmare rose in my mind. I hadn't thought about that night in years, but the memory was so vivid, I could almost smell the pile of bodies. Maybe King Zaid's death had conjured it, or my own near end. But as I dug my nails into the irritated skin of my neck, another thought occurred to me. One that made my blood chill.

Athar was the God of Mischief and Dreams. He was also Shaya's son, and my half brother. It was possible he had sent me the memory. That he wanted to help me reach our father.

Sacrifices are necessary to reach him. You know that. But I needed a bigger one for this.

Jasim glanced over at me, holding the camels' reins. "Ready?"

I stared at him as the thought took shape, calcified into a plan. I had intended to take Nasir's best calf from Reeda and spill its blood in the Temple of Shaya. But if my nightmare had been a message from Athar, a cow would not be enough. I needed something bigger.

That horrible feeling crushed my chest again. Heavier. My ribs groaned beneath it.

As Jasim helped me onto the camel, careful of my wound, careful not to hurt me, my eyes burned, and an epiphany settled on my shoulders as loud as the cicadas chittering around us. Funny that I had never realized it before.

I was a really, really bad person.

THIRTEEN

SAMIRA

I opened my eyes and stared up at the logs in the ceiling with furrowed brows. My room didn't have logs in the ceiling. It was smooth, made of brown clay. I turned to ask Nadia—

I lurched upright.

The too-soft bed.

The bathing tub.

My queen's nightgown discarded on the floor.

I wasn't in my room in Khada Palace. I was in Kaldfold. *Kaldfold.*

Events flooded back to me with startling swiftness. I swung my bare feet to the warm floor and willed my racing pulse to calm, drawing several deep breaths. Velka said the king would explain everything today. Rade had seemed . . . more reasonable than I'd expected. Even if he hadn't anticipated Queen Amunet being here, I didn't think he wanted to kill me. If he had, he would've done it the moment he saw me. He certainly wouldn't have unchained me and let me enjoy pork and kefir in the privacy of my own cabin.

No, he wanted something else. Something he needed me alive for.

Nerves slightly more settled now that I'd come to a decision, I did up the clasps of my tunic, stuffed my feet into boots, and knocked on the door.

The lock clicked, and then I was staring up into Keir's smile, bordered by twisting blue tattoos. The morning sunlight peeking through the clouds behind him attempted to soften his harsh features. A useless endeavor. This man was anything but soft. "Morning, Majesty."

I jutted my chin in the air as confidently as I could. "I wish to see the king."

"That's nice."

"Will you . . . take me to him?"

"No."

My bravado evaporated instantly. "Why not?"

"Uh, because you're a prisoner. Was that not clear?" Keir crossed his arms over his chest, the sword at his hip flashing in the morning light. "Plus, he's occupied."

I nodded meekly and moved to shut the door. That had been a terrible idea. Making demands, as if I were Amunet. Keir could probably smell the lie of my bravado. I'd just have to wait in my room until I was summoned.

Keir's foot wedged in the doorjamb. "That's it?"

I paused. "What do you mean?"

"You're just giving up?"

"Is there a point in fighting you?"

Keir's eyes flickered analytically over my face. A skilled warrior who didn't miss a thing. "Why didn't you run?" Those kohl-rimmed eyes met mine in a probing stare. "You started to, but you stopped. Why?"

"You would've killed me if I had."

"So you—what? Realized your mistake after making yourself bleed?"

"Yes."

His nostrils didn't flare, he didn't sniff, yet somehow I knew he was scenting me. He was searching for the truth, eyes raking over me. We stood like that for a long moment, my face consciously relaxed. I wouldn't so much as twitch wrong. If there was one thing

I'd learned in service to the Gods-Chosen, it was how to endure scrutiny. A probing stare was nothing new. I reminded myself that I was still in her service, and right now it was my duty to convince them all that I was Queen Amunet, at least until I knew why I was here.

I squared my shoulders the way I'd seen her do thousands of times, and asked, "Why did you tell me you weren't cannibals?"

"We had a deal, and I'm a man of my word."

"You could have just said you wouldn't kill me. But you specified cannibals."

Predatory amusement glinted in his amber eyes. "Why don't you beg me again, Majesty? Maybe you'll get another answer." He tilted his head. "But this time I'd like to see you on your knees."

I stiffened, throat closing up. My queen wouldn't have begged the first time. She certainly wouldn't lower herself to her knees before a Kald—before anyone.

"No? Don't feel like flashing those big doe eyes of yours today?" He shrugged and leaned his shoulder against the doorjamb, cloaking me in the smell of mulberries. The scent niggled at a memory. Something blurry, just out of reach.

"Here's another question," he mused, as if we were talking about the weather. "Why did the Gods-Chosen, Queen of Ashorah, daughter of Shaya, and infamous pain in the ass bother begging a Kald at all? Just to know what was waiting for you here? I would've thought it would take a lot more to break you."

I had to fight not to flinch at that. I wasn't sure why it came as such a shock. I would be hard-pressed to find a single slave in Khada Palace who *wasn't* broken. And yet when Keir said it, it hit me like a punch to the chest.

But quickly following that was fear. That he would find me out. That between my decision not to run and my complete lack of pride, he would realize I wasn't Queen Amunet. Keir was unpleasant, unhinged, but not unintelligent.

I swallowed past the lump in my throat and said, "Maybe you shouldn't believe everything you hear about me."

"Right. And what is it you call us? The cannibals in the north?" He scoffed and straightened away from the door, mercifully offering me a bit of space. "Rade will call for you when he's ready."

I blinked, glancing over his shoulder at the longhouse. I would have thought the Kaldfolk king would have been rushing to speak with the Gods-Chosen. But I supposed I wasn't going anywhere anytime soon . . .

My eyes trailed back to Keir. "You're going to stand here the whole time?"

"Thinking of running again, are you?"

"No," I said quickly. "I just . . . Won't you be bored?"

"Why?" His grin spread, making his yellow eyes gleam wickedly as he leaned forward again. "Are you volunteering to entertain me?"

Ice flooded my veins. "No."

He leaned even closer, until I could feel his supernatural body heat. "Because there are a few things I'd like to do to a Khada—"

I put my hand to his chest and pushed.

Keir glanced from my face to my hand, laughably small in the center of his barrel chest, and I could practically read his thoughts in his face. My pathetic show of resistance would mean nothing if he decided to do—whatever he was thinking of doing.

A low chuckle rumbled out of him. "Some fight at last. I was beginning to think we took the wrong queen."

My stomach dipped. Such an innocent sentence, and yet it filled me with dread.

Keir studied me a beat longer, but I couldn't decipher his look. If he was going to push his way into my cabin anyway or if he'd scented my reaction to his words and I'd already failed my queen—

A shout went up from the longhouse. I jerked my head toward it. "What was that?"

"Not your concern."

Before I could question him more, Dalla came rushing up to him. "Keir, you should come."

"Can't," he responded, hooking a thumb my way. "Babysitting."

Dalla's flinty eyes moved to me for only a second before she said, "It's Hedin."

Keir swore. "Bain knows?"

"You could say that." She looked purposefully toward the longhouse as people started rushing inside, their faces twisted in anger. It looked like a mob was flowing into the large cabin.

"Fine," Keir said. "You stay with the queen. I'll try to—"

"Oh, no." Dalla was already backing away with a grin, the expression unsettling on her severe face. "I'm not missing this."

"Dalla!"

Her laugh echoed as she turned and ran back to the longhouse.

Keir swore again, much more colorfully. Then he took my arm and pulled me out of my cabin.

I might have been curious about the shouting, but now that Keir was taking me there, it was the last place I wanted to go. Dragging my feet, I asked, "What are you doing?"

"I can't leave you unguarded," he answered. "Don't worry, Majesty, you'll enjoy this."

FOURTEEN

SAMIRA

A large crowd had gathered in the longhouse, roiling and shouting. Keir guided me along the perimeter, heading toward the dais. People parted for Keir like he was a rock in a river, opening a route to the front where I could see Rade and Bain facing off, the king on his antler throne and Bain staring up at him defiantly. A man I hadn't seen before stood beside Rade, his entire face covered in blue tattoos. It made him look even more frightening than Keir.

Bain was red in the face as he turned to address the crowd. "Alarik's only been dead a week! If our king can really replace him that easily, what does that mean for the rest of us?"

A shout of agreement went up.

"It has to be seven," the king yelled above the din. "Alarik isn't being replaced. A new member is being added—"

"Bullshit!" Bain whirled on the king. "We'd get along just fine with six."

Rade's jaw clenched. "This is your final warning, Bain. Stand. Down."

Bain pointed at the man with the face tattoos. "I do not accept Hedin as my Second."

"Shit," Keir murmured beside me as a battle cry went up among the crowd. Those had been official words. A declaration.

Rade's nostrils flared, the first real sign of his fury. Just then he looked as dangerous as the rest of them. And when he looked out over the mass of cheering like he was ready to breathe fire, a chill walked down my spine.

Keir leaned down and spoke directly in my ear so I could hear him over the shouting. "Try to run and I'll take my sweet time bringing you back," he said. Then he released my arm and stepped forward. "Let him earn it," he roared over the cacophony of the crowd.

The audience quieted and looked to Keir. He kept his arms crossed as he strode to the dais, the picture of unconcern. "The Seven are Kaldfold's strongest warriors," he said. "Our hierarchy is one of command, not strength. Each one of us could go toe to toe without gaining the upper hand." He jerked his chin at Hedin. "Let's see if he can."

Rade shook his head. "I'm not going to make him fight—"

"I accept!" Hedin boomed over the king. The crowd applauded.

Keir raised his eyebrows at Rade as if to say, *See? They love it.* "Bain was the one to object," he said. "So you will fight him. If you can hold your own for—what do you think?" He turned to Bain. "Ten minutes?"

Bain grinned, a wolf baring its teeth. "It'll only take five."

"All right. He stays on his feet for five minutes, and we will accept him as our new Second." He looked back to Hedin. "Yes?"

Hedin didn't back down from Bain's malicious smile, matching it with his own. "That sounds more than fair."

There was venom in Rade's voice when he barked, "Clear the area." His hand had been forced. He would have no choice but to oversee the fight. And even from a distance, I could see it outraged him.

I glanced back at Velka. She was biting her lip anxiously, but there was no hiding the excitement shining in her yellow eyes. It was reflected in Dalla's beside her, and in every other Kald here. My heart began racing, though it was certainly not excitement pumping through my veins.

Bain passed his fur cloak off to Keir, who resumed his spot beside me as Bain stepped into the clearing to face Hedin. They were well matched in size and strength, though Bain's eyes gleamed brighter than Hedin's, a touch of madness. Rade's Fourth stood in the center of the circle and waited, an axe and a blade strapped to either side of him.

Hedin paced, not able to match Bain's quiet menace. "How would you like your ass handed to you?" he taunted. "With swords, fists, or claws?"

Bain just kept grinning, the expression looking more and more twisted the longer it remained. "Your choice."

Hedin unsheathed his sword and tossed it aside. "Fists, then."

Bain's axe and sword clanked against the ground after his, fingers twitching eagerly at his sides. He didn't need weapons. He *was* a weapon.

I'd seen violence many times in Khada Palace and been on the receiving end of it more than I liked to count. But this . . . this was a different kind of violence. It wasn't punishment bestowed by the Gods-Chosen to teach a lesson. This was about to be vicious for no other reason than one man's dislike of another. If it was going to be anything like the night the Kaldfolk infiltrated the palace, I didn't want to see it.

Keir was focused on the fight. I could easily slip away and hide in my cabin.

But then Rade held his arm above his head and brought it down sharply. "Begin."

Hedin didn't hesitate. He launched himself at Bain. I flinched as Hedin's fist crashed into the side of Bain's face, snapping it to the left. And he didn't stop there.

Bain didn't even try to defend himself but took each hit. To the face, the jaw, the stomach. The crowd screamed with each blow, so loud I could barely hear my own breaths sawing out of my chest, but I didn't think Bain so much as grunted. Suddenly, I found myself rapt in morbid fascination, unable to move even if I wanted to.

"Come on!" people shouted.

"What are you waiting for?"

"Fight back, Bain!"

But he didn't. Hedin continued to pummel him. The more he was hit, the angrier the crowd grew. They wanted to see a fight, not this beating. I didn't like Bain, but it was difficult to watch him get hit over and over. I knew he could defend himself. *Everyone* knew he could. So what was he doing?

Hedin eventually had to pause to catch his breath, hands on his knees, and Bain straightened. Even though he'd just had the life kicked out of him, he seemed to tower over the gasping Hedin. A gash split Bain's right cheek, a bruise was already blooming over his jaw, and one of his eyes had swollen shut. He turned his head and spat out a glob of blood.

When he faced Hedin again, he smiled with bloodstained teeth.

Hedin scrambled to stand up straight, but he wasn't fast enough. Bain rammed his fist into Hedin's face, an uppercut that sent him stumbling backward. The crowd went crazy, a cheer loud enough to rock the mountaintops, and I realized this was as much a show as it was a fight. Bain had been biding his time, letting Hedin tire himself out before coming down on him with a wrath to rival the gods'.

Bain advanced slowly, a casual stroll, like he had all the time in the world. Hedin shook his head sharply as he tried to bring the world back into focus. But Bain had already reached him, pulling his arm back and sinking his huge fist into the side of Hedin's head.

He stumbled again, this time landing hard on his knees, eyes rolling.

Bain maneuvered around him and leaned over his shoulder to say something in his ear. It made Hedin's eyes widen, and he yelled out "No—" Bain wrapped one hand around his chin, and the other grabbed him by the back of his head. With a quick jerk, he snapped Hedin's neck, the *crack* reaching over the cry of the crowd to my ears.

I gasped in horror as Hedin collapsed on his face. He didn't move again.

Bain had killed him with his bare hands right in front of everyone.

And they were *cheering*. My stomach turned over and bile built in the back of my throat.

"Time?" Keir asked Velka.

She smirked, and it almost looked like pride as she gazed at Bain. "Four minutes, fifty-three seconds."

Bain grinned. "Like I said."

Keir sauntered into the ring to clasp Bain's hand. Bain laughed, high on the thrill of the fight. No one seemed to care that there was a dead body lying at his feet, someone whose only crime was not being liked by a group of six people.

Keir turned, and his eyes grazed over mine, smile falling away. I couldn't interpret the meaning in them. But newfound terror, sharp and consuming, sparked through me.

"Keir," Rade snapped. "My chambers." Without waiting for a response, he stalked down a hallway behind the throne.

Keir pulled his gaze away from mine to look at his friends and rolled his eyes, making Velka, Dalla, Cano, and Bain laugh—Sillia watched with a small smile against her best efforts—and then he followed his king down the hall.

They *laughed*. At murder.

At some point, I'd started to think Velka could be my ally here. *Foolish.* Somehow I'd forgotten that there had been a castle full of bears the night I was taken. None of them had acted on their own. None of them would be in Rade's Seven if they weren't equally vicious. Maybe Keir hadn't been lying when he said they weren't cannibals, but they were certainly monsters, all of them.

I didn't wait for Keir to return or for the others to finish celebrating. I spun around and ran back to my cabin, slamming the door shut behind me. If I could, if the gods hadn't picked me for this task, I would've run straight through the Frozen Sands, back to Ashorah. Instead, all I had was this small cabin that locked from the outside and a bloodstream full of fear.

I wiped the burning tears from my cheeks and dropped down beside the fireplace, knees pulled so tightly to my chest it was hard to breathe. Nausea swirled in my gut.

Please, I prayed. *Ketet, Phadar, someone, anyone, save me. Get me out of here.*

No one came to save me. No one ever had.

I was alone in a nest of monsters.

FIFTEEN

AMUNET

It was night by the time I drew my camel to a halt at the top of a hill outside Reeda. Mercifully, we'd not run into any other assassins. Either the one from the trading post was a shit tracker or the broken nose was enough to put him off the job entirely. Whatever the reason, I drank in the sight of the town below as if it were an oasis snug between the dunes.

Minus the water. And the lush trees. And beauty in general.

I'd accompanied the Khada Guard on patrols, many of which went to the principalities, multiple times in my ten years of training, but Reeda was smaller than I remembered. Lanterns and the moon offered just enough light to see the houses built of straw along gravel roads, and a few people in poorly stitched linens milling around. The consistent sound of *chink, chink, chink* resounded over the city like its personal orchestra, from a mine located somewhere to the west.

"We'll draw less attention if we enter on foot," Jasim said as he dismounted. He pulled on my camel's reins, guiding it to lie down so he could help me. His hands were careful of the still-healing wound in my side, and he released me the moment I was on my feet. Just as he'd been doing for the past several days since the near chimera attack, he avoided my eyes.

It rankled me. As Jasim tied our camels to a post, my annoyance rose until I could taste its sourness on the back of my tongue. His eyes were always on me. I wanted them back. Especially now. "What is it?"

He paused. Didn't turn around. "What?"

My nails dug into the back of my neck. The itch was now a consistent burning, my blinks synced up to the claws tapping in my ears. "You've been acting weird for days. Why?"

He shrugged as he gathered our supplies off the camels. "Just trying to prepare myself."

Ice sliced through my veins. He knew my plan. Somehow, he knew.

But then he said, "You're going to negotiate with Prince Nasir. Figure that'll be easier for you without any romantic entanglements to worry about."

My shoulders lowered as his meaning hit me.

Earlier I'd said there were two thoughts about the Gods-Chosen. Spawn of evil or savior. I lied. There was a third: supernaturally divine fuck. And the three categories were not mutually exclusive. Many men were easily able to think of me as a demon and something pretty to stick their dicks into, and I was not above using their simple animal brains against them. A flirt, a smile, a touch. If they weren't a total piece of shit, maybe I actually would let them into my bed.

I just . . . hadn't considered I'd have to do so with Nasir. It aggravated me that Jasim had.

I scratched harder. "Right. Thanks for being so accommodating."

He glanced over his shoulder at me, brown eyes reflecting the stars above. "You're angry," he stated incredulously.

"Well, should I be happy you called me a whore?" I bit out.

Jasim turned around, giving me his full attention, and I really was a twisted bitch because part of me preened to have it again. He strode back to my side, pausing a handful of inches away. "Should I ask you nicely not to fuck him? Should I bother? We both know you'll do what you want anyway."

An uncomfortable heat rose in my cheeks. Vicious, cutting words filled my mouth. I clenched my jaw against them, trying to think around my temper.

The princes were scheming. The Kaldfolk were hunting. Shaya was waiting. We were about to enter Nasir's territory without any guarantee about how he would react. Jasim was my only protection. And when we reached the Temple of Shaya, I would truly need him then, too. I could not spew venom at him. I needed him close, loyal, docile.

I drew a single breath. It burned like fire. "Ask me."

Jasim stared at me a beat before he huffed a humorless laugh. With a shake of his head, he said, "You force me to speak, get angry at what I have to say, and then mock me for it? Fine. Let me just save us both the time, shall I? You will tell me that this is necessary for our safety, that I am pathetic for allowing any entanglements to jeopardize—"

"Stop using that word."

"It's *your* word!" he burst out with enough vehemence to make me flinch. "You'll tell me that I have no say in this because you are queen, you are Gods-Chosen, and I am nothing, so why make me say it at all?"

I stared up into his face, his chest rising and falling with the force of his emotion, but in the tightness around his eyes, I saw hurt. Something inside me twinged at the realization.

Jasim was my personal guard. He was there every moment of my life, for every wooed adversary, every man I'd marched past him into my room. He'd never said anything about it until now. I didn't know what made Nasir different, but the fire of my temper dwindled.

Quietly, I ordered, "Kneel."

Confusion broke through Jasim's righteous fury. "What?"

"Now, Jasim."

For a moment, he looked like he might disobey. Silence descended between us as his throat worked, the muscle in his jaw feathered furiously. But he balled his hands into fists and slowly lowered himself to his knees in the sand. He stared through my sternum. "Forgive me, my queen," he said. "My outburst was unfair. I should not have said—"

"Now ask me, Jasim."

His eyes snapped up to mine.

I stared right back.

"I'm on my knees. I've apologized. You don't have to humiliate me further—"

"Jasim." I cupped his jaw and leaned closer. My voice was a gentle murmur when I repeated, "Ask me."

His brows twitched toward each other as his gaze flicked all over my face. Looking for deception or laughter.

While I was still furious at his implication, it was not based on thin air. And it was not necessarily a bad idea, either. Seducing Nasir Miqaf might, in fact, be the fastest route to the Temple of Shaya. But after days in the wilderness, with a gash in my side and persistent bees stinging the back of my neck, I was not much in the mood for it.

Not to mention the wounded gleam in Jasim's eyes that made my chest feel too tight . . .

I shook myself. More important was securing Jasim's loyalty. Yes, much more important.

Jasim's jaw popped beneath my palm. He whispered, "Don't. Please."

"Then I won't."

"Really?"

"Really."

His eyes bored into mine for several seconds before he saw that I meant it. Then they dropped to my lips. "Thank you, my queen," he rasped.

My gaze dropped, too, to those full lips I'd tasted more times than I could count, and a flush spread over my skin. Unconsciously, my thumb grazed his bottom lip, and they parted ever so slightly. He hadn't kissed me after the chimera attack, but he'd kiss me now. All I had to do was lean down one more inch. In that moment, with him looking up at me as if I were one of the stars in the night sky, recalling how much he loved being on his knees for the Gods-Chosen, I wanted nothing more than to indulge in the oblivion his dark gaze promised.

But a strange pit in my stomach blocked the heat in my blood from funneling any lower. A gnawing sensation that felt a lot like guilt. I was no longer thinking about how messy it'd be to fuck in the sand but rather what expression he'd wear when I put him on his knees in the Temple of Shaya. If it would be that same wounded look. If it would be so much worse.

I swallowed hard and pulled away. "Come on. Before someone sees us." I turned and strode ahead into Reeda, not waiting to see if he followed me. I knew he would. He always did.

That gnawing feeling remained, infuriating me with every step. I shouldn't care about wounded looks or a kiss. I *didn't* care. I cared about Shaya and what *he* expected of me. I cared about feeling his breeze again, feeling his love, his security, his acceptance.

Nothing else.

Because if I did . . .

I scratched my nape. Hard.

We headed toward the largest house in the center of the city, with a pair of guards posted outside the door. Their leather armor was Reeda orange, with a vague rendering of a man with suns for eyes in the center. Ketet's husband, Phadar, God of the Sun. They watched our approach with narrowed eyes.

When we were close enough, I pulled off my wig and proclaimed, "I am Amunet Khada, and I'd like an audience with Prince Nasir Miqaf."

Shock flashed across their faces, and the guard on the left dropped his gaze to Jasim's scimitars' hilts, where the royal seal was stamped, a lotus flower floating in a lake of fire.

"Of course, Your Majesty," he said quickly, and opened the door that led into the entryway—if the cramped space could even be called that.

A glance to the right revealed a sitting room. There wasn't much in the way of furniture or decoration, and what was present was unimpressively fashioned out of wicker. The cushions were thread-bare, feathers or cotton puffing out of the holes like they were actively fighting their fabric prisons.

But the guard turned to the left and announced, "Queen Amunet Khada to see you, my prince." Then he stepped aside, and I entered the dining room.

A table with a meager six chairs swallowed the space. Five of the occupants wore the Reeda uniform. Prince Nasir was easy to recognize, with the pointed ears that poked through the forest of braids hanging on either side of his face and the gold-flecked brown eyes that hinted at the jinni magic in his veins.

Those unique eyes flew wide at my appearance. "My queen!" Nasir exclaimed in shock before lurching to his feet and slamming both his legs into the table, sending bowls of indeterminate food sloshing. I cringed.

The prince swore as he staggered back and hit the wall behind him. He was a slender but tall man about ten years older than me with dark skin. He had to stoop so his head wouldn't hit the low ceiling. A female guard beside him put out a hand to steady him, but he batted her away and straightened, smoothing his hands down his shirt before he plastered on a smile, blinking like a blinded owl. "My queen," he said again, bowing so deep that a few of his braids fell into his bowl. "You're . . . here. In Reeda. Alive."

"Indeed I am."

"What a . . . delight. Yes, of course, I am delighted to see you! It's just that . . . we had word from Ketopolis that the Kaldfolk infiltrated the palace and took you prisoner. It was our assumption that you'd been killed, like the king."

Taken prisoner? That meant the Kaldfolk had left Khada Palace *and* my decoy could still be alive. If that was the Kaldfolk's plan, they must have a bigger purpose for the Gods-Chosen. My decoy's deception couldn't last much longer, and when they finally realized the truth, they'd come for me again. Not to mention that news of Zaid's death had evidently beaten us to Reeda. If it had reached Nasir, it could have reached Ilias, Anwar, and Sen, too.

I did not even have Shaya to protect me. Jasim would do his best, but we'd gotten lucky to escape Khada Palace with just a few scratches. Without my father's help, I didn't think we'd be lucky a second time.

I needed to get to the Temple of Shaya. Quickly.

"Clearly I'm not dead," I replied to Nasir.

He smiled. "No. Though someone should check you're not a ghost." He laughed and made a move as if to check for himself but knocked his knee on the table leg, sending more food splattering over the tabletop. "Shit," he muttered, while the gathered soldiers did their best to right the mess.

I swallowed a sigh. Somehow I'd misremembered Nasir as only slightly clumsy instead of the bumbling buffoon he was.

This was my salvation. How comforting.

Before I could demand supplies or a small contingent to take me to the Wastelands, Nasir said, "You must be exhausted from your long journey. We'll have rooms prepared for you right away. In the meantime, please, eat." He flapped his hands frantically at the girl in fighting leathers beside him, whose hair was wrapped in a headscarf.

She sent me a dirty look as she rose and grabbed a plate for me, and the back of my neck burned. I fisted my hands at my sides to keep from scratching—and to keep from lashing out at her. King Zaid would have her punished for such a blatant display of disrespect. But I didn't think a show of brute strength would win me any favors. Biting back my anger, I watched her assemble bits of chicken, flatbread, and what could be either watery cheese or congealed milk. My nose threatened to curl, but I fought it, nodding my thanks as I accepted the plate.

Another guard vacated their seat, and I took it, sitting directly across from Nasir, who managed to lower himself back into his chair without spontaneously combusting. Jasim remained at my back. A glance out of the corner of my eye showed he was firmly gripping both scimitars.

I dipped the bread in the cheese milk and used every trick I knew to keep my disgust from showing. Sour. Chewy. The meager crumbs Jasim and I had been living off for the last week were preferable to this. Still, I swallowed it and smiled. "Thank you."

Nasir's smile was crooked. "I know it cannot compete with the palace's cooks, but hopefully it is tolerable."

The bread scraped along my throat all the way down. "It's great. In fact, I'd like to pack some of this with me."

Nasir's brows rose. "Leaving already, my queen?"

"I'd like to make a sacrifice at my father's temple before the Igniting."

"But . . . the temple is in the Wastelands," he stated. As if I were an idiot who did not know the location of my own father's temple.

The burn at my neck intensified. It took everything in me not to scratch. "Yes. My father wishes for a personal visit."

"Goodness," Nasir mumbled as he lifted a bite to his mouth, a dollop of that cheese milk landing on his shirt. He didn't notice. "A demanding father, the God of the Underworld, eh?"

I smiled stiffly. "I'd like to take a small contingent with me. In addition to supplies. The temple is not too far into the Wastelands, but I would like to err on the side of caution. That is, if you find that amenable," I added begrudgingly. Oh, so very civilized and behaved.

"I would love to help you, Gods-Chosen. It would be my greatest privilege. But . . ." Nasir winced apologetically. "Sending my people to the temple puts them at risk. A hefty one, if I correctly recall King Zaid's time in the Wastelands. And as you can probably see, we don't have much to spare, in supplies or warriors. Not to mention that housing you for even a night brings the danger of the Kaldfolk's return." Nasir pressed a hand to his heart and peered at me with those owl eyes. "I'm afraid I cannot, in good conscience, order my warriors into the Wastelands. It would have to be their choice."

It took far too long to remind myself that queens did not lunge across tables. "Do you not have control of your own people, Nasir?"

"He's not a dictator," the female soldier bit out, accusation shining in her eyes.

"They could be convinced," he said quickly. "Couldn't you, Sara?"

The female soldier crossed her arms and sat back in her chair.

I nearly ordered Jasim to slice her hands off. Better yet, slice the back of my neck to stop this fucking *itch*. "What do you want, Nasir?"

Excitement lit up his face, and he leaned forward, hands clasped loosely on the table, looking me in the eye. A disconcerting look, with the bits of golden magic floating in his irises. "I want my land back," he said. "Along the Lotus River."

I nearly laughed. The last time I'd been to Reeda, the prince had been nothing but strictly cordial and agreeable. Everything I'd said had been met with a *Yes, my princess.* But he'd always been cunning, despite his lack of hand-eye coordination. It was why he'd never revolted, even after the king had kicked his family off their land and his father had been slaughtered by the Khada Guard. Why he'd allowed me to enter his home at all when he knew I'd yet to be officially crowned queen and the throne was empty. Fighting would not help his people.

But this. This would.

"Fine," I said. "The Miqaf Estate in exchange for my safe journey to—and *from*—Shaya's temple."

Nasir smiled, bits of gold alight in his eyes. "You truly are sent by the gods, my queen."

My smile was thin. I couldn't bask in the victory; it was taking every ounce of concentration not to just scratch, scratch, scratch. And those claws on glass were doing more than just tapping; they were scraping. A shudder slithered down my spine.

Nasir pushed back from the table and stood, causing minimal damage this time. "Allow me to show you where you'll be staying for the night. Tomorrow, your escort will be ready."

Nasir took me up a flight of stairs, Jasim just a step behind. The prince opened the door to a modest room—though, compared to the rest of the house, it was large. Windows along the right wall let in the humid air, ruffling the linen sheets on the bed in the center. Faded paintings decorated the walls, mostly landscapes of the Lotus River and the Miqafs' old home.

"I hope it's to your liking, my queen."

I offered Nasir my most winning smile. "Yes, thank you."

The moment he was gone, my eyes locked on the wall sconce. I chucked my wig aside and yanked the candle out, the flame flickering precariously.

"What are you doing?" Jasim asked.

"I have to try again."

"Try what?"

"I should've tried before." I dropped to my knees, eyes closed, and clutched the candle tightly between my hands.

Baba, please, I prayed. *Please talk to me.*

The wind that blew through the windows was heavy and humid. Not Shaya's.

My neck prickled again. I clenched my hands hard, feeling the hard wax dig into my palms as I redoubled my focus. *Baba, I'm sorry. I've angered you. Please forgive me. End this punishment. Get rid of this itch and this racket. I can't think. I can barely breathe without wanting to flay myself.*

No response.

Jasim ventured, "My queen?"

"Shut up!" My voice came out high-pitched. Even I could hear the hysteria in it. My chest constricted, stomach curdling. *Baba, please. I miss you. I need you.*

I barely breathed as I waited. And waited. There was no supernatural breeze. No sign at all that my father had heard me.

My eyes opened. The candle's flame burned, hardly even flickering in the desert wind.

Taunting me.

"My queen." Jasim crouched on the other side of the candle, brows drawn closely together, questions chasing each other in his eyes.

Both my hands went up to my neck. "He's not answering." The itch persisted. In fact, it seemed to intensify with every pass of my nails. "Why isn't he answering?"

"Stop that." Jasim pulled my hands away from my skin, held my wrists in one hand while his other angled my head so he could see the back of my neck. "Gods," he breathed. He held up my hands. There was blood under my nails. "What have you done?"

It had been too long. My body was rebelling at Shaya's absence. Everything that I was, my eventual power, my goals, my very existence, was because of Shaya. The parent that never left me. The one that wanted me so badly he'd struck a deal with King Zaid.

Did . . . did he no longer want me?

My heart threatened to crack at the mere thought.

"My queen. My queen. *Amunet.*" I looked up at Jasim. He still held my wrists, dark eyes boring into me.

"He's punishing me."

Jasim shook his head. "What? Who?"

"Shaya."

"Why?"

"I don't know."

"Amunet." Jasim pulled my fingers away from my neck again. I hadn't even realized I'd jerked them out of his grip. He held my hands firmly to the wooden slats of the floor, trapping them between us. Even though his grip was unforgiving, his voice was gentle. "Why didn't you tell me you couldn't reach Shaya?"

Because it can't be true.

Because he chose me. He *chose* me. He wouldn't just leave me.

"Amunet," Jasim whispered, and cupped my face. "You're shaking."

"I have to get to the temple. Please understand, I have to do this. I *have* to—"

"Hey." He tilted my head back so I was forced to meet his eyes. Familiar and beautiful brown. "I'm going to get you to the temple. I promise."

My fingers curled into his tunic, clinging to him like he was a lifeline.

He tugged me into him and wrapped his arms around me. Though tremors still racked my frame and fear churned in my gut, I melted into his embrace. It wasn't fair of me, but he was warm and safe. I buried my face in his neck, his beard scratching comfortingly against my shaved head, and breathed in the fresh woody smell of river reeds. For just the briefest moment, the claws in my head quieted.

Jasim held me for a few moments before he murmured, "You're tired. Get some sleep. I'll keep watch."

I smiled slightly against his skin. "You haven't slept, either."

"I'll be fine." Still hugging me, he helped me up to my feet.

Perhaps it was a good thing I couldn't reach Shaya. If he saw me now, unable to make it to the bed not five feet away because of something as trivial as *fear*, he'd probably disown me.

The thought sent ice through my veins.

Was that what this silence was? Had he disowned me? Why? What could I have done that was so unforgivable he wouldn't *speak* to me before abandoning me?

Fear turned over my stomach.

Who was the Gods-Chosen without the god that had chosen her?

SIXTEEN

SAMIRA

My cabin became a chamber of echoes. Screams as guards were ripped apart, the snap of a neck, the jeering of a crowd. They surrounded me. I heard the horrific sounds again and again, feeling as if I were slowly going mad. I was trapped in a reverberating cave of torment.

A shadow fell over me, and I flinched.

Keir lowered himself into a crouch in front of me. Those searing yellow eyes level with my own where I was curled up beside the fire. I hadn't realized it was night until then. The corners of the room were dark, save for this one patch before the hearth. Hours had gone by since I'd witnessed a man's senseless murder, yet it felt like mere moments.

I tightened my arms around my knees and ducked my head. "Please leave." My voice was hoarse but not weak, thank the gods.

Keir's clothes shifted. Something clinked on the floor beside me. Against my better judgment, I lifted my head.

A tankard of kefir.

"Not thirsty," I said.

"It's not for thirst." He jerked his chin toward it. "Go on. It'll make you feel better."

I made no move for it.

Keir stared at me a beat longer, and some reckless, rebellious corner of my brain that had forgotten sixteen years of conditioning refused to be the first to look away this time. I wanted him to see the blame, the contempt, the devastation. Maybe the Kaldfolk felt no remorse for murder, but they should. *He* should. I looked into the suns of his eyes, let them burn into me, and sent fire right back.

He looked away.

Satisfaction momentarily outshone my despair.

Keir scrubbed a hand over his cheek. "I thought you went on raids with the Khada Guard," he said to the wall. "I thought you'd be used to violence. I didn't think it would . . ." I waited for him to finish the sentence, but he didn't. Just continued to look everywhere but me.

"I've seen a lot of violence," I said. "Doesn't mean I'm used to it."

He nodded. Slowly, his gaze dragged back to mine. His brows were pinched as he studied me. As if a particularly difficult question had been posed to him. His nostrils flared slightly. "You smell so sad," he murmured, so quietly I wasn't entirely sure I was meant to hear it.

My throat closed up. This time, I was the one to drop my eyes.

I *was* sad. Devastatingly so. I hadn't known Hedin, but I had known Tabia and Chef Nena and Nadia. Any of them could have been ended just as brutally as he had been. Maybe the Kaldfolk had laughed as they'd done it. They'd definitely laugh when they snapped my neck.

They would laugh, and no one would cry. My queen had given me up *to* die. Not even she would mourn for me. No one would care. And the realization made me inexorably sad.

"I put honey in it."

My head snapped up.

Keir gestured to the tankard. "Makes it go down smoother."

"Why?"

"I don't know, I guess the honey outweighs the alcohol—"

"No, I mean, why did you do that?"

He rubbed his cheek again, eyebrows still knit together. I wondered if that was the same question he'd been pondering. "Your sadness smells a lot worse than your fear."

Heat crawled up my neck. It was a weird thing to be embarrassed about. I wasn't even sure why I was, but I found myself mumbling, "I'll take another bath."

"Won't help," he replied, voice like hard gravel.

"Oh."

Keir's eyes roved over my face with that same searching stare. Something about that look made my heart beat a little faster and goose bumps ripple down my body. Keir's chest expanded on a large inhale and didn't sink again for a prolonged beat. I felt trapped in his luminous gaze. He'd just told me that I reeked, and yet the way he seemed to be savoring that breath . . .

Keir jerked up to his feet, and I jolted out of my trance. "Drink it," he ordered, not unkindly, before he strode out of the room, steps rushed.

My gaze dropped to the kefir. Hands unsteady, I picked it up and tipped its contents back.

Smooth. Sweet. Warm. It melted into my bones and wrapped me in a ribbon of comfort.

I stared at the closed door. I struggled to make sense of the interaction, of the burn in my cheeks and the subtle pounding of my pulse throughout my body. The way he had looked at me, how he seemed just as confused as I was. The peace offering with honey held in my hands.

For the time it took me to drink the kefir, I was too baffled to be sad.

Early the next morning, there was a knock at my door. Energy shot through my veins, and I lurched off the bed and grabbed the empty kefir tankard, brandishing it over my head. But it wasn't Keir. "Amunet?" Rade called. "May I speak with you?"

With a sharp exhale, I set the tankard back on the nightstand, not really sure what I'd planned to do with it if it *had* been Keir. Clearing my throat, I called, "Yes."

Rade opened the door. Neither Keir nor anyone else was standing guard. I thought I spotted Velka racing by, but Rade shut the door again before I could be sure.

I kept a studious distance between us, remembering his frightening display of rage yesterday. While he might not have instigated yesterday's murder, he hadn't stopped it. He held a hefty share of the blame.

Which he seemed to realize as he gazed at me with remorse weighing down the edges of his lips. "I would have come sooner, but I thought you might want some time to yourself." He sighed and scratched his beard. "You shouldn't have witnessed the fight. That was not the introduction I wanted for you. If I'd known you were there . . ."

He would've called it off? Had me forcibly removed? But he didn't finish the sentence, and I was too frightened to ask.

He dipped his chin. Drew a deep breath. "I know what Ashorans say about us," he said, "and I was hoping to change your mind." The king huffed a sad laugh and shook his head. "I guess that's not going to happen now, is it?"

I wasn't sure how to respond. Lie, or risk his wrath? I still had no idea what the red marks on the side of his head meant. Blue clearly represented a Shifter, but I hadn't seen what black and red could do yet, and I didn't particularly want to find out.

Rade saw the flightiness in my gaze and saved me from answering. "I don't want you to be afraid of us, Amunet. I'm sorry that you are. Keir never should have forced you here."

He sounded genuine. But I knew better than to trust a Kald. Somehow I found my voice enough to ask, "Then why have you kept me here?"

Rade scratched at his beard again, a nervous tic, his sheet of black hair rippling down the left side of his body like a silken river of night. There wasn't a trace of the fury I'd glimpsed during the fight. That didn't mean it wasn't carefully tucked away and just waiting to jump out.

"You can leave," he said suddenly.

My body jolted as if it would take off immediately.

Rade's light brown eyes bored into mine. "Once I show you why Keir did what he did, you can leave. I will not be your captor. I just—need you to understand."

"Understand what?"

"What we're up against." He took a small step forward, just the barest approach. I didn't back away. Was it some sort of heretic magic that was putting me at ease? Maybe that was what his red tattoos signified. He was a witch, using his power to make me relax. Because I couldn't deny there was something about Rade that made the tension in my back lessen and my heartbeat slow just the slightest bit. The softness in his oak-colored eyes, the crookedness of his smile, the calm radiating from him.

"My Seven . . ." he started. "They are the best and worst of us. Strong, loyal. But they're all . . . *broken* sounds too harsh. *Cracked* might be better. There is a crack inside all of them. It's what makes them the best at what they do. But we are not all like them. *I* am not like them." He shuffled a few steps closer, until I had to tilt my head up slightly to meet his gaze. "All I ask is that you wait to condemn my people until I have explained. Please."

I was wrong; it wasn't softness in his eyes but desperation. Desperate for my help—for Amunet's help. Whatever he wanted to convince me of, he *needed*. Very, very badly.

I swallowed hard. "What do you want to show me?"

He drew a deep breath. I could feel the nervousness surrounding him, a nearly tangible cloud. "It will be a lot," he warned. "But I will protect you. I promise." He held out his hand. Asking me not to fear him, to come with him, to trust him.

I couldn't do most of those things. He could be lying about letting me go. But if he wasn't, all I had to do was take a look at whatever put that panic in his eyes. And then I'd be free. I would have done my part to keep the Gods-Chosen safe without having to die.

I slipped my hand into his.

SEVENTEEN

SAMIRA

A handful of Kaldfolk came riding up to the longhouse, faces flushed with cold and exertion. Each rider carried at least two or three more people on their horse. Urgency marked their every movement. They barely paused to deposit their passengers before turning their horses around and bolting back down the hill, sending frozen earth exploding up around them in a wave.

Rade led me through the unfolding chaos, steps hurried as he dodged rushing Kaldfolk.

"What's happening?" I asked.

Rade stopped beside an idle horse. "The Shroud."

Before I could ask anything further, he hefted me onto the horse. I scrambled to grab hold of the saddle's pommel and pull myself the rest of the way. Rade climbed up behind me, arms encircling me as he grabbed the reins and dug his heels into the horse's sides. We took off like an arrow down the hill from the longhouse. My heart lurched against my rib cage, and I held on to the saddle's horn for dear life.

We raced away from Frostguard. A shadow loomed at the horizon, growing as we drew closer. A wall of darkness.

That allure I'd felt in the forest, which made my insides clench and gooseflesh break out all over my body, stretched from the ground far, far into the sky. A writhing mass of solid black. Like the night sky had become a living thing.

We came to a stop when we reached flat land, a town full of thatched homes. Kaldfolk ran wildly. A woman cried out as she was knocked off her horse by a young man. He seized the reins and kicked the beast into a sprint. The woman paused to look back at the impending darkness. The terror melted away for a moment. Her eyes became shiny, and her face went slack with awe. She took a step *toward* it.

Sillia raced up to her. Scooped her up, deposited her into a different saddle, and smacked the horse's hide, sending her sprinting back up the hill. Then she turned to help the next person.

The living shadow pulsed, reaching toward us inch by inch, swallowing the settlement more with each second.

"What is that?" I asked breathlessly, not taking my eyes from the horrible wall.

"That," Rade said as he slid off the horse, "is the Shroud." He gazed up at me, eyes imploring. "See this, Amunet. See what's happening." Then he turned and ran to where a figure was standing much too close to the darkness. One look at the swinging braid, the yellow eyes stark against the night backdrop, and I recognized Keir.

Velka raced by me on horseback, as fast as the wind. She jumped off her steed, grabbed two more people who appeared enthralled by the darkness, both of whom were marked with black tattoos, and deposited them on the back of a horse. When the horse took off back to Frostguard, she stooped to the ground. Before she even landed on all fours, she was a bear, paws streaked with blue like the tattoos on her hands. She chased after the horse.

I slid off my horse on shaky legs, lips parting as I took in the Shroud. Keir and Rade were just ahead of me, and I suddenly noticed there was a third person with them. An elderly man in a wooden rocking chair.

"You have to leave," Keir was saying to him. "You have to go now—"

"I already told you, I'm staying right here," the man responded. Unlike the others, he didn't look like he was in a trance. But he was resolute in remaining in that chair.

Keir turned to Rade. Where his First always possessed an air of total control, now he seemed frazzled, wide golden eyes stark against his kohl-painted face. "Do something."

"It's his decision." The king said the words tiredly. Like it was a conversation they'd had many times before.

"He has a granddaughter. I can't find her. It's possible she's already been taken to Frostguard, but he's not—"

"It's his decision."

"He doesn't know what he's deciding!" Keir burst out. He grabbed Rade's shoulder with one hand, the fabric of the king's shirt bunching beneath his grip. "Please, Rade."

Rade hesitated a moment more, eyes darting to the Shroud, which was only a couple of yards away now. Then he looked at the old man. "Come on, Finan. Get up."

"My wife was taken by this thing twenty years ago," the old man replied stubbornly. "I want to see her again."

"Your wife is *dead*, Finan. Your granddaughter isn't."

"You'll look after Milena." Finan set his jaw and faced the darkness. Which had scuttled even closer. The hairs on the back of my neck stood on end, and my feet shuffled with the desire to carry me toward it. Consciously, my mind was awash in terror, yet I couldn't shake the need to feel those tendrils wrap around me. Ice slid down my spine, and I studiously avoided looking at the Shroud, as much as I could avoid looking at a looming wall of darkness.

A muscle feathered in Rade's jaw, and he snapped his eyes shut.

The tattoos on the side of his head started to glow the bright red color of a sunset. When he opened his eyes again, the brown had transformed to the same shade of red and shone, too, like his irises were lit from within.

I gasped. I'd suspected he might be a witch, but I wasn't truly prepared to see magic.

The old man jolted to his feet, yanked by an invisible string. "No," he said as he took a step forward, stiff, his feet moving against his will. Just like the stories I'd heard. Kaldfolk power that made a person a slave in their own body. It was chilling to behold.

As Finan took another involuntary step, he looked up at the sky. "I'm not lost!" he shouted. "Do you hear me? I'm not lost!"

Like his puppet's strings had been cut, Finan slammed back down into the rocking chair. At the same time, Rade let his breath out in a sharp gust. His shoulders slumped in defeat, tattoos returning to their dull ink and eyes a normal brown. He looked to Keir. "I've done what I can. As long as he's thinking clearly, he's allowed to make this choice. But we have to leave. Now."

Keir growled in frustration and took a threatening step toward the old man. "I'll throw you over my fucking shoulder!"

But Finan just took Keir's large hand in his shriveled one and patted it softly. "It's all right, my boy. It's all right."

"No—" Keir began.

Rade grabbed Keir's arm. "Let him be. It's time to go."

Keir released Finan's hands almost violently. He spun around, anger and defeat in his eyes—and then his gaze caught on me and widened. "You brought her—"

"I said we're leaving! Now, Keir!" roared the king.

Like a turned dial, the frazzled energy left Keir. The muscles in his neck bulged as his face elongated. Fur sprouted, claws burst forth, and when he landed on all fours, he was an enormous bear. I balked, momentarily stupefied. I'd witnessed Velka shift just minutes ago, but there was something vicious about the way Keir shifted. As if the beast was not coaxed forward but tore free of his human skin.

"Amunet!" Rade was already in the saddle, hand held out toward me. I let him pull me up behind him and wrapped my arms around his waist as Keir took off, our horse following him—

"Grandpa!"

I stiffened and twisted to see a little girl who couldn't have been older than five. I didn't see where she'd come from, but she must've been hiding when people began stampeding out of the village. She approached Finan, frightened tears rolling down her face. The old man pulled her into his lap. Was he going to let her be devoured by the Shroud, too?

I'd spent my entire life fearing the Kaldfolk. Hating them. But that little girl, so helpless . . . she reminded me of my first night in Khada Palace all those years ago. I'd cried just like that, calling out for Mama and Baba.

Finan had made his choice. But I wouldn't let the little girl be taken by the darkness.

"Wait!" I shouted, and pointed.

Rade twisted around, black hair a banner that whipped against my cheeks as he spotted the little girl. "I can't risk your safety!" he said. "We're out of time!" And maybe he was right. The Shroud was licking at the old man's feet.

But the little girl's eyes were wide with terror and confusion as she gazed up trustingly at her grandfather.

I sent a prayer for protection up to the gods and threw myself off the horse.

"Amunet!"

The ground slammed into me so hard my teeth rattled in my skull. Pain shot through the right side of my body as I rolled, but the moment I got my bearings, I jumped to my feet and ran toward the darkness, fighting every primal part of me that screamed at me to stop, and the inexplicable part of me that wanted to dive into its inky depths.

The old man was hugging his granddaughter tight as she clutched a doll to her chest, her cheeks still wet with tears.

My boots slid on the frozen ground, coming to a stop inches away from her. "Come on," I said, "we have to go."

"But, Grandpa—"

"You're Milena, right?" I interrupted, eyes darting to the Shroud.

"Yes," she sniffed.

"Milena, we have to run. Okay?"

"It's all right, baby," Finan told her. "Go with the Gods-Chosen."

A beckoning touch caressed my back, and I gasped. It was like the Shroud had tentacles and was trying to wrap them around me. Trying to reel me into the wall of night. I staggered back a step. The gentle tendrils weren't cold, like I'd imagined, but soft. Coaxing. Like I could lean back and they would cushion me—

"Amunet!" I glanced up to see Rade several yards away, his horse shifting nervously. "We have to go *now*!"

Terror clogging my throat, I mentally shook myself. I hooked my hands under the girl's armpits, heaved her into my arms, and ran as fast as I could.

"Grandpa!" Milena screamed, reaching an arm over my shoulder.

I tucked her head into my neck, holding her even tighter. "Don't look."

She cried as she obeyed, tears burning into my skin, her doll held in a death grip. Rade vaulted off his horse, clutching the reins with one hand even as he extended his arms for the little girl. With a wild whinny, the horse reared back, wrenching the reins from Rade's grip.

Rade swore viciously as the horse ran away, blind with panic. The two of us stood there, the little girl with her face buried in my shoulder, watching it disappear. We'd never catch up to it. I couldn't help a glance at the darkness. Finan was gone. The darkness had devoured him, and he hadn't even screamed. My arms tightened around Milena.

"Keir," said Rade. I wrenched my eyes away from the darkness to see a bear barreling toward us. He reared up onto his hind legs, shrinking into the shape of a man. In a blink, I was staring up into Keir's enraged face.

"Are you insane?" he snarled at me. But he took the little girl with surprising gentleness and nestled her against his chest.

He turned to the king next. "No," Rade said in between pants. "Amunet first."

"Rade—"

"*Now*, Keir!"

With a growl, Keir threw me over his shoulder. I yelped as the world turned upside down, clinging to his back as he ran with supernatural speed.

Even as the Shroud grew smaller, I could see it clawing farther over the settlement, swallowing homes, plants, claiming more and more of the land into its unnatural depths.

We rounded a bend, and suddenly I was on my feet again, head swimming as the blood rushed away.

Velka, back in human form, held Rade's horse by the reins.

Keir ordered me, "Get on."

I clambered into the saddle. Keir handed Milena to me, shifted, and took off back toward the Shroud. After several breathless moments, he returned with Rade riding atop him, as if Keir were another horse instead of a bear. Keir didn't bother pausing to put Rade in the saddle behind me. He just kept running. Velka shifted, too, her paws thundering as she followed Keir, and my horse brought up the rear.

Milena clung to me, arms around my neck, squeezing hard. But I mumbled that it would be all right as I held her close with one hand and strangled the reins with the other. I'd never ridden a horse by myself, and we bounced horribly, the wind tearing at us.

When we reached Frostguard, I barely had time to stumble off the horse before one of the healers tried to take Milena from me. "No," the girl shrieked, hands fisting in my hair.

"It's okay," I assured, smiling calmly. "Go with her. I'll come check on you, okay? I promise." Milena's fingers relaxed slightly. "Go on. It's okay." Slowly, the little girl allowed the healer to lead her away.

I stared after her. So small, so vulnerable.

Suddenly, I was standing in the streets of Ketopolis. Men had appeared out of the shadows when Baba's back was turned and had thrown a burlap sack over my head. I was brought to a room with other little girls, all of us trembling. Guards loomed over us, shoving uniforms into our hands and barking rules. They had whips and mean faces. No Mama, no Baba. When they gave me orders, I was too scared to move. A whip cracked as it came down on my back—

Shouts exploded out of the longhouse, and I sucked in a sharp breath as I was wrenched back to the present. Milena would be looked after. There were no men with burlap sacks here. No mean guards with whips. And I would look out for her. I wouldn't forget her.

But first I had to deal with the bellowing inside.

I cringed and took tiny steps toward the door.

Rade's cheeks were red with rage as he squared off against Keir. "Next time you want to force my hand, don't do it feet away from the Shroud when the Gods-Chosen is right th—"

"She shouldn't have been there!" Keir fired back. "That was your fault, not mine."

"I promised to protect her, but your constant need to undermine me put her directly in harm's way!"

Keir opened his mouth but then thought better of it and snapped it closed. He set his shoulders and stared straight ahead. I'd seen that stance in the guards at Khada Palace. A soldier at attention while being addressed by his superior. "I am sorry, my king. It won't happen again."

"Am I, Keir? Am I your king?" Rade got directly in Keir's face. "Because you have given me more and more reason to doubt your loyalty."

Keir's nostrils flared as he struggled to rein in his temper.

The floor creaked under my foot, and I winced as they both whipped in my direction. Keir's eyes flashed. "She wouldn't have been in harm's way if she hadn't been reckless enough to throw herself off a sprinting horse."

I replied, "I couldn't leave her behind. She would have died."

He blinked once. Hard. Almost a flinch.

The ire in the king's eyes melted away as he gazed at me, and he let out a slow breath. He looked drawn, aged five years in the span of a few moments. "Keir, get Velka," he instructed. Then, to me, he said, "I promised you an explanation. It's time you heard it."

EIGHTEEN

SAMIRA

The king's room was expansive, located down the hall behind his throne, within the mountain. An enormous four-poster bed, a fireplace, bookshelves, and a sitting area made up the suite, just about as large as my queen's room in Ashorah. Wolfskin rugs covered the stone floor, leading to a desk littered with papers, feather quills, and small figurines.

Rade gestured for me to sit in one of the large chairs in front of the fire, its wooden arms and legs thick like tree roots, while he went to his desk.

Velka dropped into the seat across from me, exhausted. I wondered how many trips she'd made. I'd only done the one and it had drained me.

Keir remained standing beside the door like a sentry and didn't take his eyes off me. I fought to keep my spine straight under his blazing stare.

Rade rummaged through his desk, papers rustling. He finally found what he was looking for and sat in the chair beside mine, figurines held between his fingers. He offered one to me. It was small, about the size of a thumb, but it was sturdy. When I turned it over, I gasped.

Decorative metal armor, slitted eyes, and curling feline smile. *Shaya.*

"How do you have this?" I asked, examining it from every angle, as if it would stop being Shaya if I just turned it the right way. The Kaldfolk were heretics. Monsters who had turned away from the gods. Had one of the Seven stolen this when they'd snatched me from Ashorah? But why? What would a figurine mean to heathens—

"The Seven Monarchs," the king began. "All holy, all sacred, but only two of them are Uncreated, existent since before the dawn of time." He placed another figurine in my hand.

She was beautiful, a laurel wrapped around her head, one of those leaves serving as a patch over her missing right eye. Twin braids hung down to her navel, slightly lifting off her body, like they were floating in a breeze.

"Ketet, the Mother, Goddess of Earth and Sea," I murmured. But . . . but the Kaldfolk were *heretics*. That was one of the first things I'd ever learned in Khada Palace. King Zaid had fought and beaten back *heretics*. He'd been charged with that mission by the gods themselves. I'd even seen evidence of that heretic magic today, when Rade had turned Finan into a puppet.

But I was holding renderings of Ketet and Shaya in my hands, whittled out of wood, which meant the carvings could not be Ashoran. Every statue we had was molded out of clay or carved from stone. More durable, longer lasting, like the gods deserved.

No, these couldn't have been taken from the palace.

These were Kaldfolk statues.

"Ketet and Shaya," Rade said with a nod. "Life and death. They have existed since the beginning and will exist after the end. Which makes your father one of the most important deities we have. I'm sure you know their story well."

The exact same doctrine we had in Ashorah . . .

Rade waited for my response. I swallowed hard and said in a hoarse voice, "Ketet and Shaya used to rule together as husband and wife. Ketet gave life in this realm and Shaya watched over it in the next."

Rade nodded. "Until Ketet's love for humans began to over-shadow her love for Shaya. She plucked out her right eye, wrapped it in fire, and placed it in the sky to create Phadar, God of the Sun." His voice was soothing as I listened to the familiar story. "Human life was sustained longer because of him, weakening the Underworld."

I stared, breathless. "We believe the same in Ashorah."

"You sound surprised," Keir said, and I couldn't miss the accusatory tone.

"Hush, Keir," Velka murmured.

"What do you know of the War of the Ancients?" asked Rade, drawing my attention back to him.

"The War of the Ancients," I repeated blankly. "Is that what the Shroud is? Left over from the war?"

"Not exactly." Rade's gaze dipped to the Shaya figurine. "Ketet and Phadar were bound together by their love of humans, a love Shaya could not understand. While they work to keep us alive, Shaya works to kill us. Fundamentally opposing forces. He watched his wife slowly fall in love with the sun god. Shaya was losing his realm and his lover at the same time. The death god grew vengeful."

I had heard the story of Shaya's wrath countless times from the Gods-Chosen herself. "He gave up half his soul to create the moon goddess, Ayeen," I said, "to fight against Phadar's light. And then he gave up the other half of his soul to create the jinn, led by his son, Athar. The tricksters worked to lead humans to an early death, which started the war."

"No," Rade said. "That was not enough to start a war. Phadar lengthened lifespans, the jinn shortened them. When the balance started to tip, one of the gods would send a Gods-Chosen to restore it. The world remained in equilibrium. But Shaya's magic corrupted the earth, infecting every living thing. Humans, animals, plants. It twisted them until they were monsters, little more than mindless beasts fighting over territory and food. He had changed the beings that Ketet loved so dearly, and *that* was not balance. She wouldn't stand for it."

"Why are you telling me this?" I asked. "What does the War of the Ancients have to do with the Shroud?"

"You know that Ketet and Phadar's children and their children's children fought Shaya until they managed to lock him—and most of his monsters—in the Underworld and seal the Gate. Except for jinn and Shifters, who got stuck on this side of the Gate, their powers significantly dampened. Jinn couldn't cause the same havoc they had before, and Shifters were no longer slaves to their animal halves. Shifters don't serve Shaya anymore, but the jinn are part of Shaya's soul. They continue to work for him, help him. And what does someone in prison want more than anything else?"

A chill stole over me. "Freedom."

Rade nodded darkly. "The jinn offer Shaya a foothold in our realm. And he has been using that to his advantage since he was imprisoned."

"Are you saying the Shroud is jinn's dark magic working to free Shaya?"

"Worse," Velka answered. She licked her lips nervously, yellow eyes troubled. "The Shroud is a bleeding wound. But instead of blood, it's leaking the Underworld."

My heart stopped in my chest. "What?"

"We're not entirely sure how it's happening," Rade said, "but we think it's the equivalent of banging on a door enough that it cracks open. The Underworld is seeping into our realm."

Holy gods. "How is that possible?"

"Shaya has always been powerful," Velka reasoned. "If he can never leave the Underworld, he might have just thought to move it. As an Uncreated, he's probably one of the only gods who could actually manage such a thing."

Move the Underworld? Move it *here*?

Ketet and the other Seven Monarchs had imprisoned Shaya because of his greed for human souls. If the Underworld crossed over into this realm . . .

My blood turned to ice. "Why have I never heard of this in Ashorah?" If anyone should know about Shaya's realm bleeding into ours, it should have been his Gods-Chosen.

They exchanged a look that I couldn't decipher. Rade said, "It started slow. No one even knew what the Shroud was until it was too late. And it isn't fully the Underworld. At least not yet. It's seeping in bit by bit. First its darkness, then its creatures. By the time we realized what it was, it was already too big to fight back." He scratched at his beard. "Some of the Kaldfolk refused to believe it was happening. Some cannot resist its call. You saw what happened today."

I thought of that first woman's wide, shiny eyes. Finan sitting stubbornly in his chair. My own temptation to draw closer. I swallowed past the dryness in my throat.

"Over the last two decades," Rade said, "the Shroud has sped up. As it claims more land, more people, it grows stronger and it—it thinks."

I stilled. "What do you mean?"

"I have my people watching it constantly," he replied. "We monitor it. It doesn't continuously spread. It . . . it's like it strategizes. Decides which town to take and when. It should have continued north, to the coast, where all settlements had already been evacuated. But it seemed to know that, and instead it turned east. After we began work on the tunnel through the Frozen Sands a few years ago, its movements grew even more erratic. For now, Netherridge, the village we just evacuated, seems to have sated it, and it isn't spreading farther. But that won't last long."

The Underworld was Shaya. Shaya was the Underworld. If the Shroud was the claw of the Underworld reaching into this realm, it made sense that it was as sentient as its ruler, even if it appeared to the naked eye to be just a writhing wall of night. A shudder worked through me.

"Even with all its pauses, our experts estimate we've got six months until all of Kaldfold will be swallowed. By then, the rate at which it moves will be so fast that it could take Ashorah in less than a year."

My fingers tightened around Shaya's figurine, a splinter digging into my skin. I'd only just learned about the Shroud. It had never been spoken of in Ashorah. Did my queen know of it? Or was she just as ignorant as I had been? I licked my dry lips. "What happens to people in the Shroud?"

Rade's eyes dropped to his lap.

"It twists them," Keir answered in a low voice. "Not right away. But living creatures are not meant to encounter the Underworld. Its darkness infests a person, and once it claims them . . ." He shook his head, eyes haunted.

And Finan had chosen that. Been ready to condemn his own grandchild to it, abandoned her in favor of it. He must have known all this and yet . . . Anger rose inside me, sudden and acute. An incomprehensible decision, choosing the dark over his family. A horrible, evil decision that spat in the very face of Ketet.

With physical effort, I pulled my gaze back to Rade. "You wrote to King Zaid about this," I said, recalling what Keir had said that fateful night in the throne room.

"I did," he confirmed. "Multiple times, in fact. He never answered my letters."

If the king had known, had Amunet? But that didn't make any sense. It was true that no Ashoran would stick their neck out to help the Kaldfolk, but if the threat was coming to us, and so swiftly, Amunet would have done something with that knowledge. Organized the Khada Guard on her own if she had to. She was stubborn. She would have acted. And unlike King Zaid, she would not have kept us ignorant of the threat that affected all of us.

Would she?

Guilt curdled in my stomach at doubting the Gods-Chosen for

even a second. It didn't matter what King Zaid had or had not done, my queen was nothing like him. That I knew wholeheartedly.

And yet.

The Kaldfolk weren't cannibals. They weren't heretics. Two of the three things I'd always been told were lies.

The Shroud was real. I'd seen it with my own eyes, felt its call. Rade clearly had magic, but he'd have to be incredibly strong to fabricate an illusion that massive. He hadn't even been strong enough to remove an elderly man from his rocking chair.

Unless that was just part of the ruse, to make me *think* he wasn't strong enough.

But the fear in Velka's eyes, the unease Keir was doing his best to hide, those didn't look fake. They had seen monsters. They had seen tragedy. Rade said every member of the Seven was cracked in some way. Maybe the Shroud was why.

Trying to undo the knot of thoughts swirling around my mind, to sniff out manipulation or untruths, was giving me a headache.

I asked, "So why am I here?" I was looking at Keir, who had made the decision to kidnap the Gods-Chosen. He met my stare unflinchingly.

But Rade was the one who answered. He leaned forward, elbows on his knees, light brown eyes boring into mine. "We've tried everything," he insisted. "Spells and incantations. Prayed to Ketet. Pleaded with Shaya. Nothing has worked. But"—he licked his lips nervously—"there is one thing we haven't tried."

"What?"

He glanced at his friends before scooting closer, our knees brushing. "I wasn't chosen as king for my fighting ability. Any of the Seven—any Shifter in Kaldfold, for that matter—would have me beat there. I was chosen for my magic, gifted to me by Eira."

One of Ketet's daughters, Goddess of the Lost.

I gaped. "You are Gods-Chosen?" I could not remember a time the gods had sent two of their children at the same time.

He huffed a laugh. "No. Not chosen. Blessed." His face grew serious. "There is no one more lost than those trapped in the Shroud. Eira sees that, and she entrusts me to save them."

Gods-Blessed. I had heard of people who had been touched by the gods. Different from King Zaid's blessing to rear Shaya's daughter. More tangible. Usually reserved for healers, seers, or soldiers. Or . . . a king.

Now I understood the weight on Rade's shoulders. It was the responsibility for his entire people.

"Can't you just pull people out of the Shroud?" I said.

"If I'd been king when the Shroud first took hold, maybe. But now I'm not strong enough to do it on my own."

"That's where you come in," Velka said.

My heart skipped a beat at that. Rade took my hands in his. "You are of Shaya's blood." Eagerness coated his every word. "His power flows in your veins, the same power that makes up the Shroud. If we were to combine our magic, I think we'd be strong enough to close the wound, as it were. Plug the leak."

I nearly choked. "Combine our magic?"

He released my hands abruptly and returned to his desk.

I looked at Velka and Keir. Keir's face was tight, but Velka was watching me with unveiled hope.

"There is a ritual. Our ancestors called it the Merging," Rade explained as he opened an old tome, its spine near disintegration. He thumbed delicately through the pages until he landed on the right one. "It hasn't been used in ages because it is only fit for those with power—power that hasn't existed among humans since the War of the Ancients—but the chieftains of the old world swore by it."

He held the book out to me. I took it with unsteady hands, the vellum cover rough beneath my fingers. I didn't bother looking at the words—as a slave, I had never been taught to read—and instead focused on the drawing in the center of the page.

It showed two people, a man and a woman, with red tattoos all over their faces. Their palms were pressed together, and a red glow emanated from between them, swirling up and around their heads.

"Back then," Rade said, "every ruler was blessed by the gods, and the Merging ensured that the ruling pair were equal, power shared between them so that they would lead as one."

I studied the drawing. The light around their heads seemed gentle, soft. Like an embrace. And the hands that were pressed together showed matching rings around their fourth fingers.

Wedding bands.

"This is a wedding ceremony," I stated dubiously as Rade resumed his seat beside me. When he didn't respond, I looked to Keir. "You brought me here to marry him?"

He didn't even flinch. "Yes."

I almost laughed. The Kaldfolk, instead of fleeing the palace when the Khada Guard turned on them, risked life and limb to kidnap my queen—not to eat or kill her, but to *marry* her.

But my laughter fizzled before reaching my lips.

It was too . . . small. That couldn't be the whole plan. There was something here I wasn't seeing. If Queen Amunet were here, she would know it instantly. Even if the Kaldfolk weren't heretics, even if they hadn't torn me apart like they'd done to those guards—

A wedding.

A merging of magic.

Because they wanted my queen's power.

That was what this was about. Not uniting against a common foe. This was about power. A wedding ceremony that would bind magic . . . merge it as one. If Rade had access to the Gods-Chosen's power, if he could use it however he pleased, he could drain her entirely.

He could steal it.

Why should I trust their story? Maybe the Shroud wasn't the Underworld. Maybe it was just a blight affecting Kaldfold, some corrupt magic left behind by their strange powers. That certainly seemed a lot more probable than the Underworld bleeding into our realm.

This might just be an elaborate ruse. Rade wanted to scare Amunet so that she'd feel she had no choice but to unite her magic with his. And with the Gods-Chosen's power at his fingertips, who knew what the Kaldfold king would do? Take revenge against Ashorah, for sure.

That was a plan worth drilling into the Frozen Sands for, worth months—if not years—of preparation, worth the risk of infiltrating Khada Palace and its legions. The Kaldfolk wanted the power of the Gods-Chosen.

Though Rade's gentle eyes didn't look like a thief's . . .

"I needed you to see it for yourself, Amunet." His breath brushed my cheek. I hadn't realized we were both leaning over the pages until then. "To see the threat. The magnitude of it, and understand that no army would be able to stop it, no *one* person, either." He lifted his eyes from the book to meet mine. "A Gods-Chosen and a Gods-Blessed. If we don't do it, your people and mine will be doomed to the Shroud, to that perpetual night stuck between realms, a fate so much worse than the Trench."

My gaze caught on another drawing, and my mouth went dry.

The man and woman lay on altars, head to head, with their arms hanging limply over the tabletop. Blood streamed from slit wrists.

"What is that?" I asked.

"The last part of the Merging," Rade replied. "It looks much scarier than it is. Our magic will protect us from the wounds."

"But I—I—" I grappled for an excuse. "I haven't gone through the Igniting. I don't have access to any power for another—"

"Twenty-two days. I know. If we begin quickly, the Merging will end on your birthday, when you'll have your powers. It's perfectly safe. You could save us immediately, before any more are lost to the Shroud."

I shook my head again. This was how they'd find me out. It didn't matter how much he pleaded, what he said. I didn't have that power. The ritual would kill me. I couldn't do it. I couldn't—

I drew a deep breath, staring down at the book, and forced my panicked thoughts to calm.

I could leave. That was what Rade had promised. I could turn my back on all this. It wasn't something I could fix anyway.

But my queen had twenty-two days left. Still plenty of time for word of her location to reach the Kaldfolk, for them to track her down and steal her power.

And then it hit me.

I didn't actually have to finish the ritual.

All I had to do was stall.

If they believed I was Queen Amunet for twenty-two days, if I could keep their attention fixed solely on me for twenty-two days, then the Gods-Chosen would be able to claim her birthright and Rade wouldn't have a chance to steal her magic.

If what Rade said was true, if the Shroud was the Underworld reaching into this realm, my queen would fight it off. She may have been chosen by Shaya, but her purpose was to save *us*. She wouldn't let this darkness spread and claim her people, no matter who was at the root of it. And with her powers, she wouldn't need a Kald at her side to do it.

I looked up into Rade's eyes and squared my shoulders. "What do I have to do?"

"Does . . . does that mean you'll help?"

"Yes."

Velka yipped joyfully, clapping her hands on her thighs. The tension drained from Rade's shoulders as a wide smile spread over his face. "Thank you," he breathed, voice thick with emotion.

But when I looked at Keir, he was silent, face utterly blank and yet probing. It made the hair on the back of my neck stand on end.

Three weeks. I just needed to last three weeks.

NINETEEN

∧∧∧∧∧∧∧∧∧

AMUNET

When my eyes fluttered open the next morning, it took me a moment to figure out why I felt so strange. The bed beneath me was cozy enough, blankets all the way up to my chin. It was still early enough that the insufferable heat had yet to take hold. My mind felt pleasantly drowsy and . . .

Silent. No tapping or scratching. And the itch at the back of my neck was little more than a distant hum.

Maybe Shaya didn't hate me after all, if he'd provided this small reprieve.

Gentle, gray morning light trickled in through the windows, outlining Jasim in its soft, silver glow. He sat beside the bed in a wooden chair that didn't look particularly comfortable, picking out twigs from my wig. I took a moment to just look at him.

His brows were pulled tight, eyes trained with singular focus on his task. There were small bags beneath those eyes, but that was the only sign of exhaustion. His gaze was clear, body upright. The sleeves of his ratty tunic were rolled up, and I ate up the sight of those powerful forearms, the veins that ribboned them like vines. His bottom lip was snagged between his teeth as he worked. For some reason, the sight made me smile.

The morning possessed a quiet, almost dreamy quality. Maybe I was delirious with relief to finally not want to claw my skin off, or maybe I was just a nosy bitch, but I found myself asking, "Where's your family?"

Jasim jolted, nearly dropping the wig. He swore, "By the Trench." His head whipped to me with a huff. "A little warning, my queen."

I grinned and snuggled deeper into my pillows. "You must have them, right? A family, that is. But you've never told me about them."

"You never asked." He rubbed a hand down his face.

"I'm asking now."

Jasim looked at me, a searching glint in his eyes. I *had* to be delirious, because I felt completely at ease beneath his gaze. "You feeling better?" he asked. "Last night, you . . ."

"I feel fine." The back of my neck buzzed with slight discomfort, but I could easily ignore it. Without the racket in my head, I felt better than I had in almost two weeks. "Tell me, Jasim," I murmured. "Please."

He was quiet a moment. A light wind ruffled the thin curtains over the windows and blew a few stray curls across his cheek. "Yes," he said eventually. "I have a family. They live in Masser, near the dam."

"That's far."

He nodded.

"Do you get to see them?"

"Not often. Twice a year if I'm lucky. Guarding the Gods-Chosen is a full-time job. But they write to me every week."

I frowned. It made me sad he didn't get to see them. An odd feeling. I think I'd felt it once before, when I'd learned of King Zaid's death. But I didn't try to stamp it out. I asked, "What are they like?"

He studied me again, those chocolate-brown eyes scouring my face. Quietly, he asked, "What is this, Amunet?"

Now I knew I was delirious: I smiled at my name. If I were in full use of my faculties, I'd have waved him off and changed the subject. Gone to look for Nasir and demand we leave for my father's temple immediately.

If I were kinder, I'd have left Jasim alone.

But even half mad, I was not kind.

"I want to know."

He hesitated a moment longer. His throat bobbed. But he set my wig carefully on the end table and angled his body toward me, elbows on his knees. My whole body lit up at his undivided attention. "Well," he began, "I have six sisters."

"Six!" My brows shot up. "Is that . . . Do people usually . . . ?"

Jasim's lips curled at the corners. "You mean, is it typical among lowly commoners to procreate like rabbits?"

"Yes."

He chuckled. "Can be. Just so happens that my parents loved each other. Too much and too often."

What a peculiar concept. I never knew my mother, but by all accounts, her marriage to the king was a political one. It was a miracle they had even one child. A literal, Gods-Chosen miracle.

"I'm the only boy, born second to last," Jasim continued. "Baba used to joke that the gods had finally taken pity on him when I was born, giving him another man in the house." His gaze took on a faraway look, a soft smile hovering over his lips. "It drove my mother and sisters mad when he'd make comments like that. We all helped out in his tannery, so it wasn't as if he was lacking anything without a boy. Which my oldest sister, Andra, pointed out all the time. Still does, honestly. But I think he just liked watching Mama's face turn red." He huffed a small laugh, and I grinned. Then his smile dimmed. "Of course, I was only eight when he died, so . . . Didn't really make it to the man part with him." He shrugged, like it didn't bother him, though it obviously did.

"I'm sorry." The words came out without my approval. But I found I meant them.

He looked down at his hands. Flexed and clenched them compulsively.

"How'd he die?" I asked softly.

"He was bringing home our water rations from Ketopolis. Someone followed him. Stabbed him and stole the water. We found him a few days later, Andra and I."

My heart was so heavy it struggled to remain in my chest instead of sinking to my feet. I reached out of the cocoon of my blankets and took Jasim's hand. His was coarse and rough from years of training, while any calluses I might have earned had been smoothed away with tallow. Gods forbid a royal might appear to have done some work.

Jasim stared at our hands, a line between his brows. "I joined the Khada Guard shortly after that. I send what I can back home to Mama and the girls. Most of them are married off now, but every little bit helps."

I nodded, even though I could not imagine the life he described. And I wanted to. The buzzling at the back of my neck was getting a little bit stronger, but I just clutched Jasim's hand tighter. "The king used to beat me," I blurted.

Jasim's deep brown eyes lifted to mine. His thumb smoothed gently over my knuckles as he softly said, "I know."

Of course he did. He'd helped me hobble back to my room more than once.

"It . . . it upset me, I think." I frowned as I tried to articulate a feeling I had not bothered to dwell on since I was six. "He used to be so kind. One time, he took me to the Ketopolis Market just because I'd mentioned I wanted baklawa and the palace chef didn't know how to make it. Then one day, he just . . . hated me."

Clink, clink, clink.

I winced at the whisper of a noise at the back of my head. "I can't remember if I did something to him. I might have. But it bothers me that I don't know if he changed first or if I did." I rubbed my chest where I'd felt that weird pain at the news of his death.

Jasim rose from his seat. He stretched out in the bed beside me, the warmth of his body tickling my skin, and gazed across the pillows at me with soft eyes. That *look*. But I didn't revile it this time. When he pulled me in and wrapped his arms around me, I melted into his embrace, burrowed into his neck. "You're a good person, Amunet," he murmured against the top of my shaved head. "You didn't deserve that."

I laughed hoarsely. "I'm not a good person, Jasim."

"You're a Gods-Chosen," he replied. "Of course you are." He kissed my temple.

I was going to miss him.

The realization hit me like a punch to the gut. When we made it to the Temple of Shaya, when this was all over, when I . . . did what I had to do at the temple, I was going to miss having this devout man at my side. His misplaced adoration. His ready excuses.

I would miss Jasim.

Clink, clink, clink.

Fire spread up from my nape to the crown of my head.

Ugh. Break was over. It was nice while it lasted. I reached my free hand up to scratch.

Jasim gently pulled it away and gave it a squeeze. "Come on. Let's go talk to Shaya."

Despite the return of extreme discomfort to my body, I smiled and let Jasim pull me out of bed.

TWENTY

∿∿∿∿∿∿∿

AMUNET

Nasir wasn't in the house. I asked one of the guards who stood by the front door where to find him, and he directed me down the street. "Seeing to the final preparations," he said mysteriously.

Jasim shadowed me as I wound through the streets. The coarse wig irritated my inflamed skin. The itch was loud, demanding my attention, nearly as loud as those claws against glass. It was as if the reprieve this morning had been the calm before a storm. The claws were no longer just scratching; they were breaking through. The sound of splintering glass crashed through my head. The distant mine's persistent *chink, chink, chink* only seemed to accentuate it. So much noise, so much distraction—

Amunet.

My head snapped to the left.

People bustled about. No one so much as glanced in my direction.

"My queen?" Jasim's hand landed on his scimitar. "What is it?"

The voice had been so clear. Yet the space before me was empty.

A chill washed over me. I scored my nails over the back of my neck, readjusted my wig, and kept moving. My jaw was clenched so hard, my molars threatened to crack. Jasim's eyes seared into the side of my face, but I kept my gaze studiously ahead.

We turned a corner and came upon the mine.

The crater plunged eternally into the ground and spanned a few miles in diameter. Men and women currently hung into the gaping maw on thick ropes, sweating in the early morning sun, the sound of their pickaxes ricocheting against the walls and up into the air. The hole was so deep, no one had ever reached the bottom.

Supposedly, the crater was a remnant of the War of the Ancients, like the various megaliths that dotted Ashorah's landscape. On my first patrol here, Nasir had told me some of the theories for what could have left such a scar on the world. An arrow forged of stars. A catapult that had launched the sun itself.

Or a fallen god.

The story went that somewhere in the dark recesses of the never-ending hole slumbered a fearsome god—a god that had been forgotten since the War of the Ancients—just biding its time until it unleashed itself upon the world.

I found myself staring into its black depths. The sun struggled to penetrate very far. How anyone could voluntarily lower themselves down there, and for what, I didn't know. It looked far too similar to the suffocating darkness that haunted my nightmares. Goose bumps spread down my arms. Fuck, I hated the dark.

"Queen Amunet?"

I looked up. Nasir stood a few yards away from the crater with his guards—including the insolent female one—constructing a pyre. He waved me over.

It looked like the pyre was nearly finished, and there were fifteen bodies lined up in front of it. They'd been draped in sheets of varying faded colors, but their faces were left exposed. If not for the grayish pallor to their otherwise dark skin and their purple lips, they would've looked like they were merely sleeping. Many of their faces were mottled with sunburns.

It was Ashoran custom to embalm the dead and place them in tombs. All Khadas were laid to rest beneath the palace, while advisors were allowed use of the mausoleums speckled throughout

Ketopolis. And the everyday Ashoran . . . well, I didn't know what they did exactly. I doubted they could afford tombs. Maybe they just stuffed their loved ones in a mountain.

But these bodies didn't look as if they'd been embalmed at all. There was no smell of myrrh, cassia, or any other typical spices.

Nasir noticed my curious gaze and explained, "Heatstroke and dehydration."

I nodded. That was how most people died in Ashorah. "They shouldn't be left in the heat without being embalmed." It was a miracle they weren't already rotting and rank.

Sweat stained Nasir's tunic, visible even beneath his leather armor. "They won't be embalmed." He nodded to the pyre. "We burn our dead."

I glanced sharply at him. "You what?"

"We've run out of places to bury them in the small territory you've allowed us. We have no choice." The smile he gave me was flimsy. "Of course, we are grateful to have any territory at all, my queen."

"But how will they reach the After Realm without their bodies?"

Nasir drew in a deep breath as if it was a thought that had haunted him for some time. But he only repeated, voice tight, "We have no choice."

No wonder Shaya had been so silent. His very essence was tied to death, to the people who came to his realm. If the other principalities were also burning their dead—if people in Ketopolis were, too—then Shaya had very little to draw from. He was weak.

A bigger sacrifice than a candle would be needed, indeed.

Nasir accidentally stepped on a woman's burial shroud as he faced me. "Walk with me?"

Jasim instantly fell a few steps behind, right beside the female guard, Sara. The jinni-descended prince fussed with his braids, pushing them back and then pulling them forward again. He appeared perpetually frazzled. It seemed the panic of being forced into the role of prince after his father's untimely death had never quite dissipated. Some men were just not meant to rule.

I twisted my fingers together to stop them from twitching. "So when do we leave?"

He didn't respond for a long moment, lips screwed to the side, the only sound the crunch of sand beneath our sandaled feet. Finally, he asked, "Do you know how we pass our time here?"

I blinked, caught off guard by the question.

"In Reeda," he clarified. "Out here in the middle of nowhere. When we're not mining or battling the desert heat."

"No, Nasir, I don't know your people's hobbies."

"Stories," he said. "There's an amphitheater not far from here where we put on plays. They're delightful, my queen. We've got all the usual fairy tales with scimitar fights and vanquished beasts. But every single story shares the same theme." Nasir paused a few feet away from the crater. Too close for my liking. Sara, too, seemed nervous, and stepped closer in case she had to yank the ungainly prince back to safety. The darkness seemed to yawn up at me like a hungry mouth. I shifted away as Nasir said, "Justice."

"Justice," I repeated blankly.

His gold-flecked eyes gleamed. "There is nothing a people who have suffered so much *in*justice value more."

I studied the prince, but his shimmering eyes gave nothing away. "I've already promised to return you to your home. What more do you want?"

"I'm very grateful for your generosity, my queen, and I would never presume to ask—"

"Out with it, Nasir."

"A position in court." He tipped his chin haughtily in the air. "I am of noble blood. I deserve a place in the palace."

He was delaying my trip to my father's temple because of petty politics. I nearly throttled him. But I figured that would only prolong my delay. So I smiled and nodded. "Sure. A position in court it is."

But he did not look appeased. Those gold-flecked eyes narrowed.

I swallowed a sigh.

Jinn-descended did not have as much magic as their full-blooded ancestors, but that didn't mean they were entirely without. The princes each boasted specific gifts, individual to the jinni they were descended from. Ilias in Wethai had control over the elements—water, fire, earth, wind—while Anwar in Haisab held powers of empathy, capable of turning one's emotions against them. No one knew what Sen of the Dry Lands had, but I knew that Nasir's power was truth. He could pick out a lie as soon as it left my mouth.

And one just had.

For fuck's sake.

"Yes, you can have a position in Khada Palace," I said again. I had no choice but to mean it.

What fun times lay ahead.

Amunet.

I flinched at the voice but didn't look away from Nasir. It was trying to distract me—whatever *it* was. It wasn't real, there was no one there. I trained my eyes on the prince and waited.

Nasir's eyes darted all over my face, gold flecks sparking like fireflies as his magic flared, searching for deception. But there wasn't any.

At least, for now.

In a month's time, who knew what would change, or what Shaya might disagree with? If my promise fell apart then, I didn't think Nasir would complain. Not when I'd have the power to flay him on the spot.

Amunet. A bit firmer, a bit more impatient than the last time. The glass in my mind splintered further.

I fisted my hands. *Go away,* I mentally thought at the voice, keeping my gaze easy and calm. No trace of potential deceit, no trace of anything amiss.

The prince studied me with a deep intensity. Then an easy smile spread over his face. "Excellent. We'll stay for the funeral, and then we'll go."

I ground my teeth. "No. We'll leave now."

"I cannot abandon my people when they are in mourning." He gave me a reassuring smile. "It will only take a few hours. I'll make sure my soldiers are ready to depart as soon as it's over." Before I could argue further, Nasir jogged back to the pyre, Sara on his heels.

My eyes did not leave him. "Jasim."

"Yes, my queen." He was at my side in an instant.

"I want you to talk to Nasir's soldiers."

Jasim frowned. "About what?"

"This is the second delay he's caused us. I want to know if he's keeping us here just because he's greedy and stupid . . ."

". . . or if we need to run," he finished for me. I nodded. "I doubt they'll tell me very much, but I'll see what I can do. While I'm gone, stay in your room. Door locked. And keep this"—he thrust a dagger into my hands—"on you at all times, plus a scimitar. And we'll brush up on your training." He was already undoing one of his scimitar sheaths.

"I don't need a refresher course."

"You haven't practiced in almost two years." I opened my mouth to respond, but he wrapped the leather belt of the sheath around my hips. His arms went around me as they met at the small of my back, nearly bringing our bodies flush, and the smell of him—sweat, the fresh woody smell of river reeds, and something headier that was purely *him*—surrounded me.

Deep brown eyes bled out the rest of the world as he dipped his face down toward mine. "Ashorah is your realm," he said, "but your safety is mine. If I tell you to carry a blade, then you do. If I tell you to train, then you *do*. No arguments. Understand? My queen." The last part added as an afterthought.

I should have laughed at his attempt at assertiveness and thrown off his hands, which had already finished securing the belt and now merely rested against my sides.

But I didn't.

Something had shifted between us this morning. I could not pin-point it exactly beyond a peculiar fluttering in the pit of my stomach. But it prompted me to nod silently.

Jasim gazed at me a moment longer, lips thin within his beard, before he finally nodded and stepped away.

Able to breathe again, I pulled my eyes away from Jasim and set them back on Nasir.

It was probably nothing. But we should have been several miles closer to Shaya's temple by now. Something just did not feel right.

I wanted Nasir's help, but if I had to make do with just Jasim and whatever we could scrounge up, I would.

A chuckle sounded. Not from Jasim or any of the miners. A mocking chuckle. A familiar one that left me feeling cold. That dis-embodied chuckle reverberated around me, like the strikes of the pickaxes against the crater walls.

TWENTY-ONE

SAMIRA

Sitting with my legs crossed on my cabin's hard wooden floor, the chill of the earth below seeping into me, I gazed absently into the fireplace. Just as I had been for the past several hours. But no matter how long I sat by the blaze, the ice in my bones wouldn't thaw.

There were three parts to the Merging. Now that I knew exactly what was going on, Rade saw no need to wait, so the opening ceremony would happen tomorrow. I wondered if it would become obvious then that I was a fraud. If it did, I hoped they would just kill me. A hanging or beheading, perhaps—not something worse.

Accompanying that fear was an inexplicable guilt. The Kaldfolk were meant to be demented beasts, as animalistic as the Shifters' bear forms. But not all of them were Shifters. Some, like Rade, held no beast form. And among those who were, Keir and Bain were the most frightening of the bunch, but for all their threats, even they had left me alone—mostly. Granted, it had only been a handful of days since I'd arrived, but they didn't seem like beasts. They were just . . . people. Magical, Gods-Blessed people.

And my lies could get them all killed.

My deception was wasting valuable time, and when the twenty-two days were finally up, it might be too late to stop the Shroud.

No, I tried to assure myself, *Queen Amunet will receive her powers by the Merging's end, and she'll save everyone. From drought and famine, and from the Shroud.*

They didn't need Samira. No one ever really had.

Except Queen Amunet.

I rubbed at my tired eyes. I'd barely managed an hour of sleep before giving up entirely. Dawn wasn't too far off now, and I couldn't stay in this room any longer, with my thoughts chasing each other round and round. I slipped my feet into boots, grabbed a fur cloak, and knocked on the door.

Nothing happened.

I knocked again. "Keir?"

No response. Not even a growl of annoyance.

Hesitantly, I reached for the doorknob and turned—

The door opened.

Barely breathing, I peeked my head out.

Keir wasn't standing there. *No one* was guarding my door. Had he forgotten to lock it? Or had I earned some goodwill after offering to help? Whatever the reason, I thanked the gods for the small mercy as I stepped out and shut the door softly behind me.

Frostguard was painted in a gentle ocean-blue light, the last of the fading moon's rays casting a sad pall over the place. The winding paths throughout the city glowed with torchlight.

Although I'd always hated Ashoran summers, I missed the blaze of the sun. It could be smothering, but it was home. And so much more bearable than this unyielding chill. I pulled the fur cloak tighter under my chin.

Two children scurried away from the longhouse, one of whom I recognized. Milena.

She followed a little boy into the nearby trees, where a fire's glow stretched out like rays from the sun. Curiosity curled up in my chest, and I went after them.

Singing swirled toward me on the next breeze, soft and delicate.

Kaldfolk were gathered around a bonfire. Men and women of all ages, eyes closed. Milena and the little boy settled among the group, letting their lids drift shut, too. I paused just outside the fire's circle and peeked around a tree.

The bonfire stretched several feet high, crackling loudly. And a body wrapped in a plain black shawl lay beside it on a makeshift table. Hedin's body.

A woman with black markings curling up her neck stood in the center of the crowd, tears squeezing past her shut lids as she sang, swaying slightly. She didn't have an extremely skilled voice, but there was something enchanting about her song all the same. Like the words were coming from the very depths of her soul. I didn't know the language, but the notes of sorrow and pleading in her voice resonated deep in my bones.

A drum pounded out a beat in time with her, and when I peered farther around the tree, I saw Keir. He sat on a log outside the circle, a simple, beat-up drum held between his knees. He didn't wear his normal fur cloak, and I could see those fearsome tattoos on his neck stretching past the V of his neckline as he tapped his hands on the instrument. With his eyes closed, his face looked different. His strong jaw, slightly crooked nose, and hulking frame seemed softer. Almost . . . appealing. If a monster could ever be such a thing.

The rest of the Seven were gathered around him, too. None of them bothered to close their eyes. Flames reflected in their yellow irises as they gazed at the body beside the bonfire.

"Hedin's mother," said a voice behind me, and I jumped.

Moonlight reflected off Rade's brown eyes.

"Sorry," I said quickly, moving to go back to my cabin. "I didn't mean to—"

"No, please." Rade caught my wrist. His long hair was pulled back into a bun at the nape of his neck, making his already kind face appear entirely open as he guided me back to his side. He released my wrist and nodded toward the singing woman. "Her name is Dara. She's giving Hedin's elegy. When she finishes, we'll bury him in the White Horn Mountains."

"Oh." I shouldn't have been here. This was a private moment.

But Rade leaned closer, eyes on the funeral in front of us. "Mother, hear the cry of the damned," he translated quietly, his breath tickling my ear. "Mother, save those who bless your name. We submit to you, we love you, we need you. Mother, hear the cry of the damned." His eyes glittered as he stared at the woman. "It's a prayer to Ketet that's been passed down through the generations from the ancient tongue. We say it every time a village is evacuated. Dara's using it to honor her son *and* the people of Netherridge."

The prayer was a call for help. The guilt returned, a knife to my gut, twisting deeper.

"Bain's here," I whispered.

Rade's gaze shifted from Dara to Bain. "It was an honorable fight," he said, voice tight. "A challenge issued and accepted. Dara will not blame him for besting her son."

I studied the king's clenched jaw, the anger in his eyes, and found myself asking, "Why did you let him do it?"

He sighed. "Because they all wanted it." When he looked at me, his gaze was clouded with grief. "I don't want to replace Alarik. He was my Second for so long. Picking anyone else . . ." He shook his head as if he could prevent the eventuality with that movement alone. "I've been king since I was twelve. What twelve-year-old is ready to be king?" He shrugged, then scratched at his beard. "I have to pick my battles. Everyone wanted that fight. I had to let them have it."

"But you're Gods-Blessed. You're more powerful than all of them. That alone should make them listen." Amunet hadn't even come into her Gods-Chosen power yet, and the whole world bent to her will.

"Maybe. But they wouldn't like me very much." He smiled tiredly. "I've been hated and adored. I'm not ashamed to admit I prefer being adored far more. For as long as it lasts." Beneath the thickness of his beard, I could make out a dimple in his left cheek. He gestured to the clearing. "Would you like to join? You can sit beside me."

"No," I responded quickly, taking several steps back. Spying seemed wrong enough. I didn't think the gods would forgive me for sitting among them. "I just needed some air. I should go back to bed—"

"Amunet," Rade said, taking my hand in his warm one. With the last of the moonlight reflecting in his light brown eyes and his short beard framing his sharp jawbone, he was beautiful. Not at all like the nightmare I'd been promised. "I know this must be a lot to take in. But you have my word that nothing will happen to you. We will enter each trial side by side, and I will make *sure* that you are safe."

I nodded, though I wasn't fully reassured. I didn't think I would breathe normally again until I was back in Ashorah. Or in the Paradise Fields.

Rade's gaze dropped to my hand in his. With furrowed brows, he turned it over and ran his thumb over the calluses on my palm. "You have rough hands," he murmured in surprise.

Panic sparked in my veins. I snatched my hand away. "Yes. Yes, we royals . . . we . . . work."

"Ah yes. You trained with the Khada Guard, right?"

"I—yes." I swallowed hard and thanked the moon goddess, Ayeen, for hiding the flustered blush in my cheeks. Glancing back into the clearing, I saw Keir lift his head. Those sunny eyes scanned the area, drawing closer to where I hid.

I stepped back deeper into the shelter of the trees. "Forgive me, Your Majesty, but I should—"

"How many times must I ask you to call me Rade?" His lips quirked to the side.

A shy smile curved my lips. "Sorry. Rade. I should go before anyone notices me."

"I think they'd be happy to see the Queen of Ashorah taking an interest in our customs."

"I doubt that."

Rade smiled sadly but said, "I'll walk you back."

It was actually rather pleasant walking by his side. Rade had a calming presence, a stillness within that stretched to encompass those around him. It was comforting.

He stopped outside my door. "I've instructed Keir to keep this unlocked. Feel free to walk around anytime."

"Thank you."

Before I closed the door, Rade blurted, "Wait."

I paused.

He rubbed the back of his neck and laughed self-consciously. "I just . . . I know this is a wedding ritual, but it's important that you know I wouldn't—expect anything of you. That I would never . . . force myself on you, either. That's not a, um, requirement of the Merging."

"Oh." A fierce heat stole over my cheeks. I hadn't thought that far ahead. And with his power, I supposed Rade *could* force whatever he wanted. I didn't put much stock in a Kald's word, but for my own sanity, I chose to believe him. "Thank you."

He laughed softly. "You really don't need to thank me for that."

My cheeks flushed even hotter. "Right."

Rade started to back away, a smile still playing on his lips. "The day is yours to do with as you like. I'll see you at dinner."

I nodded, and he turned and strode into the trees, back to the funeral. I watched after him for a moment before softly shutting my cabin door.

A husband. I hadn't even had a suitor. They were prohibited among the Gods-Chosen's maids. Too much of a distraction. And now I would have a husband.

No. No, I wouldn't make it that far.

I sat on the edge of my bed and stared down at my callused hands.

I'd never given them much consideration before. All slaves had hands like these. Rough skin, cracked and dry. When we'd bathed Amunet, I'd never even noticed the difference between her smooth, unblemished skin and mine. But Rade was right, my hands were . . . they were disgusting. Used, chapped.

If Rade had picked up on something so small, what else might he see? My whole body screamed out that I was a liar, that I wasn't special or chosen or royal. I could not hide that forever.

Maybe that was why Keir hated me so much. Maybe his Shifter senses could smell the filth I'd tried so desperately to wash away in the saltwater bath. Maybe when he looked at me, what he saw was the many, many things I lacked.

TWENTY-TWO

SAMIRA

I spent the day walking aimlessly through Frostguard. Keir followed several feet behind but mercifully didn't attempt to speak to me, even as he wore a pinched expression on his face, almost like he was in pain. I didn't comment on it, and he didn't explain.

I mostly stuck to the border of the village and watched the Kaldfolk go about their lives. Women hung the wash on clotheslines, men swept wayward leaves out of their homes with brooms, children roughhoused. Smoke drifted up from chimneys, and despite the ever-present cold of this place, there was a warmth to the scene.

It all seemed very . . . normal. Pleasant, even.

I passed a brewery, where I spotted Bain. He dipped a finger into a vat of the milky white kefir and brought it to his lips. His chiseled face tightened with a hard cringe, and then a cough racked his lean form.

The brewer beside him, an elderly woman with snow-white hair and hands as large as plates, cackled and clapped him hard on the back.

I became hyperaware of Keir at my back. My mind could not help but think of the other night. The kefir he'd brought me. That small bit of kindness.

Neither of us had acknowledged that moment. Granted, there

had been far more pressing matters to deal with, but now all the questions that had crowded my mind rose up again.

When I turned around and met Keir's glittering gold gaze, they tangled up on my tongue before I could voice any of them. His brows lifted in a question.

I blurted the first thing that came to mind: "I took a bath."

He blinked. "Congratulations?"

The tips of my ears burned. "No, I . . . I know you said it wouldn't help. With the smell. My smell. But . . . I tried . . ." My words trailed over a cliff and died, and I almost wished the Kaldfolk would go ahead and kill me.

Keir studied me in that piercing way of his. It took great effort not to let my eyes dart away. "Did you think that would hide your scent this morning?"

The burn in my ears spread to my cheeks. "I wasn't trying to hide."

"No?" Keir tilted his head in a poor imitation of innocent curiosity. "Then why didn't I see you?"

"You didn't look hard enough."

He took a step closer, making me crane my head back to maintain eye contact. "Believe me, I did," he said. Every inch of me became alert, some primal instinct warning me I was caught in the sights of a predator. My heart pounded in my ears. "What were you hoping to see, hm? Hedin being roasted up for a nice meal? Or maybe something more important you could use against us when you bring your Khada Guard back here?"

"No! No, I . . . I didn't want to upset anyone. It was obviously a private event. I hadn't even meant to be there. I saw Milena running into the woods and I followed her—"

"Milena," he repeated.

"Yes." When he just stared, I awkwardly added, "The girl from Netherridge?"

"You remember her name."

I frowned. "It's not a particularly difficult one."

Keir's nostrils flared. Scenting me. What he was looking for, I didn't know. But I watched him draw a deep inhale and hold it, just like the night in my cabin. The longer he held it, the hotter my face felt. When he finally let it out, it caressed my cheeks.

"You know what I smell?" he asked quietly. The dangerous whisper of a leopard moving through grass. "Beneath the sadness and fear and attempted friendliness. Beneath . . ." He inhaled again. "Beneath everything else."

"What?"

He leaned in so that his warmth tickled my skin and his sunny eyes branded themselves on the backs of my lids. "You smell like you're hiding something, Majesty."

My stomach plummeted. My blood, molten just seconds ago, turned to ice in my veins.

He hummed in approval when he scented the shift. "Tell me what it is now," he murmured, "and I will show you mercy."

Horror blared through every inch of me. I'd failed my queen. I didn't know if it was one thing in particular or if I'd never stood a chance. What I did know was that a confession would not grant me mercy. The beast in front of me would take great joy in delivering my punishment.

"Come on, Majesty," he coaxed, soft, seductive. "Secrets are so heavy, aren't they?"

They were. I hated lying. But my queen needed this from me. The gods needed this from me, and I had let them all down—

Majesty. Keir had called me Majesty. Whatever he suspected, whatever he smelled, he didn't know who I really was. Which meant I hadn't failed. Not yet. Relief made my head feel light.

"I'm sorry I was there this morning," I said in my most measured tone. "It was not my place. I did not mean to upset you. Please forgive me."

Instead of smoothing out, the line between Keir's brows deepened further. He studied me, like if he just looked long enough, he could drag my secrets out of me. I held my ground, hands fisted at my sides and face carefully neutral, the way my queen looked when she had to deal with a particularly difficult advisor. He could probably hear my heart slamming against my rib cage, but I tried to take slow breaths to calm it.

Keir said, "You—"

"Your Majesty!"

Both our heads snapped up at Velka's call. She approached with a wave.

I took a large step away from Keir, breathing easier, and smiled gratefully, beyond relieved to be saved from this conversation. "Hello, Velka."

Velka wore a bright smile, cheeks rosy from the chill, and gestured to the brewery. "Did you want to go in? Don't listen to Keir, you're allowed to approach. Venna loves to talk all about her *craft* to anyone who will listen."

Keir grumbled darkly beside me as he fiddled with something under his cloak. His jaw tightened, muscle feathering in his cheek. That wince of pain again.

Maybe if he hadn't spent the last five minutes threatening me, I would have felt bad.

Instead, I turned all of my attention to Velka. "Maybe later."

Velka nodded but fell into step beside me. Though I did my best to keep my shoulders low, my insides tensed. She hadn't done anything to me, but she'd laughed and applauded Hedin's snapped neck as much as everyone else. Though, so had Keir, and I'd had no trouble talking to him just now.

Probably because I expected him to act like a monster, while Velka seemed so . . . nice.

She pointed to a hut with a line of gutted fish hanging from its open front. "That's Aurel's smokehouse. It's his first month having a go at running the place on his own. Used to be him and his father, but the man's a little . . ." She gestured vaguely to her head. "Hasn't been fully there since the Shroud took Pinethorpe. But he's doing a fine job. You've tasted his dishes firsthand."

I'd had fish a few times now. It seemed to be the most readily available meal. And it was almost always smoked. Not as good as the pork my first night, but definitely better than the slop from Khada Palace.

"Was everyone here displaced by the Shroud?" I asked.

"Not everyone." Velka angled her head toward a cluster of cabins. "We call that Founders Street. Their families have been in Frostguard for generations—they claim since the War of the Ancients, but I think that's a bit of an exaggeration."

I vaguely remembered her mentioning she wasn't from Frostguard, and asked, "You're not a founder, right?"

"Lived here over ten years, but no. I'm luckier than most, though. My family got out of the Pillars before everything went to shit."

"Your family is here in Frostguard?"

She nodded. "Blacksmiths by trade. Papa claims to run the smithy"—she lowered her voice conspiratorially—"but everyone knows it's my big sister, Aisling, who's really in charge."

I couldn't help but grin.

Her gaze shifted over my shoulder. Mischief glinted in her eyes. "Feel like losing the warden?"

"Um . . ." Considering the less-than-pleasant conversation we'd just had, I didn't think it smart to taunt him. But when I chanced a peek back, I saw Keir was talking to Sillia, their faces severe. They didn't even bat an eye in our direction.

In the last few days, all my survival instincts must have truly vanished. First, I'd walked willingly toward the Shroud, and now I nodded to Velka, agreeing to poke an actual bear.

"When I say so," Velka whispered, hooking her arm through mine, "cut left."

My heart pounded. We walked a few more feet, steps hurried.

Keir shouted, "Velka!"

"Now!" she ordered, and yanked me to the left.

I heard Keir swear before we turned the corner into a small alley between cabins and ran. Velka careened around another corner, into what seemed to be a makeshift courtyard where drums thundered, boots stomped, and hands clapped. Kaldfolk marched in a circle around a flagpole, the Kaldfold bear flag waving from the top. They were chanting—and they were *loud*.

I slapped my hands over my ears. "What is this?" I yelled over the din.

"Birthday party!" she replied. I spotted a little boy among the crowd, wildflowers tangled in his hair and smiling widely as he was hauled into the circle.

Velka tightened her arm around mine and jerked me through the mayhem.

Before we disappeared around yet another bend, I saw Keir rush into the courtyard, his enhanced Shifter's senses unable to pinpoint us among the cacophony. He searched blindly. "Velka!"

"Come on," she urged, and then we were running down a different alley.

We didn't stop until we reached a tall tower made of stacked logs, with a ladder leaning against its side. Velka climbed without hesitation, and I followed.

She collapsed on her back at the top, laughing, and I paused on my hands and knees beside her, chest heaving as I struggled to catch my breath. But I was laughing, too. "Did you just get us in trouble?"

She waved her hand dismissively. "It's our favorite game. Or—I guess it's my favorite game that I force Keir to play."

I laughed again. I couldn't remember the last time I'd laughed, but it felt good. Like a small weight had been removed from my chest.

Glancing around, I spotted a row of arrows, and beside them

an assortment of bows. A long horn rested against the line of weapons. Meant to sound an alarm. Banisters wrapped around the square space, but there were no walls. The wind whipped through here easily. A watchtower.

Velka got to her feet and rested her forearms on the railing, jerking her chin to gesture outside. "Come look."

I stood and moved to her side. The Shroud was the first thing I saw, malicious and twisting.

"Not there," Velka corrected. She pointed south. "There."

Kaldfold stretched before me. The drought had taken its toll on this place; what I was sure had once been lush, full trees were now mere spindles with only the most stubborn leaves still hanging on, and the once-vibrant grass was now an anemic spread of brittle weeds.

And yet, somehow, there was still beauty here. Birds soared overhead, a handful of deer disappeared into the forest. The overcast sky was like a comforting blanket over all of it. The wonder of Ketet's work, no matter how hard Shaya sought to diminish it, held true.

And if I strained my eyes to the horizon, I could make out the tan color of sand. No buildings, no vegetation dotting its surface. Just sand. "Those are the Wastelands," I breathed.

Velka nodded.

Ashorah was too far west for me to make out Khada Palace or even the Frozen Sand Mountains, but just that small glimpse of the Wastelands, of terrain that was recognizable, was enough to settle me. No, I had never set foot in the Wastelands—and I never would, if I could help it—but it was only a hundred miles away from Ketopolis. Home.

"You can come here anytime."

I blinked at Velka.

She smiled. "I'll let the others know. Whenever you need to take in the view, feel free."

Free to look toward my home whenever I wanted, whenever I

needed reminding why I was doing this, whenever I needed to draw strength.

"Why are you being so nice to me?" I couldn't help but ask. "Even on the journey from Ashorah, you were kind. And now this . . ." I looked back toward the Wastelands.

Velka studied her clasped hands hanging over the watchtower's banister. "If our roles were reversed, if you were holding me in Ashorah, would you treat me like one of Shaya's leftover monsters? Or would you be kind?"

My answer was instant, but I bit it back. If Amunet got hold of a Kald, there would be no mercy. And I don't think I would've felt bad about it, either.

Velka's lips curved grimly at my silence. "My mother always says that people want to learn, they just don't want to *feel* like they are. But if you want a better world, people must learn how to be better. So we have to show you how to be better, Your Majesty," she said. "And maybe, at the end of this, when you're in charge of the largest empire on the continent, you'll have learned how to make it better, too."

I swallowed and looked away, cheeks heating with shame. Shame that I had allowed myself to be swayed into believing they weren't people but mindless animals. They had magic—just like my queen would in a few weeks. They weren't all pleasant. They were certainly flawed. Cracked, Rade had said. But Velka had never treated me like a monster, even when she thought I was responsible for so much pain and fear in her home.

She was right. She was better than me.

I was quiet for a moment. Then I broached, "Velka, could I ask you something else?"

"Sure."

"There was an old man in Netherridge—Finan. He let the Shroud take him."

"Ah, Finan." She sighed mournfully. "The promise of reuniting with a loved one can be all too tempting." At my look, she elabo-rated. "Some people feel drawn to the Shroud. We're not sure why not everyone succumbs to its call, but we think its darkness calls to the darkness in us. Those with more darkness feel the pull stronger."

My skin prickled, and dread fell like a stone in my gut. That wall of night stood tall and proud. While it looked frightening, I couldn't deny that I found it alluring, too. A desire to feel its gentle touch on my skin again. *Those with more darkness . . .*

"Do you mean . . . the Shroud only calls to evil people?" I asked in a small voice.

Velka shook her head. "We all have darkness in us, Your Maj-esty. Some just have a greater propensity for it. We think the Shroud exploits that. That's how it gets its claws in. And once it does . . ." She shrugged sadly. Oblivious to my mounting unease, she went on, "Finan's wife walked into it years ago. I imagine he hoped she was still in there, the way he remembered. But she's not."

I recalled, "Keir said the Shroud infests people."

"It does. And he would know better than any of us."

I frowned. "Why?"

"Because he—"

"Velka!" a furious voice barked. We peered over the edge to see Keir seething up at us.

"There you are," Velka called back. "We were looking all over for you."

"Get down here *now*."

She rolled her eyes. "Fun's over. Let's go, before that vein in his forehead explodes."

My conversation with Velka plagued me the rest of the day and well into dinner. What did she mean, a *greater propensity for dark-ness*? Velka hadn't seemed to think too much of it—but then again, she and her friends were tried-and-true killers. I was nothing that horrible. Other than lying for the Gods-Chosen, I had never done anything bad in my entire life. The gods were strict in their expectations, and they wanted their children to act with honor, kindness, and obedience. Which I tried to do. Always.

Part of me thought I should tell Velka I felt that call, so that she could tell me what to do to combat it. She'd help me.

But maybe she was wrong. After all, she had also said they weren't sure. So maybe it had nothing to do with darkness. Maybe it was arbitrary. A sorry luck of the draw. That felt like a better fit. The very fact that I was in Kaldfold was a testament to just how rotten my luck was. Unlucky, but not a disappointment to my gods.

None of my reassurances loosened the knot of dread around my chest.

TWENTY-THREE

〰〰〰〰〰〰

AMUNET

The crackle and pop of the pyre was a consistent roar in my ears, mercifully drowning out the scraping in my head. The only mercy the giant flame would bestow on me. Prayers rolled through my mind like sand down a hill, gathering grains and speed, one plea following the next. Yet the back of my neck continued to burn.

The way I'd figured it, a pyre was like one huge candle, with the bonus of fifteen sacrificial bodies. It was worth a shot to try to reach out to Shaya here.

On the other side of the flames, Nasir spoke with families of the deceased, gold-flecked eyes glittering with sympathy as mothers cried in his arms. It appeared genuine.

Not too far away, slightly distorted by heat waves, Jasim struck up conversations with soldiers to figure out why the fuck we were still here. The bodies were burned to scorched crisps. Funeral was over. Time to move.

With each extra second, my paranoia rose, and my side throbbed with the reminder of the assassin's blade. The sweat searing its way down my neck wasn't helping matters. My whole body shook as I resisted the urge to scratch. Thousands of scorching pinpricks crawled farther up my skull. I'd chucked my wig to the ground some time ago, unable to handle even that minor touch. Comfort seemed like a fairy tale, like something I'd never known.

A deep, familiar chuckle sounded directly in my ear. I flinched and squeezed my eyes shut. Just another symptom of my separation from Shaya, like the itch, like the claws in my head.

Yet the feeling of eyes on me lifted the hairs along my arms.

I blew out a hard breath through my nose and focused on the roar of the pyre, on the heat of the sun on the top of my shaved head.

Stop this, Amunet, chided a familiar, creaky voice. *You look like a fool.*

I bit my lip harder against the answer that jumped to the tip of my tongue. He wasn't here. Talking to him would only make—

You know why Shaya's not answering, King Zaid goaded. *He's not punishing you. He doesn't care enough to punish you. He's moved on. After all, twenty years is a long time to wait for someone to become useful.*

He was wrong. He hadn't moved on. I was his daughter.

Like you were mine?

"I was never your daughter." The words were out of me before I could stop them.

Ah, that's it, is it? That's why you're out here pouting? His chuckle sounded again, shuddering down my spine. *Better to think I was the villain and Shaya the hero than to accept that I simply did not love you.*

"Shut up." My cheeks felt hot, my chest tight. I tried to push his voice away, to focus on my prayers, to generate a plan for how Jasim and I would make it to the temple without Nasir's help. But I thought I felt the king's breath brush against the side of my face, could almost see his smile within his gray beard, his vindictive green eyes.

I tried, Amunet. But there's nothing about you worth loving.

"Stop it."

You think Shaya's different? You think he will stand beside you? You think he loves you? Oh, you poor, stupid little girl—

"Shut! Up!" My eyes burst open.

Sara stood a few feet away, eyes wide and brows low.

No King Zaid. Of course.

My cheeks were hot for a different reason now. I reached up and slashed my nails across the back of my head. "What do you want?"

"Who were you talking to?" Sweat darkened the orange of the headscarf around her face as she surveyed the space around me. The clearly *empty* space.

"I'm praying." I infused my words with as much impatience as I could muster, all while fighting the tears that threatened to well in my eyes. Tears of fear, frustration, hurt.

The guard approached me. Hatred gleamed in her hazel eyes.

Nothing new, is it? King Zaid whispered in my ear, and my body stiffened. *If not irrationally devoted, like your little pet, hatred is the only other option.*

Go away! I mentally shouted at him.

"I didn't realize our deaths affected you so much," Sara said blandly.

"Any Ashoran death affects me. I'm a Gods-Chosen."

King Zaid cackled, echoed by Sara's scoff. "Come off it, Your Majesty. You don't give a rat's ass about us out here." I didn't even see the dagger in her hand before it was pressed to my throat. I went very still. "Your presence at their pyre is an insult," she snarled. "You don't care about any of our dead. You don't care about Ashorah at all." Her eyes flashed, the brown momentarily outweighing the green. "There's only one reason Shaya would sire a child, and it doesn't take a genius to realize it has nothing to do with saving Ashorah. Quite the opposite, in fact." She bared her teeth at me. "You're going to free him."

As much as I was loath to admit it, King Zaid was right. This was nothing new. It was an accusation that had been thrown at me numerous times in Khada Palace. If someone thought of me as the spawn of evil, then they were also incapable of thinking Shaya could be something more than the villain. That he could care about the living as much as he cared for the dead.

But if I was being honest, I didn't care. If Shaya wanted me to save Ashorah, I'd do it. If he wanted me to free him from the Underworld, I'd do it. If he wanted me to burn the whole world to the ground, I'd do it. I sent those words toward the pyre, hoping Shaya would hear them. If he didn't, I'd repeat them at his temple.

"I made a deal with Nasir," I told Sara. "And if you don't remove that knife from my throat in three seconds, I'll tell your prince the deal is off and *you* are to blame."

"Can't do that with a hole in your throat."

My hand shot up to grip her jaw, nails biting into her cheeks. She flinched, knife jerking against my throat. "Do it," I snarled. "Deal ends either way."

She ripped her face out of my grip, angry red slashes now adorning her cheeks from my nails. "I might hate you, Your Majesty, but I know you're smart. It doesn't matter what truth Nasir heard in your deal. I've known him my whole life. There are ways around his magic, as I'm sure you've already figured out. Your words mean *nothing.*"

"I didn't realize people here had such little trust in their prince."

"I don't trust *you.* Deal or no, you'll betray us. My parents were screwed over by you Khadas. I will *not* let it happen again." Keeping her eyes locked with mine, she walked backward, Phadar's sun on her chest catching in the midday light, a promise in her hostile face. Her sandals crunched in the sand as she finally turned and strode back the way she came.

She certainly seems to think your precious Shaya is the villain, the king mused.

"Just stop," I said under my breath, turning my gaze back to the pillar of fire as if it were the king himself. "Please, just stop."

He didn't. *Every story needs a villain, Amunet. And make no mistake, the Gods-Chosen is a story. A nice little fable to give the people hope.*

"It's more than a story," I gritted out.

Wake up, you stupid girl, he spat. *If you were Shaya's beloved daughter, why would he abandon you? It's a lie. You are a lie.*

"No." I shook my head hard, trying to clear it. The voice might be the king's, but the doubts were my own, simmering somewhere deep in my mind for weeks. They were heresy, sacrilege. They would only push Shaya further away. I could not allow them into the light of day.

Fine, he went on ruthlessly. *If you're so sure Shaya isn't the villain, and I'm already dead . . . what characters remain in your story? Who is left to play the villain? Except you.*

"I am *not* the villain. And this isn't a fable. I exist because of *your* deal with the jinn. I am a solution to *your* mistakes, *your* ineptitude."

The king didn't respond. There was no chuckle, no breath against my cheek.

The quiet was more foreboding than the rasp of his voice.

"Hey."

I gasped with a flinch.

But it was just Jasim. He paused a foot away. "What's wrong?"

"Nothing," I replied instantly. My mouth was dry, my chest heavy, and there was a dull ache in my throat where Sara's knife had nicked me. But I sank into two decades' worth of training and schooled my face into one of smooth indifference. "Did you find out anything from Nasir's soldiers?"

He observed me a moment longer.

The truth attempted to sidestep my training and spew from my lips, anticipating his strong arms around me, the warm press of his body against mine. I clenched my jaw tight. This habit of wanting to tell Jasim things was . . . new.

Eventually, he said, "We're leaving."

"Anything more specific?"

"Now." Jasim jerked his chin over my shoulder.

I turned to find a collection of Reeda soldiers, perhaps twenty or so, waiting in disciplined rows. Beside them were a couple of wagons holding jugs of water rations, sacks of food, and supplies for shelter. Sara joined the militia with a line of goats in tow for sacrifice.

"Queen Amunet." Nasir approached with a boyish smile, though there was a heaviness to his gaze. A smudge of dullness to his gold-flecked irises. The weight of his people's deaths. He tried to stand tall as he swept his hand toward his waiting soldiers. "Shall we?"

We were going to the Temple of Shaya. I really was just being paranoid. As I followed Nasir to one of the wagons, I waited for the relief to set in.

It never came.

First the itch. Then the claws. Now irrational paranoia and ghostly voices. What would come next? How much worse would this get? And for how much longer?

Because I didn't think I could survive the rest of the month like this.

TWENTY-FOUR

SAMIRA

Change quickly," Velka told me. "We start at the sun's zenith."

Her face was caked with white clay, which cracked slightly when she smiled at me, and her light brown hair was braided differently, twisting around her head in a crown. She wore a tunic with open sleeves, joined by a small piece of fabric at the elbow. I could see the rest of her blue tattoos, swirling from her fingers all the way to the tops of her shoulders.

She held out a tunic for me to wear. I asked her to look away as I changed into it, not from any modesty, but so that she wouldn't see the scars on my back and chest.

The tunic was similar to hers, but my open sleeves were bound at the wrists instead of the elbows. When I moved my arms, the thin fabric billowed out like wings. It was entirely too thin for the cold, but Velka instructed me to leave my cloak behind. Instant gooseflesh spread over my body as I stepped outside.

Keir waited there, a statue beside Velka. His face was also painted in that white clay, nearly hiding the tattoos along his jaw. A stark contrast to the black that usually covered his face.

Velka took my arm and led me away, with Keir falling into step behind us. I could feel his eyes burning into the back of my head.

A crowd of Kaldfolk had formed in front of the longhouse, a line on either side of the dirt road, creating a path that led down the hill to where a larger mass of people waited.

All staring at me.

"Go ahead," Velka whispered.

"What?" I turned with wide eyes. "Aren't you coming?"

"You outrank us," she said. "We'll follow you."

I faced the path again. So many eyes, all searing right into my face. They wore laurels of woven twigs but no smiles and none of that white face paint. Serious as could be. My heart stuttered in my chest.

Velka whispered encouragingly, "It's just a few yards."

Right. Just a few yards. I faced forward again and pressed my shaking hands against my thighs. Amunet had paraded through crowds like these many times. It was just one step at a time.

My boots crunched loudly over the frozen earth, as if I were stepping on shattered glass.

That was the *only* sound. The silence was like molasses, thick, suffocating, coating every single person. My breaths seemed to echo. I tried not to let my shoulders hike up. *Walk like a royal,* I reminded myself.

When I finally reached the bottom of the hill, Rade was waiting.

His body was covered in that white clay, but two red streaks cut through it just under his eyes. His tunic was sleeveless, showing off the muscles in his arms.

I stopped beside him, and he gave me a reassuring smile as he gestured to the woman on his other side. Her face was painted in a reddish clay, and her hair fell in dark dreadlocks down her back. "She's a priestess," Rade explained.

I barely had time to nod my understanding before the priestess boomed to the crowd, "We begin when Phadar is at the height of his power, when the sun god is most awake, to awaken our soon-to-be queen."

A solid *boom* ricocheted down the hill, startling me. I turned.

Keir and Velka stood in line with the Seven, all wearing that white paint. They held wooden shields in their hands and slammed their swords against the wood again, letting out another *boom* that vibrated in my skull.

The priestess reached behind her and held up a bowl filled with that white paint. "Your power has been asleep for nearly twenty years," she told me. "No longer. Today you will end its slumber. You will journey into night with the protection of the sun."

She passed the bowl to Rade. He faced the crowd. "Come forward," he commanded.

Cano approached first. He dipped his fingers into the paint and then reached for the side of my head. "Cano of Netherridge," he proclaimed as he smeared the cold, sticky paint over my right ear and then the left. "I offer the strength of my ears, that your power might alert you of danger before it's near." He gave me a small smile before he stepped aside.

Dalla came next, a thick line between her brows as she took the bowl. "Dalla of Keenforge. I offer the strength of my feet, that your power might be felt with every step." She knelt and spread the paint from my thighs to the tips of my toes.

And on it went.

"Bain of Blackstone. I offer the strength of my arms, that you wield your power as a mighty fist." He didn't meet my eyes.

"Sillia of Netherridge. I offer the strength of my hands, that your power might flow from your fingertips."

"Velka of the Pillars. I offer the strength of my voice"—she coated my throat with paint—"that your very words may shake the earth."

Despite my nerves, my lips twitched up at that.

But then Keir stepped forward, and my smile dropped. "Keir of the Wild Valley." His voice was softer than the others', quieter, meant for my ears only. He didn't look away from me even as he reached to dip his fingers into the paint. "I offer the strength of my eyes," he said.

I had to close my eyes as he spread the paint over them, his large fingers surprisingly light, their heat a sharp contrast to the chill of the day. A shiver slid down my spine. He made a long line of paint on either side of my eyes and then swept under them as well. "That you might see through dangerous deception."

My eyes popped open. Keir's yellow gaze was unflinching, missing nothing.

When he rejoined his group of Shifters, it was a struggle to turn away from him, to give him my back. He was just trying to scare me. And I was sad to admit it worked.

Rade put both hands in the bowl of paint and scooped it out. Then he dripped it across my collarbones. "Rade of Frostguard. I offer my heart," he said, and instantly I stiffened. But there was nothing I could do as he touched a finger to the trickling paint and used it to draw a symbol over my pounding chest. When he skimmed the raised flesh of my scar, his eyes flicked up to mine questioningly.

I tried not to react, tried not to give anything away.

Mercifully, he didn't comment as he focused on finishing the symbol. "That your power will guide and fortify you through all your difficulties," he said. When he pulled his hand away, I could see the curiosity wending through his mind. First my callused hands and now my chest. Neither of these marks should be on a queen. I waited for him to say it, to declare it, for Keir to seize me by the arms and haul me back to the longhouse.

But the king said nothing. He simply turned to face the priestess.

The priestess spread the remaining paint on any piece of flesh not already touched and stated simply, "That you might be a light strong enough to face the night." She placed the bowl on the wooden table behind her.

The Seven mounted horses. Two more were brought forward for Rade and me. "What's happening?" I whispered to him.

"The first ceremony."

"I thought that's what this was."

"No." He gestured for me to get on the horse. The paint made my legs stick together as I climbed up. Rade got onto his own horse and echoed the priestess, "Now you must face the night." And he gazed pointedly ahead.

At the writhing, dark wall of the Shroud.

TWENTY-FIVE

SAMIRA

I pulled my horse to a stop several yards away from the Shroud. There was no trace of Netherridge, or evidence that a town had stood here at all. The dark tentacles writhed against the clouds. My body swayed toward it, the pommel of the saddle digging into my stomach. Only sheer willpower kept me seated.

"I thought you said the Shroud twists those who enter," I squeaked.

Rade dismounted his horse beside me, and so did the Seven. "We'll be fine as long as we're only in there for an hour or so."

"An *hour*?"

Rade placed a reassuring hand on my skittish horse's neck, quieting the anxious animal, and gazed up at me. "We are awakening your magic, Amunet."

I just shook my head, grateful when my horse danced a few inches away.

We all have darkness in us, Your Majesty. Some just have a greater propensity for it.

It didn't matter that I had decided Velka's explanation was wrong. I didn't want to test it. The pull I felt toward the Shroud from the outside . . . What if, when it surrounded me, I didn't want to leave?

Keir sauntered up on my other side and crossed his arms over his massive chest. "I'll make it easy for you, Majesty," he said. "Either you get down from that horse, or I'll get you down."

"Keir," Velka hissed behind him.

He just shrugged.

Something about that unfeeling gesture, the dare in his eyes, made me face forward again and draw a deep breath. Queen Amunet was frightened of no one and nothing, so that was what I had to be, too.

I slid off the horse and pretended my legs weren't shaking beneath me.

Rade gave me an encouraging nod. "We're going with you."

Velka appeared at my shoulder. "And we won't let anything happen to you."

Keir took up the spot behind me, and the rest of the Seven fell into rank around me. A wall of muscle. It should have been reassuring.

It wasn't.

My heart clawed at the cage of my ribs as I stepped forward, roaring at me to stop. But I took another step. Then another.

And then I was engulfed by the darkness.

I stepped into a cloud. The black smoke of the Shroud grazed my skin like downy feathers. A gentle, warm breeze made my tunic flutter around my shins, so at odds with Kaldfold's climate. I drew a deep breath, limbs inexplicably lighter.

Around me sprawled the night sky itself. Glittering purple dust spun through the air like stars, blinking in and out as it drifted from tree corpse to tree corpse. Branches stretched and twined with each other like broken fingers, unnatural and sharply bent, not a leaf in sight. Yet I found it . . . beautiful.

A small laugh huffed out of me. There was nothing to fear here. It was wonderful. Ethereal. A dream in the flesh.

"Majesty." A hand clamped around my elbow.

I jerked to a halt. I hadn't even realized I'd wandered forward until then.

Keir's gaze was firm, those pretty eyes shining out of a luminescent face. I gasped, hand drifting up to his cheek. Rough from rising stubble and sticky with clay. "You're glowing," I murmured in awe.

His jaw worked beneath my fingers. For some reason, that made me giggle. His fingers curled around my wrist and gently pulled my hand away. "So are you, Majesty."

"What?" I glanced down and startled. My skin was indeed glowing. Or at least the clay they had coated me in was.

Rade stepped up beside me, his skin lit up, too. When I glanced around, I realized we were *all* glowing. "Fire doesn't burn here," he explained. "So no torches. This is the only thing that works."

"We're like fireflies." I laughed. No one else did. I didn't mind.

Rade gave me a tight smile. "Stay close, okay? Keir—"

"I got her." His hand settled on my back, urging me forward. I beamed up at him and sank into his side. Surprisingly cozy for a man made of such hard muscles. I snuggled into him as we walked and his hand smoothed around my waist. Pleasant shivers spread through me.

Even Keir was nicer here. I liked it. I would stay—

A sharp pain shot through me.

"Ow!" I turned to Keir with wide eyes, rubbing my side. "Did you just pinch me?"

"Pain breaks through the haze."

Even as he spoke, I recognized the ache in my cheeks from smiling, the foreign giddiness in my stomach. I swallowed hard, feeling suddenly ill.

"It's okay," Keir assured me softly. "Just keep moving." His hand flattened against my back again, and I let it anchor me as we pushed on. The urge to laugh bubbled up a couple of times, but I focused on the throbbing pain in my side instead.

The darkness rippled away, cringing from our light, creating a reluctant path. In the shadows, I heard shuffling, like something was following us. Tracking our path. In the distance, a crazed laugh sounded.

"How do we awaken my magic?" I whispered to distract myself. Feathers rustled above our heads as an unseen bird took flight.

"You must receive your runes from the Seer." Rade gestured to the red tattoos—runes—on the side of his head. "They will center your power there, so the priestess will know where to pull it from when we are joined."

"Will mine be red, too?"

"Probably."

Velka offered, "Red runes signify a god's blessing. Blue marks us as Shifters. Black means no magic."

I tripped over a root that seemed to appear out of nowhere. Black meant no magic? I was going to emerge from the Seer with black runes, and they'd discover me here, in this place stuck between our realm and the Underworld. Maybe they'd just leave me here to be twisted.

If I even got that far. Would the Seer need to bestow runes on me before she outed the truth?

Gods-Blessed and originally from Ashorah, Zarqa was as famous as any legend. The only Seer currently living, blessed by Ayeen, Goddess of the Moon, with powers of prophecy. It was rumored she'd left Ketopolis years ago, but I never imagined she'd exchanged it for . . . this.

"How can she live here without being twisted like everyone else?" I asked.

"Zarqa is under Ayeen's protection," Rade replied. "The Seer is most powerful in the night, when her goddess rules the sky, so she has decided to live within the Shroud, a perpetual night, and the goddess's shield allows her to move through it without suffering its effects or being in danger by others who have already succumbed."

As if on cue, a scream exploded out of the trees, and I whipped my head in its direction, the hair on the back of my neck standing on end. The Seven closed ranks around Rade and me, all of them baring their teeth in a growl, axes and blades at the ready.

Something moved. Two blue flashes in the dark—eyes.

And then four. Six. Ten. More and more eyes, all focused on us. Surrounding us.

One stepped forward.

A woman with nearly translucent skin, veins creating a purple labyrinth of lines, showing clear through her flesh. Ethereal blue eyes beamed out of sunken sockets, and black hair fell in thick, matted cords around her face. The creature was hunched over, her joints so badly twisted that she was incapable of standing upright.

She looked right at me and grinned.

Rade whispered, "Don't move."

My muscles locked up, rendering me motionless whether I liked it or not.

The creature walked right up to the Seven and tilted her head at Keir curiously. In the shadows of the Shroud, her companions snickered, the sound like rodents scurrying.

And then the creature stepped *through* Keir. As if he weren't there at all. Even he couldn't hold back a shudder.

The ghostly figure stopped in front of me next, blue eyes so bright they were nearly blinding.

The Seven didn't turn to watch the creature, didn't attack, but their muscles were tight, prepared to spring into action at any moment.

I clamped my lips shut against my frightened whimper as the creature stepped close enough for me to feel the intense cold leaking off her. Colder than anything I'd ever felt before. It wasn't a physical cold. It was a cold that had seeped into this creature's very being. Leeched her of her soul. It was the cold of absence.

She leaned forward and sniffed me.

I struggled not to tremble.

"I was wondering when we'd meet you." Her voice was like nails scraping against ice. Sharp, grating. It made my insides quake.

Then, faster than my mortal eyes could catch, Keir launched his blade into the Shroud. It glittered briefly as it spun away before disappearing into the dark. An animal's cry bleated through the silence. He'd hit something.

The creature's head snapped away from me. She let out a sharp keen, blasting my eardrums, the sound was picked up by the rest of her pack. Then she bolted into the dark.

"Run," Keir instructed.

Rade grabbed my arm and yanked me into a sprint.

The sound of the creatures' keens followed us for what seemed like miles. A horribly sad, devastated sound that rattled my bones while also breaking my heart. I couldn't help but wonder if one of those sad cries belonged to Milena's grandfather. I shuddered that I had thought about staying here for even a second.

The screams ended with a last strangled shriek, the sound reverberating in the darkness and my eardrums. I finally drew to a panting halt and turned to Rade. "What were they?"

"Ghuls," Rade answered, his breathing only slightly quicker from our mad run through the darkness. "Human souls trapped between our realm and Shaya's."

A shudder went down my spine.

"Come on," said Rade. We kept moving.

"What did she mean when she said she'd been wondering when they'd meet me?" I asked.

"The creatures are mad," Keir responded from behind me. "She probably wasn't even seeing you. Her words were nonsense."

Rade looked at him over his shoulder, a wealth of meaning illuminated by the glowing paint on his face. A look only they could decipher. But Rade faced forward just as a small hut materialized out of the darkness, and my concerns instantly shifted from the ghuls to the Seer.

Golden light shone in the windows. Someone was home.

Rade paused by the rotted wooden steps leading up to a door with chipping green paint. "You have to go in alone."

"What?" My eyes darted to the house fearfully.

"Getting your runes—and the fortune they come with—is a very personal matter. The Seven have been instructed not to listen, but we will remain right here." He took my hand and squeezed. "You will be all right."

They'd all gotten runes. They'd all been to see the Seer, I told myself. All of them. And they were all standing here, completely fine. I would be, too.

Until I came out with black runes.

But if I refused to go inside, I would be just as damned. I didn't have a choice.

Swallowing past the dryness in my throat, I stepped up to the door and knocked. No footsteps approached on the other side. All was silent. I raised my hand to knock again—

The door creaked open slowly.

No one was there.

I glanced back at Rade. He gave me an encouraging smile.

My gaze drifted behind him to Keir, who flicked his hand twice at me, waving me inside.

Fisting my hands at my sides, I stepped into the hut.

TWENTY-SIX

SAMIRA

The door shut on its own behind me.

The inside of the Seer's hut was cramped. The rotted wood filled the space with a moldy smell, making my nose curl. There was no furniture. The room was completely bare. And the pull of the Shroud seemed incapable of penetrating the thin walls; the urge to frolic and giggle dissipated the moment the door closed.

"Hello?" I whispered.

A delicate pink light sparked to life down a hallway to my left. Beckoning.

I steeled myself and headed in its direction.

I entered a kitchen. Rusted pots and pans hung from the ceiling alongside various herbs, an unlit oven beneath them.

The pink light was coming from a lantern on the low wooden table at the center of the room. But there wasn't a flame. It was almost as if the lantern gave off the light on its own.

Movement caught my eye, and I startled. A cloaked figure that hadn't been there seconds ago sat at the table, cross-legged on the floor. The hood fell back as she tilted her head up at me.

Her eyes were clouded with blindness, and wrinkles puckered around her mouth. But that was about as much as I could tell behind the countless red runes that covered her face. Even the edges

around the whites of her eyes were red with them, like the tattoos
had bled into her eyes.

She gestured to the other side of the table. "Sit," she ordered,
voice rough with age.

I licked my lips nervously and quickly obeyed, folding my legs
under me.

"You've come to ask Zarqa for a fortune you do not care to
see," she stated. "But you will receive it all the same." The Seer
reached into the baggy sleeve of her cloak and pulled out a filled
chalice.

I blinked in surprise. How could she have that in her sleeve
without spilling it?

In the dim pink light, I couldn't make out exactly what was in
the cup save for small leaves floating at the top.

Zarqa brought the cup to her lips and took a hefty gulp. Then
she held it out to me.

With shaky hands, I accepted the cup. Brought it to my nose
and sniffed. It was a sharp smell, almost like mint, but with a strange
follow-up odor that nearly brought tears to my eyes.

"Drink," she said.

Bracing myself, I took a sip—and nearly gagged. The heady
odor punched me in the back of the throat and burned all the way
down.

"All of it," the Seer instructed.

I didn't give myself time to think before pinching my nose and
downing the rest. It clung to my tongue, making each taste bud
pucker in horror. I dry heaved.

Zarqa ignored it as she put the chalice aside. "Give me your
hands."

Still coughing, eyes watering, I reached across the table, and she
clutched my hands in her leathery ones. She tilted her chin up, her
long gray hair stirring in an unseen wind. Two pinpricks of light

pierced through her cloudy eyes, and she looked right at me. Her voice came out in a quiet hiss. *"Samira."*

Gooseflesh popped up all over my body at the use of my real name.

I tried to lower my gaze, to look away from that piercing knowledge, but . . . I couldn't. I had the horrible sensation of falling. Right into those twin lights. Deeper and deeper, until I didn't see the pink hue of the lantern, didn't feel the rough wood of the floor.

I was falling, falling, falling . . .

And then a hot breeze whipped around me, and sand tickled my cheeks.

I blinked and turned my head, lips parting in shock.

I wasn't in the Seer's hut, though she still held my hands in her unwavering grip. When I looked out, I saw sand for miles and miles. Dunes stretching to meet the horizon.

"It was greed that brought you here," Zarqa said in that same disturbing hiss. As she spoke, the wind intensified, kicking up the sand around us, stinging my skin.

But the Seer appeared unaffected. Her lit-up eyes stared, unblinking. *"It is greed that will seek you out. Greed destroys, greed burns."*

The sand was nearly a cyclone around us, doing much more than stinging. It scraped over me so rapidly, it burned. Blood ran down my arms, and when I opened my mouth to scream, sand funneled in. Choking me, suffocating me.

I turned to run—my feet wouldn't move. I looked down and saw that I was sinking. I jerked against the sand, but some unseen force kept me locked in place.

Zarqa's grip on my hands became a vise. I cringed as the bones in my fingers groaned.

The sand was up to my knees, my thighs, my hips. It crushed my chest, and I couldn't breathe. When I gasped for air, there was only sand.

And then the blaze of the sun vanished as I was swallowed up.

Silence. Deathly silence. A tomb's silence.

Zarqa's voice whispered by my ear, *"But out of fire were you born, out of water were you found. To both must you return before all is razed to the ground."*

I lurched, digging into the sand. I didn't know which way was up or down, but I dug and dug and dug. My nails cracked, my skin bled, my lungs burned. And still I dug and dug—

My head burst through the sand. I gasped and felt like sobbing when oxygen surged past my lips. I tried to open my eyes, but they stung with the sand cascading off my head.

I forced them open all the same.

Zarqa was gone. I wasn't holding her hands anymore. But I was holding *something* . . .

I held up my hand, and a chain unraveled, a large spherical pendant hanging from it. An amulet. A globe glinted at its center, reflecting a glare. I shielded my eyes with my hand and turned my head—

My jaw dropped.

To my right, at least a mile or two away, stood walls. Bright, metallic walls made of gold. They encircled a city. I could just make out the domed roof of a citadel at its center. It glinted against the sun's rays, made of bright gold. The *whole* city was made of gold. I had never seen such a place before.

But I had heard stories of it. Legends. And so had King Zaid.

The Buried City. Filled with more riches than anyone could count even if they lived three lifetimes, meant to be paradise on earth. Within its walls, there was an abundance of livestock, water, shelter. There was no famine, no disease, no evil. No dehydration.

And it stood *right there*.

But then a shadow loomed over me, stretching impossibly tall, a line of black coating me. Stomach dipping, I turned.

A being of darkness rose up behind me, like a shadow come

to life. It was giant, only its torso rising out of the sand as if the world couldn't contain its full form. I craned my head far back but couldn't make out its eyes—if it even had any.

"Hello, Samira," it greeted me. Its voice was an indistinguishable wheeze, rasped out with great effort, a person's dying breath.

A chill passed over me. This being knew me. "Who are you?"

The shadow curved forward so it blocked out the sun, the sky, until I was bathed in its cold darkness. "You know who I am, Samira. But you do not know yourself. Let me show you."

My bloodstream flooded with adrenaline. Though it didn't make any sense, I did know this creature. I couldn't recall how, but I *did*. And instead of fear, intense anticipation lifted the hairs on my arms. The desire to follow the creature came over me swift and fast. I wanted to remember how I knew this shadow. I wanted to know what this creature knew about me.

When the shadow reached its enormous hand toward me, I reached back.

Then Zarqa was in front of me, her threadbare cloak billowing as if in an angry storm, her glare shooting twin beams of crimson light straight through me. She snatched my hand and jerked me away from the shadow. Sand swelled up, surrounding us. With a gasp, I lifted my arms to cover my eyes.

When I lowered them again, I was back in the Seer's hut.

Adrenaline made me lightheaded, and my insides contracted tightly in fear. "What . . . what was that?" I asked breathlessly. I could still feel the sun baking my skin, taste the sand in my mouth. And when I looked down, the paint on my arms was indeed chipped.

"The realm of visions is volatile," she replied, as if that were an answer, and then began whispering fervently under her breath. She lifted her hands away from mine slowly, and as our palms pulled apart, glittering emerald rays stretched out. As the Seer moved her hands farther away, I saw they weren't just rays. They were symbols, delicate swirls that I didn't recognize. I didn't think I would've been able to understand them even if I knew how to read.

The Seer lifted her hands until the symbols were levitating in the space in front of our eyes. They bathed the entire room in their gentle green glow.

Then, in a sharp movement, the Seer's hands flexed, palms out to my face.

The symbols shot at me and slammed into my forehead, knocking me on my back.

It was like someone had brought a branding iron down on me. I squeezed my eyes shut and screamed, clawing at my forehead as the symbols burned into me. I saw them on the backs of my lids, felt them burrow into my skull, my brain.

When I opened my eyes again, green light beamed out. I slapped my hands over my eyes and writhed on the floor as another shriek cracked out of me.

I was burning from the inside out. My blood was on fire. My *bone marrow* was on fire. I was going to die. I was dying. I was—

It stopped. Just as quickly as it had come on, it all just . . . stopped.

The heat died, leaving a dull throb above my eyebrows. No light beamed out when I opened my eyes this time. Even the pink light from the lantern had gone out, stranding me in the quiet dark.

Struggling to catch my breath, I grabbed the edge of the table and pulled myself up.

Zarqa was gone; I was alone.

I stood—too quickly. Vertigo enveloped me, and I reeled backward into the wall of pans, which clanged loudly. I waited for the spinning to subside, but it didn't.

Holding my breath, I pressed my shoulder against the wall and slid along it, staggering to the front door.

When I emerged from the hut, everyone turned to me.

My legs gave out, and I vomited.

Rade was at my side in an instant, rubbing my back and mumbling soothing words.

I didn't hear a single one of them.

Every time I tried to stand, I saw double and my stomach turned over. I vomited again.

Suddenly, I was being lifted and cradled against a strong chest. I dared to crack open my eyes and recognized Keir's face above me.

"Keep your eyes closed," he warned a split second before he took off, bolting impossibly fast. I squeezed my eyes shut and clung to the fur of his cloak.

Hurried shuffling followed us within the darkness. It kept speed with Keir, and a vicious laugh sounded very close by, watching from the shadows. But Keir's arms tightened around me, and he didn't slow.

The wind whipped my hair against my cheek, and before I knew it, sunlight warmed the backs of my lids.

He didn't bother asking if I was well enough to ride on my own. He just settled me into the saddle and then climbed up behind me, clutching me to him as he whipped the horse's reins. We took off like an arrow out of what had once been Netherridge.

I must've passed out, because the next thing I knew, I was lying in my bed.

Keir stood at the edge of the bed. Sweat glistened on his face, and he was staring at me with wide eyes.

A healer slid her hand under my head and put a vial to my lips. I drank its contents without question, not even cringing against the tang.

"Don't fight the sleep," the healer told me.

I didn't. When I felt the drowsiness creeping up on me, I jumped happily into it.

TWENTY-SEVEN

AMUNET

Jasim's scimitar knocked into my khopesh hard enough to make me stumble. He clicked his tongue. "Your footwork is sloppy."

I huffed. "My footwork is fine."

He gave me a look.

Begrudgingly, I adjusted my stance. Jasim nodded, satisfied. Then he came at me again. It was harder to keep up with him than I wanted to admit. Sweat dribbled down my face, intensifying the burning itch that had melted its way down my arms. Even my lack of sleeves didn't help. Just the air tickling my skin was enough to make me want to claw down to the bone.

Traveling with Nasir through Ashorah's heat for a whole week was horrible enough, but each day seemed to bring some new torment. I felt halfway to madness.

Only halfway? King Zaid snorted.

Jasim knocked my blade to the ground.

A growl erupted from my lips.

He retrieved it and held the hilt out to me. "You're distracted."

I snatched it with a glower. "I'm just out of practice."

Better be nicer to the soldier, King Zaid clucked. *Chase him off and you'll be shit out of luck when you reach the temple.*

I hated that a disembodied voice might have a point. Sucking in a breath through my nose, I softened. "Sorry. Maybe we should stop for the night."

"It's barely been ten minutes. You agreed to an hour."

"I'm tired."

Jasim narrowed his eyes at me, the lantern light painting his golden skin in flecks of amber. It was his idea to train at night, when neither Nasir nor any of his soldiers would be around to question it. Each night we made camp, we'd turned Jasim's tent into a make-shift ring. The opportunity to hit something had done me good at the start of our journey, the familiarity of exchanging blows with Jasim almost therapeutic, but now not even the clash of blades was enough to keep my symptoms at bay.

"All right." Jasim tossed his scimitar aside and crossed his arms. "What is it?"

I sighed. "I already told you—"

"Are you sick? Is it something to do with the scratching?"

Stubborn little pup is onto you, King Zaid taunted.

My head twitched in a subtle attempt to dislodge him. He cackled.

"That, right there." Jasim pointed at my face. "What was that?"

"Gods, enough, Jasim. I'm tired, I'm going to bed. That's all." I turned to flee for my tent, but he caught my elbow and reeled me back, close enough that his chocolate-brown eyes consumed my world, firelight dancing in their depths.

"I watch you, Amunet," he told me. "All day, that is what I do. I have memorized your every facial expression. Your eye rolls and your fake smiles and your sad sighs. I know them all because it is my job to know them all. But this . . ." His grip on my elbow softened and his other hand came up to just barely graze my jaw. "This is different. Something is wrong. Tell me what it is so I can help you."

Yes, tell him how you only brought him along to sacrifice him. That'll go over so well.

My throat constricted. Jasim was more perceptive than I gave him credit for. He'd done more than watch me; he'd learned me. And he was still here. Still trying to help me. Words tried to slip past the vise of my throat, and I realized I *wanted* to tell him the truth. I knew it was stupid, knew King Zaid was right, but the weight of my inflamed skin, of the clamor in my head, had grown too heavy to shoulder alone.

I'd always been alone. I didn't want to be anymore.

I whispered, "I think I'm losing my mind, Jasim."

His brows drew together. "What do you mean?"

"I—"

Selfish to the end, eh? The king tsked. *Tell him this and you'll have to tell him everything. It'll hurt him. But of course, you don't care about that, do you? No, you enjoy torturing the pup. Sadistic bitch.*

I flinched hard.

"Amunet?" Jasim cupped my cheek, eyes desperately searching my face.

When King Zaid had forced me to accept Shaya, I'd felt as if there wasn't enough room for me in my own body. It was a horrible, claustrophobic, violating feeling. One I had never wanted to experience again. But gods, it *was* happening again.

"I, um . . . I think you're right," I said, my voice wavering. "I think I'm sick."

The king snorted. *You can say that again.*

Jasim put a hand to my forehead. He didn't feel any fever, but still he said, "We'll turn back. Find you a healer—"

"No," I cut him off sharply. "I have to speak to Shaya."

"Amunet . . ."

"I'll be fine once I speak with him, I just have—"

Once you kill Jasim, you mean.

I hope you're rotting, I snapped at the king viciously. *I hope your blood is staining that throne you loved so much. I hope the Kaldfolk*

*slit your throat—or worse—and I hope it hurt. I hope you were in
agony.*

King Zaid merely laughed.

"Amunet." Jasim's gaze was penetrating, fingers pressing
into the skin of my jaw as if he could keep my mind from slipping if only he held on tight enough.

My legs tensed with the instinct to run. I couldn't tell him. No
matter how much I wanted to. No matter how much the *look* tried
to draw me in. The moment he knew, the look would die. Its promises, its comfort, it would all vanish before my eyes, and I'd be alone
again.

Normally, I would be relieved to be rid of the look's lies, but for
one foolish moment, I wondered . . . what if it wasn't a lie?

King Zaid's snicker mocked the naïve hope. Fine, maybe the
look was a lie or an illusion, but I was hearing the dead king's voice
in my head. What was one more illusion?

I curled my fingers into Jasim's tunic. "Do you remember a few
years ago, when we were forced to train in the height of summer and
I got heatstroke?"

Confusion twisted his features, but he nodded. "You passed out
in the middle of the ring. Training ended early because of it."

I smiled slightly. "No one could wait to go inside, where there
were fans and ice, but you were there when I woke up. You didn't
leave. You never leave."

Loyal pup that confuses beatings for love, the king quipped.

Squeezing my eyes shut, I breathed, begged, "Stay with me."
My knuckles turned white from how hard I gripped Jasim's shirt.
"Please, stay."

"Of course I'll stay." Jasim rested his forehead against mine. "I'll
always stay, Amunet."

*Gods, forcing him to make a promise like that while marching him
to his death. You really are evil, aren't you.*

I shook my head as tears welled up.

"I'm here." Jasim wrapped an arm around me and drew me into him. "I won't leave you."

It was selfish. It was evil. It was everything Zaid said, everything I thought about myself, but I let him make that promise. I savored it. Cherished it. Basked in the security of it.

Then I tipped my face up to his and kissed him.

TWENTY-EIGHT

ᴧᴧᴧᴧᴧᴧᴧ

AMUNET

The world melted away under that tender kiss. The itch disappeared. King Zaid's voice faded into oblivion. Finally, after days of endless racket, there was nothing but blissful silence.

A whimper of relief slipped out of me.

"Amunet," he whispered, his own broken plea.

I wrapped my arms around his neck and hauled him against me, molding our bodies together. My tongue darted out, coaxing his lips apart. He immediately parted them, and the moment my tongue touched his, he groaned softly and the tenderness vanished.

He walked me back until my spine pressed against the wide beam holding up the tent, one hand splaying by my head while the other rested low on my hip. His mouth consumed me, tongue tangling with mine. His taste was warm, familiar, safe. His hand on my hip slid to the small of my back, pulling me against him, while one of his muscular thighs slipped between mine. Heat pooled low as my senses came alive.

He drew back, breathing heavily. "If you want to stop—"

"Don't stop."

He looked at me, those brown eyes heavy-lidded with desire yet making certain I knew what I was asking. "Don't stop," I repeated firmly.

And like the loyal soldier he was, he obeyed.

His lips were on mine again, one hand going to my jaw, tipping my head back to better plunder my mouth while his other held me close. His tunic was thin, and through it, I could feel all of him. Every toned, muscled inch. Could nearly feel his heart thundering, just as mine was.

Jasim's lips were hungry, his touch greedy, as his hands smoothed down my shoulders, my back. He abandoned my mouth for my jaw, my throat, beard scratching deliciously as he went. I buried my fingers in his silky black curls, clutching him as his lips trailed over my skin.

He nipped at the juncture between my neck and shoulder, and I gasped as he soothed over with his tongue. Jasim hooked a finger under my dress strap and pulled it down. My neckline sagged, and his lips followed it, tasting down my collarbone, my sternum, pausing just above my chest wrap.

My breasts heaved over the fabric. His eyes met mine as he pulled my other strap off. The whisper of my dress hitting the ground seemed to echo around us. He reached behind me for the knot of my chest wrap.

I relished the simplicity of the sounds around me. My galloping heart, our panting. All so mercifully normal. So blessedly familiar. My world narrowed down to Jasim and only Jasim.

My chest wrap landed beside my dress. Jasim's callused palm cupped my breast. Just coarse enough where it ran over my sensitive flesh that my breaths turned ragged, my skin hot. His thumb brushed over my nipple before he rolled it between his fingers, making me suck in a breath, but his lips were there to swallow the sound. Hot and demanding, as if he wanted to devour me. His hand at my back trailed down, smoothing over my backside, my thigh, stopping to grab my knee and hook it up around his hip, opening me up to him. When he pressed into me again, I moaned. He was hard, his hands rough against my bare thigh.

This. This was why I always came back to him. He consumed me like he wanted all of me. Not just the queen. Not just the Gods-Chosen. *Me.* Heady and addictive, and an utter relief.

His mouth left mine in favor of my breast. Tongue circling, teeth scraping over the hardened peak. I arched against him and dug my heel into the top of his thigh, pulling him impossibly closer. He groaned against me and rolled his hips into mine, his hard length rubbing against my core and dragging a gasp from my lips.

I reached for the hem of his tunic and wrenched it over his head, revealing the expanse of his beautiful tan skin. A constellation of scars crossed his chest and stomach, bumpy beneath my fingers, my lips. I kissed each mark, hand traveling down. His stomach muscles tightened against my palm, his arousal straining beneath his trousers. "Amunet . . ." His fingers flexed on my upper thigh, pausing centimeters away from where I ached.

"Stop now and I'll kill you."

His laugh was gruff. "Yes, my queen." And he slowly sank to his knees.

My pulse ratcheted higher as he eased my undergarments down and tossed them aside before guiding one of my legs over his shoulder, eyes never leaving mine. Soft lips pressed kisses above my knee, moving higher at an agonizing pace. I groaned in frustration.

Jasim's breath was hot against my center as he chuckled, sending a shiver ricocheting up my spine. "Always so impatient," he murmured before his tongue parted me in one long swipe.

He and I swore in unison, and my head fell back against the post. He moaned, "Amunet," into my flesh before he set to devouring me. A breathy sound fell out of me. My fingers found their way into the soft locks of his hair, gripping tightly as he reached the bundle of nerves at my apex. A flick of his tongue sent sparks spiraling through my body, and my toes curled.

He took hold of my bucking hips and forced them still as he repeated the gesture and then sucked.

"Fuck," I burst out, straining against him. He slid a finger into me, and my knee nearly gave out. Jasim supported me, as he always did, and hummed in approval against my folds, the sound vibrating through me. There was nothing but Jasim and his tongue and his finger—gods, *fingers*—as I squirmed and liquid heat rose and I—

I resisted. Tried to focus on the roughness of the pole behind me, the discomfort of dirt in my sandals, anything but the—

Jasim crooked his fingers inside me, and lightning zipped through my veins. A broken sound escaped me. He commanded, "Stop fighting me, Amunet," before he sucked again. Hard.

I had no choice but to obey. My body tightened and the world fell apart in a burst of stars that robbed me of breath. My knee buckled. Jasim caught me before I collapsed, guiding me down slowly until I straddled his lap, shaky and dazed. His arousal was hot against my stomach, kept away from me by his infernal trousers.

"Gods, you're so beautiful," he breathed, and kissed me. I tasted myself on his tongue, but I didn't mind. My insides felt unsteady, fluttery, my mind was utterly blank. Jasim broke from my lips to kiss his way to my ear, where he panted in a raspy voice, "I need to be inside you."

My voice was gone, but I nodded instantly. I'd agree to anything that kept this moment suspended in time. Anything to keep him touching me, kissing me.

I reached for his trousers, but he was already there, fumbling with the ties. With some maneuvering, he managed to slide them down without removing me from his lap and his length sprang free between us. My hand drifted to it of its own accord, my fingers wrapped around the hot flesh. I squeezed the way he liked it, stroked the way he'd taught me years ago.

Jasim hissed, and his eyes wrenched shut as liquid beaded the tip. I smiled.

"Evil woman," he groaned. My grin spread.

We both held our breath at that initial stretch and then let it out on a sigh as I sank down onto him. Jasim had fucked me many times over the years, but it felt different tonight. Maybe my mind was just adrift on pleasure. But when he gazed up at me, eyes twin pools of black, reverent and worshipful, I did not revile it; I reveled in it. I didn't look away as I lifted and then slid back down, admiring the way his face slackened, the flush that stole over his dark cheeks, the dangerous clench in my stomach that warned another tailspin would take almost no effort at all.

Jasim gripped my hips, my backside, as I moved. I tangled a hand in his hair while I dug my nails into the skin of his shoulder blades with the other, burying my face in his neck as I moved faster, harder. My eyes slid shut as sensations passed through me, fluttering and light and—

"I love you," Jasim breathed.

I froze.

A beat later, he tensed, too, realizing what he'd said.

Slowly, I pulled back. His chest heaved, but his eyes flicked over my face fearfully. His fingers tightened on my hips. Jasim shook his head. "I didn't mean it," he rushed breathlessly. "It just slipped out. Forget—"

"Tell me again."

Jasim blinked. Later, I might call myself stupid or selfish or any number of horrible things. And they might all be true. But in that moment, my insides lit up in a way I had never felt before. Those three words—such simple ones, and yet I had not heard them in a very long time, couldn't remember ever hearing them. I wanted to hear them again. I wanted them to be true.

My hips resumed their rhythm. "Tell me again," I whispered.

Jasim's lashes fluttered. His arms banded around me, holding me so close I almost couldn't breathe. "I love you."

My lips brushed his. "Again."

"I love you, Amunet."

"Again."

We moved faster, and he breathed his love into my neck, my shoulder, my breast, my lips. Emotion swelled in my chest, blooming into something I did not recognize but made no attempt to stop. It made me feel weightless, thrilled me, brought a smile to my face. And when I went over the edge again, it was so much more intense. I clung to him, arms tight around his neck, face buried in his hair, as it pummeled me.

Jasim trembled through the last of his pleasure. His hands were gentle as they stroked up my spine. He could sense that something had happened, and he was trying to soothe me, holding me as if I were delicate, precious, lips peppering soft kisses up my neck.

I couldn't lose him.

The thought blossomed in the pit of my stomach as we sat there, breathing hard. More than that, I didn't *want* to lose him. My only friend. The only person to love me in years, besides Shaya. And where was Shaya? My mind was fracturing, and he was nowhere to be found.

But Jasim was *right here*. He loved me. He'd watched me, he'd learned me, he knew *me*, and he was still here. He loved all of me.

"Jasim," I said, voice hoarse, "there's something I have to tell you."

He shook his head as he pulled back, eyes gleaming. Gods, the *look*. So much stronger than before, kicking up wings in my stomach. "You don't have to say it back," he said.

"No, that's not— When we reach the temple . . . I—"

Thunder rolled outside. Loud. Insistent.

And getting louder.

We stared at each other, lips swollen, bodies glistening with sweat, and listened.

Jasim's brow creased. He pecked my lips before gently guiding me off his lap and yanking up his pants. Unsheathing his scimitar, he parted the tent flaps and peered outside.

Flames of irritation melted down my skin, begging my nails to scratch, and King Zaid's voice surged back into focus. A cacophony of beratement, of laughter, of blame. A sob crawled up my throat.

Jasim's face went bone white.

"What is it?" I ignored all my discomforts as I pulled my dress back on, grabbed my undergarments, and hurried to his side. Then my heart dropped into my stomach.

Small circles of light bobbed against the black night sky. Torches. So many of them. And they were growing larger with every second, moving too fast.

Rolling toward us in the darkness was the rapid pounding of hooves.

"Horses," I said. Not camels, not merchants. *Horses.* Running full sprint at our camp.

TWENTY-NINE

AMUNET

The torches were far—but not far enough. They must have lit them when they knew they were too close for us to flee.

A battle cry rang out among the thundering hoofbeats, dispelling any hope that they could be additional soldiers from Reeda or wayward travelers. No, they were coming here to kill us. We had fifteen minutes at best.

Nasir, Sara, and a handful of soldiers raced up to Jasim's tent. The prince held a scimitar in one hand and a khopesh in the other, and his gold-flecked eyes gleamed. Whether with fear or focus, I wasn't sure. "Get the Gods-Chosen out of here," Nasir ordered Jasim and Sara without preamble. "Take the camels. There's a small village not too far away. Go there and wait. Do not leave until you hear from me."

"Look at the flags," I said. The horde was closing in, moonlight illuminating gold and blue. Like an ocean at sunset. "Those are Haisab's colors." *Prince Anwar.* Who had sent the assassin after me.

Nasir's eyes narrowed as he sought the masts with the flapping banners. When he spotted them, his face became ashen. "Impossible. You've only been with us a week. It would take Anwar longer than that to travel from Haisab to Reeda—"

"Not if Prince Anwar was already on his way here."

He met my stare with wide eyes.

Perhaps that was why the assassin at the trading post hadn't made another attempt on my life. The little minion had run off to tell the prince where I was. That far east of Ketopolis, it would have taken no real puzzling out to realize I was headed to Reeda.

"We're running out of time," Jasim said roughly.

Nasir grabbed Sara by the bicep. "I don't care what you think of her," he said. "You protect her with your life. Do you understand?"

Her chest rose and fell with harried breaths before she said, "I'm sorry, my prince."

"Wh—"

He didn't even get the whole word out before she smashed her scimitar hilt into his temple. Nasir dropped like a pile of rocks.

I stared, shocked into stillness as I struggled to process what just happened.

But Jasim wasn't. His blade was already in his hand, and he swung it at Sara.

Before he could make contact, a soldier locked his arm around Jasim's windpipe and jerked him back, squeezing until Jasim's eyes bulged and his face turned red.

That shook me out of my stupor. Ten years' worth of training with the Khada Guard rose up as I snatched a dagger from the soldier's belt and plunged it into his side, right between the ribs, before wrenching it back out with a wet squelch and doing it again. The man's eyes flew wide, crimson spreading like a plague across his armor.

With a cry, I shoved him off Jasim. The man fell to the sand with a dull thud, writhing and gurgling uselessly, blood trickling from his lips.

Jasim gasped and coughed, staggering.

I rushed to him. "Jasim—"

Sara blocked my path, scimitar aimed right at my chest. I drew up short, mere inches from being impaled.

"*Amunet!*" Jasim roared behind her, slicing his scimitar at the soldiers surrounding him. Several fell to his blade, but there were too many, and the number was growing as soldiers boasting Haisab gold and blue joined Reeda orange.

A fist slammed into Jasim's face, and he went down. I couldn't see where he landed behind the mass of armor. Alarm blared through me, my ears ringing with the force of it. "Jasim!" I made a move toward him.

"Don't even think about it." Sara's blade dug into the base of my throat, her hazel eyes aflame. "Move, and I'll gut you."

I guess you should've been nicer to her, mused the king.

I bared my teeth at her. "Traitor."

She chuckled. "Can't betray someone you were never loyal to."

"Not me, you fucking idiot. Nasir. Your people. You were going to get your land back, a position in my court, unrestricted access to the Lotus River. And now you—"

She grabbed my collar and jerked me closer. The blade sliced against my throat, sending a ribbon of pain through me. "I'm doing this to protect my prince *and* my people. We won't let Shaya be freed. And Reeda will not be a pawn in your game, Gods-Chosen."

"Anwar won't let you return to the Lotus River."

"Neither will you."

"I will. Once I've—"

"Save it," she spat. "If Anwar refuses to give our land back, at least we'll be fighting a *human.*"

"Jinni-descended," I corrected.

"Weaker than you," she fired back. "You would have turned on us as soon as you were too strong for us to resist."

"You stupid bi—" I didn't get to finish my uninspired insult because she rammed her hilt into my head just as she had with Nasir's.

Everything went dark.

THIRTY

〰〰〰〰〰

SAMIRA

I came back to consciousness reluctantly, bracing myself to be sick again. But when I opened my eyes to the log ceiling, I thanked the Mother that my stomach had settled. My forehead tingled and throbbed softly.

Every muscle was sore, and I groaned as I pushed myself up to a sitting position.

Velka and Keir were seated in front of the fire, and they turned sharply when they heard me. They'd washed off the white clay, and a quick glance down showed I had been cleaned, too. Velka and Keir appeared like they usually did, Velka with her braid slung over her shoulder and Keir with the top half of his face darkened by kohl.

"You're awake!" Velka exclaimed, and rushed over to me. "Are you all right? How do you feel? Are you in pain?"

I smiled at her fretting. "I think I'm all right."

"Thank the gods. I'll get Rade." She bolted out of the room.

Keir stood, and my eyes flicked to him, immediately on guard. He watched me carefully, head cocked to the side.

I waited for him to ask me what I'd seen, to reveal they'd disobeyed Rade's command and overheard the whole thing, to accuse me of being called Samira and having black runes, to demand I tell him about the Seer's words, those horrible sand dunes, the amulet, the being of shadow.

It was greed that brought you here. It is greed that will seek you out. Greed destroys, greed burns. But out of fire were you born, out of water were you found. To both must you return before all is razed to the ground.

Zarqa's words echoed against my skull. Meaningless, I tried to reassure myself. A fortune for a dead girl was meaningless. And yet immediately following that was, *You do not know yourself. Let me show you.*

I had wanted to see it, whatever the shadow meant. I still did. When that shadow creature had reached out to me, it was the first time in a long time I hadn't felt scared. I hadn't realized until that moment how badly I hated this fear that plagued me even now as I waited for Keir to speak. I wanted that again, that confidence, that courage.

Keir pulled me from my thoughts as he crossed the room toward me. He didn't say anything. Made no accusations or threats. He simply moved to my bedside, picked up a cup of kefir from the end table, and held it to my lips.

I hadn't even realized I was thirsty until then. I drank greedily, noting the subtle taste of honey. Keir's hand came up to cradle the back of my head, his fingers sliding between the short strands of my hair, and my eyes cut to his.

He remained quiet as he pulled the cup away and set it back on the end table.

Softly, I said, "Thank you."

Those bright yellow eyes didn't leave my face, fiercely intent, like he was seeing through my skin. "Your runes, they're . . ."

Here it comes. I sank deeper into the pillows, bracing myself.

"Green."

I blinked. "What?"

"Your runes are green."

Green? Ignoring my aching muscles, I slid off the bed, holding tight to the mattress as my knees buckled.

Keir caught my elbow and wrapped his arm around my waist, half carrying me across the room to the full-length mirror. Each step was on a knife's blade, my legs trembling with the pain radiating through me.

All that faded when I saw my reflection.

Strange swirling symbols curved along my forehead. Not raised like scars, but faded into my skin, as if they'd been there for years. And Keir was right; they were a deep green, like a crocodile's hide. I shook my head, leaning in so close that my breath fogged the glass.

Runes of red signified a god's blessing, Shifters' were blue, and regular mortals' were black. I didn't have magic, and I certainly wasn't a Shifter, so . . .

My eyes met Keir's in the mirror. He wore that stony expression, giving nothing away. My heart galloped in my chest. "What does green mean?"

Instead of answering me, he moved in front of me, large body blocking the mirror as he leaned forward and sniffed my forehead, nose grazing my skin. I held perfectly still while he inhaled a second time. His eyes turned a molten gold.

He'd scented me a handful of times before—that I was aware of. His nose was probably always trying to sniff me out and catch me in a lie. But there were only two other times he'd scented me like *this*. Just before we were about to cross that bridge to Kaldfold, when I had begged him, the first real mistake I'd made, and after Hedin's death. His eyes had darkened then, too. The widening of his pupils over the brilliant yellow irises were like twin eclipses.

His hands settled on either side of my neck, hot—the intense heat of a Shifter—and callused, scratching gently against the sensitive skin there, sending bolts of lightning shooting through my body. His thumbs applied just the slightest bit of pressure to my jaw, tilting my head back as he drew in a third inhale, and my heart pounded in the silence.

I couldn't hear the sounds of Frostguard through the windows or the soft crackling of the hearth. It was just Keir's deep breaths and my pulse rushing in my ears. Absently, his thumb smoothed against my jaw in a single stroke that I felt all the way to the tips of my toes.

"Keir?" I whispered.

His searing eyes fell from the runes to mine and melted the rest of the world away. Keir's gaze was always probing, always seeking more, and it felt as if he were actually succeeding now. My cheeks heated, my insides felt unsteady. When his pupils dilated further, gaze growing darker, my breath caught in the back of my throat, and I had the insane urge to lean forward.

He wrenched away from me. Suddenly, as if he'd been burned, blowing air sharply out of his nose to get rid of my scent. I could feel the exact imprint of where Keir's hands had been, a brand along my neck and jaw. A deep line formed between his brows as he stared down at me with those unfathomable yellow eyes.

"What?" I blushed harder when I heard how breathless my voice sounded.

"You . . ." His runes twitched as his throat bobbed. Before he could say more—if he'd even planned to—the door was thrown open and Rade rushed in, Velka on his heels.

"What are you doing out of bed?" he said. "You should be rest—" He stalled when I turned and he saw my runes. Questions chased each other across his face.

Velka's nostrils flared, yellow eyes landing on Keir. "What's going on in here?"

I waited for his answer, too. For him to tell her what he smelled, why he was looking at me like that. But Keir dropped his eyes, studying the floor, face twisted in consternation.

Before Velka could push for more, Rade nudged Keir out of the way and took hold of my elbow. Concern had won out against his bewilderment. "The Seer is always a trying ordeal, Amunet. You need to rest."

"What happened to me?"

He weighed his words carefully. "You are not just blessed by the gods. You are *of* them. A stronger reaction is to be expected. Which is why you need to be resting." He situated me on the bed again and offered a gentle smile.

"My king," Keir broached, "I think we should speak."

My eyes snapped back to him. Keir's hands were fisted at his sides, his body tense, and his yellow eyes were focused solely on Rade. A conscious effort not to look at me.

Nerves rushed through me at a dizzying speed. Surely if I'd been exposed, he would've already killed me. Or blurted it out here and now.

Unless he wanted me punished for my deception. Tell the king privately so I'd be surprised by the torture.

Out of fire were you born, out of water were you found. To both must you return.

Holy gods. Were they going to burn me alive and toss my body in the ocean?

And how in the world were my runes anything other than black?

But Rade responded, "Would you fetch the queen something to eat?"

"Rade—"

"Now, Keir."

The Kald's jaw locked up, eyes flicking to me, but he gave a single nod before striding to the door.

Velka stepped in front of him, blocking the exit. She forced him to meet her searching gaze. Keir gave a small shake of his head. Though I didn't know what Velka's look meant, Keir's answer was clear. *Not now.* She stepped aside, and Keir left.

To Velka the king said, "You can return to making preparations."

I pushed myself upright, feeling nausea build again. "Is the next part of the Merging already—"

"No, no," Rade said quickly. "It has nothing to do with you, I promise. Rest for as long as you need."

I settled back against the pillows with a sigh of relief. If I'd had to go through something like that again so soon, I wasn't entirely sure I'd make it. And Queen Amunet needed me to last a couple of weeks still.

"But if you're feeling up to it by the new moon," Velka offered, "we'd be honored to have the Queen of Ashorah at the Lunar Feast."

"What's the Lunar Feast?"

"A celebration of Ayeen. Happens every new moon."

"It's for the Shifters," Rade explained. "Their animal forms get a bit restless at the start of the moon cycle. It lets them get it out of their systems."

"The Lunar Feast is in a few days, and, honestly, it couldn't have come at a better time. We could all use a bit of fun. You included, Your Majesty," Velka singsonged as she waved and left, doing her best to appear unconcerned. But I caught her frown just before she closed the door, eyes scanning for Keir.

Sand grains still crunched between my teeth, and my stomach felt one wrong move away from another tailspin. "My reaction . . ." I ventured softly. "Why was it so bad? And why are my runes green?" Fear barred me from asking about the shadow creature.

Rade's gaze drifted up to my runes. Hesitantly, he reached out and brushed his finger against my forehead, tracing the symbols. His touch wasn't searing like Keir's but careful.

Then he lowered his hand and took mine. He lifted it to the side of his head and rested the tips of my fingers against his runes. I met his gentle brown eyes in surprise. "The older a person is," he said, voice quiet, "the easier it is to receive the runes. We're not really sure why, but I think it has to do with the magic settling inside of us. Usually, it's done around the age of sixteen." He turned his head, giving me a better view.

I swallowed hard as I traced the symbols, the same way he'd just done. His were sharp and pointy, not softly curling like mine. Like they'd been carved with a blade. They cut from his temple to the nape of his neck.

"I was twelve when I got mine," he said.

My fingers stilled. "Why so young?"

"My mother . . . she was desperate to save our people from the Shroud. She thought if she conceived a child inside of it, that child would be able to stop it. So she went in, and when she came out and the healers examined her, she was pregnant."

I lowered my hand to my lap. "You mean someone inside . . ."

Rade nodded. "I've never known who my father is. And I don't think she did, either. But she'd been inside for a full twenty-four hours. She shouldn't have been able to leave, and she wasn't the same person when she returned." He bowed his head and gave another shrug, like it meant nothing. But the stiffness in his muscles said otherwise. "She wanted my magic awoken right away. If the previous king hadn't stopped her, she would've taken me to the Seer as soon as I could walk. I was lucky she waited as long as she did."

Though I didn't remember much of Mama and Baba, the few memories I had were happy. Pleasant smells, music, feelings of bliss. It was blurry, but I knew it had been a good home. I couldn't imagine what it would be like to have memories like Rade's.

"I vomited, like you. Multiple times. And I could hardly walk. I don't—I don't remember much of what happened directly after. I just know that every time someone tried to confront my mother about my being too young, she would only say, 'It worked, didn't it?'" He tried to smile but it was weak. "She was right. It did work. Even when I was twelve, my power was undeniable. The people demanded I be put on the throne. The previous king was forced to abdicate, despite being the heir to a well-established line of Kaldfolk rulers, and pass the crown to . . . me."

I processed that with a heavy heart. Softly, I asked, "Is your mother in Frostguard?"

He shook his head. "A few weeks after I got my runes, she went back into the Shroud. It had gotten into her. She said she . . . belonged to it."

For a brief moment, compassion for Rade overshadowed my fear.

"Keir's aunt Katla raised me after that. They're the only family I have." Rade blinked several times, like he was clearing away cobwebs, and faced me again. "I don't know why you had such a strong reaction to the runes when you're nearly twenty, but I can sympathize. You're in pain right now, but it will pass. I promise."

In fact, I was twenty-two, which just made my reaction all the stranger. But maybe the rules about age only applied to Kaldfolk. They were born with wild magic in their blood. Maybe my reaction was normal for an Ashoran.

"And the green?" I asked again.

"That's probably because you're a Gods-Chosen," he said with a soft smile. "But I'll check some of the old texts, just to be sure."

Obviously, that wasn't it. Amunet was a Gods-Chosen, not me. There was something else, and some instinct told me it had to do with that shadow creature. By Zarqa's reaction, I knew that hadn't been normal. Had the shadow creature messed up the ritual somehow? Confused the magic so that instead of black I was left with some indecipherable green? And the way Keir had smelled my runes . . . Did he know what had gone wrong?

Rade gave my hand a reassuring squeeze. "You will be all right, Amunet."

I looked up at the king, at his warm eyes and gentle smile that put me at ease almost instantly. He'd gotten his runes at twelve. I wondered what it must be like to have a mother abandon him for the Shroud. Rade did not seem bitter. He was friendly and kind.

Amunet had received marriage proposals from everyone with even a hint of royal blood in their veins, from jinn-descended princes to no-name emissaries. Some even came to Khada Palace to try to woo her in person. I'd always observed them to be unpleasant. Greedy or lecherous or plain cruel. I couldn't help but think that if my queen had to marry, she would be relieved to marry someone as nice as Rade.

"You're not what I expected," I confessed.

The king blew out an amused breath. "Neither are you, Amunet Khada." His fingers stroked along my palm, feeling the calluses there. "You never told me what weapon you trained with."

I could see Amunet clearly in my mind, sweaty and exhausted from training with the Khada Guard. She'd return to her room in a huff and toss the curved battle-axe—the khopesh—on the floor before flopping onto her bed, cursing the king for making her go.

"A khopesh," I answered.

Rade whistled low. "Only my Shifters are skilled enough to handle that sort of weapon."

I prayed he wouldn't ask me to demonstrate. "I never said I was skilled."

Rade laughed.

My own lips pulled up in a smile.

The door crashed open, and Keir stormed in, rage practically pouring off him. My smile slipped. He slammed a bowl of broth onto the end table beside me, some of it sloshing over the edge. Then he faced Rade. "Now that I've been a good errand boy, can we speak?"

Rade's eyes flashed, but he offered me another smile. "Rest," he said, giving my hand a squeeze, before he followed Keir out of the room.

I waited for that second click. My door hadn't been locked in days, but I listened just in case. As expected, it didn't come.

Good. Because Keir knew something about these inexplicable runes, and I needed to know what it was.

Which meant I had to follow them.

THIRTY-ONE

SAMIRA

I wrenched open the door to my cabin. Cold air hit my face instantly, making my already unsteady legs tremble harder, but I wrapped my cloak tighter around my shoulders and steeled myself.

I'd served Amunet in the midst of fever. I'd served her with lashes on my back, with a brand over my heart. I could get out of this damn room on sore legs.

Gripping the threshold hard enough to leave nail marks in the wood, I stepped outside.

The longhouse loomed a few yards away, unlit torches marking the path. I balanced against one as I caught my breath. Then lurched for the next one. Leapfrogging from torch to torch.

I paused at the longhouse's large double doors and peered in.

Velka was inside, talking to Sillia and Cano, gesturing vaguely around the space as she gave orders. I heard her mention Aurel, the man newly in charge of the smokehouse. They must be discussing food for the Lunar Feast. Then Velka turned and led them through a side door.

Once I was sure they weren't coming back, I staggered forward and held on to the long wooden table as I shuffled through the hall. There were only a handful of people in there, and they were all too busy with getting things ready to pay me any mind.

I ducked behind the throne and slid my hand along the wall, which went from wood to stone as I ventured closer to Rade's room.

I paused. Keir's enhanced hearing would certainly catch me if I continued sliding along, panting as I was. I forced my breathing to even out and pushed away from the wall. My knees groaned, and I had to work to keep them steady.

Then I was beside Rade's door, a hand over my mouth to further muffle my breaths.

Luckily, their conversation was heated enough that they didn't hear me.

"What do you want me to do?" Rade was demanding.

"*Something,*" Keir responded. "Take her back to the Seer—"

"That's not how it works and you know it."

"A priestess, then. Have one of them examine her. Her scent isn't—"

"It's a bit strange, don't you think, Keir? That none of the other Seven share your concerns. Not the priestess, the healer, or the Seer, either."

"Bain agrees with me."

"Bain says the opposite of whatever Velka does."

"Fine, but we don't know *what* the Seer said. You should've let us listen—"

"What is your goal here, Keir?"

His First scoffed. "What?"

"We need her. You know that. *You* brought her here. If her scent offends you, then plug your damn nose."

"That's not what I—" Keir sighed heavily, and silence descended. I imagined they were having a stare-off. "I am trying to protect you, my king. To protect *all* of us. You know what happened the last time her kind was here."

"Look around, Keir," Rade replied tiredly. "Do you see an army?"

"Not yet."

There was a heavy pause. "Have you chosen someone?"

Silence.

Rade sighed. "You don't want me to pick his replacement and *you* don't want to do it. Should we leave it up to Ketet?" Sarcasm dripped from his words.

Keir tried, "Why does it have to be seven? Just tell me that and I'll do it." There was no answer. "Rade, the six of us work just as well—"

"Always questioning, Keir. And when you're not questioning me, you're undermining me. I can't even pick my own inner circle for fear you'll *murder* them."

"Bain had—"

"Thank you," Rade cut him off again, voice sharp as a blade. "Your concerns have been heard." A dismissal.

As quietly as I could, I turned and started to hobble back to my room, step by limping step, going as fast as I could while remaining quiet.

I had just made it to the throne when Rade and Keir came storming in. Keir stopped in front of me, eyes menacing, so different from the heated stare when he'd smelled my runes. "What are you doing?"

My breaths were labored, and sweat dotted my forehead. I felt like I'd run a mile. Which I hoped helped make my words believable when I said, "I was looking for the healer."

Rade put his hand on Keir's shoulder, firm and commanding, and gave me a kind smile. "I'll find her for you. Keir will help you back to bed."

Keir's yellow eyes flashed, but he gave a curt nod and offered me his hand.

Swallowing hard, I took it and let him lead me out of the longhouse, back into the frigid day. The walk back felt exponentially longer than my struggle there. I kept my eyes trained on the ground, my hand light in Keir's.

"If you're going to eavesdrop," he said suddenly, "you better learn to control that rabbit's heartbeat of yours."

My head snapped up. "What?"

He smirked. "I could hear you from a mile away, Majesty."

Oh gods—

Keir stopped outside my door but didn't open it. He reeled me in close. "You already used up your one warning, remember?" he rumbled.

I stopped breathing, eyes wide as saucers. Keir's fingers flexed around my hand and even in that small movement, I felt his strength. If he wanted to, he could kill me in seconds. Less. "I am under the king's protec—"

"The king's not here, is he?"

My eyes darted around his shoulders, looking for help. But everyone was busy with preparing for the party. It was practically deserted.

"I know you're hiding something, Majesty," he said. "And when I figure it out, your death is mine. Scent or no."

My scent? My scent would . . . stop him? Rade had suggested that it was offensive, but . . .

I paused and forced myself to push my fear aside so I could think clearly.

Keir wasn't going to stop. His hatred for the Khadas wouldn't let him. Rade's desperation had forced him to put aside whatever King Zaid had done when he'd invaded Kaldfold seventeen years ago, but as long as Keir despised me, the danger he posed wouldn't end.

And I needed it to.

If I could mend whatever pain King Zaid had caused—even a little—maybe Keir would finally back off. Maybe he'd even explain these marks on my forehead.

So I licked my lips and broached, "What did my king do to you?"

He scoffed. "Figures you wouldn't know."

"I know what he did to Kaldfold generally, but I'm asking what he did to *you*."

Keir stared hard at me, yellow eyes scanning every inch of my face. I kept my shoulders low, face open. Let him see the question as genuine.

And it was. I'd been told that King Zaid had no choice but to beat back the deranged Kaldfolk. But they weren't deranged. That part of the story had been a lie. Which made me wonder what else was, and what the king had wanted to hide behind that lie.

Memory, hurt, pain flashed through Keir's gaze in quick succession. "He trapped me in a nightmare. I've never known a man as cruel as your king."

Sympathy softened my face. "Do you mean he took you captive?"

He schooled his features back into that careful smirk again. "Clever, Majesty. Tell me, if being my friend doesn't work, what will you try next? Seduction?" He leaned in, the deep spice of a mulberry tree enveloping me, bringing with it that burst of an old memory I couldn't quite put my finger on. "Why don't you give it a try? Maybe I'll be more responsive." His bright yellow eyes flicked down to my lips.

He was trying to throw me off. Maybe I should be more frightened. After all, it sounded like his loyalty to Rade was a fragile thing. Disobeying orders, undermining him publicly. And yet, for some inexplicable reason, I wasn't afraid. "I saw you drumming during Hedin's funeral."

A blink was his only reply.

"None of you liked him, but you helped his mother grieve. Helped the people of Netherridge grieve, too. It was a beautiful prayer. The people listening . . . It meant a lot to them. But you know that already. That's why you did it." I mustered up a small smile. "You brought me kefir with honey. Twice. You care for people, Keir. Is it so difficult to believe that I do, too?"

"You care for no one but yourself, *Khada*." He spat the word so venomously, his breath whipped my face.

I swallowed my flinch. "Is that why I'm risking my life to help you get rid of the Shroud? Because I don't care?"

"You're doing it because you know we'll kill you otherwise."

"Not if you catch a whiff of my scent."

A deep growl built in the back of his throat. "Don't talk about things you don't understand."

"What do you smell, Keir?" I took a brazen step forward as the wind blew through, ruffling my short hair and carrying my scent straight to Keir's nose. His chest stopped moving. He was holding his breath. I tried not to see that for the small victory that it was. "Why would it stop you from killing me?"

"It won't," he said, voice tight.

"Yes, it would. Why?"

"You have no idea what you're even asking."

"So explain it to me."

A muscle jumped in his jaw as he glared at me, lips a firm line. He glanced at my forehead, at the impossible markings that ached even now. Those gold eyes of his were hard, giving nothing away. But despite his best efforts, his chest rose on an inhale.

A small thrill zipped through my blood. "Whatever King Zaid did to you," I said softly, "you didn't deserve it." Keir would've only been around ten years old at the time of the invasion. No matter what sort of man he'd grown into, no child deserved war.

Keir's gaze seared into me, and it was like looking into two bright suns. I had that odd probing feeling again, as if he could somehow see within me. I let him.

He took a step forward, bringing us within an inch of each other, and his hand landed on the door beside my hip. My heart lurched into my throat as his body heat seeped into me. I craned my head back to look up into his face. Cold, throat cut up with blue markings, everything about him harsh and forbidding, all except those gods-damn eyes. Those were warm and encompassing, and they were focused on me as acutely as I was focused on them.

Click.

The door behind me swung open, and I staggered back. Keir

had turned the knob beside my hip. I managed to catch myself on the doorjamb before I tumbled inside.

"Don't come to the Lunar Feast," he ordered, voice like gravel.

"Why not?" I demanded, desperate for a single explanation. If not about my runes, then *anything* would do.

He didn't bother responding. Just turned on his heel, boots tromping as he stalked away.

With a sigh of frustration, I slammed the door.

He had smelled something wrong with my runes, but he'd still called me *Majesty*, so he didn't know what it meant. He didn't know who I was—or, rather, wasn't. But it didn't explain how *I* could have runes that were not black.

In fact, for all his raving about my ignorance, he hadn't offered a single thing to rectify that. How could I know something if he wouldn't tell me? It was aggravating and infuriating, and the next time he decided to help himself to my apparently *not* horrible scent, I was going to smack him. Right across the face.

Just imagining his look of shock gave me immense delight.

The young healer arrived soon after, the same one who'd given me the sleeping draught. She was younger than me by a couple of years, a plump girl with a full face and rosy cheeks. She came to my side and unfurled a rolled-up leather pouch, revealing tools and vials. Dipping her fingers into a jar, she scooped up a thick brown substance and rubbed it into my shins. It tingled as soon as it hit my skin, and the relief was instant. A numbing agent of some kind. I sighed and relaxed into the pillows. "Thank you."

She smiled and scooped some more into her hand.

"What's your name?"

"Siv of Netherridge." Her eyes darted up to mine for a split second. "My aunt and uncle are in the Seven."

Sillia and Cano were from Netherridge. She must mean them.

"I am sorry your home was lost, Siv."

"Thank you, Your Majesty." She dabbed a little more ointment on her finger and then very gently blended it into my forehead. My lingering headache completely vanished. "And thank you for saving Milena."

"You know her?"

"I know of her," she corrected. "Both her parents died when the Shroud took the Pillars, where she's originally from. But she managed to outrun it and reach her grandfather in Netherridge. He was all she had left. If you hadn't grabbed her, she would've . . ." She cleared her throat and pulled back, quickly replacing the lid and rolling up the pouch. "I came to Frostguard to study healing under my mother when I was seven. I haven't been back to Netherridge in ten years, so I don't really know her. But I'm grateful for any Kald who is spared."

Once again, my heart ached for the little girl. I hadn't managed to find time to check on her since Netherridge was lost, but I would rectify that now. "Could you take me to see her?"

Her brows rose. "Of course, Your Majesty."

Siv guided me to a tent that was cramped with cots and utterly freezing. Even through my thick tunic and fur cloak, I shivered.

A solitary girl sat on a cot, legs drawn up, spine hunched.

"Milena," I said softly, unclasping my cloak and wrapping it around her, smiling faintly as she snuggled into the warmth. Her big blue eyes gazed up at me with gratitude. So small, so helpless, so alone, and left in this ice cave of a tent. I joined her cross-legged on the cot. She didn't talk at first, so I did. I told her she'd be safe here, looked after. That I was sorry for what she'd seen. That her grandfather was happy where he was. I had no way of knowing if the last bit was a lie, but it was the first one I'd happily told these past couple of weeks.

Her shoulders relaxed as I jabbered on, and when she leaned her head against my shoulder, I smiled softly. "If you ever need me," I told her, "I'm in the cabin across from the longhouse. You can always come find me. All right?"

She nodded. "Thank you, Your Majesty."

I gave her a squeeze and left with the promise that I'd be back to check on her again. Just before I exited the tent, Milena called, "Wait, Queen Amunet, you forgot your cloak."

"It's yours. A gift."

Milena looked down at it with wide eyes and happily squeezed her doll, which I could see now was a rudimentary rendering of Ketet.

As Siv helped me back to my cabin, I asked, "Isn't there something that can be done for the people from Netherridge? A proper house to stay in? Or a fire, at the very least?"

Siv shook her head. "All the cots are made of straw, Your Majesty. It would be too dangerous for an open fire. But the king is working on finding them a permanent place to stay. They'll probably be sent to Keenforge. I think they have space there."

"But until then, they need warmth. Maybe one of the braziers from the longhouse?"

"I suppose you could ask the king." Siv paused by my cabin door and gave me a considering look. "You're not mean. Ashorans are supposed to be mean."

I chuckled softly. "Thank you?"

Siv flushed. "I didn't mean—"

"It's okay. Some Ashorans *are* mean." I looked over and noticed Keir watching me by the longhouse's entrance. Though he was speaking with one of the other Shifters, his eyes were locked on mine. "Just like some Kaldfolk are."

He cocked a brow, bright eyes searing against the kohl, fixing me with a look that reached across the dozens of feet separating us to make my face burn and my heart give a powerful kick. I knew I shouldn't antagonize him, but fear took second place to the deep satisfaction of knowing he'd heard me.

Sympathy and kindness hadn't worked. Seduction was out of the question. I guess that only left fighting back. A thought that lit up my nerves with trepidation and the slightest inexplicable hint of a thrill.

THIRTY-TWO

ᴧᴧᴧᴧᴧᴧᴧ

AMUNET

I woke with a groan, my face crushed against a pillow. Gods, I felt like shit. Someone was beating a drum in my head, and my limbs weighed a ton each. With effort, I pushed myself upright and wiped drool from my chin, grimacing. My mouth tasted like metal, and my tongue stuck to the roof of my mouth.

I blinked once, twice, three times before the room came into focus.

Dim. A single candle in a wall sconce lit the space, seeming to throw more shadows than light into the room. I could just barely make out the decrepit narrow bed beneath me, smooth stone walls, and the outline of a window that was entirely blacked out. When I squinted, I noticed the glint of metal in the window, sheets of it lined up like boards to fully block the outside world.

Events came back to me with startling speed. Instant panic, sharp and biting, burst inside me. I ran to the door and yanked—

It didn't budge. Locked.

I slammed my palms against it. "Hello?" I called, my voice cracking. I cleared it and tried again. "Hello!"

There was no response.

"Jasim? Are you there? Open the door!"

Nothing.

Sara probably killed him after she knocked you out, said the king. *You really are all alone. In the* dark. *If I recall, you're deathly afraid of the dark. Something to do with me?*

My breathing picked up speed, sawing in and out of my chest. There wasn't enough air in here. Too dark. Too much like my nightmares. I pounded both fists into the wood, wincing when I hit the slats of metal built into it. "Hello! Hello, can anyone hear me! *Hello*—"

The door opened. A man stood there. Dark dreadlocks grazed his hollow cheeks, and a beard reached to the center of his chest. Despite his malnourished frame, his immense height made him terrifying. I'd only met him once in my life, but if I'd had any doubt about who he was, the pointed ears sticking out between the vines of his hair and the gold-flecked eyes would have made it obvious. Prince Anwar Lotfi of Haisab.

I glared at him. A pathetic show of bravery when he had the power to read and control my emotions. I tried anyway. "Release me and I promise to spare you."

"Spare *me?*" He scoffed. "Oh, Gods-Chosen. I don't think you understand what's happening here."

I let out an enraged scream and lunged—

My fury guttered. A candle snuffed out. I halted abruptly. The fear remained, but the desire to tear Anwar's throat out with my teeth simply evaporated.

Anwar's gold-flecked eyes glinted with the use of his magic. "Behave, Gods-Chosen. Or I might decide to make your stay truly unpleasant."

Chills worked down my spine. "Where am I? Why am I still alive?"

"Because it'll be easier to sit on the throne if the Gods-Chosen has given her blessing."

I tried to muster up a scowl, but my facial muscles wouldn't obey. "I won't give you shit."

"No," he agreed. "But you are going to marry me. Which is just as good."

I scoffed incredulously. "I'd rather die."

"I'd rather you would, too. Unfortunately, killing you would probably bring the might of the gods down on me, which I'd like to avoid."

I glared with the force of the Trench's flames. "I will not marry you."

The dim light from the single candle made Anwar's smile look like it stretched entirely across his face. "You already have. There will be plenty of witnesses—from Haisab *and* Reeda—who will attest to it. A little persuading, and the imbecile Nasir will profess the same. All I need from you, Gods-Chosen, is for you to keep on breathing. So you will remain here. Surrounded by iron." He pointed to the door and the various metal beams bordering the room. "Even when you go through the Igniting, you will remain here, as trapped as if you were a mere jinni."

Iron could trap a jinni. But not just a jinni—it could incapacitate any creature of Shaya's.

My heart bumbled around in a panicked frenzy, slamming into my ribs, staggering up my throat. No, no, no. No, this couldn't be happening. Shaya wouldn't let this happen. He wouldn't leave this blasted moron to rule while his daughter rotted in the dark.

Maybe this is exactly what he wanted. Maybe he put you here. King Zaid snorted. *Throw you in a dark hole and forget about you. If I'd thought of it, I'd have done it myself.*

"Where's my guard?" I demanded. Jasim would get me out. He would—

"Dead," Anwar replied brightly.

That chasm in my chest yawned impossibly wider, nape and back of my head blazing with the need to scratch. They were lying. Jasim wasn't dead. He'd been fine. Unconscious but—

Alone in the dark, King Zaid singsonged.

"You will be fed," Anwar said, "as long as you behave."

"No," I stated, like it was obvious, like it was a fact. "You can't leave me here."

Anwar smiled again, that eerie, cutting line, and slammed the door.

I lunged to catch it but was too late. My teeth rattled as I crashed into it. Even though I knew it was futile, I yanked on the knob, but it was already locked again. I banged my palms on it. "Anwar! Anwar, let me out! Anwar! You can't keep me in here! Not in here! *Anwar!*"

But no one answered.

Knees threatening to buckle, I staggered back as it slowly sank in.

Shaya wasn't answering. I wouldn't make it to the temple. Anwar had taken me captive. The single candle on the wall flickered, as if it, too, were against me, threatening to plunge me into total darkness. And Jasim . . .

The backs of my legs hit the bed. A rickety, tattered thing. But I barely registered it as I sank onto its uneven mattress.

Darkness was all around me. Pressing in. Just like that night all those years ago.

The king had said there was nothing about me worth loving. He was right. Loving me had gotten Jasim uselessly killed. At least his death in the temple would have meant something, a bridge to Shaya, but this . . . there was no meaning in this. It wasn't fair. It wasn't right. It wasn't *true*, it couldn't be.

I longed for my rage. But whatever Anwar had done had left me with nothing more than heavy, suffocating fear and crushing sorrow.

THIRTY-THREE

SAMIRA

After a whole day abed, the pain in my legs had entirely vanished. Which was good for me, since it took that long for Bain to poke his head into my cabin. My heart hit my feet at the sight of his sharp face.

"Rade wants to see you," he growled.

"Where's Keir?"

"Taking a break. Let's go."

I followed Bain out of the cabin, body tense.

Rade was waiting for me by the longhouse's cedar doors, speaking to a large man with thick wrinkles roping across his forehead.

Suddenly, Bain grabbed my arm and pulled me to a stop. Before I could panic, he said, "Hedin was a traitor."

My eyebrows rose. *Hedin?* Of all the things I expected him to say to me, it wasn't this. "The man Rade was going to make Second? Why would Rade choose a traitor—"

"Rade didn't know. Still doesn't. No one did, except the Seven. We kept it a secret. We needed time to plan the best way to punish him, to make sure the death fit the crime. The fight cut our planning short. Velka thought you deserved to know." He rolled his eyes before his lips curled up into a nasty grin and he leaned in even closer, grip tightening until I winced. "That is what we do to traitors. Hedin's death was quick. Most traitors don't get that lucky. Remember that."

My heart nearly beat out of my chest. But I thought of how I'd stood my ground against Keir, how he'd backed down, how I'd made the decision to start fighting back. I adopted that same bravado now as I tipped my chin in the air and demanded, "Let go, Bain."

For a moment, his Shifter eyes flashed and he looked like he was going to refuse. I held his gaze for several nerve-racking moments before he slowly peeled his fingers off my arm. With more courage than I felt, I turned my back on him and strode forward, ordering my legs to carry me the last few feet to Rade.

The king turned to me with a friendly smile, oblivious to the silent war I'd just won or the nervous sweat on my forehead. "Amunet," he greeted me. "Thank you, Bain."

His Fourth dipped his head and ambled off. But not before shooting me one more dark look that sent my stomach into a tailspin. I might have won just now, but it didn't mean much. A snapped neck was Bain going *easy*. If he found out who I was and what I was doing here . . .

"Come on," Rade said. "There's something I want to show you."

I swallowed down my fear and forced myself to keep my chin high as I followed Rade out of Frostguard. We didn't speak much along the way. I didn't know if Rade could tell something was wrong with me or if he simply liked the silence.

Kaldfolk—Shifters, specifically—had been birthed during the Time of Night, the height of Shaya's power, the most frightening chapter in the War of the Ancients. Half animal, half man, they'd torn through mortals like they were nothing. It wasn't until after Shaya was locked away, his power significantly diminished, that they'd developed consciousness. That they'd become more man than beast. That didn't mean their wild, animalistic side was gone, though. I'd seen its strength with my own two eyes when they had invaded Khada Palace. Bain could be one bad day away from snapping my neck, with or without Rade's say-so. Or rather, torturing me and *then* snapping my neck. If I was lucky. Which I never was.

"Here we are," Rade said.

My eyes widened, and the air fled my lungs.

An enormous brass circle, large enough for a small assembly of people to stand in, was nestled into the earth, a bright emerald at its center. It almost looked like a compass, except there were far more than four directions carved into it, with those symbols I'd glimpsed during my time with the Seer. The markings curled all the way around the circle, a crisp border of black lines against the gleaming brass.

"What is this?" I asked.

"We're not sure," Rade replied, stepping into the ring, nodding that it was all right for me to follow. "We think it must be a remnant of the War of the Ancients. Look, do you see that?" He pointed to the emerald at the center.

I nodded, gaping. "That's Ketet's eye." The emerald jewel was bracketed by thick black lines meant to resemble eyelashes, a common symbol to represent the goddess's remaining eye. The lashes stretched up and drew together to form an arrow, which was aimed at one of the various indecipherable marks.

"So we unoriginally call this place the Eye of Ketet." Rade smiled crookedly.

Hesitantly, I stepped over the circle's border.

A hush fell. The hush of a sacred place. It wasn't cold within the compass. And it wasn't hot. It was comfortable. My panic and fear dissipated along with the chill.

"You feel it, don't you?" Rade said, smile stretching.

"Yes." I almost thought if I looked over my shoulder, I'd find the Seven Monarchs standing there. The circle carried the serenity I always found in prayer, calm and tranquil.

Rade nodded and approached the center. He knelt before it, resting his fingers just on the edge of the eye. "This is my favorite place in all of Kaldfold," he said softly, reverently. "Peaceful, meditative. It feels like the Mother watches over this place."

I drew to his side and lowered myself to my knees, following his movements and touching the edge of the eye. A beautiful, wonderful place of worship. An oasis, somehow shielded from nature's cruelty. The brass wasn't corroded in the least, but gleamed as if it had been placed here just yesterday instead of millennia ago.

"My mother brought me here to say goodbye before she went back to the Shroud."

I glanced up at him in surprise.

He struggled to meet my eyes. "She thought if she did it here, in this beautiful place, it would lessen the blow. And she was right. For as long as I remained in this circle, I wasn't sad. Even when I couldn't see her beyond the trees anymore, I wasn't sad. Not here. Never here."

But he'd had to step out of the circle eventually. And the shadows creeping into his face were answer enough of what he'd felt then.

Indeed, Rade seemed to feel a great deal. For his people, for his mother who had abandoned him, for the gods. I didn't have very many people to care for like that. I wasn't sure I'd have the strength to even if I did. Perhaps the burden of caring for my queen was enough.

I licked my lips and thought about what solace Amunet could offer. Rade didn't have the heightened sense of smell the Shifters did, so I didn't have to be so careful with my word choice. "My mother died in childbirth," I found myself saying. This was Amunet's story and not mine, but I thought it might comfort him just the same. "I never knew her. But I think my life would have been very different if I had."

He nodded in understanding. Then he said, "It's foolish, I know, but I . . . Sometimes, I think that if I could just get rid of the Shroud, I'll find her waiting for me." He huffed an embarrassed laugh and scratched at his beard.

A couple of hours turned a person into a ghul. If she'd been in there a decade . . .

But we all needed a bit of hope. I was not so cruel as to take that from him.

I reached across the space between us and took Rade's hand. "You are blessed by Eira, Goddess of the Lost. If there is a way to bring her back, you will find it."

Rade smiled softly. "You know, I have good memories here as well. The first time I felt like I had a family again was here. Keir's aunt took me in. Things had been difficult—for both me and Keir. But we came here and talked. We understood each other. And I knew I had not just a friend but a brother." He let out a long sigh and looked up at the surrounding trees. "Things always feel easier here."

They did. There was a lack of pressure somehow, like physical pounds had been lifted off my back as soon as I'd stepped foot onto the metallic surface.

Rade's gaze lowered to my hand over his, and his smile faded. "Keir told me you were listening to our conversation." My heart skipped a beat. "He seems to think you're hiding something from me, Amunet."

Slowly, I drew my hand away from his, blood rushing loudly in my ears.

"Ashorah is a blessed land. The Lotus River is obvious evidence of that. But this"—he ran his fingers along the edge of Ketet's eye again—"this is proof that Kaldfold is blessed, too."

I swallowed hard, struggling to look down at the emerald, no longer feeling worthy enough to do so. Out of the corner of my eye, I thought the jewel gleamed brighter. As if Ketet herself were glaring at me.

"So I will ask you this once, Amunet, only once, and I ask that here, in this sacred place, you be honest with me." He locked his eyes with mine. "Is there truth to what Keir says?"

Everything I'd been taught, everything I believed, warned me not to lie here. Not here.

But Queen Amunet still had almost two weeks before the Igniting. Plenty of time for the Kaldfolk to kill me and turn their attentions toward finding her. And by the time they managed to find her, my deception would have enraged them, made them crueler to her than they had been to me. She wouldn't be offered a warm cabin. They'd hold her in chains. And then drain her of every ounce of her power.

Bain's threat rang in my ears. I could still feel where his fingers had clutched my arm. A little more pressure and he could have shattered every bone.

As my silence stretched, Rade whispered, "I saw you."

My head whipped up.

He was watching me carefully. "I know we're not supposed to share what the Seer shows us, but . . . I saw you, Amunet. You were by my side."

"You saw me in your fortune from Zarqa," I repeated.

Rade nodded.

Me. He'd seen me. Not Amunet. "What . . . what was I doing?"

"I can't tell you that," he replied apologetically. "It's dangerous for others to know their future as someone else has seen it. Some will rush toward it, some away, and it inevitably leads to chaos. I shouldn't have said anything at all, but Keir is like my brother. I had to ask the question. I owe him that much." He waited for my answer.

I struggled to keep the shock off my face.

The King of Kaldfold had seen *me* in his fortune.

It couldn't be. He had to be mistaken. I hadn't seen him in my vision. I hadn't seen anyone, except a gigantic being of shadow that Zarqa jerked me away from. The one that told me I did not know myself.

I was suddenly very aware of the green runes that curled across my forehead. Runes that couldn't really belong to me. There had to have been some mistake that resulted in me, a slave from Khada Palace, having unique green markings.

Unless . . . unless they somehow—improbably, *impossibly*—weren't a mistake. Unless they meant something. Something that had rankled Keir. That summoned a great shadow into my vision. That had caused Rade to see me in his.

It did not make any sense. I didn't feel any different.

But Rade had seen *me*.

My breathing quickened. The glow from Ketet's eye in my peripheral vision became more insistent, and I slowly lowered my gaze to the small emerald. It had to be the sun's rays refracting off the jewel that was causing its shimmer. If it were actually glowing, Rade would comment on it, but he only continued to study me.

I stared into the eye of the only mother I had ever relied on, and a blanket of warmth seemed to envelop me, more than just the gentle serenity of this place. The Mother herself, I thought, wrapping her arms around me. *Tell him,* I could almost hear her whispering in my ear. *It will be all right. You will be safe, Samira. You can tell him.*

The truth leaped into my mouth. I barely had time to clamp my lips shut against it.

It wasn't the Mother talking to me but my own cowardice begging me to come clean. Fear of Bain's violence. Fear of being the reason the Gods-Chosen never reached the Igniting. Fear that Rade would stop looking at me with those bright, hopeful eyes.

"No," I breathed. "There is no truth to what Keir said."

The light in the emerald guttered, and cold washed over me. The X throbbed over my chest as my heart cracked, and my skin felt like it was shriveling up against my bones.

Rade scanned every inch of my face, hardly blinking as he searched for the truth. But then he nodded with a smile and stood, offering me his hand. I let him pull me up, but he didn't step away. "We are a team, Amunet," he said. "That's why I saw you in my fortune. That's what this whole ritual is about. Fortifying us into one unit. Gods-Chosen and Gods-Blessed, bound together. A marriage at its most basic definition."

I didn't know what to say, what to do. I only managed to whisper, "Yes."

"From here on out, it is you and I."

"Yes."

"You will be acknowledged as my queen. And I, your king."

"Yes." The one word I was capable of uttering, apparently.

That easy smile spread wider across his face, revealing that dimple in his left cheek. "Good," he said. He looked down at my hand still in his, his thumb smoothing over my knuckles once before he brought them to his lips and kissed them, his lips soft and warm. Then he released me and guided me back to Frostguard.

I hardly managed to wait until Bain shut the door behind me before I lurched for the chamber pot and vomited. I only allowed myself to cough once, not wanting Bain to hear me. And as soon as I finished, I lit a fire in the hearth to chase away any odor.

My insides felt weird, like they'd shifted to the wrong places. Lying on that hallowed ground, seeing the light go out of Ketet's eye—even if I'd just imagined it—it was like something had been severed. I didn't know what exactly, but I felt an intense absence that stretched to the deepest parts of me.

I whispered a soft prayer, but there was none of that comforting calm that usually accompanied the words. Nothing at all. Just a horrifying, disturbing silence.

What if—what if that *had* been Ketet and I'd denied her? Rejected her? I clapped a hand over my mouth, muffling my sobs even as the tears burned rivers down my cheeks.

Greed destroys, greed burns.

My greed. I had told myself that I was here to protect my queen and die for her if need be. But was that really why I'd kept silent with Rade?

No.

As frightening as the Kaldfolk were, this was still a much better life than the one I'd had in Khada Palace. I was ashamed to admit it, so, so ashamed, and I hadn't even realized it until I was given a warm room here, with consistent meals and a saltwater bath whenever I wanted, but it was possible that I . . . I might not have liked my time at Khada Palace.

No, I knew I hadn't.

I'd *hated* it.

I didn't want to give up my cabin, my smoked fish, my honey-laced kefir. Velka's smiles. Rade's trust. Even Keir's harsh challenges. And I'd been selfish enough to choose that over a goddess, the only mother I could remember, the only constant in my life.

She was gone. And she'd taken the comfort of the gods with her.

THIRTY-FOUR

∧∧∧∧∧∧∧∧

SAMIRA

The Wastelands were just a speck on the horizon, yet I hadn't looked away from them for nearly an hour. I'd stared at that hint of desert for so long, I saw it on the backs of my lids with every blink. I didn't mind the wind, the chill, or the way the wooden banister dug into my forearms as I leaned against it. I hadn't felt so alone since those initial hours after my kidnapping.

Velka and Rade had checked on me often over the last couple of days, and I made sure to visit Milena every chance I got, but it was as if I were trapped on one side of a glass window while they simply waved at me from the other side. Separate.

The Trench was where the worst souls were sent after death, where they suffered for eternity, severed forever from the gods, left only with Shaya. Where the death god let his soulless mind run rampant with ideas of torment.

One lie. That was all. I could feel it like a literal stain on my heart. One lie, that was the price of my soul.

I traced a finger over the *X* on my chest, almost thinking I'd push too hard and my chest would cave in like a rotted log, utterly hollow.

From the ground below, Keir called, "Nearly done up there, Majesty?"

"No," I replied flatly.

"Going to be much longer?"

I rolled my eyes. "You don't have to stay."

He didn't respond. I thought he must've left, until the ladder groaned and his yellow eyes appeared in the square door in the floor. "The Lunar Feast is tonight," he said. "If you don't mind, I'd actually like to go. Which I can't do until you're tucked safe and sound in your cabin."

Evening was still hours away. I didn't bother pointing that out. "Just give me five more minutes." I dropped my chin into my palm and brought my eyes back to the Wastelands. The life I'd had was so far away. A life I no longer yearned for but despised. My memories of my time there seemed to contort and shift as the truth slipped out from behind the mask of my zeal.

Keir climbed fully into the watchtower and warmed the space by my side. "What's wrong with you? Is it your power? Has something happened?"

"Can't you just sniff me and magically know?" I asked sarcastically.

"That's not exactly how it works." He paused. "Plus, I tried that already."

I huffed a humorless laugh. "Of course you did."

"What is it? You've been acting weird all week."

"I'm really not in the mood today, Keir."

"If it's something to do with the Igniting—"

"Could you please just—" I cut myself off when I heard my voice echo out over the hill. I drew a deep breath. While there was a good deal I wanted to rage at Keir for, the current cause of my anger could only be blamed on myself. With conscious effort, I uncurled my fingers, which had made themselves into fists, and spoke in a more measured tone. "Five more minutes and I'll come down. I won't make you late for your party. I promise."

His brows arced in surprise, but he didn't say anything. I didn't have it in me to feel triumphant at rendering him speechless.

I followed the thick line of clouds back to the Wastelands, which burned away the closer they got to Ashorah's searing sun, until there was nothing obstructing the sight of the gentle blue sky. Deceptive, that gentle blue, since working under it felt like being broiled alive.

And in the opposite direction . . . the Shroud. I tried to avoid looking at it, but my gaze was inevitably drawn to its inky depths. I couldn't shake the feeling that those swirling tentacles were every bit as aware of me as I was of them, like they were looking right back at me. But it didn't unnerve me. Rather, I had to fight to keep my lips from stretching into a smile and my feet from carrying me to its doorstep.

"Always there, isn't it?"

My eyes slid to Keir.

He'd turned to rest his elbows on the banister, too, gaze trained on that writhing wall. "Even when you're not thinking about it, you can always feel it trying to pull you in. Right here." He rubbed the heel of his palm against his sternum with a frown. Exactly where I felt that indescribable tug.

My brows lifted. "You feel drawn to the Shroud?"

He nodded, expression unreadable. A breeze ruffled the rope of his braid, shifting it a few inches over his shoulder blade.

I didn't bother being surprised that he knew I felt it, but I was taken aback by the fact that he'd decided to share *he* did. "Velka thinks it means we have a greater propensity for darkness."

He smiled ruefully. "That is the prevailing theory, yes."

"You don't agree?"

"The Shroud isn't about darkness. It's the Underworld. Death." There was something in the way he said it, a weight to the words, that had me studying him closely. There were a handful of scars peppered around his face that I'd never noticed before. Small silver lines along his jaw, just above the runes, and a few that chipped down his throat, slightly distorting the strong blue lines. "I think we're drawn to the Shroud," he said, "because some of us are closer to death."

A small shiver passed through me. Given my current predicament, that made an awful sort of sense. One wrong move was all it would take for a blade to come down on my neck. The Underworld could be anticipating my arrival and was calling me to it.

Keir shrugged. "But what do I know?"

My brows drew closer together. Along with the scars, there was a weathered appearance to Keir's face that I only just recognized. It was in the heavy lines of his brow, the pinch at the corners of his eyes. "I have a feeling you know a great deal," I murmured.

He glanced over at me, yellow irises startling against the dark kohl. They moved over my face, examining me just as carefully as I'd just done him. Voice sincere, he asked again, "What's wrong, Majesty?"

I dropped my gaze to my hands and swallowed. The truth would get me killed but . . . perhaps a partial truth would suffice. "I learned to pray beside the Lotus River," I said quietly. "It was so long ago, most of my memory is blurry, but it was my father's favorite place . . . I think." The memory was too frayed to gather more than a few impressions. "The river was loud, I remember. And there was a tree nearby that kept it from being too hot. Praying there . . . it was peaceful."

Mama had been there, too. Vaguely, I recalled a gentle voice reciting the worshipful words, the soft spray of water as the river splashed over the bank. "Prayer brings me back to that peace. When my thoughts are too loud or when I'm scared, Ketet comforts me with it. But now that I can't reach her, I don't . . ." Emotion clogged my throat. It felt like losing the gods and that last connection to my parents in one fell swoop.

Gently, he prodded, "What's stopping you from praying?"

"I try, but it's not . . . working. There's no peace, no comfort, *nothing*." I fiddled absently with a splinter sticking out of the banister. "I don't know how to live without my prayers."

The wind whistled between us in the ensuing quiet. Keir gazed stoically out over Kaldfold. "It's a blessing and a curse, isn't it?"

I glanced up at him curiously.

"Hope," he elaborated. "At its core, that's what prayer is, right? Hope that the gods are listening. Hope we're not alone. Hope that they'll help. It's a painful thing to lose." Tendrils of brown hair whipped around Keir's face, deepening the line between his brows.

"How do I get it back?" I asked.

He looked at me, gaze heavy. "When I figure it out, I'll let you know."

My throat was suddenly tight. "Hope will come," I whispered, defending my queen even now. She was all I had left. "The Gods-Chosen will save your people."

"See, you say that," he said, and angled his body toward mine, "and I can hear the truth in your words, smell it in that distinct scent of yours. Everything about you compels me to believe you." He was so close that his supernatural warmth wrapped around me, blocking out the wind. "And yet that rabbit's heartbeat . . . why does it scream out that you're lying?"

I took several breaths. Maybe it was my bad mood or the isolated quiet of the watchtower that gave me a surge of confidence, but I found myself blurting, "I want to make another deal."

He frowned. "What?"

"That day on the horse, you gave me an answer in exchange for hearing me beg." The memory sent heat crawling up my neck. "I want another answer. Preferably without the humiliation this time. You have questions, too, so . . . an answer for an answer."

He observed me for several seconds, during which time I didn't breathe. He was probably scenting me for deception. It was risky to promise him answers, since I knew exactly what his question would be. But my soul felt empty without Ketet, the Underworld was counting down the seconds until it claimed me, and there were unexplained markings on my forehead. I *needed* answers, and if this was the only way I'd get them, then so be it.

Keir gave a curt nod. "Ask your question."

Victory filled my lungs. I faced him fully. "What do you smell in my runes?"

His face shuttered, all traces of softness gone. "Ask a different question."

"No."

He stared at me, and I stared back. Anticipation and fear twined together inside me. I feared that look in his eyes, but I thought of the strength I'd felt when the shadow creature had offered to show me who I was. How light I'd felt without this burden of terror hanging around my neck all the time. I tried to harness that feeling and stood a little straighter.

A muscle in Keir's jaw popped. Then, "Cinnamon."

I blinked. When he said nothing more, I dumbly repeated, "Cinnamon."

He nodded curtly, that muscle in his jaw bulging again.

"That's . . . it?"

"Mostly. There are some other notes in there that are specific to you. Can't really pinpoint what they smell like. But they've gotten stronger since you got your runes." There was a slight tinge to his cheeks. From the cold, I assumed.

I waited for him to say more. Something like *And also the odor of a liar* or *You reek of heresy,* but he offered neither of those. His throat bobbed beneath his runes.

Cinnamon. Not scary. Not indicative of something deeply wrong with me. Not an answer for why my runes were green or why there was a shadow creature in my fortune. Just . . . cinnamon. "But then why did you react so—"

"I answered your question. Now it's my turn." When he faced me again, the yellow of his eyes seemed deeper. Closer to smooth honey than the sun.

I braced myself. I'd have to answer very carefully so that he wouldn't smell the lie.

His gaze fell from my face to my chest. "What are you tracing?"

My brows slammed into each other.

He nodded to where my fingers were unconsciously drawing over the grooves of the scarred X.

I dropped my hand quickly. "That's your question?"

Keir was intensely focused on that spot. I wondered when he'd first noticed that habit of mine. And why he cared. Why he'd waste his question on anything other than *What are you hiding?* But he didn't clarify. Simply insisted, "A deal's a deal, Majesty."

"It's . . . it's . . ." I hadn't anticipated this question. I wasn't prepared for it. I didn't have another answer lined up. "A scar."

He was quiet a moment. Then he asked, "Can I see it?"

My eyes snapped up to his. His voice had been exceptionally soft. So soft, in fact, that I could almost mistake it for kindness. The ice had melted from his gaze, leaving behind glittering eyes and an open face. A face that, when it wasn't glaring or sneering at me, was quite pleasant to look at.

I'd answered his question. I'd upheld my part of the deal. I could shut him down and walk away. I'd revealed too much already anyway.

But my hand had a mind of its own, because it drifted up to my collar and pulled it aside.

A thin line formed between Keir's brows as he studied the mark. As if his hand suffered from the same affliction as mine, he reached out to gently touch the mottled skin, fingertips rough and warm. Goose bumps spread over my flesh. "It's deep," he murmured.

My throat had closed up, so I could merely nod.

His index finger smoothed down the harsh line, pausing at the top of my breast, before he repeated the motion with the other line. "How did it happen?"

I stole a cup of water from the kitchens because I was so dehy-drated I'd started to see spots and couldn't walk a straight line. But stealing that cup had robbed someone else as equally thirsty as me and went against the Gods-Chosen's explicit rules.

I'd thought about the lesson I'd learned that day often, but not the event itself in years. The flash of the knife seconds before it cut into my flesh. The look in Amunet's face as my blood had run down her hand. The burn of the blade, the fever that didn't go away for days as infection set in. My failure and shame forever sliced into my flesh.

I answered hoarsely, "Disobedience is punished."

Keir's eyes flicked back up to mine. I felt their touch every bit as much as the coarse tips of his fingers against my chest. They brushed over my burning cheeks, grazed over my clenched jaw. "Zaid did this?" he asked in that same, infinitely soft voice, yet there was an underlying anger to it.

"Yes."

His fingers stilled. "Whoever would do this to you is not worth that lie, Majesty."

The humiliation I'd wanted to avoid speared through me. That feeling so familiar, that had walked in step with me since I'd gotten the scar. I hadn't noticed its absence over the past few weeks until that moment, but now it covered me like a blanket of stinging wasps. Keir could not know what I had done to deserve something so ugly, and explaining it to him was as mortifying as it was impossible.

I stepped back, and his warm hand fell away. "I answered your question. I want to go back to my cabin now."

He observed me for a long moment, but I would not meet his eyes as I rushed past him.

Keir became a quiet presence at my side as we trekked back to the central square. The heat in my cheeks seemed to rise with each painfully silent moment.

Before I could push into the sanctuary of my cabin, Keir caught my wrist. "Wait, just—" He blew out a sharp breath. "We all have scars, Majesty. I know—"

"I don't want to talk about it—"

"Don't give us hope," he blurted. "Any other lie can be forgiven, but don't give us hope if you won't—if you can't—" I thought I felt his hand tremble just the slightest bit where he held me. "It will break us."

He was begging me. Keir of the Wild Valley was begging *me*.

Guilt was a blade through my innards.

I slipped my wrist out of his grip. "Enjoy your party," I mumbled. The cabin door shut behind me with a dull thud.

It will break us.

A plea, not for himself, but for his people.

But as he'd established on the journey here, when I hadn't hesitated to beg *him* for answers, I was already broken. I had been broken that first year in Khada Palace. Maybe if I were stronger, like Velka or Sillia, I wouldn't have been. But I wasn't. I was the kind of girl who stole water rations from another. The kind who lied to a goddess's face. And now I was beyond helping anyone.

THIRTY-FIVE

AMUNET

I huddled underneath the single candle, my frame racked with shivers as I tried to focus on prayer. Every time I shut my eyes, all I saw was darkness. Suffocating, horrible darkness. At least with my eyes open, there was the slight flicker of the candle. But then I was all too aware of the complete lack of air in here.

Baba, please help me, I implored. *I tried to fix whatever I did to wrong you. I tried to get to your temple. I failed. I'm sorry. Really, really sorry. But* please *don't make me stay here.*

Do you know what the definition of insanity is? King Zaid asked.

My breath stuttered on a whimper. My nails reopened the scabs on the back of my neck.

Doing the same thing over and over and expecting a different result.

There were no mirrors in here, but I could feel the bags under my eyes, the crustiness on my lashes, the dry skin peeling on my lips. Meals were brought, but I had no appetite. In fact, I felt ill. Bile was a consistent burn in the back of my throat, and a corner of the room reeked where I'd vomited a few hours ago.

I bent my whole self into my prayers, the only option left to me. All my attention was focused on them so that I wouldn't miss the brush of my father's breath when it finally came. So I wouldn't have to think about Jasim or the horrible emptiness in my chest.

But it was no use. There wasn't even the weakest stirring from Shaya.

It's a fitting punishment, King Zaid pointed out. *For all the pain you've caused others. That maid you sent to the Kaldfolk, Jasim, Nasir.*

I winced at the mention of Jasim. "I didn't do anything to Nasir."

Of course you did. He's a prisoner now, just like you. All because he wanted to get his people back home. He tsked.

I squeezed my eyes shut, the pain of Shaya's absence ripping through my abdomen.

Darkness. Suffocating darkness. So much worse with my eyes closed. *Can't breathe, can't see, can't—*

My eyes popped back open and searched for the light of the candle. Some of its wax dripped off the sconce and landed on my shoulder. I hissed at the burn but let the pain center me.

You are all I have, Shaya. You are my entire family. I know you remember how it felt to be abandoned. How it broke your heart when Ketet locked you away. I will never leave you, Shaya. So please, please don't leave me.

I hated to remind him of that time. Ketet and Shaya had been family before she decided to create a new one without him and sought to humiliate and denigrate him at every turn, resulting in the War of the Ancients. A war that was so violent, so hate-filled, it spilled from the After Realm into this one and necessitated Cilene, Goddess of War, sending a son as Gods-Chosen to save us mortals. And then Ketet—the woman Shaya had loved, his wife, the mother of his child—locked him away for eternity.

That was the story of the family that created our world, tragic, heartbreaking. It hurt my father. But if I couldn't reach him through my love, maybe I could reach him through his rage.

I prayed reminders of Ketet's betrayal toward him and received not even a whisper in return. King Zaid snickered.

The hours—days?—since I'd been locked away dragged by at a snail's pace, and my mind flipped between terror and despair.

Not for the first time, I wondered why I should be bothered with saving any of these people. Why, when they were so spiteful to me, when they made their hatred so obvious, was I meant to do anything to help them?

The candle went out with a hiss as loud as a death knell.

King Zaid's taunting laugh surrounded me just like the darkness, wrapping around my throat. A snake's vise. I couldn't breathe. All I could see was that inky blackness from my nightmares, crawling over a pile of bodies, bringing awful cold with it. Reaching for me, getting rid of me—

Blindly, I staggered to the door and banged on it. "Hello! Hello, please! The candle—I can't—someone—"

The door opened, letting light flood the room in a solid, miraculous beam.

I blinked as my eyes worked to adjust.

A guard stood there. He wore Haisab's colors of blue and gold. "What is it?"

I drank in the sight of the hallway behind him. Countless torches burned along the walls, bathing the space in light. Unintentionally, my feet shuffled closer.

The guard drew his scimitar and leveled it at me. "Don't."

I retreated and worked to swallow past the dryness in my throat. "I need a new candle."

The man looked past me to the dark room and nodded. "Back up. Forehead against the wall."

Though all my instincts urged me to run, I turned and pressed my forehead to the scratchy wall on the opposite side of the room. The guard's sandaled feet padded toward the sconce. There was some fiddling as he replaced the old candle and then the hiss of a match. Dim light bloomed.

My body trembled with the desire to fight. My knuckles yearned to drive themselves into the guard's nose and dash madly past him to freedom. But I wouldn't make it even an inch before his blade stopped me.

I drew several deep breaths, shoring myself up.

There were three takes on Shaya's Gods-Chosen. When in doubt, the third never failed.

I hesitated a moment, remembering the way Jasim had spat the words at me when he thought I'd seduce Nasir. *Should I ask you nicely not to fuck him? Should I bother? We both know you'll do what you want anyway.* My stomach knotted, so disgusted with myself for a moment that I tasted bile at the back of my throat.

But Jasim was dead. He wasn't here to care.

So I did my best to ignore the chattering in my head, the burn in my skin, as I smoothed a hand across the wall. I only dared a brush of my fingertips against his wrist. He tensed.

I turned my head, all my movements slow and nonthreatening. "Thank you," I breathed.

The guard's face was plain. It was hard to make out anything concrete in the pathetic flicker of the candle, but I thought he might be older than me by a half dozen years or so. He kept his expression stoic, but he didn't pull his hand away.

I offered a flimsy laugh. "I'm afraid of the dark, if you can believe it."

His lips pressed together while he debated whether to engage. He'd probably been given strict instructions not to. But I kept my face open, head tilted just enough for the candle to catch the brightness of my green eyes. The guard said, "I'll make sure to check the candle more regularly."

My smile was smooth as honey. "What's your name?"

Another moment of hesitation. "Malik."

I turned fully. Malik's muscles locked up, scimitar held aloft. But it was no longer aimed at my heart, just hovered in the space between us. "You have kind eyes, Malik."

He blinked. His eyes were actually relatively bland and brown, but I gazed into them as if they held the secrets of the After Realm in their depths. Hesitantly, I lifted a hand. He tracked my every move but did not flinch away as I cupped his cheek. "Beautiful," I murmured, like he wasn't meant to hear it.

Malik's throat bobbed.

I shuffled a half step closer. "Very few people treat me with kindness. Did you know that, Malik? Oh," I said with an embarrassed laugh, "I suppose you do."

"Gods-Chosen, you . . . you should get some rest." His voice was hoarse.

"It's so dark in here, Malik," I whispered, pressing closer, molding the front of my body to his, and his breath caught. He was already hard. Normally, I would have rolled my eyes at how easy it was, but now I thanked the gods.

I smoothed my hands up his chest, over his shoulders, working my way inch by inch down to his brandished right arm. If I could get the scimitar out of his hand, I could get out of here. But I kept my eyes trained on his. Tilted my face up so that my lips were a hairsbreadth from his as I breathed, "Help me, Malik."

"I . . ."

"Please," I murmured as my hand slid down his forearm. Nearly to the wrist. Almost—

"No!" He shoved me so hard, I slammed into the wall with a gasp. The sharp end of a blade scraped my throat yet again. A habit that was getting on my last fucking nerve. Malik glared at me with those unexceptional eyes. "Get away from me, demon."

Demon. King Zaid snorted. *Humiliated yourself for nothing.*

I swallowed, cheeks searing. "Malik—"

"Stop." He backed away, scimitar still brandished. "I will not betray my prince."

"That wasn't—"

The door slammed, and I flinched. My hope crashed like a bird felled mid-flight. I stared blankly, stunned, as the dead bolt slid into place, locking me back in this tomb.

I stared at the candle until my eyes burned, until I saw it on the backs of my lids with every blink, and I prayed hard. Every dribble of wax that melted down its side, every millimeter of wick that burned away, I offered up to Shaya. And still I felt nothing.

My leg bounced anxiously, and I dug my nails into the skin of my arms. My fear had turned to rage. White, blinding rage.

A cage. Shaya was imprisoned in the Underworld, and I was imprisoned in an ugly, magic-proof iron cage. It was shameful that the two of us should be brought so low. He and I were the most powerful of our kind, yet he was left to while away his eternity and I was sitting here staring at a melting candle.

If it weren't for the meals that came like clockwork, I'd have no way to tell the time. I was due for supper soon, which was how I knew it had been three days since Anwar had captured me.

Captured. Like an animal.

I scratched harder and turned to look over my shoulder.

The door was still closed. Just like it had been every time I looked back there.

Knots curled in the wood. They almost looked like eyes. Watching me. Anwar was watching me—or maybe someone else. These eyes were brown, the same shade as the door, not gold-flecked. But then whose were they? And why wouldn't they look away—

I dug the heels of my palms into my eyes and forced myself to draw deep breaths. They weren't eyes. It was just a gods-damn door. That's all.

You're going mad, said the king.

No, I wasn't mad. I just needed to talk to Shaya.

A click sounded. It might as well have been a cannon for how hard I jumped.

Malik appeared with my supper in hand—a plate of unseasoned chicken and a cup of olive juice. I was instantly on my feet.

He brandished his scimitar. "Get back against the wall, Khada."

My hands curled into fists so tight, my palms ached. But good behavior was important. I obediently turned and pressed my back against the wall under the sconce with the melting candle, several feet away from the door.

He didn't take his eyes off me or lower his blade as he slowly crouched and set the plate on the floor at his feet.

"Could I speak to the prince?" I asked. For good measure, I added, "Please."

"He's busy," he answered brusquely, and turned for the door.

"Wait! I'll make a bargain with Anwar," I rushed to say. "A real one. Tell him that." A jinni bargain was something that couldn't be broken. I'd swear to whatever he wanted, if he would let me out of here.

Malik shook his head as he backed out of the room. "Why would Prince Anwar make a deal with you when he's already won?"

Another failure. King Zaid clicked his tongue. *Add it to the list.*

I stood in the center of the room, chest heaving. Whatever magic Anwar had used to tamp my fury had vanished long ago and now it rose like a tidal wave. I let out a scream that was part shriek and part roar. If there had been anything in the room, I would've broken it, shattered it, sent my fist sailing straight through it.

I kicked the plate of food and watched the olive juice splatter against the wall. But it wasn't enough.

I threw my body at the door. Each impact against the metal beam sent pain smarting through me, but I didn't care. I did it again and again, taking a small amount of pleasure in the pain, in the resound-ing *boom* I made each time.

When the right side of my body throbbed and ached, I stopped. Bruises were already forming along my arm and hip.

I backed away from the door and stared at the knots in the wood that looked like eyes, at the wrinkle beneath them that curled like lips around a smirk.

Just as fast as the rage came over me, it receded back into its fiery depths, and I grew very quiet. Deathly quiet. A predator's silence. Barely even breathed.

I was Gods-Chosen. I was Queen Amunet Khada, daughter of Shaya, heir to Conqueror Zaid. I would not be caged.

I looked at the smirking door and smiled right back.

THIRTY-SIX

〰〰〰〰〰〰

SAMIRA

Queen Amunet had many parties over the sixteen years I'd served her. Even just circling with trays of food or wine had been fun. There was dancing, spectacularly vibrant clothes—and music. Gods, I loved the music. Flutes and harps and drums, they filled the space with an energy unlike anything I'd ever experienced. Sometimes, I'd pretend that I was a guest, a shy wallflower, observing my friends and waiting for someone to invite me to dance.

The Lunar Feast didn't sound anything like Amunet's parties.

There were no flutes or harps, only drums. Some were a deep thrumming to match my heartbeat and others were as high as a bird's trills, the rhythm changing every few minutes. I couldn't help but wonder if Keir was responsible for one of them, which made me think of our conversation earlier today. What he'd said about my runes. How he'd looked at my scar, the brand of my shortcomings. The fire of mortification started to climb its way up my neck again, so I crumpled the memory into a ball and chucked it into the farthest corner of my mind.

Wild laughter rose above the drums, high-pitched and rowdy, and roars drowned out all the rest. Roars I hadn't heard since that night they'd come for the Gods-Chosen. Bear roars. Low and hungry and frightening.

The fireplace painted my room in a comforting warm glow, but it didn't help chase away the memories that wrestled forward, no matter how hard I tried to crumple those up, too:

Amunet's green eyes, wide and frantic.

Tabia's apologetic smile as she left me.

Men torn to pieces.

Bright yellow eyes in the darkness.

A knock sounded at the door, and a little girl's voice called, "Queen Amunet?"

I shook off the bad memories and opened the door. "Milena," I greeted her, doing my best to sound chipper. "Is everything all right?"

She was bundled in my fur cloak, the hem of it a train behind her, and her blue eyes were panicked. "Everything is so loud and I—" She cut off with a gasp when another bear's roar rocked the longhouse behind her.

"Come in, come in." I stepped aside quickly.

Milena scurried in, clutching her Ketet doll in a white-knuckled grip. Her skittish eyes kept darting to the door. Sympathy swept through me.

"Would you like to sleep here tonight?" I asked her gently.

In answer, she scampered to the bed and burrowed into the blankets.

Smiling, I crawled in beside her. It didn't make much sense, but I suddenly felt a lot better having someone else in the room with me. Even if that someone was a five-year-old girl.

Milena blinked. "Are you crying?"

"No," I said, and quickly wiped away any evidence to the contrary. "Just yawned."

Milena took my hand under the covers, eyes knowing. "I don't like the noise, either."

I laughed softly and gave her hand a squeeze. Another roar blasted, and she ducked under the covers.

Protectiveness rose up inside me, momentarily chasing away my self-pity as I stared at her quivering form. Milena had been ripped from her family not once but twice, and those gods-damn Shifters were making her new home a terrifying hell.

Before I knew what I was doing, I was out of the bed and wrapping a coat around my shoulders.

Milena bolted upright. "Where are you going?"

"To see if I can get them to quiet down." When her eyes widened impossibly farther, I said, "Don't worry. I'll be right back. Try to sleep."

I waited for Milena's hesitant nod before I opened the door and stepped out. Alone in the dark, my bravado evaporated, and all I could hear was Keir's warning, *Don't come to the Lunar Feast,* ringing in my ears.

But there was a little girl trembling anxiously in my room . . . and a stirring of curiosity in my chest.

I straightened my spine and walked to the longhouse.

It had been entirely transformed over the past few days. Lines of wildflowers hung from the ceiling. Statues carved of wood were posted along the walls, each a different face of the moon goddess, Ayeen. One for each phase of the moon.

Kaldfolk stood on the tables. They were writhing against each other in time to the drumbeats. Some were truly entangled in each other, wearing very little clothing despite the chill of the night, and showing off their black runes, while others stumbled drunkenly, mugs of kefir in their hands, as they shouted words to some song I didn't know.

Despite the decorations hanging from the ceiling and Ayeen's statues, the hall was a mess. Like an animal had torn through it. Or multiple. Claw marks marred the tabletops and walls. Food was strewn across the floor and trampled. And some of the Kaldfolk were bleeding from scratches on their exposed flesh.

But no one had blue runes. No Shifters.

Rade was among the revelry, a crown of wildflowers around his head, eyes glimmering as he moved through the rapid steps of a dance. Sweat glistened on his face, and a smile stretched across his lips as he threw back a cup of kefir. He looked freer than I'd ever seen him.

I slipped through the crowd, tucking my elbows in close to avoid any bodies. "Rade."

He turned to me with delighted surprise. "Amunet! I thought you weren't coming."

"I'm not, I just—"

He grabbed my hands and pulled me to his side. "I'll teach you the dance. It's very simple."

"I'm sure it is, but I really just wanted—"

"Your Majesty!" Velka tumbled into me on drunken legs, giggling, eyes gleaming with something akin to madness. Her braid was undone, hair a wild dark mess around her head, and she'd stripped down to her undergarments, which were slashed through, leaving very little to the imagination. I noticed a black tattoo different from her other blue runes nestled just over her heart. It looked like a very large bite mark—I guessed a *bear's* bite.

Velka noticed my gaze and waved dismissively. "It's just a mating mark."

"A wha—*oof.*"

She yanked me into a tight hug. I could feel the scrape of claws against my back, as if she were not fully committed to her human form. "I'm so glad you're here!" she gushed.

I surveyed the longhouse, looking for signs of the rest of the Seven, but it was only Velka. A small relief.

"I was just trying to get her to dance," Rade told her.

"Oh yes, you must, you must! It's so—" Her head snapped in the other direction, as if she heard something I couldn't, and a wicked smile broke across her face. She let out an excited yip and shifted into a bear, barreling on all fours out of the longhouse, claws tearing apart the wooden floor.

I set my chin and refocused. "Rade, it's so loud that—"

"Here, kefir," he shouted over the drums as he thrust a cup of it at me.

"No, I don't want—"

A woman caught his hands, and he laughed as he swung back into the dance.

I huffed in annoyance and set the kefir on the nearest table. One of the dancers kicked it over, splashing white all over my coat. I gasped and stumbled back a step. They all merely laughed and carried on. With a glower, I tore off the dripping coat and folded it over my arm.

The Lunar Feast was meant to be an event for the Shifters, for *them* to lose control. With animal spirits, complete abandon made sense. But Rade was just as bad. So were all the Kaldfolk with black runes. The cups of kefir were probably to blame.

Parties in Khada Palace were never like this. I could hardly hear myself think.

When Rade swung close enough, I snatched his shoulder, dug my nails in, and pulled him out of the line of dancers. "It's scaring Milena," I yelled directly into his ear.

"What is?"

"The noise!"

"If I ask them to stop, they won't listen."

"Could you try?" Now that I said it out loud, it did sound rather ridiculous.

Rade shrugged. Took my hand and led me to the circle of drummers, where he repeated my request. The drummers—none of which were Keir—just laughed and pounded harder. The sound reverberated in my head.

Rade gave me a crooked grin. "See?"

I shouldn't have been surprised. And really, I wasn't. Of course they wouldn't quiet their party for one scared little girl—or for me. But at least I could tell Milena I'd asked.

I turned to thank him, but he was already swept back up into the wild crush of bodies. With a sigh, I fought my way through the chaos. When I burst out into the night, I tilted my face up to the sky and greedily drank in the freezing air, for once grateful for the chill. Inside was far too suffocating.

I crossed my arms tightly over my chest and lowered my eyes, ready to trudge back to my room, an apology for Milena on my lips—

I drew to an abrupt halt.

Bain stood in my path.

THIRTY-SEVEN

ᴧᴧᴧᴧᴧᴧᴧ

SAMIRA

Enjoying yourself, Your Majesty?" he asked, craning his head slowly to the side. His tunic was torn at the seams, and it billowed out around him in the cold night breeze. His blazing yellow eyes appeared even crueler in the starlight, and when they scanned over me, I felt like meat he was about to carve up. The sound of a neck snapping echoed in my ears.

"I—I'm just going back to my cabin," I stuttered, making to move around him.

Bain matched my step. "*Your* cabin? Made yourself right at home, didn't you." His teeth were pointed bear's teeth. "All is forgiven, then, eh? Marry our king, get rid of the Shroud, and we'll pretend your lot never rounded us up."

"Rounded you up?"

He laughed, ducking his head low, glaring at me from under his eyebrows. He didn't answer me. Instead, his face elongated, fur sprouted, and he landed in front of me as a bear. Fear choked me.

When the Kaldfolk had reached me in Amunet's room, there hadn't been much time to observe their animal forms up close. And even when they'd evacuated Netherridge, I was more concerned with the darkness of the Shroud than I was with a pack of bears.

But a Shifter bear was *big*. Really big. Much larger than a normal bear. One bite of those massive jaws, and he would take my entire head off.

Running would do no good. I fisted my hands in my balled-up coat as I struggled to control my trembling. Just over his massive body I could see my little cabin, where Milena waited for me. But it was still a good several yards away.

Teeth flashed as Bain let out a roar and lunged.

Even knowing it wouldn't help, I dropped the coat and burst into a sprint, but I didn't even fully turn around before he slammed into me, claws like blades impaling my shoulders as I crashed onto my back. The smell of copper filled the air, and blood leaked down my arms. Hot air and spittle shot into my face as Bain roared again, his weight crushing. His jaws gaped open.

My arms came up, hands shoving his face, keeping his enormous teeth from my jugular. He thrashed, claws digging even deeper. Pain speared through me, and I cried out, eyes squeezing shut.

The Seer had gotten it wrong. I wasn't going to burn. I was going to be mauled to death.

I worked my legs up under his stomach and pushed with all my strength, trying to topple him. If I could just get free for a second, I could get to the longhouse. He wouldn't dare attack me in front of Rade. I just had to get inside.

But the bear was too heavy. Bain roared into my face again, blasting me with his rancid breath, choking me—

Something crashed into the bear, knocking him off me.

I gasped, my lungs finally able to expand again. My shoulders were slick with blood, but I hardly felt the fresh wounds as I bolted up to my feet.

Another bear had its teeth locked around Bain's neck. Every time Bain tried to stand, the second bear smashed his face back down to the earth and snarled. *Submit,* it seemed to demand. Saliva dripped from Bain's teeth, bloodlust still in his eyes as he looked at me.

The second bear's teeth tightened around Bain's neck, pushing him deeper into the ground until one of his eyes was forced shut. If it bit any deeper, it would break flesh.

Bain finally whimpered and went limp. The teeth released, and Bain staggered up to his paws.

My rescuer stood in front of me protectively, possessively, and snarled.

Bain glared but obediently ambled off, disappearing back into the dark.

Leaving me alone with my rescuer.

This bear was somehow *larger* than the first, its shoulders reaching much higher than my head. It turned slowly, yellow eyes locking on my still-shaking form, the fur on its neck blue. Without breaking eye contact, it rose up on its hind legs and shifted.

In the next breath, Keir stood in front of me, trousers tattered and bare chest heaving. His tan skin glistened with sweat under the light of the stars, and despite the pain lancing through me, my eyes ate up the sight of him, the immense strength and power that radiated off him. His large biceps flexed as he pushed his long braid over his muscled shoulder, veins cording his forearms like vines, and his massive chest rose and fell with each jagged inhale.

My own breath hitched as my gaze lowered. Above the rows of strong abs, huge white scars slashed along his rib cage, and bone peered out through the flesh, stark against his skin. Not a fresh wound. Not even a few days old. The puckering of skin around the exposed bone looked like the scars on my back, on my chest. Old. Smoothed by time.

We all have scars. That was what he'd said this afternoon after I'd shown him my *X*. But these were not just scars. Incredulously— impossibly—he'd healed with bone bared. Gods, the agony he must feel every hour of every day . . .

He cocked his head and approached. Stalked closer, until he was mere inches in front of me. His nostrils flared as he took in my scent, a piercing odor of fear and pain, I was sure. I kept my eyes trained on his torn chest.

Then he reached up and smoothed a thumb under my eye, wiping away my tears. The touch was so gentle, so unexpected, my gaze drew up to his.

Keir's eyes were suns. Scorching as he looked at me. "I told you not to come tonight," he rasped, voice more guttural than usual, like the night in Amunet's room, caught between beast and man.

I said nothing. He might have just saved me, but the way his eyes raked over me, I thought it might have only been so he could devour me himself.

And then he moved. Circled me. Every step that of a predator.

I held my injured arms close to my sides and kept perfectly still.

He paused behind me, so close his inhuman body heat seeped into my back, chasing away much of the night's chill. From the corner of my eye, I watched his hand lift to my shoulder—an entirely human hand, I marked gratefully. Slowly, he pulled my nightdress's strap to the side, revealing my torn shoulder, and I winced. "You're hurt," he murmured.

There was something in his voice, something I'd never heard before, and I chanced a look back.

He stared ahead, into the night. The kohl that encircled his eyes and crawled up his forehead made his gaze look murderous, but it wasn't for me. It was for Bain. He almost looked like he'd tear off into the dark after him.

Then his eyes dipped back down, and his expression changed. The anger faded away, replaced by curiosity. Like my shoulder held the answer to a question he knew he shouldn't ponder, that he fought with every shred of willpower. A war waging in his mind.

A war he lost as he lowered his head to my skin and inhaled deeply, just as he'd done to my runes a few days ago.

Run, the rational part of my mind urged. *Get back to the longhouse or to Milena.*

But I couldn't. I could only watch as Keir's eyes guttered, so dark there was almost no trace of their bright gold. His hand hovered beside my arm a moment before drifting down again, stroking me without so much as touching me. A shiver racked my body, though I was anything but cold. In fact, my skin felt flushed, and a deep heat was curling low.

"That scent . . ." he rumbled, his nose skimming against the curve of my neck, making goose bumps pucker over every inch of my flesh. "Gods, that scent . . ."

Keir didn't touch me, barely even allowed his face to graze mine, but I felt the phantom brush of his lips against the back of my neck, and my breath stuttered, the earthy spice of a mulberry tree filling my nose. Keir chuckled, a rough purr that tightened my insides. "Always so scared, aren't you, little rabbit?" he whispered.

"I—I'm not scared of you."

He inhaled again, and another deep laugh rolled out of him. "I suppose you're not." He lifted his head, and his bottom lip accidentally brushed the shell of my ear. I felt the touch all the way down to the tips of my toes and bit my lip, that swirling heat unfurling entirely, filling me with a deep pulsing want. Another rumble of a laugh. "No, you're not scared at all, are you. The scent of fear is nowhere near as tempting as *this*."

"Tempting as wha—" I turned to face him, but his hands clamped down on my hips.

"Don't," he said sharply. I heard him swallow, his fingers flexing against my sides as he struggled for control, kneading my flesh. "Don't move." Haggard breathing stirred the tips of my hair.

"Why?" I asked, voice little more than a whisper.

He didn't say anything for a long time. The skin under his unforgiving grip throbbed, a sensation that spread through my whole body. Keir hated me and I hated him. Yet there was an unmistakable heat growing between my legs, anticipation beating in my veins.

Keir's right hand released its grip on my hip to slide to my stomach. He applied just enough pressure to ease me back a single step, and then our bodies were flush. Suddenly, my heart was trying to beat its way out of my rib cage. Keir's body was a furnace. His chest expanded against my shoulder blades with each unsteady inhale, restless energy emanating from him in waves, like he was one second away from pouncing. He ducked his head to speak in my ear. "Because," he finally said, breath hot on my neck, "you're already hurt, and I don't want to make it worse."

I angled my head toward him, our cheeks brushing. "I told you, I'm not scared of you."

"I guess I'm not making myself clear." His lips skimmed over the spot behind my ear. Almost a kiss but not quite. His palm against my stomach drew me even closer, and I sucked in a breath when I felt something hot and hard dig into the small of my back. Fire melted down my spine, centering in my core. Keir took hold of my jaw and turned my face so I was looking straight into those simmering eyes. "Clear enough?"

Oh yes. He was very, very clear.

Keir wanted me. It should have disgusted me or frightened me. And yet, against every instinct, every ounce of common sense, every logical corner of my mind, a thrill shot through me. My gaze lowered to his lips, so close his breath dusted across mine. All I had to do was lean an inch closer, and I'd taste them—

Keir ripped his hands away and stepped back, cold filling the sudden space between us. He stared at me, brows high, chest rising and falling rapidly. Almost as if he'd heard my thoughts. Or rather, smelled them.

Voice shaky, I ventured, "Keir?"

"I'll get the healer."

"Keir—"

Paws hit the earth in seconds as he shifted and bounded away.

I stood there, with only the dim torches and stars for light, and fought to catch my breath. My face felt too hot, my insides were on fire, and my legs were like a newborn colt's. For some reason, I felt embarrassed, though I wasn't entirely sure why. Wasn't entirely sure what had just happened in general. Why had Keir . . . and why had *I* . . . ? I could still smell mulberries, a cloud around me pulling at that memory I couldn't quite see. At once comforting and intoxicating.

I shook my head, trying desperately to clear it, and practically sprinted back to my cabin.

Siv came and patched me up. But even after she made assurances that I'd be all right, even after she agreed not to tell Rade what had happened, and even after Milena had fallen asleep curled up beside me, I could still feel Keir's breath on my neck, his heat against me, his rough voice in my ear.

I didn't sleep at all that night.

THIRTY-EIGHT

AMUNET

I stood with my back firmly pressed against the wall beside the door, waiting like a snake in the grass.

Anwar kept my meals regular. Three times a day, never missed.

I'd started counting the seconds in between meals. Timing them with exceptional precision. An obsessive, needlelike focus. I didn't hear any of Zaid's taunts, didn't bother scratching at my inflamed skin.

I waited. And I waited.

My concentration was honed by fury. I didn't lose my place in tallying the seconds even once. Not even when I thought the door was watching me. I was more than irate; I was boiling with all the flames of the deepest pit of the Trench.

I counted. And counted. Until I was absolutely sure.

Five hours between breakfast and lunch, and lunch and supper. Thirteen hours between supper and breakfast.

Which meant my next breakfast was coming in exactly twenty-three seconds.

The tips of my fingers tingled with anticipation.

Click. The lock. And then the knob turned.

Malik was instantly alert when he didn't see me waiting like a good little pet on the other side of the room. His scimitar zinged as he brandished it. "I won't search for you, demon," he barked. "Come get your food now, or wait until sup—"

I whipped around the door and slammed my elbow down on Malik's wrist with a battle cry. The scimitar fell into my waiting hand, and while the guard was still stunned, I plunged it into his throat.

Malik stumbled sideways into the wall, mouth gaping open. I grinned, hoping he saw the face of my father's demons reflected in my eyes, and cut the blade to the right, severing his artery.

The guard choked, and blood spurted out, bathing my face. The metallic smell lunged up my nose. I inhaled deeply and licked the blood off my lips, copper and salt filling my mouth.

Malik collapsed, his head attached to his body by only a few resolute tendons.

I bolted out the open door, up the stairs, slammed into the door at the top—

The door crashed back into me. My foot slipped, and I hurtled down the steps with a shout, the uneven wood leaving angry scratches on my skin. My head cracked against the hard floor, and stars burst across my vision. I lay there in a daze, blinking hard to bring the world back into focus.

Another guard bore down on me. Without waiting for me to catch my breath, he hauled me up by the collar. My legs struggled to work, but he didn't care, letting me stagger drunkenly behind him. Then he tossed me back into my dark room.

I landed in a heap on the floor, a groan rumbling out of me.

There was a crash from somewhere outside. The guard's head whipped that way, listening, before he quickly grabbed my wrist and carted me across the room, to the bed. From his waistband, he pulled out a pair of manacles and clapped one around my wrist and the other around the post at the foot of the bed.

"Meals have been reduced to once a day," he intoned unfeelingly, and rushed back out the door, slamming it shut behind him.

I gave the shackle an experimental tug and sighed at its lack of give. I couldn't even make it onto the bed now. I'd have to sleep on the floor. Like a dog.

My eyes alighted on the puddle of blood beneath Malik's body across the room. I could still feel its stickiness on my face, taste its copper on my tongue.

An idea popped into my head. I rose up onto my knees, the hard stone of the floor digging into my skin, and held my hands at my sides, palms up, eyes shut. I fought the instinctive fear at the suffocating darkness behind my lids and did my best to welcome it, to welcome him.

Baba, I prayed, *accept this sacrifice from your most humble servant. See the bloodshed as my devotion to you, as my plea for your help.* Tears built behind my closed lids. *I am only trying to do as you wish, Baba. I search for your presence so that when you grant me your power, we can work as one.*

I waited breathlessly, my words reverberating in my head, eyes squeezed tightly shut, hoping and hoping and hoping—

A warm breeze stirred against my face.

My eyes popped open. And my breath caught.

The air in front of me moved. A wave stretched up from the ground, hovering in midair. Almost like a heat wave but standing upright. It distorted the room in a single vertical line. Small particles of light shone along the edges, like glittering dust.

Shaya.

I stood and took a step—my chain pulled short. I snarled in frustration.

Outside my prison, I heard shouting and metal crashing against metal. But I ignored all of it as I focused on the line of light shimmering in front of me. Gentle and delicate.

It drifted closer. Paused inches away.

Hesitantly, I reached out.

My hand disappeared into the light.

I quickly pulled it back out. But my hand was fine. Unharmed. I extended it inside again—and felt a warm breeze on the other side.

It was a door.

I laughed incredulously. Thrust my hand into it. Took another step, straining against my manacle.

My prison door flew open, and a man stumbled in. Bloodied, bruised, white-knuckling a scimitar. He looked like he'd fought his way through the Trench itself.

Shock nearly stole my voice. All I managed was a breathless, "Jasim?"

Jasim's eyes went straight to the floating light. "What is that?" Before I could answer, shouts thundered from the hall, accompanied by heavy footfalls. It startled me back into motion.

"Come on." I held out my hand.

One arm around his midsection, he stumbled toward me and took my hand just as the miraculous door drifted closer. It swallowed us up in a flash of light. The strain on my manacled wrist vanished.

It was like finally breaking the surface of a lake after drowning. The unsteadiness fled my limbs, my mind settled, the itchiness disappeared from the back of my neck. I could finally breathe again.

Rocks and twigs dug into the soles of my sandals. The sun bathed my face in blessed, merciful light. When I opened my eyes, I wasn't in the cell anymore. The shackle was around my wrist, but the few inches of chain that had come with me through that strange doorway hung uselessly from it. Beside me, Jasim was hunched over, catching his breath.

Jasim.

Without thinking, I threw my arms around him.

He hissed in pain.

Instantly, I released him. "Oh, fuck, sorr—"

His arms went around my waist and crushed me to him, and he buried his face in my neck. I curled my fingers into his tattered shirt, relief nearly sending me to my knees. A wave of hysterical laughter rocked me. "I thought you were dead," I breathed.

He smiled against my cheek. "I already told you, I will never leave you."

I squeezed Jasim tighter as another amazed laugh bubbled out of me. Over his shoulder, the wave and sparkling dust were gone. As if they had never been there at all.

Shaya had saved me. He hadn't abandoned me. He still chose me. And he'd blessed me with Jasim's life.

"Are you hurt?" he asked, beginning to pull back. "Did Anwar—"

I held on tighter. "I'm fine." He smelled of sweat and blood—and familiar river reeds.

Jasim was okay. We were both free. A pressure lifted from my chest and relieved tears pricked my eyes. *Thank you, Baba.*

Jasim tensed. "Amunet."

Something about his voice made me lift my head. His eyes were trained gravely on something behind me.

The sandy earth stretched out in front of us, leading to a chain of mountains that were split down the middle, forming an entrance. On either side of the entrance was an enormous statue, identical and towering as high as the mountains themselves. A man with feathered wings curling over his shoulders, their tips nearly touching his crowned head. I knew exactly who was depicted there.

Athar. Shaya and Ketet's son, God of Mischief and Dreams.

And through the entrance, beyond the mountains was a sea of thin, tall trees. The forest stretched out as far as the eye could see. Despite the blazing sun, fog drifted along the forest bed.

My sweat dried cold on my back. I'd seen drawings of this place, had been warned against venturing this far south by every tutor, every nursemaid, by the king himself.

I was facing the Border Mountains. And past that, Dead Man's Forest.

"Shit," Jasim muttered.

My curse was much more colorful.

THIRTY-NINE

∧∧∧∧∧∧∧∧

SAMIRA

Velka was posted outside my door instead of Keir, her braid a frazzled mess around her face, and her eyes glittered with residual wildness from last night. She greeted me with a hoarse voice.

"Where's Keir?" I asked.

"He, uh, he got a bit out of hand last night," she replied. "Shifter stuff. Rade sent him to cool off." She waved her hand like there was nothing to worry about.

A blush found its way to my cheeks as I recalled Keir's fingers digging into my hip, his haggard breath in my ear. He'd been near snapping. I couldn't deny that the possibility had, for a thoughtless moment, excited me. But along with the deep desire I'd glimpsed in his eyes burned wrath. If he actually had snapped last night, but not on me . . . gods knew what he'd done to get put in a time-out.

"And Bain?" I asked, tone consciously casual.

Velka paused. "What about Bain?"

Keir hadn't told her. After what had nearly happened, I definitely wasn't going to be the one to do it. "Never mind."

The wild glint in her eyes faded for a moment as her gaze lowered to my bandaged shoulders. "I heard Siv came to see you. Did Bain . . . ?"

"I'm fine, Velka. Just got caught up in the Lunar Feast." Which wasn't a lie, since the phantom hardness of Keir's body still tingled against my spine.

Oblivious to my rapidly heating blood, Velka nodded and waved for me to follow her.

She led me to another cedar house with a straw roof. Though not as large as the longhouse, it certainly overshadowed the other huts in Frostguard. Inside was a collection of bunk beds, all of which were empty. A small kitchen at the back needed tidying—clay bowls were strewn over every surface, and the quaint sitting area off to the side was arranged haphazardly. Lived-in but unkempt. I peeked through another door and saw an array of weapons hanging on the walls. A training room.

Velka went directly to one of the bunks and reached up, feeling around the blankets. She moved about the space with such familiarity that I asked, "Is this your cabin?"

"Shifters' Lodge. For the Seven. Ah, there it is." Velka pulled her hand back from the bed. A strange chain hung from her fingers, made of molded brass with little pouches hanging from it. She walked around me and fastened the chain around my neck.

A terrible odor drifted up from the pouches, and I nearly gagged. "What is that?"

"Sheep dung mixed with herbs. To hide your scent."

That scent . . . Gods, that scent . . .

I shook my head to clear it and faced Velka. "And you keep this in your bed?"

"It's Alarik's old bed. The others thought it would be a funny prank on the new Second." She shrugged like it didn't bother her, even though it clearly did.

"Rade's chosen a new Second?"

"Yeah. He did it while Keir and Bain were . . . occupied. Probably for the best."

I nodded and flicked one of the pouches on the strange collar. "And why do I need to hide my scent?"

"For your own safety. You can take it off once you're out of the water."

"The water?"

Velka stopped, finally seeming to realize I had no idea what she was talking about. "Rade didn't tell you?" I shook my head. "Well, you won't come fully into your power until the Igniting, but your magic should be alive and moving through your veins. It will meet Rade's for the first time today, and over the next few days, it will grow to know him well. So that when you're bound together, your magic will recognize his and meld."

"Wait, did you say over the next few *days*?"

She nodded.

"How many days is this part going to take?"

"Three."

My eyes nearly fell out of my head. *Three days* pretending to use magic I didn't have. And there would still be nine left before Queen Amunet came into her power.

Fear rose up inside me. It wouldn't take three days for me to be found out. Only a few moments, at the most. Then they'd know I was a fraud, and they'd go after Queen Amunet, steal her power, and I'd be sent to the Trench.

"Hey." Velka took my hands in hers and gave them a squeeze. "It's all right. Magic is instinctual. You'll know what to do when you're there."

"What if I don't?" I whispered shakily.

"Rade will be with you. Today is just about trust and collaboration. You'll be fine."

I should tell her now. I should confess the way Ketet wanted me to in the Eye. They were going to find out as soon as this trial started anyway. When they realized I'd deceived them, that I couldn't help them against the Shroud . . . maybe they'd do worse than tear me apart. But maybe if I came forward, they'd be merciful. I opened my mouth—

"I'm sorry, Your Majesty," Velka said.

I choked.

She lowered her eyes shamefully. "When Keir first proposed this plan, we were all against it. An Ashoran queen was just as likely to murder us all in our sleep as she was to save us. We heard such stories about you, and I . . . well, I thought you would be completely different. After what your king—" Velka shook her head and gave me a crooked smile. "Anyway, I'm sorry. For kidnapping you and scaring you, for putting you through this ritual. And thank you. For proving us all wrong."

I took in the emotion on her face, the earnestness in her eyes, and I couldn't get the confession out. It was stupid and dangerous, but I couldn't make my lips form the words. I was greedy—greedy for her trust. For the goodwill in her eyes . . .

"What happened when King Zaid came to Kaldfold?" I asked softly.

Velka waved her hand dismissively and put on a smile. "Not today. Today is a happy day. Come on, they're waiting for us." Without giving me time to respond, Velka strode out of the lodge.

She led me to where five Shifters stood in a line, their horses at their sides, Keir noticeably absent. There was a new face among the Seven. The man I'd seen Rade speaking to before he'd taken me to the Eye of Ketet. He had brown hair the color of tree bark and a deep set of wrinkles in his forehead. Sillia's age or older.

"Senko of Crestbane," Velka offered without my having to ask. "The new Second." The skin around her eyes tightened. She certainly didn't look happy about it.

Neither did the rest of the Seven. My eyes landed on Bain first, but he gazed straight ahead, not looking at me, showcasing his profile— along with the large bruise covering his jaw and the teeth marks on his throat. Probably the reason Keir wasn't standing with them now.

My shoulders still ached, my back still smarted, and not for the first time, I found myself feeling grateful for Keir of the Wild Valley.

I climbed onto the stallion Velka designated as mine. The Shifters led the way, but instead of heading down the hill like we usually did, we went up, toward the White Horn Mountains.

A trail curled its way higher, steep and unforgiving, and eventually opened into a clearing bordered by sheer mountainsides that stretched high above our heads. There were no trees here. No ice, either—nothing except for a lake in the center.

A placid lake without so much as a ripple, despite the wind. It was still—too still. And so deep blue it was nearly black. I couldn't see anything beneath its glassy surface. Velka had mentioned water, but that couldn't . . . I couldn't be expected to get into *that*.

Like last time, the priestess was there, Rade beside her. But no crowd, save the six Shifters. Thank the gods.

I dismounted and walked cautiously around the lake to stand beside Rade, only daring to look up at him in darting glances.

He didn't appear any worse for wear from last night. His brown eyes were honey warm, and he smiled easily at me, his hand brushing mine in silent support. A foul-smelling chain was wrapped around his neck, too, and he carried a waterproof oiled supply bag on his shoulders.

"We began with Phadar," the priestess said, "God of the Sun, to guide you on your way through the darkness. Now we turn to his wife, Ketet, Goddess of Earth and Sea, for your journey through her realm of water. Ketet and Phadar, the Holy Pair. You are to emulate them here on earth, and you will begin by fighting side by side. From comrades to lovers, as our Holy Pair were." The priestess pointed at the too-silent lake. "Enter Ketet's realm together."

I stared at the glassy surface, knees trembling.

"Amunet," Rade said, gently taking my shoulders and turning me to face him. I swallowed my wince when he touched my wounds. "It's important you understand this part. All right? This lake is not a normal lake. It has existed since Ketet shaped the earth. There is one way in and one way out."

I locked my knees to stop their shaking. "What do you mean?"

"We'll enter here," he explained, "but we must exit at the bottom." When my breath caught, he smoothed his thumbs back and forth over my shoulders, sending trickles of pain down my arms.

"We'll drown," I said. Maybe Rade had magic that would help him breathe. I did not.

He nodded. "We'll need air to make it to the bottom. We'll take it from the Behemoth."

My heart pounded. "The what?"

"It's a creature that lives in this lake. Its blood will help us breathe underwater."

Tell him, Samira. Tell him right now that you can't fight any sort of Behemoth, that you have no magic, that you're a fraud. Tell him, tell him, tell him!

"The Behemoth is large. Obviously," Rade went on. "It'll smell us, like a shark. Its size will slow it down. But these will help us approach without being scented." He pointed to the pouches on his collar. "I'll use my magic to stun it, and you use yours to penetrate its scales. One sip of blood is all we need. That's all we have to do."

That's all? Dear gods, I was going to be sick. "But my power—"

"It will work," he assured. "It was the same for me when Eira blessed me. You may not have full access, but when danger arises, it will rise in return to help you. Think of it like an intention to Shaya, an explanation in your soul. When your father hears it, he'll help you."

Tell him!

"The lake will let out at the end of the mountain chain, and then it's a three-day walk back to Frostguard." He smiled at me. "We can do this, Amunet."

Tell him, tell him, tell him!

But the words wouldn't come.

I couldn't tell if it was cowardice or bravery when I nodded my head and turned toward the lake. Though, if I was honest, being swallowed by a Behemoth somehow sounded less frightening than facing the hurt my lies would bring. Coward it was, then.

Rade took my hand. "Ready?"

Of course not. But I just clutched his hand and nodded again.

Then we jumped into the lake.

FORTY

ᴧᴧᴧᴧᴧᴧᴧᴧ

SAMIRA

The water was like ice. Instinct alone prevented me from sucking in a huge gulp. And it was instinct that made my legs paddle back up to the surface.

My head slammed into a wall.

I looked up, very easily making out the sky above, could even see the Seven peering down at us. But when I touched the surface, my hand pressed flat. Not ice. The lake's surface had become a barrier.

One way in and one way out.

Something touched my arm, and I whipped around, little bubbles bursting out of my mouth in what would have been a yelp. But it was just Rade. He held up his hands in a placating gesture. *Relax,* his serene brown eyes seemed to say. *It's just me.* Then he waved me to follow as he swam deeper. My wounded shoulders throbbed as I paddled after him.

From the shore, the lake had seemed dark, but the sun managed to shine a spotlight straight through. We hovered atop a sandy cliff, and beyond that was a nearly fifty-foot drop.

At the bottom was an archway.

The way out.

I'd hoped we wouldn't really need the Behemoth, but we definitely couldn't swim all that way on one breath.

Pressure was already building in my chest as we swam toward it. A mass of seaweed stretched out of the sandy wall. Its inky leaves waved as if there were a current—but there wasn't. It felt like swimming through molasses.

I winced as my shoulders gave an angry pulse. A glance toward them showed red billowing out like twirling ribbons. My wounds had reopened, and the salt in the water was sharpening their burn.

Rade stopped suddenly and looked to the left, where an enormous shadow disappeared around a corner. I couldn't make out any distinct features other than fins and a large tail.

A very large tail.

Rade's runes glowed a deep red, and his hands twitched in front of him, fingers curling in, like he was pulling on a thread.

The shadow reappeared, drawing closer and closer, swimming into the sun's beam.

I slapped a hand over my mouth.

The Behemoth was a cross between a shark and a whale. Large black eyes on an enormous ivory body, its puffy mouth gaping open and showing off razor-sharp teeth. Nostrils were cut under each eye, and they flared as it scented us. It blew out an angry string of bubbles when it caught the manure.

But still, Rade's fingers curled, and it drew closer . . .

The Behemoth dwarfed us to practically the size of ants. I watched with horror as the ribbon of my blood made its way through the water to the monster. Its nostrils flared as it inhaled, and its pupils dilated. Adrenaline flooded my system when its mouth gaped open—

Rade's runes pulsed, and then a bright red light shot out of his hands, slicing through the thick water and crashing into the Behemoth's eye.

It roared viciously, the sound slamming into me with a wave of fury. Another blast of Rade's runes, and light was shooting toward the other eye. Rade's lips formed the word *Now!*

My lungs constricted painfully, demanding oxygen. Stars popped up across my vision, and my feet tried to kick me back up to the surface—the surface that was a ceiling over our heads.

Instinct was driving my every move, filling me with panic.

I had to do something, I had to—but there was nothing I could do—I had no magic—I couldn't stop—couldn't kill—I needed air—needed it now!

A nick. That was all. A nick, and then there would be air in that monster's blood.

Ignoring the call of the surface, I swam down, deeper, straight for the Behemoth. It hardly even noticed me as it struggled to open its eyes against Rade's assault. I reached its dorsal fin, grabbed it.

Opening my mouth, I dug my teeth into its scales. Hard. It was like biting into leather.

The Behemoth spasmed in pain, its powerful body trying to thrust me away. But I kept my hold and clenched my jaw tighter, teeth groaning in protest. Tighter. Until I felt the scales give way and a metallic taste flooded my mouth. My mind balked, but I swallowed.

Instantly, the pressure on my chest eased. I took another gulp and my vision cleared. It wasn't much, but it would be enough to reach that archway below.

Rade appeared beside me. He drank from the dorsal fin, several quick sips. Then he met my eyes and pointed down, at the exit. I took one more drink of the Behemoth's blood and nodded. Together, we pushed off and swam toward the sandy floor.

The Behemoth gave an enraged cry that filled the water with an unearthly sound, and when I glanced back, it was following us. And it was *not* slow.

I grabbed Rade's sleeve and pointed. His eyes widened, and he kicked his feet faster. I matched him, rowing my arms frantically, my wounded shoulders bleeding in earnest now, but I fought through it. Faster and faster, channeling all my strength into my legs.

Agony shot through me, and I cried out, losing the precious oxygen I'd gained.

The Behemoth had caught my ankle in its mouth. Its eyes were entirely black now. Its nostrils flared wildly as it released my ankle—only to clamp its teeth higher up my leg, digging into my knee, shredding my flesh. A cloud of bubbles burst out of me as I screamed, vision blackening.

Red light exploded, and then the Behemoth released me with a roar.

I tried to swim away, but my shoulders throbbed with each movement, and my right leg wouldn't work. It weighed me down like an anchor. There was no more breath in my lungs.

I was going to drown. I was going to die. I was going to the Trench.

An arm wrapped around my chest. Rade, hauling me toward the exit, paddling as hard as he could with one arm. The light from the archway was spotted with stars as I struggled to hang on to consciousness.

We broke the surface.

I gasped, hacked, sucked in as much air as physically possible, scrambling onto the rocks, already shivering against the horrific cold of the lake.

Rade sputtered beside me, water sluicing off him as he struggled to catch his breath. "Your magic," he panted. "What happened?"

But I couldn't answer him as pain ripped through me. I cried out and turned on my back to see the damage.

My leg was a mess of blood, and I thought I saw the white of bone at my ankle. My hands quaked as I pressed them against the wound, trying to stop the bleeding, but another bolt of agony just sliced through me.

Rade's eyes widened as they landed on my wound. "Shit!"

The pain was fading—and so was the world. I fell back against the stone floor as darkness encroached along the edges of my vision.

"Amunet? Amunet, look at me! Amunet, I need you to stay awake." He tapped my cheek, light but firm. His eyes hovered over mine, his hair a sopping curtain around us. "I have to set the bone. All right?"

I heard his words, but they didn't make any sense.

The darkness closed further around me.

"Bite this," Rade ordered. Something rough was shoved between my teeth—and then fire blasted against my ankle. Melting me from the inside out.

I lurched upright, biting down hard on the leather belt as a screech tore out of me.

Rade's runes glowed as he wrapped one hand around my ankle and the other around my knee. Wave after wave of excruciating pain radiated up my leg.

My foot snapped back into place, and the world went black.

FORTY-ONE

ᴧᴧᴧᴧᴧᴧᴧ

AMUNET

Wethai is a few days' walk north of here," Jasim said from where he sat at the base of one of Athar's statues. "It'll be risky, but now that Anwar has made a move, Prince Ilias may be in the market for a royal ally."

I gazed up into Athar's face. He had the same curling lips as Shaya, the same regal nose, but his eyes weren't slitted, and his cheekbones were rounded where Shaya's were sharp as a blade. Despite his mischievous smirk, Athar's face was soft. Open. All bits of Ketet. "We can't go to Wethai," I answered absently.

"I'll do better this time. No more distractions. And you'll make a real jinni deal so he can't go back on his word—"

"No, Jasim."

"What do you want to do?" he demanded, lurching to his feet. "Walk into the mischief god's playground? Try your chances against people with half a face or music that comes from nowhere and drives you mad? Only a handful of people have ever gone in there and lived to talk about it, Amunet, and anyone unfortunate enough to survive has entirely lost their mind."

I rolled my eyes. I knew all of that already. Dead Man's Forest and the Dry Lands had featured prominently in my tutoring as forbidden landscapes. Dangerous, deadly places, only slightly less feared than the Wastelands.

The Temple of Shaya might as well have been a world away. But that was all right. My only reason for visiting the temple was to reconnect with my father. Which I had, seeing as I had been magically transported thousands of miles away. And I'd done it by sacrificing Malik instead of Jasim. A mercy from my father.

"Shaya brought me here for a reason," I said. "He wouldn't have rescued me just to thrust me into danger. We have to find out why."

Jasim turned me to face him. "If we go in there, we might not come out."

"I know—"

"You have to live, Amunet." His fingers spasmed on my shoulders. "Nothing else matters. I can't lose—" He cut himself off abruptly. One of his eyes had swollen shut while his other one was shot through with veins of red.

I took a moment to examine him more closely. He really was in bad shape. His entire right arm was slick with his own blood. Sweat rimmed his ashen face, his thick curls hung limp and matted, and the left side of his face was swollen and splotched in purple and blue.

Concern etched my brow. "What happened to you?"

A muscle in his jaw feathered. "They left me in camp when they took you. Probably assumed I was dead. When I woke up, everyone was gone, but their tracks were easy to follow. Sara brought you to some outpost where Anwar was waiting. It took some time to stake the place out, and I probably could have done with a bit more planning, but I didn't know what they were doing to you. It's possible I wasn't thinking clearly." He winced.

He'd survived that first attack. He could have left me. Instead, he'd risked death again to save me. The words of love he'd whispered just before the night had gone to shit swirled through my mind, and my throat constricted. When I spoke, it came out in an emotional whisper. "I've treated you horribly for years, but you still . . ."

Jasim looked away from me toward Dead Man's Forest, yet I got the impression that he wasn't really seeing it. Staring through it to a different place, a different time altogether. "I have spent the last thirteen years with the Khada Guard, and it is . . . not a nice place. Everything about it is meant to harden us into ruthless warriors. I learned to wear the mask. To be ruthless, to be aggressive, to be worse than everyone else just to survive. I got so good at it that I never took the mask off. Maybe I forgot how to. It became a part of me. And then . . . I met you." He looked at me, eyes crinkling at the corners as he smiled. "You wore a mask, too, and I could see it. You wanted people to think you were ruthless, too. But sometimes your mask slips. And when it does . . ." His shoulders lowered as he gazed at me. "You're magnificent."

I shook my head wordlessly, eyes burning.

Jasim reached out his uninjured arm to cup my cheek. "I know you have your demons, Amunet. I know being a Gods-Chosen isn't easy. But beneath that mask, you are *good*. You try to be good every day. I see it."

I was a creature of the Underworld. I was a girl willing to save the world or burn it down if her creator asked her to, because Shaya was the only one who truly knew me and truly loved me. That was what I'd always believed.

But maybe . . . maybe Jasim was right. Maybe I'd concocted a mask for myself to protect me from Zaid's cruelty, from those who would use me, from those who hated me because of my father. Maybe everything I'd done—throwing a servant to the Kaldfolk, making false promises to Nasir, conspiring to sacrifice Jasim, nearly decapitating Malik—maybe none of that was really *me*. Maybe whatever goodness Jasim thought he saw in me wasn't an illusion at all. My face was still awash with Malik's blood, but maybe the creature full of rage and violence was the true illusion.

A smile lifted my lips, fragile, new, a little shaky. "Thank you for coming for me."

Jasim's eyes softened. He tilted my face toward his and pressed a tender kiss to my lips, one that lit a spark in my chest. I shifted closer, and Jasim inhaled a pained breath. I broke the kiss with a soft apology. Then I said, "We have to go into Dead Man's Forest."

"Amunet—"

"We can't trust any of the princes anymore. And this is where Shaya sent us. So it's where we'll go. Just keep your scimitar handy. Okay?" I waited for his agreement. If we were going to move forward together, then I wanted it to be *together*. Not because I had decreed it.

Jasim let out a long breath, studying the intimidating entrance. After a moment, he reluctantly nodded. "Stay close."

If we'd had any supplies, I would have suggested patching him up first, but the most I could offer was an arm around his waist. Then Jasim and I hobbled into Athar's playground.

FORTY-TWO

SAMIRA

I was lying on a blanket on the floor of a cove, a smooth slab of rock in the mountain. The lake's water didn't ripple beside me, silent as ever, and a campfire blazed a few feet away. Beyond it, stars sparkled in the night sky, the wind whistling.

Blinking blearily, I tried to sit up—but stopped with a hiss when my leg gave an angry throb.

"Easy," Rade warned from where he sat next to me, feeding the fire. He wore only a flimsy cotton shirt, and I realized it wasn't a blanket I was lying on after all but his tunic. He smiled tiredly. "How do you feel?"

"Okay." My leg tingled and pulsed, but as long as I didn't move it too fast, that horrible pain was gone. "Did you heal me?"

"The bones only. Skin will take longer."

The wounds on my knee, ankle, and shoulders were wrapped in bits of fabric, which Rade must've torn from one of the many layers he always wore. A sharp, minty smell reached my nose, and I spotted a bit of green peeking out from under the binds.

"Neem leaves," Rade said in answer to the look on my face. "Helps numb and disinfect."

"Oh." With shaky arms, I pushed myself up, careful not to jostle my leg, gritting my teeth against the pain in my shoulders. "Thank you, Rade."

He nodded and tossed another twig into the fire. "What happened, Amunet?"

I glanced at him out of the corner of my eye. But he kept his gaze trained on the fire. "The Behemoth was faster than you said."

"That's not what I'm talking about." He meant why hadn't I, Amunet Khada, used my gods-given magic to save us. "Does it have anything to do with that scar?"

I turned to him sharply. "What?"

He nodded toward my chest. "I felt it at the first ceremony. It's right over your heart. And it's old. Did something happen to you? Did it affect your power?"

I pressed my hand over the *X* protectively. When Keir had asked me something similar, I'd owed him an explanation. I supposed I owed Rade the same, given what my misstep had cost us, but the answer planted itself stubbornly at the back of my throat and refused to come any farther. "No," I said softly. "I just haven't gone through the Igniting yet. I tried to warn you."

He didn't say anything for a moment, debating. But then, like he couldn't help it, he said, "We're relying on you, Amunet. You know that, right?" His brown eyes seared into mine. "All of us, all of Kaldfold. We're relying on your power."

It will break us. Guilt ate away at my stomach lining.

He blew out a sharp breath. "Sorry, I— That's not fair of me to—" Rade fixed his face into another smile, though it didn't fully reach his eyes. "I'm glad you're all right."

I returned his tight smile and wrapped my arms around myself. The campfire did nothing to chase away the chill in my bones.

Rade cleared his throat. "We'll arrive back in Frostguard a little later than expected, but we should still have a full week to recover before the final ceremony."

That picture from the ancient manuscript of the pair bleeding out flashed behind my lids.

"It'll be easy," Rade assured. "No gigantic monsters to fight—

and no more venturing into the Shroud. The final ceremony is about struggling with inner demons. Though I suppose that might be scarier than a gigantic monster." *For the both of us.*

I let out a long breath, sagging against the rock wall behind me. "And then it'll be over." All the lying, the ridiculous rituals, the guilt, the unending questions. It would all be over after that ceremony, and I would face Shaya in the After Realm.

"It'll just be beginning," Rade corrected.

"Right. Of course."

He tilted his head to study me, the firelight flickering gently over his red runes. Then his eyes dipped to my neckline. "If you won't tell me about that scar, can you at least tell me what happened to your shoulders? Those look fresh."

Bain waiting for me in the dark, his claws sinking into my skin, blind terror.

"Amunet . . . they look like claws," he said as if he could see the memory, too. Rade's face darkened. "Tell me which of my people did it, and I will see to it that they are dealt with. You are under my protection."

My eyes flicked up to the king, at the intensity in his eyes. Though I'd been taught to fear him and his people my entire life, I always felt safe with him. Even now, with an injured leg and the closest civilization more than three days away, I was glad for his comforting presence.

I—I wanted to tell him. Not just how I'd gotten hurt, but my name, my history. I wanted to tell him everything.

But as I ran my finger over the *X* again, I heard the warning as clearly as if Amunet had shouted it in my face. Tell him, and he'll hunt her down. His intentions might be good, but Amunet's power was hers by Shaya's decree. Not his to take.

And I couldn't tell him about Bain. If "dealing" with him meant Rade would have him killed, the Seven would have to face another loss—and I couldn't do that to Velka. Plus, reliving that night meant

I'd have to think about how Keir had saved me. How he'd wiped away my tears, how he'd stood close, his breath on my neck, heat at my back, and inhaled my scent. How it had turned my insides to lava and made my pulse race. How I'd nearly run just to see what he'd do when he caught me.

I had no desire to think of that.

Shoulders curling forward, I mumbled, "I'll tell you after the final ceremony." A ceremony I wouldn't survive.

Some of the tension leaked out of Rade. "Deal."

That guilt climbed up from my stomach to lodge itself in my throat. He was looking at me like I'd agreed to save his people all over again. The rage he'd feel when he found out . . .

"Tell me about your training," he said, yanking me out of my spiraling thoughts.

"What?"

"It's one of the few things I know about you—that you trained with a khopesh. Do you enjoy weapons training?"

"Oh, um, not particularly, no."

"What *do* you enjoy?"

I looked into Rade's face, our shoulders almost touching, and found myself answering as Samira. "Bread."

A surprised laugh huffed out of him. "Bread?"

"Fresh bread," I amended. "When it's just out of the oven." I could practically see Chef Nena standing in the middle of that kitchen, kneading the dough. The flour would puff up around her until she set to digging her fists into the pile of dough, wrestling it into submission. It would suck up all the flour and was almost a living thing when she tossed it into the open-faced oven.

I'd watched Chef Nena do it many times while I'd waited with Tabia to bring my princess's tray up to her room. My voice was a distant whisper when I said, "When you crack it open, steam wafts up, straight to your nose, and that steam has a *smell*. Gods, a wonderful, homey smell. And then the taste—" I drew to a stop as I noticed Rade staring. "Sorry, that was—that was probably not what you were—"

"No, please, go on." He chuckled as he turned to face me more fully. "I've never heard anyone speak so passionately about bread."

My face heated, and I glanced away shyly. "I don't get to have it often, so . . ."

"Can't you ask for it whenever you want?"

Yes, *Amunet*, you can. "It takes water to make bread," I quickly covered.

"Right." Rade stared at me a beat longer before he turned to the waterproof oiled bag sitting beside him and rummaged around. "Now, it's not fresh," he warned. "In fact, it's probably a bit stale—and made with salt water, so it's . . ." He pulled out a hunk of bread. Thick, instead of the flat disk I was used to.

My eyes widened all the same.

That last night in Khada Palace, I'd very nearly snatched it off the princess's discarded plate. Just a nibble. That was all I'd wanted. And here . . . here was a piece so big I needed both hands to hold it.

"We also don't make it often," he said when I stared in stunned silence. "Only on special occasions. But it was left over from the Lunar Feast, so . . ."

Mama had made bread once—or at least, once that I could re-member. In my memory, there was no face to accompany the worn hands that held it out to me, but I knew she'd had a bright smile. And Baba's warm laugh had echoed around me as I dug into the bread with both hands, dipped it in whatever curry Mama had made that night.

Just hours before I'd been taken.

I'd never resented my life in Khada Palace while I was there. Or at least, not since the inclination was beaten out of me. I was lucky to serve the Gods-Chosen, to have access to water and a safe place to sleep.

But between my revelation in the Eye and this log of bread, the sound of Baba's laugh fading into the whistling wind, I loathed the life I'd had. And yearned for the one that had been stolen from me.

"Sorry," Rade said, eyes darting all over my face. "I thought it would be nice—"

"It is nice." I took his hand and squeezed, even as a ridiculous tear trailed down my cheek. "Thank you."

His smile was soft, sympathetic, and he nodded toward the bread. "Try it."

I smiled and took a bite. Despite the protection of the bag, it was damp from our swim, the crust too chewy, the inside too spongy. "It's delicious."

FORTY-THREE

SAMIRA

I fisted my hand in the fabric of Rade's tunic at his shoulder as I hobbled over a particularly large rock. The clouds blocked out the sun, and if I'd thought Frostguard was cold, it was nothing compared to the tundra of the White Horn Mountains. Their peaks created a funnel of cold air that was a near-constant blast, making my ears burn and my nose run.

Our clothing was thin, a necessity for our swim in the lake, but how I longed for a fur cloak or the unnatural body heat of a Shifter.

Keir's searing chest against my back. The hot puffs of his breaths over my lips. The burning hardness against the small of my back—

Not that Shifter.

We'd been walking for hours. Those numbing leaves Rade had wrapped around my wounds had worn off, and now each step was like a blade scraping against my ankle. The trek would've been a struggle even if I were in perfect health; the terrain was rocky, the air too thin, and the overcast sun reflecting off the icy rocks was near blinding.

At least we had conversation to help pass the time. It started with Rade trying to distract me from my pain with a funny story about the first time he'd seen Keir change forms as a young boy and had screamed so shrilly, Keir still hadn't let him live it down. He continued effortlessly throughout the day, pointing out that if we were going to be married, we ought to know a bit more about each other. I couldn't correct him.

I'd never really had someone to talk to before. My friendship with my roommate, Nadia, had been one of silent understanding, and Tabia had been nothing more than a kind face most days. This was . . . nice.

"My power is part of me and also wholly Eira's," he was explaining. "With your injury, your bones were lost. Eira helped them find each other again, healing the break. But the skin was taken. Gone, not lost. So her help stopped there."

I nodded, fascinated. I couldn't help but think of the visible bones in Keir's chest. Maybe that was what had happened to him. I could ask . . . but then I'd have to explain how I'd seen him shirtless.

Instead, I opted for "When Eira grants you power, what does it feel like?"

"It feels . . ." He adjusted his grip around my waist, pulling me closer and taking more of my weight as we went over a high groove. "Like sticking your hand in ice for so long that instead of freezing, it burns. Two overwhelmingly powerful feelings at the same time."

My brows rose. "That doesn't sound very pleasant."

"Power from the gods is a weapon. Name a weapon that feels pleasant."

"Good point." I was gearing up to ask him more about his runes when he stopped abruptly, fingers tightening on my waist, suddenly on high alert. I frowned. "What—"

"Shh." He tilted his head to the sky, scanning. "Did you hear that?"

I shook my head and looked around. I didn't see anything, but unease spread through me.

Rade ushered us behind a nearby boulder. We crouched, and I had to bite my lip as my leg gave a cry of agony.

Boom. The sound like thunder. But the clouds weren't dark enough for that. And then again, *boom.* Closer this time. There was no lightning, no rain, no impending storm . . .

Boom.

And then I saw it.

Huge, feathered wings. So white they nearly blended in with the clouds. But its violet beak and talons gave it away.

A bird—larger than any I'd ever seen, larger than any *animal* I'd ever seen—hovered over us, and with each flap of its wings, a *boom* shattered the sky. Even from a distance, I could see its feathers sticking out around its head like a mane. They rippled in the wind as it circled us. Beady black eyes scanned the earth. Looking for prey.

For us.

The runes on the side of Rade's head glowed, and then a thin, scarlet film drifted over us, pulled up like a blanket. It glinted softly in the sunlight, and when Rade looked at me, his eyes were two crimson stars in his head. He mouthed, *Don't move.*

My nails dug into the rock in front of us as I stared at the creature, willing it to move on.

Its eyes landed on us—but it seemed to look through us. Whatever shield Rade had erected must have had its intended effect, because it let out a frustrated *caw* before veering north, thunderously flapping its mighty wings until it disappeared behind one of the peaks.

I shuddered in a deep breath. "What was that?"

Rade relaxed beside me, and the crimson shield faded. "The Roc," he answered. "Only one of its kind—as far as we know. One of the many creatures that roamed free during the Time of Night. It dominates the White Horns and usually leaves us alo—" He cut off sharply.

My head snapped to him. "What? What is it?"

"Your runes," he said.

I put my hand to my forehead, a useless gesture since the runes were smooth against my skin. But when I pulled my hand back, I could see a soft emerald glow reflecting against my palm. "What's happening?"

"Your power sensed danger and reacted."

I gazed at the green reflection on my palm in wonder, wondering if he was right for one crazy moment before quickly dismissing it. I had no power. The only other time the runes had glowed was in the Seer's hut when Zarqa had bestowed the markings on me. That must be what this was. The remnants of Zarqa's magic. My runes were still fresh, and perhaps the imprint of her power still lingered. That was the only logical explanation.

You do not know yourself.

Anxiety built in my chest, growing steadily as Rade's brows pulled close together, thoughts chasing each other over his face.

"Rade?"

He blinked and shook his head. "We should be safe now. I'll keep the shield up tonight just in case." He took my hand and helped me to my feet, but the line between his brows remained, and we barely spoke the rest of the way.

We made camp in a small alcove, Rade's shield a glimmering door over the opening.

While I chewed on a bit of stale bread, Rade finally spoke. "Amunet . . ."

I paused.

"The whole point of taking on the Behemoth—the whole point of this entire leg of the Merging—is for our magic to meet. I don't understand why your magic didn't react to the threat of the Behemoth but"—a smile spread over his face—"you *can* call it up."

I nearly choked on the bread. "I can't—"

"You can! That's what this was." He touched my forehead, caressed it with his fingertips. "That's why your runes glowed, Amunet. Your power sensed danger and rose up to protect you."

"Why now, and not with the Behemoth?" I'd actually been attacked by that creature, and my runes hadn't so much as flickered.

"I'm not sure. Maybe because you were relying on my power? Or had already thought of another way around the Behemoth by biting it?" He shrugged. "Either way, it worked this time, I'm sure of it. And now that it's awakened, we can acquaint our magic."

"How?"

"Through our runes." His beautiful face was alight with hope. I hadn't even noticed that hope had dimmed after the Behemoth. The desperation, the pleading in those softly glowing eyes—his magic awake as he held the shield in place—made me lick my lips nervously.

I had no magic. He'd only be acquainting himself with the fading imprint of the Seer's power. Still, the hope in his eyes blazed, and I whispered, "Okay."

Rade shifted closer, turning his head to give me a full view of his red runes. Then he gently slid his hand behind my head and drew me in.

I let him guide me into his body, softly pressing my forehead to his temple, his thick black hair tickling my cheek.

At first, I thought the warmth of his skin was just a result of his being too near the fire. But it intensified, searing against my forehead, almost to the point of pain. I gasped and moved to pull away—

Rade dug his fingers into my scalp and held me in place. When he opened his eyes, they were beacons. And then there were matching points of green light on his cheek. From my eyes.

The heat softened. Became a delicate graze against my face. That heat was like a finger—like Rade's fingers in my hair—except *more*. So much more. Ordering each hair on my arms to stand at attention.

My eyes drifted shut as that heat traced each curve of my runes, drawing and redrawing them, before melting into them. And that melting sensation was . . . oh gods, it was the most delicious thing

I'd ever felt. It trailed across my skin, my blood, each nerve, setting it all on fire.

Rade's fingers in my hair were like an extension of that heat in my skin, which was traveling deeper, lower, and when his thumb idly rubbed the crown of my head, it was mirrored by the heat inside me. A sigh slid past my lips, and I didn't even have the awareness to be embarrassed by it.

I fisted my hand in Rade's shirt, just above his pounding heart, and nuzzled closer, smoothing my runes back and forth over his as he let out a low moan. Each pass urged that heat further into my core, until my toes curled. My fingers tingled as they released their death grip on Rade's shirt, searching for his neckline, his skin, moving with a mind of their own.

The tips of my fingers brushed his chest, and his breath stalled.

I pressed my palm flat over his heart, gasping when I heard his pulse as clearly as if I had my ear pressed to it. Its rhythm echoed, throbbed beside my own.

Rade lifted his hand and slid it beneath my neckline, his callused palm scratching gently against the top of my breast as he settled it over my heart. Beating in unison, beating as one.

That heat inside me followed his hand, circled around my heart like a dog readying for sleep. With each pass, it twined tighter and tighter, my heart rate doubling with each orbit. That finger of warmth stroked the edges of my core, once, twice, until I was a throbbing ball of need. Then it pushed in, and I stopped breathing.

Rade growled in approval. "There you are."

His words were an anchor to the outside world, offering a lifeline through the haze that had settled around me. I clung to them and peeled my forehead away, breaths jagged.

As soon as our runes were no longer touching, the heat receded. I could feel its absence like a physical thing.

Rade looked at me, face flushed and eyes heavy-lidded. I was sure I looked the same.

I couldn't find my voice for several moments, the only sound the snapping of the campfire and our own heavy panting.

"What . . ." My voice cracked. I swallowed and tried again. "What was that?"

His chest heaved as he stared at me with those luminous eyes. "Our powers meeting."

I shook my head, knowing that wasn't what it was at all. No, that was . . . that was something else entirely.

My gaze dropped to where my hand still rested above his thundering heart, just as his remained over mine. "Is that what it'll feel like?" I managed. "After we finish the Merging?"

"I don't know," he whispered back, slumberous eyes locked on my lips. "No one's done this in many years but . . . I think so."

My breath came out in a stream. I didn't know what to make of that. Whatever he'd just done had felt good. *Really* good. But also . . . slightly wrong. Because this was Rade. At some point over the last several weeks, I'd come to think of him as my friend. What just happened was too sensual to be friendly.

Maids in the Gods-Chosen's chambers were not permitted suitors. Obedient worker that I was, I had not even looked at a man for fear of disappointing the Gods-Chosen and the Seven Monarchs. But as my heart struggled to resume its usual pace, I realized just how ignorant I was.

Rade had promised he would not force himself on me, and I believed him. But he thought the Gods-Chosen was going to be his wife. How many times had I seen men stumble over themselves for a mere kiss from Amunet? And how many times had I seen those same men turn cruel when they were rebuffed? Far too many. And the way Rade was looking at me . . . I recognized that look.

Giving up my body for the Gods-Chosen filled me with dread every day, but I'd resigned myself to it. It only now occurred to me that doing so might not only include death.

As if sensing my spiraling thoughts, Rade cleared his throat and pulled away. He took a few moments tending to the fire, obviously stalling, before he finally said, "It had to be done, Amunet. If our magic didn't meet, the Merging wouldn't work. I'm sorry if it was . . . unpleasant."

I gazed at him, looking for any hidden meaning behind those words. But there was no indication that he'd noticed anything amiss with my "magic." "It was more than I expected."

He nodded, face contemplative. "About half of Kaldfolk are Shifters. Just the luck of the draw. Enhanced senses, inhuman strength, deep, unfailing loyalty. I'm not a Shifter, but after I got my runes and it became obvious I'd be king, I knew I wanted Shifters in my inner circle. I bonded with seven of them. Eight, now that we have a new Second. It felt similar to this. Not totally," he allowed. "But similar."

"We're bonded?"

"We will be when we've finished the Merging." He struggled to meet my eyes. "That was just a taste."

I digested that. "Does it leave a mark?"

He tilted his head curiously. "What do you mean?"

"Like a mating mark?"

"What?" Rade startled. "Where did you hear that?"

Heat crawled up my neck. "From Velka at the Lunar Feast. Merging sounds like mating, so I thought—"

"It's nothing like mating."

"Oh." The burn of embarrassment spread higher.

A smile curved his lips as he noticed my blush, and he huffed a laugh, a bit of the tension dissipating between us. "Mating is purely a Shifter thing. I couldn't do it even if I wanted to. Something to do with their animal spirits. They bite each other to lay claim to one another's bodies . . . among other things."

"Oh," I repeated, and coughed awkwardly. I wondered who Velka's mate was. I hadn't noticed her spending significant time with anyone in particular. But to put my burning cheeks out of their misery, I changed the subject. "So you've been through all of this before."

"A version of it," he agreed. "It's faster with Shifters. All that's required to bond with them is a ride while they're in their bear forms. It requires trust and surrender from rider and Shifter. But after each ride, it felt like I got to keep a piece of them with me." Rade rubbed his chest, as if he could feel them there. "The intensity of it fades with time, but it never fully goes away."

I studied him. Despite his words, he seemed almost sad. Even with my uncertain feelings over what just happened, compassion welled within me. I reached across and took his hand.

His head jerked up in surprise. But I just gave him a small smile, his hand warm in mine. The king glanced down at our joined hands and swallowed. "It's meant to be a marriage ritual," he said. "It makes sense that it would be more . . . concentrated." He stroked his thumb over my knuckles. "I'm sorry, Amunet. I should have known. I'd have warned you if I had."

A small smile lifted my lips. "I know."

Rade returned my smile and patted my hand. "Get some rest. I'll keep watch."

I nodded and stretched out on the ground, turning over to hide my face. Exhaustion weighed me down. Not just in my fatigued limbs, but a soul-deep exhaustion that no amount of sleep would fix. A pound added every time someone called me *Amunet* or *Your Majesty*. The result of lying with my every breath.

I was so sick of it.

Nine days. That was all the time I had left. Nine days, and then my twenty-two years on this earth would be over. Forgotten. And the last thing I would have done was deceive a group of people in desperate need of help.

With Ketet having turned her back on me and the Kaldfolk one confession away from loathing me, Amunet Khada really was the only one I had left. And for the first time in sixteen years, I scorned her for it.

FORTY-FOUR

SAMIRA

When we eventually arrived in Frostguard two days later, Siv took one look at my limp and turned into a fussing hen. She moved quickly, disinfecting and stitching my ankle before checking my shoulders, which had healed some over the past few days. Still, I was grateful for the numbing salve.

After Siv left, I hobbled to the mirror.

The girl looking back was me, but not. My cheeks no longer caved in, my collarbones no longer jutted out of my skin, and I thought with a few more well-seasoned meals, I might even have curves.

But like always, the green runes, stark against my tan forehead, pulled all my attention.

I ran my fingers over their shapes. It was like they had always been a part of me. Smooth and even, no sign of that strange glow. And no tingling.

With a sigh, I lowered myself into a chair, intent on thinking over everything that had happened in the past few days. I waited for feelings of guilt or horror to bubble up at my blasphemous thoughts about the Gods-Chosen, but they never came. All I felt was hollow. The empty center of a reed stalk just one harsh gust away from snapping.

Someone cleared their throat.

I jolted awake. I hadn't even realized I'd fallen asleep, but I must've been there awhile, because my neck ached from the odd angle, and someone had draped a blanket over me.

When I lifted my head, Keir stood in my doorway.

Instantly, I was thrown back to the night of the Lunar Feast. It felt so long ago now, and yet, I could still hear his gravelly voice in my ear as he'd buried his nose against my neck, his fingers flexing against my hips, his hard length digging into my back. The heat that had bloomed in my stomach, that had settled between my legs.

His lips tipped up in a knowing smirk that made the tops of my ears burn. But he only said, "I have a message."

No apology for waking me. No explanation for his behavior at the Lunar Feast—or his subsequent absence. I tried not to let it bother me. "From Rade?"

"Obviously," he said, and I bristled, heat banking. "The king has decided that you will dine with the Seven once you've recovered."

"What? Why?"

"Ask him yourself." And he left. Just like that.

Gods, he was infuriating. The new moon must have been an exception. But sit through a whole dinner with him? Maybe it was time for me to start praying again.

I stood outside Shifters' Lodge and fisted my hands at my sides. I'd managed to put the dinner off for several days, hiding out in my cabin as my wounds slowly healed. But by the fifth day, it was obvious to Siv that I was well enough to walk on my own, and she told Rade as much. The dinner couldn't be avoided any longer.

Rade had said this dinner was to help me connect with the Seven, to let them get to know me, so they would accept me as their queen once the Merging was over. I'd done my best to weasel out of it, but I couldn't very well say it wouldn't matter if they accepted me since I wouldn't survive the last trial.

With a deep breath, I pushed open the heavy oak door to Shifters' Lodge.

It was filled with children.

I stared in stunned silence as they ran past me, chasing each other and giggling. I recognized them from Netherridge. The older townsfolk sat at the long table, or on the extra cots that had been moved in to accommodate them all.

"Queen Amunet!" I turned just in time to see Milena come barreling toward me. She slammed into me hard enough to knock the wind out of me, my still-healing leg giving an angry throb, which I ignored as she wrapped her arms around my waist. "You're back!"

I chuckled softly and hugged her. "What's going on? What are you all doing here? Where are the Seven?"

"We were moved here while you were gone."

"Really?" Rade and I had spoken about Netherridge and the Shroud a few times on our journey, and I'd mentioned the unfit conditions of the tent, but he hadn't told me he'd already seen to it. Though I shouldn't have been surprised.

Milena nodded. "The warrior said we'd like it here, and he was right. It's a lot better."

I frowned. "Which warrior?"

"The really big one with the runes on his neck."

Keir. "Well," I said, surprise evident in my voice, "that was nice of him. Where is he now?"

"The Seven switched with us! They're in the tent."

Keir had moved them all to that small, frigid tent? It was . . . uncharacteristically kind. Although, as I thought back to his drumming at Hedin's pyre, his pleading for his people before the Lunar Feast, the kefir with honey, I thought perhaps it wasn't so uncharacteristic. A smile hovered over my lips.

I gave Milena another hug and stepped back into the night's chill.

Even from several yards away, I could hear the Seven. Their laughter and chatter practically boomed out of the thin fabric walls. I steeled myself and pushed the flap aside.

Warmth was the first thing I noticed. It had been a glacier when I'd visited Milena, but now it was toasty, as if there had been a fire burning all along. But there wasn't one.

The second thing I noticed was the distinct smell of kefir.

The Seven were sprawled in various positions. Velka lay on her back, a tankard in her hand, cackling at a joke Dalla had just told. Cano giggled beside them, while Sillia leaned against the pole holding up the tent, large arms crossed over her chest, a small smile on her face. Senko of Crestbane sat separate from the others. He kept a bland smile on his face if only to look like he was part of the group, but it was obvious he was on his own.

Keir was on one of the cots beside Bain, whose jaw had fully healed. Neither of them bothered to look at me. They were too busy chuckling together. Clearly, what had happened at the Lunar Feast was behind them.

I should've thanked Keir for standing up for me. But between his aggravating behavior and my trek through the White Horns with Rade, it had slipped my mind.

"Your Majesty!" Velka exclaimed much too loudly as she staggered to her feet. "We're so glad you came!"

"Thank you for having me," I replied stiffly.

Velka threw her arm around my shoulders and whisper-shouted in my ear, "Sit by me."

I didn't even have the chance to respond before she yanked on my arm. I dropped onto the pile of hay beside her, trying and failing to swallow my wince as the movement pulled at the still-tender wounds in my leg and shoulders.

"Oh gods, I'm so sorry, Your Majesty," Velka gushed.

"It's all right. I'm fine." I shifted to get comfortable. Despite Velka's drunkenness, I was grateful she was there. Especially when I glanced around the room and found only one other smile sent my way, from Cano.

"Hey, Your Majesty," Bain called from his spot on the other

side of the tent—not far enough to warrant a shout. "You ever try moose?"

"Excuse me?"

"Moose," he repeated, and I just stared. "As in, the animal?"

"Oh. You mean—you mean have I eaten moose?"

"I'll take that as a no."

Keir snorted into his cup. I gritted my teeth as my shoulders drew up. Keir could be kind; he could also be a complete bastard.

We didn't have moose in Ashorah. There was no reason I should have tried such an animal—never mind on a slave's limited menu. Still, I felt as if I'd failed some test.

"We're eating it tonight. You'll like it," Velka said quickly. "In fact, I'll go get it."

I snatched her wrist as she stood. I didn't bother whispering, knowing every single Shifter in this tent would hear me, but I hoped the desperation in my eyes conveyed, *Don't go.*

"I'll be quick," she assured me before stumbling out of the tent.

Throat dry, I turned back to the pack. They were suddenly all very silent, watching me, yellow eyes bright as stars. Predators observing prey. It made the hair on my neck stand up, and suddenly I was in Amunet's room again, surrounded by the monsters of every scary story I'd ever been told.

I coughed awkwardly and ventured, "Thank you for letting the others use your lodge."

Keir's gaze was made of stone, offering absolutely no insight. None of the Seven said anything, either, letting the silence gather weight. I clenched my hands so tight, my knuckles turned white.

I couldn't understand how this could be the same man who had sacrificed the comfort of his lodge for strangers—or how this could be the same man who had cradled me against his chest and looked at me with irises made of heat and want. Now he looked at me as he had that first night by the Frozen Sands. With disdain.

It bothered me that it bothered me.

Come on, Velka. Hurry up.

Sillia suddenly said, "My niece told me you were worried for the Nettheridgers." Her niece, Siv. "Why?"

"Because they were cold and scared," I answered honestly. "It's not so cold in here anymore, though."

Bain replied, "Shifters run hot." He waggled his eyebrows, making nearly all the Shifters chuckle. My gaze inadvertently slid to Keir. He raised a single brow at me, and my face burned. I swiftly looked away.

"Where are our manners?" Keir said. He grabbed a tankard that was already full and held it out to me. "For you, Majesty." He passed it down the line until it reached me. I accepted it and took a sip.

It was rancid. Like curdled milk. Sour and bitter, stinging the back of my throat. It took every shred of strength not to choke. My eyes watered slightly and I gulped it down hard. "Delicious," I croaked.

"No, it's disgusting," Cano corrected.

"Pure filth," Dalla agreed.

"Hey!" Bain gave everyone a mock glare. "I spent five weeks on that batch."

"Should've made it six," replied Senko, cringing as he took another sip. Keir laughed.

Bain turned to Sillia. "Your taste is much better than these rats'. What do you think?"

"Last time I drank one of your concoctions, I had diarrhea for a week," the warrior deadpanned. "I'm not touching it."

I couldn't help but grin, relaxing a bit—though I didn't take another sip of Bain's kefir.

Velka mercifully returned with a large plate of meat. A loud cry of celebration rose from the group, and Keir snatched the dish and yanked a dagger out of his waistband to carve it. He passed out massive hunks, which everyone accepted with their bare hands.

Moose tasted remarkably similar to cow, if a little gamier, and whatever spices had been added made it rather pleasant.

Velka pulled her piece apart. "What'd I miss? Did you already tell them about your khopesh, Your Majesty?"

"What khopesh?" Keir asked.

Velka hooked her thumb at me. "The queen's weapon of choice."

"*You* are trained with a battle-axe?" demanded Dalla, impressed despite herself.

"Bullshit," Keir laughed before I could respond. I struggled to meet his eyes.

"It's true," Velka answered for me. "Rade told me himself."

"Well, Rade is mistaken," Keir fired back. "I know a warrior when I see one. Sorry, Majesty, but you're not one."

My heart rate started to pick up even as Velka persisted, "Rade said she's got the calluses to prove it."

Sillia strode toward me suddenly, and I tensed when she dropped into a crouch and seized my wrists. She turned my palms over and frowned. "A queen's hands should be smooth. No matter the training. A mark of your luxury." Her grip on my wrists tightened, and I winced. "So why do you have calluses?"

"Because I—I trained hard—"

"They wouldn't have let you. Not this hard."

Velka was suddenly at my side. "Sillia, let her go."

But she didn't. The blaze of her eyes bore into my face.

This was how I'd be found out. By one stupid, insignificant lie. I thought about the promise I'd made to myself to fight back against Keir, but I couldn't muster up any indignation or anger. Not when I was surrounded by Kaldfold's deadliest Shifters. My eyes flicked to Bain. He'd planned Hedin's death for whatever betrayal he'd committed. If they discovered mine, they'd think up something much worse. *Oh, gods.*

"Rade said she's not to be harmed," Velka reminded, her voice a warning growl.

"Sister," Cano said softly, putting his hand on Sillia's shoulder, "stand down."

Her grip on my wrists tightened further, making my bones groan.

"It's an easy enough thing to sort out," Keir said, and Sillia glanced at him over her shoulder. He got to his feet, the torchlight flickering menacingly over the tattoos on his jaw. "Let's get the queen a battle-axe."

"What?" I exclaimed.

"Absolutely not," Velka said.

"Keir." Senko stepped in front of him. "No."

"You've been here five minutes," Bain snapped. "You don't get a vote."

"I'm not going to hurt her." Keir rolled his eyes. "Just see what she's made of."

"I think it's an excellent idea," Bain agreed.

"Shut it, Bain," Velka bit out.

"What? I'll even let her use mine."

"Even if this wasn't incredibly inappropriate, the queen is injured. It wouldn't be a fair fight, Keir, and you know it."

"So I'll go easy," he countered.

Velka bared her teeth at him. "That's not the point—"

Sillia stepped forward again, and the tent fell silent. She might be Fourth now that Senko had officially been appointed above her, but her commanding presence was respected by all. She pulled an axe from her waistband and thrust it toward me. An order.

I stared at the weapon, struggling to control my breathing. I'd never even held a weapon before. I wouldn't win a fight against a fly, let alone Keir.

But when I looked up into Sillia's dark face, craning my neck against her enormity, my throat closed up, and I found myself reaching for the axe.

Keir grinned. "Excellent."

FORTY-FIVE

AMUNET

I wiped the sweat from my brow, feet throbbing dully as pebbles dug into my sandals' thin soles with every step. When I glanced up, I spotted a tree with a strange red substance leaking from it, too vibrant to be normal sap, and my heart sank. "We've come this way before," I panted. *Three times before* to be exact.

Jasim sat on a boulder, the same one he'd rested on yesterday. Hand tight around his midsection, face pale. My brow creased with worry, but he waved me off. "I just need a minute."

I pursed my lips.

Dead Man's Forest was foggy but not dark, thank the gods. Leaves rustled over our heads, but that was the only noise. A forest this large, there should have been creatures scurrying, insects buzzing. Instead, silence pressed in, and even though we'd used the sun as a compass, we'd been going in circles. It was fucking eerie.

I took advantage of the break and felt for Shaya's breeze. Hoping for some sort of guidance. But there was nothing. Still, I didn't lose heart. He must've expended a great deal of energy to transport us, out of an iron cage, no less. He would find me when he was able.

I sat on the ground at Jasim's feet. "Let's stop here for the day."

"I'm fine." He stood, the movement stiff. A muscle in his jaw bulged as he tried to hold back a groan.

I reached for his hand and gave it a little tug. "Please. I'm tired."

My lie was hardly convincing. A small laugh huffed out of him, but he slowly lowered himself to the ground beside me. I braced him as best I could, though I wasn't sure I offered much help. I'd inspected his wounds earlier, so I knew he wasn't bleeding anymore, but each day out here, he slowed down a bit more. He needed a proper healer.

"We have to find water," he said as he rested his head back against the boulder.

"I know." It had been a few days since my last cup, and I imagined the same had to be true for Jasim. "With this much living vegetation, there has to be a water source somewhere close. We'll find it."

Jasim nodded. Then his eyes drifted shut.

Sympathy lowered my shoulders. He was exhausted. I was, too, but with his injuries, it was a wonder he'd passed the sun's zenith without collapsing.

I curled up beside him and rested my head on his shoulder, gazing out at the leafy branches and fog surrounding us. In my gut, I knew I had made the right decision leading us in here, but . . . the silence was unsettling. I wished my father's aims were clearer.

"I would take you to the market," Jasim mumbled.

I gazed at him in surprise. His eyes were still closed, but a faint smile turned up his lips. "If I'd been allowed to court you. The first place I'd take you is the Ketopolis Market. A new baklawa stall opened last year. Nena's daughter runs it."

My heart warmed as I settled back into his side. "Why would we get baklawa from the market when we have a cook who can make it?"

"Because the market is the only place you still smile." He rested his cheek against my head. "Sorry you have to settle for a creepy forest instead."

I smiled and cuddled closer. "This is much more memorable."

He chuckled. My smile stretched.

"Sleep. I'll keep watch."

He was tired enough that he didn't argue. I slipped Jasim's scimitar out of his callused hand and settled it in my lap as I trained my eyes on the crawling fog around us.

A twig snapped.

My eyes burst open.

I'd fallen asleep. Fuck!

Night had turned the trees into towering shadows. The temperature had dropped with the sun, and my breaths puffed in silvery wisps of vapor. Mercifully, the moon remained bright, chasing away the horrible dark. The moon goddess protecting me when her husband could not.

The space beside me was empty. The scimitar was gone.

My heart plummeted into my stomach. "Jasim?"

Another twig snapped, drawing my attention several paces away. Jasim's form was barely more than a silhouette, but his blade glinted in the moonlight. It hung limply from his hand, tip scraping the ground.

I lurched up to my feet and hurried to his side. "Jasim, what are you doing?"

His eyes were wide, hardly blinking as he stared into the trees. "I saw her," he whispered.

A chill passed over me. "Who?"

"Andra."

"Your sister?"

Jasim nodded.

I frowned and peered into the trees. "Where?"

But he didn't have to answer. Out of the darkness, an eye gleamed. The moonlight gilded the side of a woman's face, the resemblance unmistakable in the curve of her cheeks, the tilt of her lips. A whimper broke out of her, like that of a wounded animal.

I shook my head, bewildered. Jasim said his family lived near the dam. Dead Man's Forest wasn't as far as Ketopolis, but it was at least a week's journey from the dam. Not a place someone would accidentally venture.

The hairs along my arms rose. Something wasn't right.

Jasim didn't notice. He staggered toward his sister. "An, how are you here? Are you hurt? Is Mama here, too—"

"Wait." I caught his elbow and jerked him back.

A split second before Andra lashed out at him. Her hand swiped through air as she stumbled forward into a beam of moonlight.

Horror shot through me.

The other half of her face, which I'd thought shrouded in shadow, was nonexistent. As if someone had sliced a blade straight down the center of her body. Half a nose, one eye, one ear, a single arm and leg. Her insides were exposed along the line of symmetry, organs pulsing and bones flashing.

Below her knee, her leg ended in a fleshy tail. She balanced on it but still put her hand out against a tree to right herself after her lunge.

Almost instantly, the tree disintegrated under her touch.

My eyes flew wide. "Nasnas," I breathed.

Jasim blinked rapidly, struggling to make sense of the image. "Andra?"

I dug my nails into his arm. "That's not your sister. It's a nasnas!"

The creature hissed at us and pounced again, propelled by her tail.

Jasim moved on instinct. His scimitar slashed. Half a head hit the ground. The feminine features slipped away until a deformed monster was left in its place, with gummy, razor-sharp teeth and bulging, veiny eyes.

Jasim stared at it, breathing hard. "Holy gods."

Athar's playground.

My pulse rushed in my ears. "Are you okay?"

"Yeah, I'm—"

Branches rustled. Jasim yanked me behind him just as an inhuman cry echoed. Eyes reflected moonlight out of the trees. Another nasnas burst forward. It wore King Zaid's face, white hair almost silver under the moon, skin sagging with age, but its tail shot it forward an unnatural distance.

I balked. Jasim twisted away before its deadly touch could turn him into a pile of dust, too, then stabbed his blade through the creature's chest. It gave a shrill scream. Jasim wrenched his scimitar out, blood black as tar coating the metal.

But there were more coming.

"Run," he said. *"Run!"*

We spun around and took off blindly through the forest.

Pounding tails thundered behind us as they gave chase.

Baba, please! I shouted in my head. I had no idea where I was going and barely managed to dodge the trees that seemed to pop out of nowhere. *Please, Baba! Please, help us!*

We turned a corner—

And burst out of the trees into an unnatural clearing. Stone rose before us. Not a mountain. A wall. It stretched impossibly long to either side, blocking off an escape.

A dead end.

"Shit!" I spun around, ready to run in a different direction. Jasim stepped in front of me, scimitar brandished, ready to take on the whole pack if he had to.

Nasnas glared from within the trees, their eyes like embers against the shadows. My heart thundered in my ears. We had to do something. It couldn't end like this. It couldn't—

"They're not coming any closer," Jasim panted.

He was right. They snapped their teeth at us, growled menacingly, but they didn't approach. I pressed my back against the rock wall, cringing, bracing myself.

A few more tense moments went by. Then the nasnas gave a last resentful hiss and loped off into the fog. The night swallowed them up.

Silence blanketed us. Adrenaline replaced my blood as I waited.

But they didn't come back. "Why did they leave?" I asked, dread knotting my stomach.

Jasim shook his head. After a few more minutes, it became obvious they were really gone. He lowered his blade but didn't sheathe it as he turned to me. "We should . . ." His words trailed off as his eyes shifted behind me and widened.

I didn't even have time to question him before I felt something jab at my back. Jasim caught me as I stumbled. When I looked behind me, the breath caught in my throat.

Something grew out of the stone wall. Something long and protruding, stretching out above our heads. A curve swept up from the protrusion. Full lips emerged beneath it, and I realized the long protrusion was a nose. Two closed eyes pressed out until a whole face had materialized. Huge, taking up the entire wall, dwarfing us. It had pointed ears. And when the eyes opened, they were twin flames. No irises or pupils. Fire for eyes.

Though I had never seen one before—had never heard of one trapped in a rock—I knew what it was instantly.

A jinni.

FORTY-SIX

AMUNET

S peak," the jinni commanded in a voice loud enough to make my teeth rattle.

I swallowed past the dryness of my throat. Jinn were minions of Shaya, created by the last embers of his soul, possessors of great power. And judging by this one's size, it was ancient.

Jasim grabbed my arms and moved as if to push me behind him. But I shook him off. He gave me a wide-eyed, incredulous look as I stepped forward. "What are you doing?"

"It's a *jinni*, Jasim." A creature capable of speaking directly to Shaya. Tears of relief threatened to well up, but I choked them back as I turned to the stony face again. "Great jinni," I greeted. "It is a sincere honor to meet you. My name is Amunet Khada."

"Khada." The jinni's flaming eyes considered me. "I am only able to grant one request for you, Amunet Khada. What is it that you want?"

Only one request. I knew jinn sometimes used their great power to help mortals—usually with another shoe ready to drop at the most inconvenient time. But I was in Dead Man's Forest, fleeing for my life. How much worse could it get?

Let me speak to Shaya.

Return me to Khada Palace.

Either one of those would have been helpful. Yet they seemed too . . . small. The jinni must have been sent by Shaya directly, that was why it had saved us from the nasnas. But I didn't think my father would waste a jinni on moving me somewhere else, when he could have just deposited me there himself. Especially not one so ancient. No, Shaya brought me to this jinni so I could ask for something specific.

There was only one thing Shaya cared about.

"I want to feel my power."

"What?" Jasim grabbed my elbow. "Amunet, no, ask it to take us home."

The jinni's blazing eyes flared until I saw their light on the backs of my lids with every blink. "The power that awaits the Gods-Chosen at the Igniting," he repeated. "This is what you want?"

"No." Jasim stepped in front of me, forcing me to meet his eyes. "You'll get your power in a few days. Shaya is giving us a way out of here. We have to take it."

I hesitated. This was what Shaya wanted of me. I knew it on an instinctual level. And the anticipation rising within me . . . It was what I wanted, too. After all the taunting from Zaid's voice in my head—voicing my own doubts—and nearly a month without a single word from my father, I needed this reassurance. I needed to know he hadn't sent me into Dead Man's Forest to throw me away. I needed to know the god still chose me. And after being locked up, after being chased by creatures with half a face, I needed to stop feeling weak.

But the imploring look Jasim was giving me . . .

We were meant to be a team now. His opinion mattered to me. I'd never felt so conflicted, weighing his want against Shaya's. The scales tipped back and forth in my mind. Goodness against loyalty. Goodness against strength. Goodness against *me*.

The jinni's eyes blazed over Jasim's head. "Is this your one request, Khada?"

Jasim murmured, "Amunet . . ."

I tore my gaze from his. "Yes," I breathed. "This is my request."

The jinni's eyes flared, a flame so bright I had to shield my eyes.

It was instantaneous. A heat settled on my skin like a blanket, seeped in, melted into me. I gasped as it skittered through my chest, calcified my heart, my lungs. A fire that warmed me from within, filled me with Shaya's spirit, brimming with his strength. Nothing like the chill on Zaid's balcony all those years ago. There was no darkness, only fire. Burning and powerful and bright. My fingertips tingled as if any second flames would burst from them. It was everywhere, raw and overwhelming and oh so delicious.

This. This was what was waiting for me. Access to *this* wonderful, crackling power.

A tear leaked from my eye as I looked back up at the jinni. "Thank—"

But the face had disappeared, replaced by smooth stone again.

"What have you done?" Jasim whispered.

A yip sounded.

We whirled, Jasim's blade flashing.

People emerged from the trees. They wore plain clothes made of leather, all earth tones of muted greens and brown. Perfect for blending in with the forest. Their heads and faces were wrapped in thick fabric. In their hands, they held spears so sharp I could practically feel their bite from several feet away. Arrows were aimed directly at our heads.

But more concerning than their weapons were their eyes. They were rimmed in kohl and beamed out of their faces.

Yellow eyes.

One stepped forward. In the gap of the mask where her eyes shone out, I could make out crow's-feet. Her shoulders were pushed back, confidence radiated out of her. The obvious leader. "You have stolen from the Cirra Tribe."

Cirra Tribe? I'd never heard of such a people. And a tribe . . . that implied . . . "Do you—live in Dead Man's Forest?" Impossible. People could not survive in Dead Man's Forest without entirely losing their minds or being gobbled up by the nightmarish creatures that dwelled there.

But judging by their Shifter eyes, they were one of those nightmares.

The woman ignored my question. "Cirra grants one request every year." Cirra must've been the name of the jinni. "Only one. And every year we wish for *rain*. Cirra gives us enough for a single year and returns so we can renew that wish. But you," she seethed, dipping her chin to glare at me over her nose. "You have stolen it."

"We did not know of your custom," Jasim replied. "It was not taken intentionally—"

"It was taken all the same." Another woman stepped forward, younger than the first. "And we will have it returned to us."

Darkly, I asked, "How?"

"You will be bled," she proclaimed. "Just enough to take the wish from your blood. We will right this wrong. Your friend"—her eyes slid to Jasim—"will be left unharmed."

Fuck that. I reached for my power, intent on dropping the whole of the tribe like flies.

I smacked into a wall. My power was there, just beyond the mental barrier, but . . . I couldn't grasp it. I should be able to snap the woman's neck with a thought. But I could do nothing as she demanded what was rightfully mine. Not for a few more days, at least.

Realization settled, and I felt like screaming. The other shoe hadn't just dropped; it had walloped me upside the head.

"*I* can give you your wish," I said, strategy pivoting. "In a few days, I will have power. I'll bring your rain."

"Amunet," Jasim hissed.

The woman cocked her head to the side. "Amunet. Khada?" She huffed, as if amazed by her good fortune. "I have changed my mind." She glanced to the younger woman at her shoulder and then to her people at large. "Kill them."

In unison, they tore off their face coverings, revealing the blue markings underneath. Tendrils of blue twisted around their mouths, trailed down their necks. Skin contracted and shifted over bone, re-arranging itself. And then one by one, their spears and arrows were abandoned as they dropped to all fours, faces elongating, ears sliding up to the tops of their heads, hands becoming paws.

In the next heartbeat, a pack of hyenas glared at us. Too large to be natural.

"Run." Jasim grabbed my arm and jerked me into motion. "Now!"

We bolted for the second time that night.

Their cackles and yips followed us, their stampede making the ground tremble.

"You should've just done what they said!" Jasim shouted.

"It's my power," I gasped as I pumped my arms faster.

"Gods-dammit, Amunet!" One of the hyenas got too close. Jasim swung his scimitar. Blood splashed. The Shifter howled in pain and fell back. We ran faster. My lungs burned, my panicked breaths drowned out the howls at our backs.

I darted around a tree—and the earth vanished beneath me.

I swallowed a scream as I slid down a small ravine and hit the bottom with a grunt. Jasim slammed into the earth beside me but was up again in the next breath, dragging me after him.

A thicket of dry branches. Jasim shoved me under it and then squeezed in beside me. My nose curled against the stench of what I prayed was a foul-smelling flower and not left over from an animal, especially as Jasim smeared it all over my body and then his to conceal our scents.

Jasim put a finger to his lips. I covered my mouth to quiet my erratic breaths and stared into his dark eyes just as I had when the chimera had approached. But there was none of that false calm this time. Both of our eyes were wide, our chests rising and falling rapidly.

Thundering footsteps neared us and paused. I imagined they were scenting the air. I clamped my eyes shut. Jasim took my hand and I clutched his.

After several breathless minutes, their steps started moving again. In the opposite direction.

My eyes opened. Jasim gestured for me to wait. We didn't move until the strange stillness of the forest settled back over us. Finally, Jasim nodded.

My breath streamed out through my teeth.

Jasim flopped against the earth, not caring that he was lying in shit. "What is wrong with you?" he demanded. Blood trickled down his arm from where one of his wounds had reopened.

"I didn't know a tribe lived in here. Or that they relied on a gods-damn jinni for water."

"That's not what I'm talking about!" He lurched upright again. Eyes nearly black with his rage. "You're getting your power in a few days, Amunet! You didn't need it now."

"But I wanted it." I crawled out of the thicket and stood. My eyes landed on a stick. I grabbed it and used it to scrape the shit off. Pointless. The pungent filth clung to me. It would take a proper bath to rid myself of it. Ugh.

Jasim's gaze followed me, lips parted in bewilderment. After a moment, he stood. "It was reckless. You're smarter than that. We could have both been killed—"

My temper flared, nerves shot by two near-death experiences. "I am Gods-Chosen," I snapped, whirling on him. "But I have spent the past month and a half unsure if that was still the case, unable to connect to Shaya, hardly able to *think* past this awful itch and all the voices in my head. I needed to know that I was still chosen and that my power still waited for me. I am and it is. That is more important than a random Shifter tribe in Dead Man's Forest."

Jasim stared at me, stunned silent.

My power wrapped protective tentacles around me, bracing me.

Residual adrenaline burned through my veins, welcoming the fight. Reckless, he'd called me. I anticipated what worse names must be on the tip of his tongue.

Finally, he said, "I didn't know about the voices."

I blinked. "What?"

"I knew about the itching, obviously, but you never said anything about voices. Is that why you did it? Because the voices told you to?"

An incredulous laugh welled inside me. "I just said it was my decision."

"This is what you tried to tell me that night, before you were taken. When you said you were losing your mind, I didn't realize . . ." He cupped my face. "Listen to me, Amunet, that wasn't you. You didn't mean it. I'm going to get us out of here and then find you a healer. It's going to be okay."

I tried to push him away, but he held his ground. "It *was* me."

"You're a good person. It was a mistake. We'll find a way to make it up to the tribe so their people survive."

"Jasim, you're not listening. I made this choice because it was what I wanted—"

"You are a *good person*—"

"Stop saying that. It's not a catch-all for every—"

"It is what I believe. What I have to believe. The Gods-Chosen is *good* and *holy*—"

"*I was going to kill you!*"

Jasim jerked as if I'd struck him.

And just like that, the illusion shattered. For both of us.

I felt stupid, so painfully fucking stupid, to have missed it before. That gleam in his eye that was just a bit too bright, the insistence on my goodness, which I was a real fool to have ever believed. It wasn't true. None of it was true.

Jasim was a zealot. I'd known it in Khada Palace. Somehow, I'd forgotten it out here.

Of course Jasim didn't love me. Like Zaid had said, there was nothing about *me* worth loving. But there were plenty of excuses to be made for the oh-so-holy Gods-Chosen.

Pain fractured my heart and spiraled through my limbs. This must be what it felt like when the insipid little organ broke.

"What do you mean?" Jasim whispered.

The laugh trapped in my chest grew hotter, grew teeth, transformed into a scream. My neck prickled with the need to itch, and the power just out of my reach roiled as if it, too, was frustrated. "Candles didn't work. I needed to make a sizeable sacrifice when we got to the Temple of Shaya. *You* were going to be my sacrifice, Jasim. I kissed you and fucked you and planned to slit your throat the whole time."

He stared at me, lips parted in shock. He shook his head.

"Go on, tell me I'm a good person. Tell me that was a fucking mistake." At his silence, I continued mercilessly, wanting to feel every bit of the pain reverberating through my chest, "I'm the spawn of Shaya. I am not a good person. I am not a hero. Maybe that makes me the villain—or maybe it makes me nothing at all. All I know is that there is one creature in this whole fucking world I love, and it is not you. It will never be you. I will pick Shaya every time. The girl you've convinced yourself I am doesn't exist. When will that finally sink in?"

The brutal words were directed as much at me as at Jasim. I was so fucking furious with myself. That fragile, misplaced hope shattered into a million pieces and scored my insides on the way down.

His usually expressive brown eyes shuttered. He took each blow with the stoicism bred into him from decades in the Khada Guard. A muscle beneath his beard popped over and over. Jasim's voice was low when he finally said, "I think it just did."

His shoulder brushed mine as he moved past me. He didn't glance back as he trudged into the forest. The fog and trees swallowed him up.

I stared after him, breathing hard. I'd finally done it. I'd finally broken through.

So why did my chest ache like a picked scab? And why did I feel so hollow? Why did I feel so . . . sad?

I waited a few moments, but he didn't come back. I'd pushed him beyond his promise until he'd finally left. Just like he was supposed to. Just like I knew he would—just like anyone would—if I weren't the divine Gods-Chosen anymore.

When a breeze blew through, it sounded an awful lot like King Zaid's mocking laugh.

FORTY-SEVEN

SAMIRA

I clutched Sillia's axe to my thundering chest as I followed the Seven to the clearing among the trees, the same place Hedin's funeral had been held a couple of weeks ago—though it felt like another lifetime.

Dalla and Cano stabbed two torches into the ground as Keir tossed aside his fur cloak. He spun his axe expertly, and it whistled as it cut through the air.

I spoke through dry lips. "I never claimed to be a warrior. And this isn't a khopesh—"

"An axe is an axe, Majesty." Keir stretched his neck, his braid swinging at his back. "First blood wins."

I blanched, even as Velka shouted, "No!"

"We swore not to harm her." Sillia patted her chest. "First contact. No blood, Keir."

"Fine." He grinned at me. A predator toying with its food. "Ready, Majesty?"

"Why are you doing this?" I whispered for his ears only.

"Because I was a fool, and now I'm fixing my mistake."

"What do you mean?"

"You don't know how to use that." He nodded to the axe I was strangling against my chest. "Admit it."

I couldn't. Not without making this whole month worthless. I racked my brain for something else to say to stop this. I should voice outrage, question how they could treat the Gods-Chosen this way. I should threaten to tell Rade of their insubordination, threaten them with punishment after I was made their queen.

But when I opened my mouth, the words died on my tongue, gagged by my terror.

Velka turned to Sillia. "I am Third, and I demand you stop this."

"Well, I'm First," Keir countered, "and I'd rather not."

"Back-to-back," Sillia ordered.

Keir approached so that we were mere inches apart. I had to tilt my head all the way back to meet his sparkling gaze. In a voice so low, I almost missed it, he said, "Your heart's going like a rabbit's again, Majesty. Tell me why, and this stops."

I ground my teeth hard enough to shatter them but said nothing. The truth would kill me as much as my silence. I had no choice. I had to do this.

He shrugged. "Suit yourself." And he turned.

So did I, and when I pressed my back to his, my head cradled within his shoulder blades, my knees nearly gave out at the strength I felt there. Keir could snap me like a twig. It wouldn't take any effort at all.

But I was trapped. Put here by my own stupidity.

We walked ten paces away from each other. Heart in my throat, I faced him again. The runes skirting down his jaw and throat made him look like he was salivating.

Sillia barked, "Begin."

Keir pounced.

I'd always been fast. I was small and nimble, and when the adrenaline shot through my body, masking the pain in my leg and arms, that swiftness was the only explanation for why my head was still attached to my body.

Keir swung his axe at my torso, but I darted away, quick as the rabbit he often called me, and spun back around to see him coming at me a second time.

Again, I dodged him, swallowing a curse when my boots slipped on the icy ground and a dart of pain went through my leg.

Keir snarled in frustration. When I tried to jump away once more, he was ready. He swept his leg low, and I went sprawling face-first, my axe flying out of my hand and pain ricocheting through my body.

I turned onto my back just as he brought his blade down. With a yelp, I rolled out of the way. The large blade lodged into the ground exactly where my head had been.

Holy gods. He was trying to kill me.

"Keir, enough," Velka called.

"Don't interfere," he snapped, and her mouth clamped shut. A primal obedience.

Keir stalked toward me, and I scuttled away on my hands until my back hit a tree. "Tell me why you won't fight," he said, and kicked my axe back to me. "Tell me and I'll stop."

I clutched the axe's hilt and glanced from the tree to Keir, an idea flaring to life. I used the tree to heave myself up to my feet, pressing my back against it as I caught my breath.

"Have it your way," Keir growled, and swung his blade right at my head.

I ducked.

The axe stuck in the bark.

Keir grunted as he struggled to pull it out.

I bolted out from under him and spun to smack the flat of my axe against his back—

His arm shot out, axe free, and slammed against mine.

The weapon flew from my hand, and I didn't even have time to gasp before he poised his blade at my neck.

A tickle of pain and then a small bit of blood trailed down my throat. Just a scratch.

I didn't move.

Keir bore down on me, yellow eyes wild and hungry, just like they'd been that night in the palace, just like the Lunar Feast. He was breathing hard—whether with exertion or restraint, I wasn't sure. With a small flick of his wrist, he could slit my throat.

His nostrils flared, and his eyes darted up to my forehead, my runes. His face changed. He pulled the axe away from my throat, and I could breathe again.

But then I watched as Keir brought the weapon to his lips.

His tongue darted out to lick my blood off the blade's edge. His normally too-bright eyes guttered to a slumbering gold and flicked back to mine.

I didn't know how to describe that look. It wasn't bloodlust or even anger. It was something else entirely, and it held me captive. I couldn't look away from those peculiar eyes. They seared into me and covered the rest of the world in a blanket of quiet, the only sound my haggard breathing and thundering heart.

Then someone was shoving between us.

"What do you think you're doing?" Rade demanded. He slammed his palms into Keir's chest, knocking him back a step.

Keir said, "She's fine." But his voice sounded dazed. Soft. Not a trace of his usual growl.

Rade glanced at me, instantly spotting the line of blood on my neck. His red runes mirrored the rage in his face. "My orders are not suggestions, Keir. She was not to be harmed. What you've done is treason."

Keir blinked, finally looking away from me as he came back to himself. "Treason?"

"I am your *king*." I'd never seen Rade so furious, but his eyes were like the flames of the jinn. "Senko," he barked, and his new Second stepped forward. "Lock him up."

Keir scoffed as Senko approached. "You can't be serious. She's fine, Rade. Look at her."

Rade turned to the rest of the Seven. "If he resists, use force."

Keir gaped as he looked from Rade to the Seven, ultimately stopping on Velka. His jaw tightened. "I told you not to interfere."

"And I didn't," she retorted as she reached his side. "The king did." She helped Senko wrench Keir's arms behind his back and pushed him forward.

But as he passed me, Keir looked me dead in the eye.

And grinned.

FORTY-EIGHT

ᴧᴧᴧᴧᴧᴧᴧᴧ

SAMIRA

Your cabin's been marked," Rade said. "The Shifters can't protect you there. Come with me." Without giving me a chance to ask what he meant by "marked," he waved me after him, leading me straight to his room in the longhouse, where Sillia and Cano stood guard.

Sillia didn't meet my eyes, Cano offered me an apologetic smile, but all I could see was Keir's grin. It flashed on the backs of my lids with every blink.

He knew.

He must've tasted it in my blood. Or rather, *not* tasted it. He knew I was a fraud. He'd probably already told Velka as she'd led him away. They could be seconds from bursting into Rade's room and telling him the truth. I was no demigod, no magical creature, no one of any importance. I had duped them all.

Rade guided me to sit on his sofa and then settled heavily beside me. His gaze was instantly on my neck. It was barely a scratch and didn't even warrant a bandage. "Keir's insolence has grown beyond what I imagined," he fumed. "I am so sorry, Amunet. I should have seen it." He reached out and ran his finger under the wound. His voice was a horrified whisper when he said, "He could've killed you."

"But he didn't," I replied softly. "He barely hurt me at all."

But Rade was right, he could have. Keir could've taken my head clean off, but he'd only left a graze that would heal in a day or two. I was lucky. For now.

"Rade," I ventured, "what did you mean when you said my cabin was marked?"

He drew his hand away with a sigh. "The night of the Lunar Feast, Keir was more—out of control than usual. And he claimed your cabin. As a bear." At my blank stare, he added, "As a bear claims its territory . . ."

I blinked. "You mean . . . you mean Keir *peed* on my cabin?"

Rade cringed but nodded. "The other Shifters recognize his scent and struggle to go past it. Even Kaldfolk who aren't Shifters can feel his claim. I can only handle it because my scent was already in your cabin, but even I can't remain there very long. That's why he was sent away the morning after. Shifters are not allowed to mark anyone without permission."

I'd stayed in that cabin, surrounded by Keir's scent without even knowing it. It was hard to name the emotion that coiled in my gut at that thought.

"When this is over tomorrow," Rade said, "I . . ." He swallowed, but his face remained stern. "I will banish Keir to the Shroud."

I started. "What?"

"Before you even arrived here, he'd done nothing but spit on my orders. It's endangering all of us. He kidnapped the Gods-Chosen, for gods' sake! If he were anyone else, he'd have already been dealt with. Brother or no, I will deal with him now." Rade's eyes glinted with rage.

Keir had tried to kill me. I should be happy he would be sent away.

But the Shroud? That dark place that turned one's mind against itself, that brimmed with Shaya's malevolence? That twisted a person into a soulless ghul? That seemed like a punishment too great—especially when Keir was *right*. Every question, every doubt, every suspicion he had about me was right. He was trying to keep his king and his people safe, he had done what he was meant to do as Rade's First, and he was going to be left to go mad, to be twisted and warped into one of those ghuls, because of it.

My stomach clenched.

Rade took my chin with his forefinger and thumb and tilted it up, looking deeply into my eyes. "I'm sorry for all of it, Amunet," he said thickly. "Your abduction, forcing you into this union—and that stupid dinner."

I tried to smile around the nauseous guilt swirling through me. "It's all right."

His face was so close, I could feel his breath against my lips, fanning over my cheeks. Those kind eyes of his dipped down to my lips, and my throat went dry. That night in the White Horns rose up sharply in my mind. The low-spiraling heat when his runes had touched mine, the brush of his fingers in my hair.

The conflicting emotions that followed.

Rade looked at me now like he'd looked at me then, those brown eyes dark with want. I could not decide if I felt that same want. If it was desire that made me want to lean in or curiosity. Or guilt.

Maybe he felt me freeze, because he cleared his throat and pulled away, cheeks faintly pink. "You can sleep here tonight. My room is not marked, which means the other Shifters will be able to reach you should anything happen. You can have the bed. I'll take the sofa."

It was definitely guilt that curdled inside me then. We'd slept side by side for the last few days on the mountain, yet it felt different here. More intimate. But with only a few hours—minutes—before they discovered I had stolen a month from them, the least I could do was not steal his bed, too. Propriety, timidity, none of that mattered now anyway. "You don't have to sleep on the sofa," I said. "If you don't want to."

His eyes cut to mine.

I tucked my hair behind my ear. "The last part of the Merging is tomorrow. There's no sense in you being exhausted from a night spent tossing and turning."

Rade's gaze darted to the bed. "You're sure?"

I nodded, and limbs shaky, I padded over to the bed and slipped under the covers.

Appearing a little dazed himself, Rade blew out the lanterns, easing the room into darkness, before he rounded the bed and settled against the pillows.

The bed was large—larger than the one in my cabin—but with him lying beside me, it felt very, very small.

"Good night, Amunet," he whispered.

"Good night, Rade."

The silence crackled with tension. I wasn't sure what I was waiting for, but my muscles were tensed, braced.

Eventually, Rade rolled over, giving me his back, and my heart rate slowed enough for me to sink into the mattress.

In a way, it was a relief that Keir finally knew, that the trick was over. I let my eyes drift shut as I savored the softness of the mattress, the pillow, the blankets. If this comforting place was the last thing I would experience before the end, I was grateful for it.

Soft morning light filtered in from under the door. No one had come for me.

Maybe—maybe they still didn't know. Maybe Keir hadn't told them yet. Which meant . . .

The final ceremony. I'd complete the Merging today, on Amunet's birthday, and my normal human blood would leak out of my body until I was nothing but an empty husk.

I'd done it. Whatever happened, I'd bought Amunet all the time I could offer.

I hoped it wouldn't hurt. I hoped they'd give me something to render me unconscious before slitting my wrists. Then I could simply close my eyes in Frostguard and not wake up.

Unless Rade spoke to Keir first. Maybe that was what Keir was waiting for, a chance to speak to the king. If Rade checked on his First before the ceremony, if Keir told him what he'd uncovered last night, there would be no peaceful easing into death. It would be violent and—

Rade's arm tightened around my waist, pulling me flush against him, and my thoughts scattered. His breaths tickled the back of my neck, his nose buried in my hair, and I stiffened.

I glanced over my shoulder, but Rade's eyes were closed. He was still asleep.

I should wake him up.

But as long as we remained here, in this bed, the terror that awaited me outside didn't exist. Rade sighed in his sleep and snuggled closer, and incrementally, I relaxed. It was nice, being held. Warm and comforting. Slaves in Khada Palace did not touch, let alone hug. So when Rade curled himself around me, a small smile lifted my lips.

But then his leg slipped between mine, and his hand drifted higher over my stomach until it rested just beneath my breast. My heart kicked into motion as I tensed once more.

"Rade," I whispered.

He mumbled incoherently and shifted again, nuzzling further into my hair, his beard softly scratching the sensitive skin there, and an inadvertent shiver worked through me. His hand on my ribs moved higher, cupped my breast, and I blurted, *"Rade."*

He stilled behind me, and the world ground to a halt. My breathing was too loud in the silent room, my heart like a drum.

After an eternity of putting together the pieces of what had been happening, he pulled his arm away, eased his body back a few inches. I cringed into the quiet. Swallowing hard, I turned onto my back.

Rade stared at me across the pillow, light brown eyes hazy with sleep—and something else. He scanned my face, which I was sure was the same shade as his runes. His thick beard framed his jaw, his full lips, and his long black hair spilled over his shoulders.

He didn't say anything, and neither did I; he didn't move, and I could hardly breathe. Then his eyes dropped to my lips like they had last night, and my breath caught.

I almost pulled away, reasoning that tonight was Amunet's Igniting, so there was no more need for a ruse. But I hesitated.

This was Rade. Beautiful, kind Rade. My friend. In a few moments, he wouldn't be my friend any longer, but right now, he wanted to kiss me. The only kiss I'd ever have before my purpose was served and I was executed. I might not have felt intense desire toward him, but I didn't think kissing Rade would be any great sacrifice. In fact, it would probably be as nice as his cuddle, as the rune-touching. A pleasant memory to cherish while my life slipped away.

Slowly, giving me plenty of time to pull back, he leaned across the pillow. I tipped my face toward his and our lips touched.

It was such a small, soft kiss. Sweet. I wasn't entirely sure what I was supposed to feel, maybe something akin to the buzzing adrenaline that had surged through me when Keir had touched me during the Lunar Feast. But as Rade swept his lips over mine a second time, all I could think was that it was pleasant enough. Rade's arm wrapped around my waist and pulled me closer, reeling me into his warmth, pressing me tightly against him. He held me like he needed me, and that, more than the kiss itself, made me relax into him.

Rade smelled like cedarwood. It reminded me of my cabin. Cozy and safe. And his body was sturdy against mine. None of Keir's knee-quaking bulk, but lovely.

It occurred to me that I probably shouldn't be thinking of Keir so much when I was kissing Rade. Trying to lock down that part of my brain, I let Rade's tongue coax open the seam of my lips. His tongue swept in, and Rade moaned softly into my mouth. The kiss shifted into something less sweet and more hungry.

His hand left my cheek, sliding down my shoulder and side. He draped my leg over his waist, fitting my hips to his, his hardness digging into my thigh. I made a small sound of surprise, which only seemed to encourage him further.

Rade rolled me onto my back and made quick work of the clasps down the front of my tunic. I detached my lips from his, breathing hard. "Rade—"

"Amunet," he groaned as he trailed kisses down my jaw, my throat, following the path of my neckline as he peeled it away.

Too fast. This was too fast. I wasn't ready—I didn't even know— it was only supposed to be a kiss—

"Gods, you're so beautiful," he muttered against the X on my chest before he pressed a tender kiss to it, working his way down my chest.

My heart thundered beneath his lips as nerves fizzled through my veins. "Rade."

"Hm?" He opened my tunic, revealing my breasts. His lips were hot as he kissed down the slope of one. When his tongue brushed over my nipple, I gasped, "Wait, stop."

He froze instantly, and his head popped up. Hair curtained half his face, billowing slightly with his uneven breaths, but the dazed look of desire quickly cooled. "What's wrong?"

"Sorry, I . . . I didn't mean . . ." Fire branded my cheeks. All at once, I realized how foolish and naïve I was. I never should have kissed him, not while in his bed. "I'm sorry," I repeated.

"Oh." His eyes widened. "Oh my gods." He rolled off me onto his back, chest heaving as he looked at nothing but the ceiling. "I shouldn't have done that. I wasn't thinking."

"It was my fault—"

"*No.*" He sighed and rubbed his eyes, pushing hard. "No, it was mine. Kaldfold isn't strict about virtue, and I just assumed Ashorah was the same. I said I wouldn't force myself on you and I just did and I'm— Fuck, I'm so sorry." When he opened his eyes again to look at me, I saw sincere regret.

Mortification branded itself into my soul as I held my tunic closed. "No, please, I didn't— It was a good kiss. I just wasn't expecting . . ." I trailed off, feeling pathetic and stupid, stomach curdling like months-old kefir.

It was true that Ashorah encouraged virtue among its women, but Amunet had never listened to those rules. She would have handled that so much better. She certainly wouldn't have shrieked in Rade's ear right after he'd called her beautiful.

This would be the memory I'd carry to the Underworld with me. Seemed about right.

I wouldn't need a betrayal to ruin our friendship; I had a sinking suspicion I'd accomplished that all on my own.

Rade looked like he was going to say more, but the door clicked open, followed by a startled, "Oh!"

I turned to see Velka standing there, gaze averted awkwardly. "Sorry, I didn't— I was told to come get you. Final preparations, my king."

I saw the scene through her eyes. The two of us breathless, Rade on his back, my unbuttoned tunic held together by my fist. The heat in my cheeks went up by several degrees.

"Amunet?" Rade ventured cautiously, his gaze burning into the side of my head.

I smiled flimsily through swollen lips without looking at him. "Go. I'll be all right."

"Are you sure?"

"Yeah."

He hesitated a moment longer. But a glance at the semi-open door, and Velka waiting behind it, made him think twice. He grazed his fingers over my hand. "We'll talk later?"

There would not be a *later*. But I said, "Of course."

He gave me one of his crooked smiles and headed to the door. He paused. I busied myself with doing up the clasps of my tunic to avoid his gaze. He sighed before his footsteps thumped down the hall.

"Okay if I come in?" asked Velka.

"Of course." I flopped back on the pillows, wanting nothing more than to bury myself under a pile of them and never see the surface again.

Velka shut the door and approached. "You all right?"

"We were just . . ." I gestured vaguely with my hand before I let it drop to the mattress. "I reacted badly."

Velka nodded sympathetically and perched on the edge of the bed. "When Bain and I were first mated, I'd yelp every time he touched my butt."

I shot straight up, pity party momentarily stalled. "*Bain* is your mate?"

"Yeah." She cringed. "Long story."

"I thought you hated him."

"I do sometimes. Most of the time." She laughed, a tired sound. "Thin line between love and hate."

I gaped. There had been a strange dynamic between them, which I'd noticed my very first night here. They were always watching each other, but I'd thought their glances seemed veiled with hostility. I wondered what had caused that rift between them. I opened my mouth to ask one of a dozen questions.

But Velka said, "Forget about Bain. I wanted to apologize, Your Majesty. Again."

I blinked. "For what?"

Her tattooed fists were clenched on her thighs. "I tried to stop him. Really, I did. And believe me, Keir will be punished accordingly. I'll see to it myself, if I have to. Sitting in a cell in the mountain is just the start."

"That's where he is?" I confirmed. "In the mountain?"

"Much deeper in the mountain than we are now," she assured me. "Rade's given strict instructions that no one is to see him until after today."

I stilled. "He hasn't said anything?"

"No. Didn't say a word the entire night I was on guard. Oddly quiet by Keir's standards. But he knows he overstepped. He's probably coming up with a scheme to get out of whatever punishment the king has in mind for him."

He hadn't told anyone what he'd tasted in my blood.

Amunet would get her powers by sundown. And I would live just that long.

My doubts, my worries, what just happened with Rade, none of it mattered. When I perished during this last ceremony, Rade would realize Keir was right, and he wouldn't be exiled to the Shroud. Everything was going to be all right.

All I had to do was die.

FORTY-NINE

SAMIRA

I stopped by Shifters' Lodge to say goodbye to Milena. Of course, she didn't know I was saying goodbye, and I did my best to keep my face from showing any distress. If the little girl noticed the stiffness to my smile, she didn't let on as she rambled about her new friends, how much nicer her old bed had been than the one she slept on now, and offered to show me how to make my own Ketet doll. I smiled the whole while, furiously battling the burning in my eyes.

I was going to leave her. I was going to die and leave this poor little girl behind. That fissure in my heart spread until it was a full chasm. But I couldn't explain any of it to her. So I just gave her a hug and told her to be good before returning to the longhouse.

Rade was waiting for me beside his antler throne, dressed in a white tunic and trousers nearly identical to my dress. Gold trimming along the neckline and hem, with little bells tinkling brightly from the belts around our waists. Even the braids in our hair were the same, albeit mine were much shorter.

We looked exactly like the drawings in the book. A bride and groom.

My cheeks warmed instantly, embarrassment rising again. But Rade just gave me a kind smile, the same he'd always given me, and held out his hand. Tentatively, I took it.

He squeezed it and whispered, "Ready?"

The band around my chest loosened marginally. He wasn't upset. I hadn't ruined this friendship. Yet.

I might not have a romantic kiss to ferry me to my death, but at least I'd have relief.

The priestess stood in front of twin spreads of blankets on the floor, with pillows laid head-to-head. Beyond her, the longhouse was filled.

All of the Seven—minus Keir—stood against the wall, eagle-eyed. The rest of Frostguard occupied the seats at the two long wooden tables or sat on the straw-littered floor.

The priestess faced the congregation, dreadlocks pulled into a knot at the nape of her neck. "One ceremony to awaken, one to acquaint, and one to bind. Today, we bear witness to the Merging of King Rade of Frostguard and Queen Amunet Khada of Ashorah."

The crowd's applause echoed the thundering in my chest.

The priestess went on. "In this ceremony, you will purify your magic by venturing into the Mirror Realm and ridding it of your mirror self—your qareen."

My head jerked up.

Qareens, our mirror doubles, which made the opposite decisions of those we made in this realm. Evil creatures who were always looking for a way to switch places with their hosts.

Why had Rade painted this ceremony as the easiest? Defeating my qareen sounded terrifying. If I failed, it would mean my qareen was free in this realm to wreak all sorts of havoc and evil while wearing my face.

"It's all right," Rade murmured beside me. "I'll cast a spell to find our qareens. Once we enter the Mirror Realm, they will be shackled and waiting for us."

I nodded. That was something at least.

Rade closed his eyes, and the runes along his temple lit up. He stayed like that for several minutes, lips twitching as he mumbled words to Eira. Eventually, his eyes opened and his runes quieted. He gave the priestess a nod. The qareens were handled.

The priestess handed Rade a cup, which he drank from before passing it to me. I took a gulp, cringing at the sour taste. The priestess took it back from me and said, "Please, lie down."

Rade reclined on one of the blankets while I took the other. The top of his head grazed mine, and it was a small comfort.

The priestess's runes glowed as she lifted her arms, palms hovering over us. "Time works differently in the Mirror Realm," she warned us. "Days there are mere hours here. When you awake, it will be as if no time has gone by, but your magic will be at its purest form. Then I will be able to bind you together."

Just a few seconds. That was all. And Rade would be with me.

I sent one final prayer of strength up to the gods, hoping they would listen just one more time, as darkness claimed me.

FIFTY

AMUNET

Dead Man's Forest felt far more menacing without Jasim. The fog slithered over the forest floor, slow and unhurried. I'd barely slept the past couple of days, my senses constantly on high alert, and it was starting to take a toll.

There was no one to rely on now but myself.

Loneliness shadowed my every step. Even at my most isolated, Jasim had always been there. Even when I thought him dead, he'd worried for me, defended me, rescued me. For that short while I'd gone willingly into his arms, I'd felt . . . happy. I cursed myself for being so fucked up that I'd lost that. Why couldn't I have just asked the jinni for what Jasim wanted? Why couldn't I be the sort of person who sacrificed? I knew *how* to do it, but why . . . why couldn't I *want* to?

With every blink, I saw the look of utter devastation on Jasim's face. The way his eyes had widened, how that spark of adoration fizzled out and died. The tense set of his shoulders as he walked away.

I hoped he'd find his way out of here. I hoped he made it back home and lived a good life. That he found a girl like the one he'd tricked himself into thinking I was and she met his six sisters and mother and they became a family. Maybe, if he was happy, the ache in my chest would go away.

As the days wore on, my tongue stuck to the roof of my mouth, my throat clicked with every swallow, and hunger gnawed at my stomach lining. Deep down, I knew that if I ran into a nasnas or another tribe now, I'd be dead. I couldn't even outrun a snail in my condition. I had to resort to lapping up what water I could from wet pools in the mud left by the fog. Like a dog. Just enough to keep me going but nowhere near enough to actually chase away the burn of my dry throat. Every step was on unsteady legs, head pounding both from dehydration and the sound of talons clawing against glass.

Why am I here, Baba? Shaya never responded, but that didn't stop me from trying. *I thought it was for the jinni, but that had nearly resulted in my death. You must have another plan. Please, show me what it is. I don't know how much longer I can last . . .*

I'd lost track of the days. Perhaps there was a single day left until the Igniting, perhaps there were weeks. Both options seemed far too long.

I needed water and I needed it now.

My stomach suddenly pitched hard, and I threw my hand out against the nearest tree as I vomited pure bile. It burned my throat and made tears burst from my eyes. Even though it was hot and humid, tremors racked my body, a chill that wouldn't leave. I leaned my sweaty forehead against the tree and drew deep breaths.

Baba, where are you? Help me. Please.

"Now, isn't this a sorry sight."

My head snapped up.

A man leaned against a tree some feet away. Though *man* didn't seem quite right. There was an otherness to him, even in the casual cross of his lean arms over his chest. His movements were too sharp, almost birdlike. His head canted from left to right, too fast, making his dark curls flop back and forth over his round, tan face, the sun catching the blond highlights. "All that calling for Father, but what if he'd found you like this? Do you think he'd be pleased?" He shook his head sadly, orange eyes beady as they scanned over me with disapproval.

"Where . . . where did you come from? Who are you?"

He put a hand to his chest as if wounded. "You cut deep, Sister." Then he pushed off from the tree, and large feathered wings unfurled from his back, curling up toward the crown of his head, blocking out the sun and dousing me in shadow as he approached.

Sister. He'd called me Sister. And I knew those hawk features. I'd passed statues of him on my way into Dead Man's Forest. This was . . .

"Athar," I breathed.

The God of Mischief's lips quirked up in a smirk at once amused and malicious. "In the flesh."

My stomach caved in.

A brush of a breeze, a rush of power, that was all the contact I had ever received from a god. Never had one stood before me. Wonder, excitement, awe all warred for attention. But it only took a few seconds for each one of them to be drowned out by fear.

Dead Man's Forest, Athar's playground. I'd already survived two of his twisted games—the nasnas and that tribe—but I very much doubted I'd manage against the god himself. Not with my mind and body already in shambles.

His silver breastplate glinted in the afternoon sun as he swept his arm toward the trees in a dramatic flourish. "Shall we?"

I took an instinctive step back.

Athar's head canted to the side. "You ask for help and then reject it?"

"I asked for *Shaya's* help," I replied.

He laughed, a squawk of a sound. "You're a rude little thing, aren't you. Instead of delivering Father's message, I ought to just leave you to my friends. I think I heard that fun little tribe skulking about not too far away."

My eyes narrowed. He was baiting me, dangling Shaya in front of me like a carrot. I knew better than to engage with Athar's tricks in this place, let alone the god himself, but my power roiled violently at my fingertips, and suddenly I found myself asking, "What message?"

The corners of Athar's eyes crinkled. "A visual one. Which

brings us back to . . ." He gestured to the trees again, one eyebrow raised in challenge.

Athar. My brother. Here. A thought as mad as a dead king's voice in my head.

I had to be hallucinating. That was the only explanation. I wished Jasim were there to tell me. Nothing good would come from listening to a hallucination in Dead Man's Forest.

Yet my power continued to writhe, slamming against its confines, begging me—no, ordering me—to go with him. So desperate that I actually staggered a step forward. Then another. Yanked so viciously, I thought it might rip me in two.

"There's a good girl," Athar said.

My power came from Shaya. It wouldn't lead me into danger. At least, that was what I told myself as I obeyed it and followed my brother.

The God of Mischief led me to a clearing bordered by palm trees—healthy, with lush green leaves. Within their circle was a large expanse of black sand as dark as the obsidian candle I used to pray with.

Athar sauntered into its center and then turned to face me impatiently, hands on his hips. For the first time, I noticed he had talons instead of nails, sharp points that clicked against the metal of his armor. "You coming or not?"

Panting with barely restrained nausea and exertion, I gritted my teeth and crossed the sand, the grains sliding beneath my feet like water.

Athar gazed down at me, eyes like two sparking embers. Anticipation seeped out of him, which only filled me with more trepidation. "What is it?" I asked. "What message does Shaya have for me?"

He intoned, "See why you were chosen."

I waited. Brows high, sun beating into my bare scalp. But Athar said nothing more. "That's it?"

"Rude *and* entitled. No wonder."

"No wonder what?"

Athar merely grinned and waved at me. "Have fun, Sister."

"What are you—" But then I realized Athar was growing taller. Looming over me.

No, wait, he wasn't growing.

I was shrinking.

I looked down as the sand swallowed my ankles. "What—" I yanked, but it was like my feet had been glued in place. No matter how hard I pulled, I couldn't get my feet to budge even a fraction of an inch.

And the sand was climbing higher, almost to my knees now.

"Help me!" I demanded.

"I am."

"Athar!"

"See why you were chosen."

"I don't know what that means! Get me out of here or I'll—"

"Don't you trust our father?"

I paused in my struggle, the sand at my waist.

Of course I trusted Shaya. I'd spoken to him almost every day of my life. I knew him. He hadn't abandoned me. Not when Anwar held me captive. Not when the nasnas had been after me. He'd brought me to this place. Not for the jinni but for *this*.

I fought the instinctive panic that rose with the climbing sand and said, "Yes."

Athar's teeth flashed as the sand moved up my chest to my neck, the weight of it crushing. So similar to my nightmare, that suffocating darkness, the way it stole my breath. But I wasn't alone this time. My brother was with me. My father had sent him. I'd be okay.

I repeated that to myself again and again as the sand closed over my head.

FIFTY-ONE

SAMIRA

A clear blue sky stretched above me, broken only by the sphere of the blazing sun. My skin was instantly slicked with sweat, the humidity a physical weight on my body.

But the stones beneath me were cool.

With a frown, I sat up.

The floor was made of solid limestone cubes—a single tile as large as my whole body. Twin marble columns stretched far above me, bordering a doorway with doors that were no longer there, reaching for a ceiling that didn't exist.

I spun around and saw a crumbling statue of a beautiful woman with long braided hair, her left eye sure and strong, her right eye covered with a patch.

Ketet.

Beside her, limestone stairs led up to nowhere, the second floor having fallen apart a long time ago. A small pool sat at the bottom of the steps, at Ketet's feet. Serene and still enough for the sun to be reflected perfectly off it, like a mirror.

This was a temple. One that hadn't been used in centuries, by the looks of it.

"Rade?" I called. But the temple was utterly deserted. No qareen. No Rade.

I got to my feet—and glanced down in surprise. My injured leg no longer hurt; the other one did. I pulled up the hem of my dress to reveal the wounds on my ankle and knee, but they had all switched to the opposite leg.

My hand immediately dropped to my chest.

The scarred *X* was still there, but it wasn't over my heart; it had moved to the right side of my chest. A quick inventory told me the claw wounds on my shoulders and lash scars on my back had also shifted.

The Mirror Realm. Everything was reversed.

A cough sounded behind me.

I whipped to the front of the temple.

A figure stood in the entrance, a mere shadow with the sun at their back, leaning heavily against the doorjamb, breathing hard.

My qareen. Though not shackled, like Rade had promised, it didn't appear to be in the best condition. If I surprised it, maybe I could—

The figure stumbled forward, face coming into view, and my brows knit together. "Keir?"

Rade's First didn't respond as he brushed past me and dropped to his knees in front of the pool, plunging his hands into the water and gulping down handful after handful.

His tunic gaped open, sweat stains soaking through nearly every inch of the fabric. His sword was sheathed down his back, but the makeup that usually painted a mask around his eyes was faded and smudged, revealing sunburns all over his cheeks and forehead.

"Keir, how are you here? Rade said he . . ."

"Locked me up?" he gasped between swallows. "He did. One minute I'm in a cell, the next I'm waking up in the sand. Thanks to your blood, I assume."

"My blood?" He'd tasted it just hours before the ceremony. My eyes widened.

"It tied us together somehow," he said as he continued to drink.

"Did you know that would happen? Is that why you tasted it?"

"Nope. Just lucky."

I recalled that image of the bride and groom bleeding out on the altar. Blood did seem to be the key to this last leg of the ritual. My blood in Keir's system must have dragged him into the Mirror Realm with me. A man who, not twelve hours ago, had tried to take my head off with an axe.

Great.

But that wasn't my most immediate concern. I glanced back to the entrance of the temple. "Is Rade with you?"

He paused, water dripping down his chin, and looked around as if just now realizing. "He's not with you?"

I shook my head, stomach tightening.

Water splashed into the pool as Keir dropped his hands. He looked around. But there was nowhere to hide in this crumbling temple. "Shit."

My boots thumped quickly against the limestones as I crossed to the dilapidated doorway and peered out.

Rocky mountains and dunes. And nothing else all the way to the horizon. "Keir," I ventured, "how long were you out there?"

"A day."

Which meant I'd been asleep for a full twenty-four hours—at least as this realm counted time. My heart plummeted.

"Rade!" Keir shouted as he climbed the stairs to nowhere and called at the top of his lungs, *"Rade!"* His voice echoed over the desolate landscape. There was no response. He swore again and jogged down the steps. "Stay here," he ordered.

"Wait, where are you going?"

He didn't respond as he staggered back out into the desert.

"Keir!" I ran after him. "Keir! Wait!" He ignored me, hand over his eyes as he strode forward. But my steps slowed as I looked around. These dunes, this sand. I'd seen them before. "I know this place," I murmured.

Keir did stop at that, squinting in the brightness. "What?"

"The fortune Zarqa gave me. She brought me here." I spun in a circle as I took it all in. Everything was the same, down to the sun's heat beating on the top of my head, the rough grains scratching against my shins.

"Here?" Keir repeated. "She showed you the Mirror Realm?"

Out of fire were you born, out of water were you found. I didn't see fire or water, besides the pool at the base of the stairs—

The amulet. There had been an amulet, too. Maybe if I found it, it would get us out of here. Or show us where to go.

I crouched to the sand and started digging.

"What are you doing?" Keir asked.

"Looking for the amulet."

"Right. Of course. The amulet." Keir shook his head and trudged away.

In the vision, I'd emerged from the sand with an amulet. But finding such a small object in tons of sand would be impossible.

Suddenly the hair on the back of my neck stood up. I turned to look over my shoulder.

Nothing. Just more desert.

And yet . . . something called to me. I shielded my eyes against the glare and squinted. Heat waves distorted the horizon, but I thought I saw something glint. It couldn't be the amulet, of course, not at that distance. Still . . .

"Keir." I scrambled up to my feet, going after him. "Keir, you're going the wrong way."

"Zarqa give you a map for this place, too?"

"Keir." I grabbed his arm and yanked.

He turned around impatiently. "Rade—"

"Rade isn't in that direction."

"How could you possibly know that?"

"I—I don't know." I glanced over my shoulder again. The horizon was undisturbed, but I felt that same compulsion to head that way. "You just have to trust me."

"Trust you?" His eyes blazed hotter than the sun. In a flash, he'd drawn a dagger and pressed its serrated edge to my throat. When I tried to jerk away, his hand grabbed the back of my head and held me in place. "*You* are the reason he's out there," he snarled. "You lied. To *all* of us. I should kill you right here." Keir's eyes shone with undiluted rage, and the dagger was sharp against my skin. Any more pressure and he would draw blood.

I was right, then. My blood had proven I was not the queen.

But I wasn't scared. "You won't kill me," I said. Perhaps foolishly, but I couldn't help thinking this was the second time he'd threatened to kill me in as many days, and if he'd really wanted to, I would already be dead.

His eyes bored into mine, trying to make me burst into flames with just a look. I held my ground, not even blinking.

Then his lips quirked up in a menacing grin. "You're right. I'll let Phadar do it instead." Just as quickly as he'd seized me, he dropped his hands. I drew in a shuddering breath.

"I'm going to say something to you that no one has ever said to you before, Majesty." He leaned in, getting right in my face. "You're on your own." He waited a beat, letting that sink in, before he turned and kept walking.

I stared at his back, heart thundering. I'd always been on my own. But that was going to change when I died. Whether I ended up in the Paradise Fields or the Trench, I wouldn't be alone. But if I died out here and my qareen managed to get free, there was no way I'd make it to the Paradise Fields. Shaya wouldn't hear a word of my pleading. I'd be responsible for whatever horrors my qareen carried out, and there would be no chance for my redemption. Not to mention if Rade died out here because of me—

My spiraling thoughts froze as my mind caught on one word Keir had said. One very important, very specific word.

Majesty.

He still thought I was Amunet.

"You don't know," I yelled. Keir was already several feet away. He didn't stop. I called louder, "Whatever you tasted in my blood, you don't know all of it. There's more!"

He froze without facing me.

I licked my dry lips and dared to approach. "I'll tell you."

Keir turned, body wound tight. His yellow eyes narrowed, tracking my every step.

I stopped a foot away from him. "I want to find Rade, too. But who knows how long he's been out there on his own? He'll need water, food—if we just charge out there, we won't do him any good. We need a plan. So I will tell you the truth." I fixed him with a stare. "If you continue to uphold the order you were given."

"And what order was that?"

"To protect me."

His brows lowered.

"Rade ordered you to guard me that first day. Swear that you will until we kill my qareen."

"Let me get this straight. Your bargain is to tell me what I've already figured out in exchange for helping you continue to deceive my king."

"You haven't figured anything out."

"I know you don't have any magic." Keir's eyes glittered triumphantly. "You're mortal, Majesty. Chosen by no god. You've put all of my people in danger—"

"Like I said"—I crossed my arms over my chest—"you haven't figured anything out."

He scanned me from head to toe, and I could see the calculations in his eyes. Trying to figure out what other lies I had told, what else he needed to know to keep his king safe. "New deal," he countered. "Tell me now, and if I believe you, then I'll help you."

"No."

"Have it your way." He turned to leave again.

"Kill me," I blurted, and he stopped. "When it's all over, execute me in whatever way you like. Gut me with your dagger, behead me, hang me. I won't fight you or even speak a word in my defense." *Because I'll already be bleeding out of my wrists by then.* "But help me now. For Rade."

Keir studied me a moment longer, a muscle in his jaw flexing furiously under his runes. But I saw the decision in his eyes before he snapped, "Fine." He brushed past me as he returned to the temple.

I gazed after him, breathing hard with relief and anger, eyes drifting to the horizon again.

There was nothing within those heat waves. No indication that it was the right way to go. But that strange feeling stirred in my chest, drawing my attention beyond the crumbling temple.

Stuck in a deserted wasteland with Keir was about as bad as it could get. I'd spent the last month doing everything for the Gods-Chosen, but if these were my last moments, hours, days in this world, I would use them to do what I could for Kaldfold, for Rade.

And Rade needed his strongest warrior. With my qareen lurking somewhere out there, I did, too.

Even if that warrior would be plotting ways to kill me the whole time.

FIFTY-TWO

〰〰〰〰〰

SAMIRA

I stood at the top of the staircase, staring hard to the west, at that inexplicable metallic glimmer, while Keir tried to figure out how to carry water without a canteen, muttering curses to himself the whole while. But he'd made it very clear he didn't want my help, and I was content to watch him struggle.

Rade's power came from the Goddess of the Lost, so no matter where he'd been dropped in this place, he should be able to find his double. He might've thought I'd done the same and already returned to Frostguard. In which case, Rade might not even be in the Mirror Realm anymore. Or maybe he'd asked Eira to help him find me. Maybe he was headed this way right now.

When I'd voiced that possibility to Keir, he'd dismissed it. "We can't just sit here and wait for him to *maybe* turn up," he'd said.

Though I loathed admitting it, he was right. Rade could be lying helpless in the sand somewhere, slowly roasting under the sun's flames. Something had obviously gone wrong. Not waking up side by side with our qareens bound at our feet was the least of our concerns. There could be dangerous creatures out here, and with Rade all alone . . . We had to move fast.

There was sand and gravel in all directions. As far as I could tell, the abandoned temple was the only thing in this wasteland. Though that compulsion drew me to the west, I knew better than to insist without some proof to show Keir. Intuition certainly wouldn't be enough. Which was why I'd trained my eyes westward, trying to decipher—

I straightened as it suddenly occurred to me. Miles and miles of sand, a large dirt-encrusted mountain, and that glinting. A reflection. A *roof*. Right where it was supposed to be.

"Keir!"

He'd taken off his boot and dunked it in the water, the clear liquid streaming over the rim. A sorry excuse for a canteen. His frown suggested he thought the same. But he looked up when I called. I waved him over, and he climbed the steps to stand beside me.

"Look." I gestured to where the sun winked off the metal roof.

Keir's brows drew closer together. "Another temple?"

I shook my head. "Ashorah."

He stilled as he took in our position, making quick calculations, before his eyes settled on the horizon again. "If you're right," he said slowly, "that means we're—"

"In the Wastelands." My heart gave a fearful kick.

His face tightened. "Humans can't survive more than a couple of days in the Wastelands."

"I know." King Zaid had nearly died here four decades ago, saved only by his bargain with the jinn. "Keir, if Rade is out there . . ."

"Fuck." Keir whirled around and smacked his palm into the nearest column. The *boom* echoed out over the desolation. He kept his head lowered, powerful shoulders heaving up and down as he struggled to stay calm.

Then he drew a purposeful breath through his nose and schooled his features as he turned to me. "Rade is lost. So Eira will find him." He stated it like it was a given, nodding several times, reassuring himself. "If he hasn't killed his qareen yet, she'll have guided him toward Ashorah, too. He might already be there. We'll go that way. Either we'll meet Rade on the way, meet him there, or we can stock up in the city before we conduct a more thorough search for him.

Gather food, water, camels." He crossed his arms as he did the math. "Under normal conditions, that would be a two-day journey, but with the heat and the sand, I'd say our travel time will be doubled."

"We'd go faster if you shifted."

His head snapped up, and I cringed. "Absolutely not."

"Keir, if Rade—"

"No." A hammer falling down, ending the argument.

Part of me wanted to shout at him that it didn't matter. That we could be risking Rade's life—not to mention our own—by spending more time in the Wastelands. That we didn't know what sorts of creatures lived in the Wastelands or the Mirror Realm.

That whatever King Zaid had done to the Kaldfolk had absolutely nothing to do with me and that he didn't have to be so remarkably horrible every chance he got—especially when I was spending the last few days I had trying to save *his* king.

"Say it," Keir dared. He stepped closer, that challenge shining in his yellow irises. "I can feel you censoring yourself. You've got something to say, say it."

"Fine. I think it's stupid to risk death—ours and Rade's—instead of shifting."

"He's not going to die."

"But if he does—"

"He *won't*," he snapped, voice dipping to a threatening growl.

"I know about the bond," I said, and felt slightly victorious at his surprised blink. "And I don't particularly want to be tied to you, either. But I think it'll be worth it if it means getting out of here faster."

"What you think doesn't matter," he retorted. "You are not entitled to the bond, and I refuse to let you have it. Eira will keep Rade safe, and we will walk. End of discussion."

We stared off for another few moments, both our glares strong enough to melt flesh from bone. He was being proud and stubborn, and it was going to get all three of us killed.

Finally, I bit out, "We'll need water."

"We'll use our shoes."

"Our feet will burn on the sand."

"Then we'll burn our feet." He slipped off his other shoe and headed back for the pool.

By the time Keir allowed us to stop walking, the pads of my feet were a blistered mess. I'd only hissed with that first step onto the simmering sand, but I'd gritted my teeth and choked back any other sound. Contrary to Keir's belief, I had experienced plenty of pain in my life. I wouldn't give him the satisfaction of thinking I couldn't handle it.

We trekked through the Wastelands well into the night, making the most of the hours without the sweltering heat, and some of the tension bled out of my body as the sand cooled. But like this place was some cruel joke, once the sky darkened, the temperature plummeted. I suddenly wished Keir had his fur cloak. I kept my arms crossed tightly over my chest, but with no help from my flimsy dress, I couldn't stop shivering.

It wasn't until the full moon shone brightly that Keir finally slowed. "We'll need to start again before the sun is up," he said. "But we can rest a few hours."

I dropped to the sand without a word, carefully placing my water-filled boots beside me, and drew my knees as close to my chest as possible. Every inch of my skin was sticky with dried sweat, and I could still feel the hot touch of the sun on the top of my head despite the chill.

Keir lowered himself easily. If it weren't for the vicious sunburns marking every visible part of his body, I would've thought he was absolutely fine. With an exhausted sigh, he turned to me. "How much do you know about this place?"

I shrugged. "Not much."

"Your king nearly died out here. Surely he shared some tips for staying alive."

I gave him a bland look. "You know how he stayed alive."

"He didn't tell you anything that might be helpful? Some place he took shelter, maybe? Or what food he scavenged?"

I'd been racking my mind for those same answers for hours, searching the recesses of my memories for any tidbit that could tell us where to go or what to do. But I'd never personally spoken to King Zaid, and all the stories about his time in the Wastelands were focused on the jinn that had appeared to him. It was a story of Shaya's benevolence, not survival.

I shrugged helplessly. "He was only in the Wastelands for three days."

"Did you never ask what it was like?"

"We didn't have that sort of relationship."

He shook his head with a dark laugh. "Unbelievable."

I bristled. "What?"

"This is your fault. The least you could do is offer some knowledge on your own land."

"My fault?" I sputtered. *I'm not the one who forced you to lick my blood off that blade.* I drew a slow breath before I launched us into another argument. With forced calm, I said, "The Wastelands are not Ashoran territory."

"Oh, please. When you were homesick, you looked here. To the Wastelands."

"Because it was as close as I could get—"

"You knew." He glared at me, accusation shining in his gold eyes, and I knew we were no longer talking about the Wastelands. "You knew you had no magic. How could you let it get this far?"

That emptiness inside me lifted its slumbering head, awoken by the deep pang of guilt that reverberated through me. "I didn't have a choice."

"Bullshit." He dug his fingers into his hair, not caring that it messed up the long braid. "I begged you, Majesty. I begged you not to give us false hope. You chose to do it anyway."

Claws raked across my heart like something was trying to burrow in. That hole left behind when the gods had abandoned me in the Eye of Ketet widened. I rubbed at the spot on my chest. "I'm sorry," I whispered.

"You're sorry," he scoffed, turning his eyes up to the mosaic of stars in the night sky. Then he shook his head and rolled over, giving me his back.

I stared at him for a long moment, eyes burning.

I'd tried to do the right thing. That was all I'd ever wanted to do. Do right by Amunet, by Nadia and Tabia, by Ashorah, by the gods. But I'd failed. I had lied to protect my queen and only succeeded in damning her, along with all of Kaldfold and Ashorah. I couldn't do a single gods-damn thing right.

I had the oddest sensation of being outside my own body, like I was gazing at my reflection in a mirror, seeing myself as Keir did, as everyone must. A sorry slip of a girl with unremarkable features who had let herself be broken by supervisors and overseers within a single year, who was weak and pathetic, who was now responsible for so much impending destruction.

Keir was right. This was all my fault. What happened to Rade, in here or out there, what would happen to Velka and Siv and little Milena, all of it was my fault. What should I have done? Risk the Gods-Chosen? Was that the braver thing, the right thing?

I watched myself rub at my chest again. The Wastelands would be a fitting resting place for me. I'd been alone at the start; I would be alone at the end.

As if I were standing a few feet away, I observed impassively as I pressed my hand harder against my chest, right over the X, and dug my nail in until it broke skin, until a stream of blood trickled out. The pain was distant. Like it wasn't even mine. I drew my nail down, retracing my mark of shame, renewing it.

And then I traced it again. And again. Excavating old flesh, delving deeper and deeper, blood coating my hand. The scar that marked me as lesser, as lacking. Not strong and kind like Velka. Not brave like Rade or even little Milena. Not powerful like Keir and Amunet.

Amunet had given me the *X* before, but now I bestowed it on myself.

Even as I watched tears sear down my cheeks, watched myself shiver as I lay down on the sand, I couldn't shake the feeling that this pathetic girl deserved everything she got.

FIFTY-THREE

AMUNET

Deep, impenetrable darkness. I didn't exist here; nothing did. There was no air, no sound.

And then, suddenly, there was.

A gentle breeze swept across my face. Not the warmth of a breath, like Shaya's breeze. Not the hot gust of Ashorah or Dead Man's Forest. No, this was . . . something I had never experienced before.

I blinked my eyes open to one of the most gorgeous ceilings I'd ever seen. Made of pure gold that glinted in a soft morning light, shapes of various sizes pressed in as if by a giant's branding iron. Hexagons and diamonds and circles, all outlined in polished silver—a kaleidoscope of wonder.

Brows furrowing, I pushed myself up. I found myself, inexplicably, on a luxurious mattress, with covers of pristine white drawn up over my body. Gone was the exhaustion of the past few days, along with the nausea, sweat, and buzzing in my head.

Where the fuck was I?

"Athar?" I called. The only response was my own echo.

I swung my legs off the bed, feet sinking into the plush white rug. It wasn't just the ceiling that was made of gold; the floor and walls were, too. I made my way over to the bank of windows cut into the left wall. As I leaned out, taking in the gorgeous garden, a soft wind caressed my face. I was several floors up, the perfect vantage point from which to take in not only the garden, but the landscape of vivid greens beyond it—grass and palm trees and shrubs, spreading into the distance. Alive. More than alive. Thriving. The sun was nestled like a golden egg in the blue palm of the sky. It didn't beat down but bathed. Encouraged living things to bask in it. My heart skipped a beat.

That was not *my* sun.

Which meant . . .

"Athar!" I shouted, a touch more frantic.

Nothing. Not even a mocking chuckle.

My heart thundered, breaths coming in panicked puffs. Athar had sent me here. I'd trusted a trickster god like an idiot, a gods-damned *imbecile*, and now I had no idea where I was. I spun away from the window and leaned against the cool gold wall, eyes squeezed shut, trying to find some solidity.

Power tingled at my fingertips. I glanced down in surprise. It felt . . . more tangible now. No longer on the periphery or just beyond my reach. My breaths came easier as it wove up my arms in ribbons of comfort.

The door across the room opened, and I tensed, feet spreading into a stance that would make Jasim proud.

A girl with long raven-black hair smiled at me. "You're awake," she chirped. She held a gold tray in her hands, balancing a chalice and a small bowl of fruit. Gingerly, she set it on the ottoman at the foot of the luxurious bed. "You've been asleep for fucking ages, so I thought you might be hungry."

I squeezed my eyes shut until I saw stars. But when I opened them again, she was still there. My mind stuttered.

The gentle waves around her face were not familiar, nor was the ease of her smile or her strong frame. Her sleeveless turquoise gown showed off defined biceps and forearms crawling with veins. But the emerald-green eyes that glittered out of a tan face . . . those were *very* familiar.

They were mine.

I murmured, "You're . . ."

She cringed sympathetically. "A bit of a shock, I know. Here, sit." I was so dazed that I allowed the girl to lead me to the plush chair beside the window. When she held the chalice out to me, I took it. Clear water rippled gently within.

While I was nowhere near death any longer, I was still incredibly thirsty. But even with the shock of seeing my double, I had enough sense to hesitate.

"It's safe," the girl said. To prove it, she took the chalice and sipped it. She beamed and handed it back. "See?"

Self-preservation kicked in, and I gulped it down so fast, some of it streamed over my chin. The whole while, I stared.

She was identical to me and also incredibly different. Not just in her appearance but in the way she carried herself. No weight dragged her shoulders, no misery creased her face, no attitude shone in her eyes. She was lighter than I ever was.

"Sorry for just barging in," she said. "I should have given you a chance to prepare. Although yelling out, 'Qareen incoming,' probably wouldn't have helped." She laughed, a melodic, carefree sound. She swapped out the now-empty chalice for the bowl of fruit.

It was unnerving, looking into my own face and seeing a different person gazing back.

"What's it like not having hair?"

My brows lifted.

"Sorry, was that rude?" A delicate blush spread over my qareen's cheeks. "I'm just so curious. I never thought I'd actually get to meet you." She tilted her head like an inquisitive puppy. "I always thought I'd look ugly with a shaved head, but you're very pretty. Bet you don't get lice, either. Well, obviously, since I get them all the time." She snorted to herself. "There isn't much I'd want to trade places with you for, but lice is one of them. Agitating little fuckers. And Shaya." She gasped and leaned forward. "What's it like, being connected to him? He must be so—"

I straightened. "You're not connected to Shaya?"

She shook her head mournfully. "I tried once. Brought a goat to his temple and everything. But I just couldn't bring myself to hurt the innocent creature."

I blinked at her. Same face, same voice, and yet she was an entirely different person.

The opposite of me in every way.

Who I would have been without Shaya. Kind. Happy. Couldn't even sacrifice a goat, while I'd been ready to sacrifice . . .

I set down the bowl of fruit and drew a deep breath, pushing aside shock and inexplicable jealousy to *think*. Athar had sent me to the Mirror Realm, my qareen's presence made that much clear. My qareen, who had evidently watched over me while I was unconscious. She could have killed me then, but she hadn't, which made me think that somehow my qareen was the only one in existence who did not wish to switch places with her host. Or was too cowardly to do it.

See why you were chosen. That was what Athar had said. The message Shaya had for me. Maybe something to do with my qareen.

"How long was I asleep?" I asked her.

"You appeared in the foyer last night and slept well into the afternoon."

Hours, then. "Have you met anyone else since?"

Her brows furrowed as she shook her head. "The citadel is empty."

"Citadel?"

She nodded.

My gaze drifted back to the miraculous view outside the window. The Mirror Realm did not conjure places out of thin air, but

I didn't know of any location called *the citadel*. Wherever we were, it was not in Ashorah. Maybe it was another secret of Dead Man's Forest, like the Cirra Tribe. But if neither Athar nor Shaya had appeared to my qareen, then she was not what I was sent here to find.

Briefly, I debated killing her just to be safe. But she stared at me with wide, guileless green eyes. A puppy at the foot of its master, tail thumping eagerly, and I thought I might have better use of her.

"Is there anything here relating to Shaya? Or maybe the Gods-Chosen?"

The girl perked up. "Yes! A whole room, in fact."

Relief and a touch of excitement swirled through me. Athar hadn't tricked me after all. "Show me," I instructed.

FIFTY-FOUR

ᵕᵕᵕᵕᵕᵕᵕ

SAMIRA

W hat did you do?"

My eyes snapped open.

Keir was crouched over me, holding my neckline away from my chest and exposing my handiwork from last night.

I glanced down and choked back a curse. I'd made a horrible mess of my skin. I hadn't truly felt it last night, but now the wound burned. It looked nearly as bad as when it had gotten infected all those years ago. The *X* was outlined in an angry red. One sharp move would split the scabs, and it would start bleeding again.

Batting Keir's hands away, I sat up and pulled my dress back into place. "It's nothing. I'm fine."

"I smelled blood, but I thought it was your blisters."

"It's nothing, Keir," I repeated, standing. "Let's just go."

"Let me see it."

"There's nothing to see." I started trudging over the sand again. The sun hadn't crested the horizon yet. We could manage a mile at least before we had to bear its insufferable heat.

Keir rounded in front of me and grabbed my shoulder. "It could get infected."

I shrugged out of his grip and kept on. "We're not wasting water cleaning it."

He reached for me again. "Majesty, just let me—"

"No!" I shoved him roughly, surprising him enough that he stumbled. I folded my arms protectively over my chest, a useless shield. A small trickle of blood rolled down my breast.

Keir stared at me. "You did that to yourself."

"We're wasting time before the sun's up."

His eyes scanned my face, studying me with deep intensity. I had that acute sense of probing I often got under Keir's peculiar gaze, and it left me feeling bare, exposed. I tightened my arms around my chest.

"That's why you didn't run," he said, realization dawning. "That night with the shackles. You weren't trying to escape. You were doing *this.*"

I turned on my heel and started walking, not caring if he followed or not. I was not having this conversation.

"Why?" he called after me.

I kept my eyes trained straight ahead and said nothing, but a second later, he was next to me, keeping pace at my side. "Talk to me, Amunet," Keir pressed. "You said you got that scar because of disobedience. What did you mean?"

I focused on putting one foot in front of the other.

Keir took one long stride and cut off my path again. I barely avoided ramming into his chest. "Tell me."

I met his gaze from under my brows. "Not yet."

Keir observed me a moment longer, the fire not dimming in his eyes. "I gave you my word I wouldn't leave," he said, voice low.

"You also gave your word to Rade."

"And I kept it."

"By nearly killing me? By marking my cabin without my permission? By avoiding your post for a full week?"

"I'm flattered, Majesty. I had no idea you'd miss me so much."

"That's not—"

"Believe what you want," he interrupted, tipping up his chin and glaring down his nose at me, "but I have never broken my word.

If you'd been telling the truth about your skills with a khopesh, I wouldn't have been able to kill you." Then, as an afterthought, he added, "And I wasn't actually going to kill you."

My breaths were jagged pieces of glass in my lungs as I struggled to keep from exploding. I'd never felt rage like this. The pressure of it built inside me, and it took every ounce of willpower to keep a lid firmly planted on top of it.

"No?" I seethed. "You just drew blood because you're a twisted bastard who likes the taste of it—and oh yeah, pissing on cabins like an untrained dog?"

"I marked your cabin to keep you safe. Or have you forgotten that Bain nearly ripped your throat out that night? He would've come back the second you were alone. My scent protected you." I opened my mouth, but he plunged on before I could respond. "You're the one who lied every chance she got. The way I see it, if anyone is going to break their word, it's you."

He was right. I was already nearly laid bare before him—my lies and my guilt. Why not tell him everything? For a second, my name hovered on my tongue. But it stuck there. My last piece of protection against his full hatred.

"All I've ever tried to do is act with honor—" I began.

"Do not," he snarled, "talk to me about honor, Khada. Your people don't know the meaning of the word."

"And you know nothing of my people."

"I know that seventeen years ago, your king marched into my home," he said, yellow eyes flashing. "And he forced *my* people into the streets. He rounded them up—took *children*—and threw them into the Shroud. Then he set up a perimeter so that anyone who tried to escape met the edge of his soldiers' blades."

My anger ebbed as my brows furrowed.

But he wasn't done. "Some managed to get away before the legions arrived, but some of us"—he pulled the hem of his shirt up, exposing those slashes across his abdomen, the white of his rib peeking out through the skin bound by a leather band—"some of us went in and didn't come out for days."

I stared at the scars, fury guttering out like a blown candle, and I shook my head as if that alone would make it untrue.

"The Shroud was Shaya's will, your king decided," Keir continued mercilessly. "The Underworld god's desire to reclaim us—because Kaldfolk are demons, right? Shaya's abominations? Your king wanted to force all Kaldfolk into the Shroud, where he thought we belonged. He knew it would kill us, drive us mad, turn us into monsters, and he forced us in anyway. Now tell me, Majesty, was that honorable?"

No, King Zaid wouldn't . . . He couldn't have.

But the loathing on Keir's face, the scars on his body, those weren't lies.

"I . . . I didn't know," I whispered. But had Amunet? Had she known what her father had done? She'd only have been three at the time of the invasion—certainly not to be blamed—but if she had known, then she had lied to us.

Keir had been stuck in the Shroud. For days, he'd said. No wonder he always had that gleam of madness in his eyes. No wonder he despised Amunet as much as he did. He'd come face-to-face with monsters, in the Shroud and outside of it.

"I'm sorry," I said brokenly.

Keir stiffened.

"I mean it—"

"Quiet." His eyes strayed over my head.

The hair along my body shot up. I turned and scanned the desert. And when I saw it—only a handful of miles away—my blood ran cold.

An enormous bird with sand-colored feathers and violet talons. It didn't look exactly the same as the one I had seen in the White Horns, but there was no mistaking it.

A Roc.

My heart dropped. "I thought there was only one of its kind."

"There is."

"Then how—"

"I don't know." Keir's eyes were wide as the bird flew closer.

My breaths picked up speed as my mind raced. "We have to hide." But Rade wasn't there to pull a magical shield over us.

Echoing my thoughts, Keir said, "Not many hiding places in a wasteland, Majesty." He drew his sword from its scabbard on his back. The blade was almost laughably tiny compared to the massive beast heading our way.

My eyes darted around wildly before settling on the sand. I dropped to my knees and started digging furiously.

"What are you doing?" Keir demanded.

"It's the only option."

The Roc drew closer, eating up the distance like it was nothing. Its tan mane rippled in the wind, and it released an earsplitting *caw*.

"Fuck." Keir plunged his hands into the sand beside me. He worked much faster than me, hardly taking his eyes away from the bird as he gestured to the sizeable hole he created in mere moments. "Get in."

I jumped in and lay on my back.

Keir threw sand on top of me, head darting up every few seconds.

The Roc's beady eyes were visible now, and its violet beak dipped toward us.

"Hurry, Keir."

He finished burying me and looked up. With another colorful swear, he ordered, "Don't move."

"Keir—"

The Roc's shadow covered us. Keir let loose a vicious roar as he dropped his sword and his face elongated, his body lengthened and fleshed out, fur sprouted, claws burst out of his fingernails, and suddenly there wasn't a man standing above me, but a bear. Completely animal, save for his eyes, which burned with human fury.

He roared again—and then tore off in the opposite direction.

The bird gave chase with a shriek, beating its wings right on top of me and sending sand flying. I squeezed my eyes shut as sheets of it sprayed my face.

Then the sun blazed forth again as the Roc's shadow moved, making a beeline for Keir's retreating form.

I waited several breathless moments, the weight of the sand claustrophobic. Panic rose up in my chest. I couldn't see what was happening, but I heard Keir's bellows, the Roc's screeches.

Get up, I urged myself. *Get up and do something.*

But I didn't know how to use a sword, and I couldn't shift into any animals. Remaining hidden was the smartest thing I could do.

A gentle breeze tickled my face. Soft, delicate. A caress. Entirely unlike the hot, dry gusts of the Wastelands. It was purposeful. Like a finger against my cheek.

I blinked as I felt it again, and it trailed away from me. Like it wanted me to follow it.

Going against my every instinct, I struggled to move. The sand was a band around my chest, my arms, my legs. But I gritted my teeth and pulled hard.

My right arm burst free. Then the other. I sat up, sand cascading off me like a waterfall, and staggered to my feet, spitting out the small grains that had somehow gotten into my mouth.

That wind brushed through my braided hair before trailing away again.

A short distance from me, Keir and the Roc were engaged in a fierce battle. I scooped up Keir's sword. I had no plan, just a feeling driving me forward. The Roc had just beaten its wings against Keir, whose fur was already matted with blood. He righted himself with a snarl before lunging at the bird.

The Roc screamed as Keir's razor-sharp teeth clamped down on its shoulder, and slammed its beak into Keir's side. Keir roared in agony, releasing his grip as blood gushed out. He crashed into the sand, and the Roc was on him in an instant, tearing at him.

"Keir!" I shouted.

As I ran toward him, the wind skimmed past me again, bringing a sudden shadow. I looked up, half expecting to see another terrifying monster. Instead, where before there had been nothing but hot blue skies, a slate-gray cloud swirled, as if an invisible finger was stirring the sky. And not just any cloud.

A *storm* cloud.

I gasped as thunder rolled over the desert, loud enough to shake the earth. Lightning flashed, louder than the sound of Keir's pained roars, and then, like a bucket had been overturned, the cloud dropped a deluge of water.

I stared with parted lips at the sheets of falling water. I'd never seen rain before. Any other moment, it would have been magnificent, but right then, it was downright miraculous. Water, plummeting uninhibited, like there were endless reserves of it, pounding against the dry sand and the enormous bird.

The Roc withdrew from Keir, beating its wings awkwardly. It cawed, its feathers weighted down by the onslaught of rain. The Roc's talons grazed the sand as it struggled to stay in the air. It glared up at the cloud, then shrieked toward Keir one last time before flying away and disappearing through the clouds.

I ran to Keir as another round of thunder drummed and lightning cut through the sky, and fell to my knees next to him on the wet sand. He groaned as his features shrank back into those of a man, but it was a halting, jerky transformation, taking too much effort. Blood soaked through his tunic, and his normally tan skin was sickly pale. His eyes stayed closed as I pressed my hands to his wound. Blood instantly coated my palms. If it hadn't been for the rain, he'd be dead. I didn't know whether to be grateful or frightened of whatever wielded this kind of power—and why it had decided to help us.

"Keir? Keir! Keir, can you hear me?"

His face was slack, body limp. Blood wept out of his side. He was losing too much.

Thunder clapped and lightning shot down from the sky, blindingly bright. I cried out and threw myself on top of Keir, shielding our faces with my arms, the bolt of heat so close it nearly scorched the hem of my dress.

And then it vanished. Replaced only by the pounding rain.

I blinked my eyes open.

Keir's sword, which I had dropped in my hurry to reach him, shone a fiery orange.

I stared, breathless. Memories of my one visit to the palace barracks rose sharply in my mind. Healers had tended to large wounds with searing metal. The smell of burning flesh so horrific that I had never forgotten it, even years later.

A blessing, it turned out.

"Thank you," I breathed to whatever entity was responsible for this mercy, and crawled through the sticky sand to snatch up the blade.

Heat speared through me, and I screamed, releasing the sword. A nasty red burn bubbled up across my palm, sending streams of agony up my arm.

I gritted my teeth. A problem for later.

I wrapped my hand in the skirt of my dress and picked up the sword again.

When I reached Keir, I wasted no time yanking open his tunic, revealing his muscled torso. The blood was still gushing out, seeping into the sand beneath him. "Sorry," I muttered, and pressed the flat of the blade against the wound.

Keir didn't move, even as his skin sizzled and that horrible odor lifted into the air.

I pulled the blade away. The wound was blistered, but it was closed. And his large chest was moving up and down. Breaths shallow, but they were there.

Careful to avoid my own burn, I heaved Keir onto his side, allowing the rain to clean what it could around the wound, wash away the excess blood.

When the searing in my hand became unbearable, I lowered him back to the sand and drew my knees up to my chest, staring at him, at the runes that stretched down his jaw and stopped just above his heart, the various battle scars that mapped up and down his torso, those awful slashes across his abdomen, the leather band wrapped around his chest. *He's a Shifter,* I told myself. *Superhuman. He'll be just fine.*

I glanced from Keir to the rest of the Wastelands.

Without the sun, I couldn't see Ashorah. There was only the empty, uninhabitable landscape of nothingness. The rain no longer felt miraculous. Just cold.

I curled tighter into myself.

FIFTY-FIVE

ᴧᴧᴧᴧᴧᴧᴧᴧᴧᴧ

SAMIRA

A hiss of pain made me jerk my head up. Keir blinked hard against the sun as he came to. The rain had stopped a long time ago, leaving behind the unforgiving heat again. Keir groaned as he tried to sit up, then dropped back down with a curse.

"You shouldn't move," I warned.

"Get it off." His voice cracked on the words, shaky hands reaching blindly for his chest. For the band wrapped around it.

"How do I—"

"Buckle. On the left."

Careful of his wound, I hiked his tunic up to his sternum. The band was made of thick leather, and it was bound tightly around his ribs. Pressing against the exposed bone. I couldn't help but cringe. "Keir, what is—"

He snatched my wrist and looked up at me pleadingly. Tears pricked the edges of his eyes. "Please, Amunet. Get it *off*."

I nodded quickly and tilted my head to find the buckle. I undid it and pulled the band away from his chest.

A breath whistled past his teeth and he slumped back to the ground, eyes drifting shut. "Thank you."

I held the band in both hands. It was rough, strong, and the side that had been pressed to Keir's skin was scratchy. "Keir, what is this?"

He clenched his teeth and forced himself onto his elbows. He took one look at his cauterized side and coughed a humorless laugh. "There better be no more talk of me and my word now, Majesty." He collapsed to the sand again, breaths quick. Even that small movement had taken a lot out of him.

"Keir, why were you wearing this?" I pushed.

"I have to." His voice was softer than before. He was fading.

"What do you mean?"

"Pain . . . breaks through . . . the haze . . ." His breathing evened out as he lost consciousness again.

I glanced back down at the band. He'd said that to me before, when we'd been in the Shroud. But we'd both come into the Mirror Realm wearing what we'd been in before, which meant that Keir had been wearing this in his cell, far away from the Shroud. Why? It seemed torturous.

I placed the band in Keir's hand. The last thing I wanted was for him to wake and add theft to my list of crimes. And then my eyes drew up to where the sun was glinting off Ashorah. My brows furrowed as a thought suddenly occurred to me.

Everything was reversed in the Mirror Realm.

My scars had switched sides. North was south. But . . .

But if everything was reversed in this place, then Ashorah would be to the east.

We'd been heading west.

This was the Wastelands, I was sure of it, and the sun *was* reflecting off something out there. That compulsion in my chest remained, a gentle nudge in that same direction. But it was no longer comforting, no longer offering me the security of a plan.

Because if that wasn't Ashorah glinting under the sun, then I had no idea where I was leading us.

Keir's pained groan woke me in the middle of the night. My head popped up from where I'd been dozing beside him. "Keir?"

A sheen of sweat covered his face and his form was racked with shivers. I placed my uninjured hand against his forehead. It burned, hotter than his normal Shifter body heat. Fever. A spark of fear lit in my stomach.

I moved to reach for one of the water-filled boots, but Keir's hand shot up to catch my wrist. I gasped, startled.

Eyes still closed, he returned my hand to his forehead. "You feel good," he muttered.

"I'm just getting you some water." I cradled the back of his head and fitted the boot to his lips. Precious drops leaked out the corners of his mouth as he drank. I let him have a few swallows before I had to pull it away. We were down to only three boots now.

But when Keir's brilliant eyes fluttered open, dazed with fever, I wiped any anxiety from my face. "It's going to be okay," I told him calmly.

A large smile spread across his lips as he gazed up at me. The first real smile I'd ever seen on him, free of scorn or arrogance. Even in the dim moonlight, it made him look devastatingly beautiful.

Keir's hand drifted up to the side of my face. He pinched one of my braids between his fingers, combed through it until the strands were free. "Soft," he murmured.

I huffed a laugh. If he knew he was pawing at my hair like a kitten, he'd be furious.

Those unnatural eyes of his trailed away from my face to my neck, and his hand followed. He stroked the curve of my throat where it met my shoulder, the same place he'd buried his nose against during the Lunar Feast, and a soft heat spread through me. "Right there," he slurred, voice a hoarse rumble. "I wanted to put it right there."

"Put what?"

"But I've been thinking about it. Now I think I want to put it here." His touch trailed down to my chest, pausing just above the mess of my scar. "People won't see it as often, but you'll trace it instead of this."

A mass of goose bumps rippled down my body. Suddenly, I wasn't laughing anymore. "Keir, what are you talking about?"

His gaze returned to mine with that dazzling smile, eyes crinkling. "Say it again."

"Say what?"

"My name. I like how you say it."

I felt like I had a fever, too, skin far too warm. "Keir."

He rumbled a hum of approval that made my skin tighten. His lids began to droop once more, and I hesitantly resettled my hand on his forehead. He tilted his face up so that his nose brushed against the sensitive skin of my wrist, nostrils flaring as he drew a deep breath. Then he slumped back into sleep, lips curved up.

I stared at him. My neck and chest tingled faintly, and I felt out of breath. I knew Keir was just lost to the cloud of his fever, but what he'd said echoed through my skull. I rested my free hand over the scar on my chest, but for the first time since I'd received it, I felt no compulsion to trace it.

Keir's fever broke around dawn and he slept most of the day, only waking up a couple of minutes at a time. Long enough to take a sip of water and then pass out again. Each time, he appeared a bit more lucid.

At one point, he caught me studying him and frowned. "Why are you looking at me like that?"

My cheeks burned and I mumbled some excuse. He didn't seem aware of anything he'd done or said the night before. For some reason, it felt like my secret. I didn't want to voice it for him to somehow taint with his annoyance or anger. I cradled it within my heart and told him nothing.

During one of those brief intervals of wakefulness, I mentioned my concerns over Ashorah, but neither of us had a better option. We'd find what awaited us when we got there.

My stomach growled in hunger, and no matter how hard I clenched it, the growling wouldn't stop. If I was hungry, I imagined the man bear beside me had to be absolutely famished. I needed to find something to eat or we'd both die.

So I dug. Sifted through the sand inch by inch, the sun beating into the top of my head, burning through the fabric of my dress, roasting me.

I wasn't sure how long it was before I found a centipede. It was a quick little thing, but my desperation made me quicker. I dove for it. Pinched it between my index finger and thumb, its tiny legs pinwheeled, tickling.

If there was one, there were more, and I'd need a place to hold them. I tore the skirt of my dress until just above my knees and then dropped the centipede onto the fabric, quickly twisting it closed and tying a tight knot on top. Then I went back to digging.

By the time the sun had set, I'd found five more centipedes, a scorpion, and a handful of small spiders. Though I hadn't been a scullery maid, I'd seen Chef Nena work enough to know I shouldn't risk eating any of these raw. Which meant I'd need to make a fire.

I grabbed two rocks, but my heart sank when I realized there was no kindling. Not even puffs of dry grass to use.

Keir moaned as he woke. Just like every time, he tried to rise, and this time he managed to sit up fully. He shoved his long braid off his shoulder with a relieved breath, then frowned at my dress and the makeshift knapsack. "What are you doing?"

I locked my eyes on his braid. "I need your hair."

"Excuse me?"

I held up the sack. "To cook. I don't have enough hair or I'd do it myself."

"Sorry, why do you need *hair* for that?"

"Do you see any other way to start a fire around here?"

Keir's eyes scanned our surroundings, and when he looked back at me, they were wide with panic. "You can't cut my hair. Use my shirt."

"You'll burn faster that way and increase your risk of heatstroke. It's too dangerous." At his horrified look, I added, "It's only hair."

"No."

I blew out a frustrated breath through my nose. "You won't shift to get us there faster, and you won't cut a few inches off your *feet* of hair so we can eat. What sort of guard are you?"

"The sort that saved your life from an enormous killer bird."

"I saved your life from that bird, too," I shot back. I wouldn't let his vanity get in the way of our survival. I reached for his braid.

He smacked my hand away, and I hissed as pain rocketed up my arm.

Keir sat up straighter. "You're hurt."

I held my palm against my chest before he could see the burn. "I'm fine."

Keir took my wrist gently. I let him draw it toward him. Even in his human form, I couldn't help thinking of his hand as a paw for how large it was as it cupped mine. His thumb smoothed over my fingers, and they uncurled, revealing the burn. A muscle in his jaw popped. When Keir looked up at me again, I couldn't decipher the gleam in his tawny eyes but found I couldn't look away.

Then he released my hand and drew his braid forward. Rubbed the thick brown locks between his fingers. "A Shifter's hair symbolizes rank," he said, voice quiet. "I'm the highest-ranking Shifter in Kaldfold. Have been since I got my runes."

My face softened. "It'll grow back, Keir."

"No," he said, "it won't." But he glanced back up at me, taking in every scratch on my face, the sunburns, the blood crusted on my neckline, my injured hand, and swallowed.

Between one blink and the next, claws took the place of his fingernails. He held his braid in front of him, took a sharp breath, and slashed.

At least a foot of brown hair thudded to the sand. His lips thinned as he retracted his claws and offered it to me.

I took the rope of hair carefully, the meaning behind it making it feel heavier.

"Just because you cut it in this realm doesn't mean it's cut in our world," I said softly.

Keir smiled tightly. "Maybe."

I placed his hair on the sand and then got to work striking the two rocks together. "How's your side?"

"Hurts like a bitch," he responded. "But it'll heal." His brows drew together when he saw my handiwork on his wound. "How'd you know to do that?"

"I saw a healer do it in the palace once. A guard in the barracks." I wasn't sure why I told him. Probably a mixture of starvation, dehydration, and the reverberation of last night ringing in my head. "I had to help hold him down while the healer worked."

Keir cocked a brow at me. "What was the princess doing in the army barracks?"

The clump of hair finally caught, and I leaned forward to breathe it to life. It was a small fire, but it would do. I opened the bag of squirming insects and pulled out one of the centipedes, holding it above the modest flame. But it kept shifting, and my fingers were instantly too hot.

Keir took the centipede from me without a word, held it against one of the rocks, and smashed the other down on its head. It stopped moving. Then he reached into his hair and pulled out a pin. Part of his coiled hair sagged to the side as he held it out to me. "A spit."

I accepted it with a short nod and skewered the centipede. As I held it over the flame again, I met Keir's searching gaze. "I already told you," I answered. "There's a lot you don't know about me."

"Now would be a great time to share, Majesty."

I crossed my legs and gazed at the centipede. It slowly curled in on itself. "I worked a lot in the palace. In whatever way was needed of me. Sometimes, that included the barracks."

"And if you didn't, you were punished?" He glanced down at my chest.

I pulled my neckline aside to reveal the *X*. It struck me how easy it felt to show it to him now. "This was because I stole water."

Keir's eyes snapped back up to mine. "What?" When I kept quiet, he prodded, "But it's *your* water."

"No, it isn't." Releasing the neckline, I nodded to his other side. "How are your ribs?"

Keir looked like he wanted to insist on an answer. But after a moment, he dropped his gaze to the flame. "It's an old wound."

"It looks . . ." *Horrible. Painful.*

He shrugged. "It is." Despite his efforts to appear unbothered, the muscles in his shoulders wound tight.

Voice quiet, I asked, "How long were you in the Shroud, Keir?"

He brought his eyes back to mine, and I could see the wealth of pain in them, the gleam of ever-present madness. Years' worth of suffering held in that bright yellow gaze. When he spoke, it was a choked whisper. "Forty-eight hours."

My eyes widened.

Rade's mother had been in the Shroud half that time and had been forever changed by it. Had felt its pull even years later. But Keir had been in that horrible place for two full days. No wonder he was so harsh. Between the wound to his torso and the one to his mind, it was a wonder he could function at all.

And Rade . . . Rade had been planning to send him back. Did Keir know that as he waited in his prison in the mountain? Nausea coiled in my gut.

"What was it like?" I asked softly.

A muscle worked in his jaw. "Nice, at first. Like you saw. And then . . ." Keir squeezed his eyes shut on one very hard blink. "It taunts you with your dreams. The good ones and the bad ones. Makes it impossible to know what dangers are in your head and what are real. Turns you against yourself until you submit."

I was overcome by the horror of it. I took his hand.

His eyes opened again and landed on my touch. Slowly, his fingers curled around mine.

"And that band you're wearing," I dared. "It keeps you from going back, doesn't it?"

Keir's throat bobbed. He eased his hand away from mine. "It'll be slow, but I'll be able to walk tomorrow." His turn to change the subject. "We'll leave at first light."

I only nodded and pulled the blackened centipede off the hairpin. I didn't even taste it when I popped it into my mouth.

FIFTY-SIX

〜〜〜〜〜〜

SAMIRA

The next two days were more of the same. Trudging through sand. Sizzling under the sun. Resting. Then up to do it all over again. As we readied to make camp once more, I felt it. The compulsion—which had been little more than a nudge—strengthened, solidified into a cord in my chest.

My head snapped up.

Keir paused in unwrapping the fabric around his side. He'd torn off the bottom of his tunic and was using it as a makeshift bandage. "What is it?"

My brows furrowed as I gazed across the sea of sand. The sun was just about to dip behind the horizon, and the last of its golden light bounced off that roof in the distance. "I feel . . ."

Keir followed my gaze, instantly on alert. "What?"

"A pull." Something about that beaming structure . . . It wasn't just a beacon anymore. It was alluring. A siren's song, calling for me. Different from the Shroud. Stronger. More urgent.

"A pull. Care to elaborate?"

"We can't stop to rest tonight," I murmured, and took a stumbling step forward. "We have to keep going."

"Majesty, what are— Amunet, stop." He grabbed my arm.

I hardly even felt it. A shudder of fear passed through me, but it wasn't mine. They were in trouble; they were scared. They needed me, whoever was waiting for us there.

I tried to pull out of Keir's grip, but he held fast. "They need help."

"For the love of—" Keir growled as he placed himself firmly in front of me. "Who needs help?"

"I don't know. Someone . . ."

"Amunet, look at me. *Look* at me." He held my face and shook me until my eyes found his, the sunny irises bright with alarm. He waited until he was sure I was seeing him, until my frantic movements slowed, before he said, "We're still a full day away. You can't just take off."

I nodded, but it was like a rope was wrapped around my sternum, desperately trying to drag me away. I couldn't help but think of the shadow creature from Zarqa's vision. It had appeared out of the sand. Maybe it was the one calling to me. I shuddered. "They want me there," I whispered. "Why do they want me there?"

Keir didn't have to voice his concern. It was plain in his eyes as he scanned every inch of my face. "Am I going to have to tie you down, Majesty?"

The sun finally succumbed to the horizon, taking its rays with it. The distant gleam faded as if it had been nothing more than a mirage. And yet the pull remained. Even though my legs trembled with the effort to stay in place and not take off across the desert, if I concentrated, I could resist it. For a little while longer at least. Because Keir was right—it was madness to press on now. We had to rest. "I'll be okay."

"You sure?"

"Yes."

Keir's hands lingered on my cheeks before finally dropping down to his wound, but I didn't miss the way his eyes kept darting worriedly back to me.

His side was viciously red. Though he made a strong effort not to react, the skin around his eyes was tight with pain.

"Let me see it," I said, stepping toward him.

He shifted away. "I'm fine."

I sighed and tapped the *X* on my chest. "I have some experience with infection. Just let me look."

He rolled his eyes but removed his hands from the wrap, revealing the blistered wound. I took a step forward, and when he didn't bolt, I bent to get a good look at it in the fading light.

The bubble of a blister had shrunk significantly, which was a good sign, but the skin around it was still an angry red. I placed my hands on either side of it, and Keir hissed in a breath. "Sorry," I murmured. His skin was hot against my touch, but that was normal for him. A quick glance up at his face showed clear eyes. No fever. A stark relief.

"Give me the bandage." He handed it over without a word. There was no blood on the fabric since the wound wasn't open, but there was some discoloration from where the blister had emptied out. "Try to keep a clean part against the wound," I told him as I shifted the bandage to a spot without discharge.

"I know that," he snapped.

"So do it," I fired back. I might have pulled the knot tighter than necessary.

"Careful!"

"Sorry," I said. Unapologetically.

When Keir glared down at me, his yellow eyes were twin flames. He looked like he wanted to put his dagger to my throat again. But I straightened and didn't flinch away, daring him. He grumbled, "I liked you better when you were scared of me."

My snort was entirely involuntary. "No, you didn't."

"It made you much easier to deal with."

"Then why did you make sure I knew you weren't a cannibal? Why reassure me I wasn't in danger right from the beginning?"

"I wasn't reassuring you."

"Then what were you doing?"

"Being honest. A foreign concept to you, I know." He gave me a false smile.

I returned it. "And saving me from Bain? What about that night, Keir? How was that meant to keep me scared of you?"

His smile dropped instantly. Tension settled over us, strung tight. One sharp breath away from snapping. Suddenly, my heart was beating too fast, skin flushing hot, and I could think of nothing beyond his strong body against mine, his lips at my ear, his hands on my hips. The way his rough voice had raked shivers down my spine. Just the memory was enough to send a wave of heat to my core.

Neither of us had mentioned the Lunar Feast. Alluded to it, shot knowing looks, but never blatantly shone a light on that secret in the dark. But with his fevered words thrumming through my veins, a heady confidence seized me. Bolstered by the glint in his eyes as he stared down at me, which almost seemed like anticipation. His breaths fanned across my face, his side heaving against where my hand still rested on the bandage's knot. His nostrils flared as his eyes flicked up to my runes for just a millisecond. Then his jaw clenched, and he turned his head away.

My cheeks heated. I ducked my head and worked on double-knotting the bandage. Then, before I could think better of it, I asked, "Is it just cinnamon?"

His head whipped back to me.

I busied myself with the knot, which was obviously as secure as it could be. "Your reactions to my scent are always . . ." *That scent . . . Gods, that scent . . .* I swallowed. "Strong."

Keir's face was made of stone. He just gazed down at me with those intense eyes. But the longer he remained silent, the more the heat inside me cooled as another thought took hold. "Is there something wrong with me?"

At that, he chuckled. "There are quite a few things wrong with you, Majesty," he answered. "But none of them have to do with your scent."

"Are you sure?"

"Positive."

Some of the tension seeped out of me. "So what is it?"

"I don't know."

"What do you mean, you don't know?"

"Exactly what I said." He backed away from me, checking the tightness of the knot himself, before dropping down to the sand.

"So there *could* be something wrong with me."

"No."

"But you just said—"

"You smell good, okay?" His eyes flashed with annoyance, a hint of redness along his cheeks, before he glanced away again. "I like your scent. Fucking love it, actually. That's all. There's nothing wrong with you. Now go to sleep." He turned over, giving me his back like he'd done every night.

Slowly, I sank down a few feet away, already shivering in the desert's cold, and stared at him. Wings took flight in my stomach. I tried to tamp them down as I curled up in the sand. Somehow, that only seemed to make the sensation worse.

Rade had suggested my scent was offensive, but he'd been wrong. Keir liked it. *Loved* it. I pressed my lips together to stop them from curving as another freezing shiver racked my frame.

Keir sighed and rolled over, scooting closer to me in the sand.

My eyes snapped to his. "What are you doing?"

"Relax. Shifters run hot, remember? I can hear your teeth chattering. You need the body heat." He held out his arm.

I hesitated for only a moment. But I *was* freezing. Kaldfold had been cold, but there were warm coats and fires burning in every available nook and cranny. This was unbearable.

And Keir loved my scent . . .

Not bothering to waste any more time deliberating, I sidled closer and nestled eagerly into his warmth. Keir wrapped his massive arm around my back, cocooning me. His skin was like a furnace. It was . . . bliss.

But as I started to relax, I realized the runes on my forehead would touch the ones cutting down from his jaw. The feelings that rune-touching conjured up were too strong, too intimate. Whatever he'd confessed about my scent, I didn't think he'd appreciate such liberties. I stiffened and arched my head away.

Keir mumbled, "What are you doing?"

"Trying not to touch your runes."

"My runes?"

I could already feel the muscles in my neck cramping. I wouldn't be able to stay like this. Keir's runes stretched all the way down from his jaw to his sternum in thick, long lines. Regardless of what unnatural position I took now, there was a good chance my forehead would land on one of those lines at some point in my sleep. I should just roll over. That was the safest option for both of us. I started to turn—

Keir's hand landed on my hip, stilling me. "Nothing will happen if our runes touch."

"Yes," I stated, "something definitely will."

The moonlight gilded his amused grin in silver and reflected off his gold eyes. "Only a Gods-Blessed can do that. You're safe with me, Majesty."

I looked down at the iridescent blue marks and swallowed hard. Hesitantly, I relaxed into Keir and allowed my forehead to rest against his warm flesh. I squeezed my eyes shut and braced myself for the heat to intensify. But it never came. No searing. No fingers reaching inside me. No overwhelming ache or need. It was just the warmth of his skin, the gentle rise and fall of his breaths, and nothing else.

"See?" he said. His grip on my hip softened and slid to the small of my back. "Sleep, Amunet."

Feeling foolish, I settled with my face pressed against his chest, folding my arms tightly between us. The smell of sweat drifted up to my nose, but so did the spice of mulberries. It wrapped a cozy blanket around me and niggled at a memory until it finally, *finally* sprang free. My lips spread into a smile beyond my control. I hesitated a moment before I whispered, "Keir?"

"Hm?"

"Remember how I told you about the tree I used to pray under, beside the river?"

"Yes?"

"It was a mulberry tree." I couldn't believe I'd forgotten that wonderful tree until now. "When I was little, I used to love climbing it. I'd sit in its branches for hours. It was big and shady, and in the spring, my fingers would almost always be stained maroon from all the mulberries I'd eat. They were my favorite treat, besides bread." I glanced down at my fingers curled against Keir's chest, almost expecting them to be stained even now. My lids slipped shut, and within the quiet of my head, I could almost hear the rustle of my tree's leaves, see the light filtering through the branches, and when I inhaled, I caught its distinct earthy aroma coming off Keir's skin. I smiled wider. "That's what you smell like to me."

Keir's body was carefully still against mine except for the movement of his breaths. He didn't say anything, and I was suddenly too embarrassed to pull out of his chest to see his expression. I swallowed and awkwardly mumbled, "Just thought it was fair for you to know. An answer for an answer, right?"

He remained motionless for a moment longer. Then one of his hands left me to fiddle with something under his shirt. I recognized the gesture from Frostguard but only now realized what he was doing. Keir pinched the leather band between his fingers and pulled it tight, cinched it around his ribs. His features twitched in a wince.

I started to ask why, but his massive arms wrapped fully around me again, enveloping me in his Shifter heat as he buried his nose in my hair and drew in a long, deep breath. He didn't question whether there were mulberry trees in Khada Palace. He didn't accuse me of lying or offer an explanation. He just hugged me against him, and I burrowed into the space beneath his chin, surrounding myself in warmth and mulberries until I hardly felt the desert's cold at all anymore.

We were lost in the Mirror Realm, broiling alive under the desert sun, wounded, nearly starved, and headed toward a glint in the distance that could be anything. I had no idea if Rade was safe or dead. My qareen awaited me somewhere.

And yet, bundled up in Keir's arms, I slept more soundly than I ever had.

FIFTY-SEVEN

AMUNET

My qareen led me through the massive citadel. Apparently, when Athar had plopped me in the Mirror Realm, my double had also been torn from wherever her home was in here, and she'd spent the hours between her arrival and mine wandering in confusion. To my benefit.

We strode through rooms of immaculate white and nauseating gold. Bedrooms and sitting rooms and libraries. At the end of a corridor, a set of stairs yawned before us. My sandals slapped against them as we descended into another open space. There was no mistaking the opulence for anything other than an entrance hall, meant for receiving guests and awing them. The front double doors were massive, decorated with intricate images of the Seven Monarchs.

"This is where I found you," my qareen said with a gesture to the tiled floor. "You looked so helpless, I couldn't possibly leave you there, so I carried you upstairs."

"I'm not helpless," I said sharply.

The girl flinched and nodded quickly. "I didn't mean it in a bad way. I just—we can all be helpless sometimes, can't we? It's nothing to be ashamed of." Her eyes darted to mine and away fretfully before she opened another door. Her smile was shy. "It's in here."

Guilt pinched my chest. I hadn't meant to snap at her. The physical exhaustion of Dead Man's Forest had turned into a soul-deep exhaustion. Nearly twenty years spent proving myself. Twenty years without a restful sleep. Twenty years doing whatever Shaya wanted of me. Prayers, sacrifices, punishments. Yet it still wasn't enough, and now here I was, making nice with what was supposed to be my evil double. Except it was obvious to me now that *I* was the evil one between us.

No wonder Jasim had left.

I entered the room. And froze.

We were in some sort of gallery. But instead of paintings or sculptures, the walls were inlaid with plaques of iron. Gold filigree outlined silhouettes in the metal, the bright golden threads of light strange against the darkness of the space.

"Is this what you were looking for?" my qareen asked.

I peered closer.

The first panel was a battle scene. Soldiers firing arrows and slashing scimitars while balls of fire rained from the sky. A chaotic vision. The next panel depicted victory, a woman with a leaf for an eye patch standing atop a pile of bodies. Squinting, I could just make out pointed ears on some of those bodies. A chill went through me as I suddenly understood.

It was the defeat of the jinn. And their descendants. Which meant the woman was Ketet.

This was the War of the Ancients.

I skipped over a few panels until I found him.

Shaya looked just like my obsidian candle, save those glittering, golden eyes. Slitted like a cat's. His lips were curved in a sob, fangs glinting from where he rested on his knees at Ketet's feet. Begging.

Disgust twisted my stomach, and I took a step back. The image was . . . This was blasphemy. Shaya did not *beg*. Certainly not from Ketet. No, he raged. He fought.

In the next panel, Shaya was slumped against a set of doors engraved with bodies crawling over each other in writhing chaos. The Gate to the Underworld. Shaya pounded his fists against it.

Ketet stood on the other side with a man behind her. He had suns for eyes, the gold filigree somehow brighter here than anywhere else. Phadar.

This was Shaya's imprisonment.

My instincts—everything I'd ever been taught—ordered me to turn away. To not dishonor my father by looking a second more at this depiction. Sad, beaten, weeping. Helpless.

This was not right. This was not Shaya.

And yet, I couldn't look away.

He looked so . . . human. I loved my father. Of course I did. But he was a god. No matter how much he cared for me, looked after me, no matter how much I prayed to him, he was still *other*. But this image, this heartbreak, I understood. Very well.

Reaching up, I smoothed my fingers over Shaya's face, the bodies in the Gate, Ketet's braids. My fingertips sparked with power as I brushed Phadar's chest.

I brought my fingertip to a stop, resting it on the pendant that hung against his sternum. My eyes darted back to Shaya, half expecting him to have moved. To smile or to nod. He did neither.

But I didn't need him to.

I studied the pendant closer. It was large—really more of an amulet. On its surface, gold outlined a skull. Matching the knobs on the Gate to the Underworld.

See why you were chosen.

An incredulous laugh huffed out of me. Of course!

My enemies had always speculated that Shaya hadn't borne a child to save Ashorah but rather as a tool to achieve his freedom. Sara had said as much in Reeda. I'd always told myself that I didn't care one way or the other what Shaya wanted to do with the world. Didn't care if he wanted me to save it or throw wide his prison doors. And I'd meant it.

This amulet was the key to opening the Gate, to letting Shaya walk free once more. He'd be beside me. No more faint wisps of a breeze. No more candles or sacrifices at temples. I'd be able to reach out and touch him. See his proud smiles. Feel my father's love.

And the creatures he'd been forced to abandon would be under his command once more. The Shifters who'd dared invade my home, who'd tried to kill me in Dead Man's Forest. The jinn-descended princes who'd made me grovel for sanctuary, who'd thrown me into that horrible room, imprisoned me just like Shaya.

My father would bring them all to their knees.

I grinned. "Yes," I told my qareen. "This is exactly what I was looking for."

FIFTY-EIGHT

〰〰〰〰〰

SAMIRA

The sun had only just started to paint the sky in shades of violet. Dry heat hadn't settled its weight on my skin yet. I drew a deep breath, taking a moment to enjoy the fresh air, and let my lids flutter open.

Keir's face was tipped down, nose nearly brushing mine, his soft breaths dancing across my lips with each exhale. He looked at peace while he slept. The skin beneath the faded kohl on his forehead was smooth, his eyelashes curving gently against his strong cheekbones.

My head was pillowed by his bicep while his other arm had wrapped entirely around me, holding me tightly against him so that I could feel every dip and curve of his strong body. But none of that was the reason for the ribbon of surprise that twined around me.

It was the fact that my arm was wrapped around him, too. My hand had found its way under his tunic, palm on the bare skin between his shoulder blades. My fingers pressed into his smooth, warm flesh, muscles shifting with each breath he took, and I had the distinct impression I'd been clinging to him.

People moved in their sleep—and it had been a cold night. It was innocent, meaningless. All I had to do was sit up, then Keir would wake, and we could return to this nightmare.

But I didn't sit up. I didn't move at all. I continued to lie there in the sand with my hand on Keir's back and my head on his arm. Instead of lurching away, I studied him. His slightly crooked nose that suggested it had been broken at one point, his full lips underlined by his blue runes, the scruff of facial hair that had grown alongside those blue lines.

I wondered what Keir's runes meant. They were clearly symbols, and they never crossed over each other, as if they were spelling something out. I followed the column of his throat with my eyes to where the runes disappeared within the V of his tunic, feeling the absurd urge to trace them.

And then Keir's eyes opened, instantly finding mine, and I stopped breathing.

It was like the sun emerging from behind a cloud. Bright, sudden. A zing ripped through my blood. I waited for him to say something cruel or to shove me away.

But he simply stared at me, gaze heavy-lidded with sleep. I could see his thoughts stringing themselves together, taking inventory of our position, of *my* position, wondering how long I'd been awake. And still he didn't move, glittering cyes locked on mine. With each silent moment that passed, my skin grew warmer, my pulse grew faster.

Keir's eyes dipped to my lips, and my heart stopped.

For a moment, I thought of a different morning, waking up in a different man's arms. The moment of indecision, of panic. I felt none of that now. My tongue darted out to wet my lips, and Keir tracked the movement. I held my breath.

All at once, the heat in his gaze cooled and he sat up. My arm fell out of his tunic with a dull thud. "We should get back to searching for Rade," he said without looking at me.

Fire burst in my cheeks as embarrassment speared through me. "Right." I hardly had time to get the word out before Keir was on his feet.

*   *   *

As we drew closer to that mountain, that strange pull in my chest became stronger. But I bit my chapped lip and forced myself to keep moving at the same pace. It was a physical effort not to break into a run.

And then, there it was, the source of the glint. Still far, but finally visible: a golden roof on top of a crumbling temple, nearly identical to the one I'd woken up in. We both walked faster.

It loomed over us just as the last one had. An ancient ruin made of columns broken halfway to a ceiling that had long ago collapsed to the floor. The winding staircase was fully intact, wrapping like a snake around fierce statues of Shaya. The Underworld god stood proudly, slitted eyes gazing out at the horizon. The Temple of Shaya.

Empty. Abandoned, just like Ketet's. No city, no Rade, no one at all to help us.

"Fuck," Keir mumbled.

A sad laugh bubbled out of me. We'd crossed the Wastelands. We'd actually done it. And now we were going to die. I'd led us days in the wrong direction, probably sealing Rade's death in the process, because . . . I'd seen something shiny. Saying it to myself now sounded so idiotic, humiliation burned my cheeks and ripped another hysterical laugh out of me.

"What about this is funny?" Keir demanded.

I pointed at the ancient structure, stomach cramping as I laughed harder. I fell to my knees, tears spilling over my cheeks.

It was greed that brought you here. It is greed that will seek you out. Greed destroys, greed burns.

The Seer was right. I could have ended this all before stepping into the Mirror Realm, before I dragged Keir in with me. It was greed. My own damned greed, wanting to know what it was like to be Amunet—more importantly, to *not* be Samira—if just for a little while. At every turn, I'd been selfish and horrible and—gods, I'd made all of Kaldfold think I was their salvation.

But out of fire were you born, out of water were you found. To both must you return before all is razed to the ground.

The sun's *fire* was over my head.

I held the water-filled boots in my hands and turned them upside down, cackling at the splat of water against the hot sand. *There you go, another prophecy fulfilled.* I snorted.

"What are you doing?" Keir stared at the boots with horror. "Amunet, have you totally lost your mind?"

I wiped tears from my cheeks and gasped through the laughter, "I'm not Amunet."

"What?"

"My name is Samira." Another grin split my face. "I'm not the queen. I'm her *slave.*" And then I was lost to a fit of giggles that racked my whole frame.

Keir stared at me, lips parted, and the image was so comical, I keeled over, forehead to the ground as laughter rocked me.

His feet slammed into the sand with enough fury to shake the earth. He grabbed me by the arms, hauled me to my feet, seethed, "What do you mean? Where is the real Gods-Chosen?"

But I didn't care about his fury or his righteousness or what he'd say to Rade—because we were never going to find Rade. We were never going to get out of the Wastelands. My time was done. Served. Lies or truth, none of it mattered anymore. This was the end.

So I finally confessed, "When you invaded, Amunet asked me to take her place so she could escape. She thought you would kill her, and we couldn't let you kill the Gods-Chosen."

Keir's brows bunched together over his wide eyes. "She escap—"

Sand shot up like a geyser arouind us. It knocked us both off our feet and sent us sprawling in the sand. I grunted at the impact. But when I glanced back, my heart stopped beating in my chest.

The sand rose up and packed together to form the shape of two male bodies and one female. Faces emerged around eyes of fire. Pointed ears solidified on the sides of their heads. Fire blazed in the impression of hair, flickering in an unseen wind. The one in the middle grinned, the sand gaping into a black void in his face.

Jinn.

"Lost, little humans?" The grinning jinni's voice was rough, like a wheel over gravel.

Keir scrambled up to his feet and drew his sword and dagger. I stood, too, and stared with wide eyes.

The female jinni to the right chuckled at the weapons and sidled closer. She reached out a sandy arm and slammed her hand down directly on Keir's sword. The blade went right through the sand. The jinni pulled her hand back easily, not a scratch to be seen. "Put your blade away, Shifter."

Keir didn't. Choosing the illusion of safety. "What do you want?"

"You need help," said the jinni on the left.

"We're fine."

"You will die out here."

Keir didn't respond to that, a muscle in his jaw popping. We both knew it was true. We'd already lasted longer than King Zaid. We had a couple of days left at the most.

The grinning jinni drifted to the side to peer at me over Keir's shoulder. "We can save you, child. Would you like us to save you?"

My instinct was to immediately reject the offer, like Keir had done. Jinn were dangerous. I knew that. But they also had power. And I did not. I wasn't a Gods-Chosen; I couldn't save Ashorah. But maybe I could at least save Keir and Rade. They didn't deserve to die. And if I could do something about that, I had to.

"Can you save all of us?" I asked. Keir whipped around. I avoided his look.

The jinni's grin spread wider. "Of course."

"What is your price?"

"Amunet," Keir hissed, too preoccupied to remember that wasn't my name.

The female jinni moved toward me through the sand like a serpent, leaving a trail behind her, until she was standing beside my shoulder. "We won't ask for anything great."

"Our price is simple," agreed the male on the left, coming to my other side.

The grinning jinni said, "We just want what's in your hand."

I looked down at my empty hands and frowned. "I have nothing."

"Not now," he amended. "But later."

"No," Keir said instantly. "It's too dangerous. Too open-ended."

I agreed. But I tried to think of what I could possibly hold that would be of any value to the jinn. Food, maybe a weapon, clothes.

The amulet.

If Zarqa's fortune was true, I would hold that at some point. I didn't know what it was or what it did, but if that was what the jinn were after, I definitely shouldn't give it to them. If I agreed to this, I wouldn't be able to say no.

Unless . . .

Out of fire were you born . . . To both must you return.

Maybe this was part of Zarqa's fortune. The jinn were beings of sand and *fire*. Maybe I was supposed to agree to this bargain.

"When?" I inquired. "When will you ask for this?"

The grinning jinni's fiery hair blew toward me, and I flinched against the heat. "When you hold what we want."

"I need more."

"You won't get it, child."

The female jinni by my shoulder said, "This is our deal. Take it."

"If we leave you here," the jinni to my left added, "you will never find your qareen. Then you and the Shifter will die."

The grinning jinni asked, "Do we have a deal?"

I was starting to get dizzy from turning my head so much. Licking my dry lips, I clarified, "You will save all of us from the Mirror Realm. In exchange for what's in my hand. Mine and no one else's."

"That is the deal."

I lifted my eyes to Keir's, and he shook his head.

"If we die, Rade dies," I reminded him. Keir swallowed hard and fell silent.

I tried to assure myself the deal might not last long enough to benefit the jinn. If they got us out of the Mirror Realm, the Kaldfolk would kill me for my betrayal anyway. Then I wouldn't have time to find, let alone hold, the amulet—or anything else.

But whether or not this plan hurt me in the end, I had to save Rade and Keir.

"I accept."

The grinning jinni smiled so wide, the void of his mouth cut clear across his face. "See you soon, child." Instantly, the bodies of sand collapsed back to the earth in a pile, as if they'd never been there at all.

Keir flashed me a troubled look, but there was no time to speak of what had just transpired. The ground roiled beneath us, rippling like waves. I threw my arms out to try to keep my balance, and Keir caught my hand.

The sand caved in.

I screamed, my heart hitting my feet as we plummeted. I lost my grip on Keir.

Sand poured over us, swallowing Keir's shout. I scrambled for something to hold on to, but it was only sand and more sand, slipping through my fingers fast enough to burn.

The sky grew smaller and smaller, until it was a speck as we tumbled into the sinkhole. Sand blinded me, but I was falling so fast, I couldn't move my arms to shield myself. Careening, feet over head—

My back slammed into something hard, my bones clanging together with the force of the impact. I gasped for breath, blinking hard as I tried to bring the world into focus.

Keir was beside me, on his stomach. With a groan, he rolled onto his back. He took a few seconds to catch his breath before he asked, "You okay?"

"Yeah," I panted. "You?"

"Fantastic," he wheezed.

Walls of thick, dark sand stretched up to the dot of sky above us. Some grains still trickled down the sides as it settled, shifting noisily.

We were in a chasm.

Anger twisted my chest.

"You said you would save us!" I yelled uselessly up to the sky.

But there was no response. The jinn were long gone.

I dropped my head to the sand and squeezed my eyes shut. I'd thought I'd been so careful, but I had missed some loophole and doomed us all. For a second time. If the walls of sand collapsed on us, it would be less crushing than the hopelessness that pressed in on me now.

"Tell me your name again."

I blinked my eyes open.

Keir kept his gaze resolutely on the sky so far above, refusing to look at me.

Throat tight, I ventured, "Samira."

"Samira . . ." he repeated, trying it out. His tongue caressed the syllables in a low rumble. The first time I'd heard my name in weeks, and it was coated in so much pain and betrayal, my heart sank into my stomach. "Answer a question for me, *Samira*. Do your people hate us so much that it was easy to pretend to care for a tent full of refugees? To convince Velka you were friends? Were you laughing, *Samira*, when I told you about my time in the Shroud? How about when you got Rade to fuck you? Were you laughing then?"

Heat raced to my cheeks. "How did you—"

"Shifter hearing, remember? Don't worry, I didn't listen to the whole thing." When he finally looked at me, the yellow of his eyes blazed with fury. And something more that had his chest heaving and his brows dropping low.

"I didn't—I mean, *we* didn't—" I cut myself off. Not the important part. "No, I wasn't laughing. I wasn't pretending—"

"You went through the *whole fucking wedding ceremony!*" he almost shouted, half sitting up. "You tricked us all into thinking you were kind, that you gave a single fuck about us. You made *me* think—" Keir blew out a laugh that was nothing more than a whip of hot air and dropped his head back to the sand. "Your queen gave you an order and you obeyed. Fine. But you had a month, Samira— if that's even really your name. Should we try a few more? See which identity you prefer? I hear Leila is a popular name in Ashorah. How about that one?"

My eyes burned. "My name really is Samira."

"I gave you so many fucking chances, *Samira.*" I cringed. He threw my name at me like it was a curse. "Over and over, I begged you for the truth. None of this had to happen. You could have stopped it."

"I wanted to tell you," I whispered. "But then my runes were green, and Rade said he'd seen me in his fortune, and at the Lunar Feast, you . . ." A lump formed in my throat; I swallowed past it. "I thought I was doing the right thing. And then, I . . . For sixteen years, I mattered to no one, and then suddenly, I mattered to *every-one*. It was . . . addictive." It sounded so selfish when I said it out loud. No, I'd known it was selfish before. Despite all the excuses I'd made for myself, I'd known, and yet I'd done it anyway. The guilt was suffocating.

After a beat of silence, Keir asked, "Rade saw you in his fortune?"

I nodded.

"In what way?"

"I don't know. He only told me he'd seen me."

A long breath streamed from his nose as he considered that. He turned his face up to the sky again, eyes flicking back and forth as he processed how much of the past month had been a lie.

In a small voice, I offered a pathetic and inadequate "I'm sorry."

"You're sorry," he repeated dully, just like he had our first night in the Wastelands. "We're going to die in here while my people die out there, and you're sorry."

Tears I could not afford to lose bubbled over my lids. "There's still the Gods-Chosen." A weak consolation, a platitude that tasted false on my tongue.

He looked at me once more, and I watched the fire go out in his eyes, replaced with a tired sort of sadness. "We all have scars," he said, repeating what he'd told me after I'd shown him my *X* in the watchtower, the first time he'd really begged me. "I would have understood yours. If you had just told me."

"You would have killed me."

"No, Samira. I wouldn't have. I never could have. Isn't that obvious by now?"

Somehow, that assurance, said so sadly, so ruefully, made my heart crack wider. Confusion and despair constricted my lungs, strangling me beyond words.

Keir pressed his hands into the sand to sit up—and paused. "Is this metal?"

Sucking in my tears, I sat up, too, and dusted sand away to reveal a pristine surface with a reflection so pure, I could see my own stunned, sunburned face staring back at me. A seam cut through it, splitting the metal sheet in two. I swiped more sand away to reveal curling shapes on either side of the groove. Handles.

We were sitting on two massive doors.

I staggered upright, eyes widening as I took in the enormous double doors made of solid gold. They created the floor beneath us.

Keir quickly stood, too, wincing as the movement pulled at his wound. "What is this?"

"I don't know." But that cord around my sternum returned, gave a powerful yank toward the doors. Beneath them. "They want me to go down there."

"Who, the jinn?"

"I don't know." I braced my feet against the metal floor and tugged at the opposite handle with all my might, straining under the weight.

Keir's hands appeared beside mine. I stilled. "I got it," he said tightly.

The tension between us was thick. My heart shrank. I let go of the handle and stepped back. Keir gritted his teeth and pulled.

The door lifted slowly. Marble stairs descended beneath it, farther into the earth.

Veins bulged in Keir's neck, his arms shook. "My sword," he ground out. "Use it to prop it open."

I grabbed the sword from where it had landed a few feet away and positioned it under the door, against the corner. "Okay."

He lowered the door cautiously until it settled against the sword hilt. The blade scraped a few inches until it wedged fully into the corner. "Will it hold?" I asked skeptically.

"It'll have to. It's all we have."

Another tug at my sternum, and I ducked under the door. Thank the gods it didn't squash me like a bug. Keir followed, brandishing his serrated dagger, the only weapon he had left.

The marble stairway curved partway down, making it impossible to see what might be at the bottom. I descended as fast as my feet would carry me, the pull intensifying with every step. I rounded the curve, and gasped.

Before me spread a gleaming metropolis of gold buildings, each one more exquisite than the last. Bright green trees of all kinds lined the gold-paved streets. Palm trees, evergreens, birch, pine, ginkgo. Trees that shouldn't be able to exist alongside each other—shouldn't be able to exist dozens of feet below the earth—and above, not the dark curve of a cavern ceiling but, impossibly, the sky. And the sun. Not sweltering and cruel, as I knew it, but giving off a soft, pleasant warmth. A breeze teased the ends of my hair, the wisps that had come free of the braids, and cooled the sweat on my brow.

"What is this place?" Keir breathed.

The city was angled so that all the roads and all the buildings looked toward an imposing gold citadel with a domed roof and stained glass windows. It loomed over the entire area, demanding attention with its high columns and imposing god statues. Even from here, I could recognize Ketet's laurel crown and waving braids.

There was only one place this could be.

"The Buried City," I whispered.

The city King Zaid had braved the Wastelands for. That I had seen in my fortune from Zarqa. That was meant to be paradise on earth. We'd found it.

The city was quiet. *Silent.* There wasn't a single person to be seen.

A shudder slithered down my spine.

Keir and I exchanged a look before setting foot on the golden street before us.

As we passed bazaars and apartments, the cord in my chest strengthened further, like a solid thing, yanking me toward the citadel, impossible to ignore. I moved faster, jogging through the splendid city. Wordlessly, Keir kept pace beside me.

When I reached the citadel, I didn't hesitate. I threw open the door and skidded into an expansive entryway. Mosaics covered both floor and ceiling, and from above, all Seven Monarchs gazed down at us regally. Diamond chandeliers dangled from the vaulted ceiling, glinting in the soft light, and our padded steps echoed in the empty chamber. To the right, through a curved archway, I heard a rushing sound. The cord tugged me toward it. Another look passed between Keir and me. Whatever his feelings, he brandished his dagger and walked in front of me.

A large pool spanned the length of the wide room, glorious and sparkling, sizeable enough to swim laps. Delicate steps descended into it, disappearing into the deep blue. At the rear of the pool, a waterfall spilled from a high golden spout, bathing the whole space in a light mist.

Water.

I collapsed to my knees beside the pool and shoveled handful after handful of clear, sweet water into my mouth, and gods, it was chilled. Refreshing.

Keir's dagger clanged loudly as it hit the golden floor a split second before he dove in. Water splashed me, and I was so delirious with relief, I laughed and jumped in, too.

Each burn, each blister, each piece of torched flesh gave a sigh of relief as the water streamed through my hair, over my body, and though the cord still tugged, the bliss of the water as it soothed my wounds and slaked my thirst was for the moment stronger.

When I resurfaced, Keir stood comfortably in the center of the pool, while my toes struggled to scrape the floor. He looped an arm around my waist to hold me up. Panting softly, I set my hands on his shoulders. The last of the makeup that usually bordered his eyes had disappeared, and without it, he looked far less intimidating. For a moment, our relief outshone any jinn or lies. Keir's sunny eyes lit up with a genuine smile, his runes glistening against his jaw, and my lips stretched into a matching one.

But then, his nostrils flared and his smile dropped. He whipped around, water sloshing around him as he backed up, cornering me against the pool wall. "Keir, what—"

"Shh." The muscles in his back bunched tight. "We're not alone."

FIFTY-NINE

AMUNET

My qareen claimed to have never seen the amulet before. But it had to be here somewhere. That was why Shaya had asked Athar to send me to this strange place. He wanted me to find it.

And I would. By the gods, I would.

I'd envisioned meeting Shaya countless times. But it had always felt like a distant fancy. It didn't matter how powerful I'd be, I would never be as powerful as Ketet *and* Phadar *and* the lesser gods. There was no hope of breaking the seal on the Underworld that their joint power had created. So most of my dreams of meeting my real father had been contained to words on a breeze. A disembodied presence that was comforting, constant, but not corporeal.

But with a key . . . with a key everything could change.

No more nightmares. No more petty politics. No more itch, no more voices, no more symptoms of any kind.

No more loneliness. No more doubt. Just a father's love. Acceptance.

And all I needed was a fucking key.

I stepped out into the entrance hall to begin my search—

My power started thrashing wildly. A hound pulling at its leash. So much more insistent than when it had guided me to follow Athar.

I lifted my head.

The front door was open.

The double doors had both been shut before. But now sunlight streamed through, cutting a line across the entryway. My heart froze in my chest, thoughts emptying out.

To my qareen, I whispered, "I thought you said the citadel was empty."

She cowered behind me. "It is."

"Then who opened the door?"

She shook her head.

Voices.

My head whipped to the left. Across the entrance hall stood an archway. And out of that archway echoed voices.

"Let's go back upstairs," my qareen hissed. "Quick!"

I should listen to her. Just because Shaya had sent me here didn't mean it was entirely safe. Whoever was through that archway had been lying in wait for hours.

But I needed to find that amulet. If there were people living here, they would know where it was, surely. A few sweet promises, and the amulet would be in my hands.

I took a step forward, and my qareen grabbed my arm. "We have to hide!"

Even with all the brawn she possessed from never having ended her training with the Khada Guard, she was a coward. I was not.

"Stay here," I told her, and slipped free of her grip.

I would not hide from the echoes. I would meet them. And get what I needed, one way or another.

SIXTY

SAMIRA

Mere seconds later, sandaled feet slapped through the archway. Peering around Keir's shoulder, all I could make out were filth-encrusted toes poking out beneath a plain dress. A girl.

Adrenaline surged through me. It was difficult to make out her features beneath what appeared to be layers of grime. Her head was shaved to mere bristles, and an odor drifted across the room, so horrible it managed to span the several feet between us. It smelled like . . . feces?

Was this my qareen?

"Forgive the intrusion," she said in a sweet, polished, proper voice. "I seem to have gotten lost. You are . . . Kaldfolk, yes? Is this Kaldfold?"

If Keir responded, I couldn't hear him over the rushing in my ears. I knew that voice. Knew it better than my own. It was a voice I never thought I'd hear again. It felt like a trick. Work of the jinn, maybe.

But then Keir shifted to the side, and I couldn't deny the evidence before my eyes.

Queen Amunet Khada's clear emerald eyes were bright as ever, if a little unsure as she took in the hulking Kald in front of me. A shackle hung from her wrist, and streaks of filth covered every visible inch of her skin. There was something different about her, more than the signs of rough treatment on her body. There was a gleam in her gaze that hadn't been there before, a fidgeting in her stance, a hollowness to her cheeks that seemed more than just hunger.

Then her Khada-green eyes moved from Keir to me, darting from my ear-length hair to the runes across my forehead. Her shapely brows pulled together. "You're Ashoran," she said with surprise, her eyes flitting between me and Keir as if trying to explain to herself what an Ashoran might be doing with a Kald.

A ringing started in my ears.

She didn't recognize me.

I had spent sixteen *years* at her side. I had tended to her every whim. Dressed her. Bathed her. Fed her. I had received scars at her hands—my chest ached even now from renewing the X she'd given me. I'd traded my very *life* for hers.

And she didn't have a clue who I was. It was written all over her confused, pretty face.

She held out her hands in front of her, flexing her fingers. "My power feels stronger. Like it . . . knows you." The queen's gaze on me was curious. Calculating.

Conditioning ordered me to curtsy. Duck my head and clasp my hands in front of me. Exclaim what a relief it was to see her.

But as the ringing faded, a fire breathed to life in my gut.

She was here. Somehow, for this last leg of the Merging, she was here. She could finish this. She could find Rade. She could charm Keir. She could get rid of the Shroud. She could save everyone.

The Gods-Chosen had stepped into the story at exactly the right moment.

I wasn't needed anymore. The burden I'd been bearing all these weeks in Kaldfold was gone. I should be rejoicing. I waited for the ecstasy of relief to sweep over me.

Instead, the fire bloomed larger in my stomach, my heart pounding like a fist on a door.

"What are you doing here?" I said. My grip was so tight on Keir's arm, I could feel the give of his skin under my nails, but he didn't pull away.

Amunet's eyes narrowed to slits, and she came a few steps closer. "*Do* I know you?"

I waited breathlessly, this unnamed emotion blazing through me.

But I could name it. The heat in my gut, the tight bands squeezing my heart even as my heart beat against them. I was *angry*.

I'd given so much for this girl. More than just this life, I'd sacrificed my afterlife. The gods had turned their backs on me because of the choices I'd made. Keir despised me, the Kaldfolk would curse me. All for her. And she couldn't even bother to remember my face? She got to just waltz in at the very end and take all the credit? Take my friends, my accomplishments—and it *was* an accomplishment that I'd made it this far. I had earned the right to live as long as I had. Had earned every breath I took.

The world had always been unfair. In Khada Palace, I had found a way to live with that reality. Just keep my head down, obey, go through the motions, don't say a word. Pretend everything was fine. No, more than that, pretend to be *happy*. Grateful.

But right now, standing here, I could no longer pretend. Could no longer bear it at all.

Amunet crouched at the edge of the pool and studied me. Even with Keir between us, I locked eyes with the Gods-Chosen. I refused to be the first to break.

Her face went slack, as if she'd been hit. "You."

"Me," I whispered.

Her eyes flicked from me to Keir. Taking in his posture, his protective stance, his stare. And she laughed. "Incredible. I knew the Kaldfolk had taken you, but I'd assumed you'd only last a few days in their captivity. It seems you exceeded my expectations." She laughed again. A sound I used to compare to birdsong. Now it grated.

Keir's lips parted as he suddenly understood. "You're the Gods—"

There was a yank that wrenched Keir's arm from my grip, then a splash. Between one blink and the next, Keir disappeared underwater.

"Keir!" I screamed, peering into the deep blue, but it was impossible to see through the water. "Keir!"

The water exploded upward, and Keir went flying out of the pool. I heard something crack when he crashed down to the gold floor. He didn't move.

I swam to the steps leading out of the pool.

A creature rose up from the depths, blocking my path, its massive form shedding water. It turned its yellow eyes on me. And its face . . .

It was Keir's. But also, not Keir's. His eyes were feral, and his lips curled maniacally at the corners. Half the creature's body was a charred black. Not just burned but *scorched*.

It was Keir's qareen, already lunging across the water toward me.

There was no use fleeing. I held perfectly still as he came within inches of me, rising up to his full height, water cascading off his bare, scorched torso. He ducked his head into my neck just as Keir had done at the Lunar Feast, some of his skin flaking off, and drew a deep breath. He smiled against me.

I clenched my jaw as I fought every instinct that screamed at me to run. I wouldn't be fast enough and would probably only earn this creature's fury.

His unbound hair swung forward and curtained us off so all I could see was his deformed face as he pressed me against the pool wall, and when I felt the hard heat of him, it became startlingly apparent that he was naked beneath the water.

His large hands came up to my face, and he tilted my head as far back as it would go. His wild eyes sparkled eagerly as he put his nose to my forehead and inhaled. A moan rumbled out of him.

Then he ran his tongue over my runes, from right temple to left.

My nose curled even as my body's trembling intensified.

He dragged his nose down my cheek and neck until he landed at my shoulder. Where the wound from Bain's attack was. Keir's qareen yanked my dress strap aside, running his fingers over the spot. He took another deep inhale. "Mine," he purred—and then bit down.

I screamed as pain ricocheted down my arm and blood spilled over. He'd used his bear teeth, and they stabbed straight through my flesh. I slapped and shoved at him, but he was immovable. He bit down harder, and my eyes bulged.

A roar erupted behind him.

Keir's qareen looked up sharply, my blood trickling down his chin.

It was Keir, one arm wrapped gingerly around his abdomen. He was favoring his right leg, and I knew he had to be in pain. But his face was twisted into a look of pure rage, his dagger aloft. Amunet had moved off to the side, inching her way around the pool and out of the qareen's line of sight.

The qareen stepped in front of me and snarled at Keir. *"Mine."*

"No," he snarled right back, more animal than man. Keir hurled the dagger. It whistled through the air toward the qareen's heart, but the qareen moved at the last second, and it embedded itself in the creature's shoulder.

He let out an enraged roar as black blood dribbled out.

"Run!" Keir shouted at me before his bear form tore out of him with another roar. The qareen yanked out the dagger and let it clatter on the floor beside my head. Then he swam fast as an arrow toward Keir.

I grabbed the discarded dagger and heaved myself out of the pool—

The cord around my sternum wrenched me back, and I fell with a splash, water shooting up my nose. I broke the surface, sputtering. My chest ached from how hard the cord had pulled.

"What's wrong with you?" Amunet shouted, eyes darting from me to the qareen, though she made no move to help Keir.

I didn't bother answering her. The Gods-Chosen's arrival had been a large enough distraction to ignore the pull, but now it was yanking at me with renewed vigor. Demanding. It wanted me to go through that waterfall, and it wanted me to do it *now*.

Keir lunged, claws extended and teeth snapping, and ripped a chunk out of the qareen's abdomen in a spray of black blood. Its scream rattled the ceiling. In the next blink, there were *two* bears wrestling on the side of the pool. Blood—black and red—splattered the wall.

Keir needed my help. I wanted to help—

Now! that pull ordered.

I turned my back on Keir and lurched through the waterfall.

SIXTY-ONE

AMUNET

My maid disappeared behind the waterfall, moving so fast she almost looked as if she'd been dragged. The moment she was gone, my power threw itself against its confines. Less like a horse champing at the bit and more like a raging bull. Stronger.

Because of her. But why?

The Kald roared as his qareen slashed at him, but I barely heard it over the static buzzing in my ears. Without stopping to think, I dove into the pool after her.

A small, cavernous room met me on the other side of the waterfall. No sounds filtered past the curtain of water. It was a sacred sort of quiet. Like when I'd stepped through Shaya's doorway made of glittering sand.

I stepped out of the pool gingerly onto the smooth stone floor. Water trickled softly down my body, like it, too, knew to control its volume.

Stone walls rose up around me—so at odds with the solid gold of the palace. A large golden table stretched across the opposite wall, covered in a bright emerald cloth that billowed lightly in an invisible wind.

My maid stood over it, her back to me, staring down at the altar.

My power went wild. With each step closer, its flailing became mightier. Sweat gathered on my brow as I fought to keep myself in check.

Whatever was beneath the green cloth moved, rhythmically, up and down. Breathing. A body. Bound hands poked out from underneath the cloth.

"What is this?" I asked.

My maid didn't respond. Her brown eyes were focused so resolutely on the altar, she almost looked as if she were in a trance. Then she reached out and pulled the cloth off.

It was a girl. The *same* girl as the one beside me.

Her qareen.

Her wrists were bound tightly behind her with a thick golden rope. Her ankles were tied, too, and her nudity was covered by faintly glowing green tattoos that curved around every inch of her body, just like the ones currently adorning my maid's forehead. They were scrawled from her toes all the way up, finally disappearing into her long, dark hair.

The qareen struggled against her restraints, bucking wildly the moment the sheet was pulled away. She tried to scream, but it was muffled against the gag in her mouth.

My power burned its brightest yet. An intangible flare, yet somehow blinding. Hesitantly, I rested my hand on the qareen's arm.

A gust of power surged toward me so fast, I startled and yanked my hand away.

Then I laughed.

My power. Somehow inside this random maid's qareen. Bound there, if the ropes and gag were any indication. How or why, I couldn't know, but this must have been the other reason Shaya had sent me here. To claim it.

If my power was bound inside her, I could only think of one way to get it out. The same way the Cirra Tribe had planned to take my wish back—I'd have to bleed it out.

Something glinted, catching my eye. I turned to find my maid holding a dagger, the one that Kald had thrown, her eyes still trained on her qareen.

She had anticipated my need and acted accordingly. She was well trained indeed.

I held out my hand expectantly. "Give me the knife."

She blinked. Once. Twice. Staring at my outstretched palm.

My smile was indulgent. "You have served the Gods-Chosen valiantly. Beyond all expectations. For which you will be greatly rewarded. But I can take it from here." I wiggled my fingers insistently.

It was just the same as it had been that fateful night, when the Kaldfolk ravaged my palace. Her, gazing at me with those large frightened eyes. And me, impatient to get on with my father's plans. I really should have recognized her the moment I'd seen her.

I reached for the knife.

The girl stepped back. "No."

SIXTY-TWO

SAMIRA

The Gods-Chosen stared at me, face frozen. "No?"

My heart hammered in my chest. I had never said no to Amunet. Never. Had never even dreamed of it. But my fingers were latched on to Keir's serrated dagger and refused to let go.

It was me lying on the altar. I was looking down at myself. *My* gagged mouth, *my* glowing green runes, *my* lit-up eyes that weren't brown but a bright, piercing orange. But there were no scars on my chest or back.

She looked just like me and nothing like me at all. There was so much on her body that my own was missing. But she was *me.* Whatever pull I'd felt had lured *me* here. It wanted *me* to find her. Wanted *me* to use this dagger. Not Amunet Khada. *Me.*

"Give me the dagger, girl," Amunet repeated. "That is not a re-quest."

Girl. She couldn't even bother to remember my name.

My qareen shook her head fervently and screamed into her gag.

That same disturbing feeling of looking at my reflection in a mir-ror came over me. I gazed down at my qareen, fear making her oth-erworldly eyes bulge, her body trembling as she braced for impact. Her bucking had ceased. She was no longer trying to get away. No longer fighting. She just looked up at me pleadingly.

Passive. Resigned. Just as I'd been when Amunet had tossed me to the bears.

And she'd do it again. Right now. She would take this dagger, cut into *my* qareen, and then . . . what? Vanish. It would not be in her nature to help Keir, a Kald, against his qareen—or to help me, a slave too insignificant to have a name. Keir and I would be left alone to deal with his double. And to figure out a way home, if we were lucky enough to survive the scorched creature behind the waterfall.

I stared and stared at my qareen, and the longer I looked, the more disgust filled me. Pathetic, broken, helpless. A scared little girl always at someone else's mercy.

I hated her. I hated her fear. I hated her choked screams. I hated the tears streaming down her cheeks. It was a loathing so deep, it was an integral part of me. A hatred that had always been there, lurking in the background of my consciousness, that I hadn't spotted until just now.

"This is your last warning," Amunet said. "Give me the fucking dag—"

I slit my qareen's throat.

Glittering blood flooded out of her neck, and she twitched violently. I must've nicked an artery, because it spurted out and splashed over my chest.

The moment her blood hit me, the metallic scent punched up my nose, and my hatred and disgust drained away as the horror of what I'd done sank in. My qareen jerked harder, all the veins in her head bulging as she fought to hang on to life, choking on her own blood.

With a gasp, I tossed the knife away like it'd burned me. "Oh gods," I whispered, covering my mouth. "I'm sorry! I'm sorry, I didn't—"

"What have you done?" Amunet shrieked, and lunged at me. Grabbed me by the shoulders and sent me flying into the wall.

My head cracked, and pain burst through me.

Something sharp pricked my neck. It took several hard blinks before I managed to make out Amunet's twisted face. She snarled at me and pressed Keir's dagger harder against my throat. She looked nothing like the girl I'd served my whole life. Not the savior I'd pictured. She looked like an animal. "Do you have any idea what you've just done? That was *mine*, and you've—"

Something shifted on the altar, and she stopped. I strained past the pain and horror running through me to focus.

My qareen's blood moved. Twisted along grooves in the altar I hadn't noticed until just then, slid down to the floor, where more symbols had been carved. Glittering blood, like a river reflecting sunlight. It filled in the ruts on the floor, draining toward us.

Amunet and I watched in stunned silence as it puddled around our feet.

Then disappeared as it seeped into my skin. Only mine.

Wide-eyed, Amunet lowered the dagger and stepped away.

A white, burning pain blasted through me, like a hundred branding irons had been thrust into my core at the same time. I tried to swipe the blood away, smacking at my legs, my arms, but it was useless. It climbed up my thighs like vines, stretched across my shoulders, until it reached my chest. I screamed.

Pain and agony. That was all there was. Soul-wrenching *pain*. Bright light burst behind my eyes, and I caved forward, slapping my hands over my face. It scorched me from the inside out, eating away at my organs, evaporating my blood, turning my bone marrow to lava.

When I opened my eyes, the dead girl on the altar was missing her runes, her bronzed skin utterly unblemished.

The pain ripped through me again, knocking me off-balance. I swayed forward but managed to catch myself on the altar before I hit the floor.

With a tattooed hand.

Barely able to catch my breath, I gaped at my knuckles, my wrists. I held them up in front of me, breaths jagged. Both hands were covered in faintly glowing green runes, which reached up my arms, down my torso, painted over my legs.

Every rune that had been on the qareen's body was now on mine.

I staggered away from the altar, but pain surged up my legs, sapping their strength, and I landed hard on my knees beside the pool.

The water was calm enough this far from the waterfall for me to clearly see my reflection. My eyes weren't brown anymore.

They were orange.

And they beamed like sunrays out of my skull.

Stupefied, I glanced up at Amunet. Her chest rose and fell rapidly as she took me in. She shook her head once. "You—"

She was wrenched backward, as if an invisible hook had ripped her off her feet. She went sailing through the air, toward the wall—and then through it. Disappeared.

It was the last thing I saw before white, agonizing fire swallowed me up.

SIXTY-THREE

AMUNET

Oxygen surged into my lungs, and I sucked in the deepest breath I could, coughing violently. Sand exploded out of my mouth, and light blinded me. My thoughts were sluggish, pulse thundering in my ears. My head flopped forward, chin hitting my chest.

A rope was tied around my ribs. I was being dragged across black sand. *What . . . ?*

I looked up, and Athar was there. He grinned and waggled his fingers in goodbye.

"Wait," I croaked. Sand coated my mouth, crunched between my teeth, burned my throat with its dryness. But something was wrong. My power no longer thrashed. My fingertips no longer tingled. In fact, I could hardly feel my power at all beyond a subtle wind. A mere inkling that it was out there somewhere.

With her.

Footsteps shifted behind me. On my flimsy neck, I turned to see a woman with yellow eyes and a face covering. The one from the Cirra Tribe. On my other side was the younger girl. They hauled me toward the shade of trees.

"No." I struggled weakly. "No, let me go!" But my arms were useless, entirely drained. "Athar!" I tried instead.

But Athar was gone. Vanished like he'd never been there at all.

My head was light, chest searing as I continued to gasp for oxygen, and my legs wouldn't work. There was nothing I could do as the women dropped me unceremoniously against a tree trunk. I laid there, breathing hard, glaring up at them.

The leader loomed over me, fingers tense around her spear. "Hello, Amunet Khada."

The younger girl cinched the rope tighter around my torso, pinning my arms to my sides. Behind her, men and women from their tribe stood. All armed. Some still in their hyena forms.

The younger girl passed the rope to a man while she pulled out a curved bowl and fitted it to the side of my neck as the leader twirled her spear. She stopped with the razor-sharp edge against my jugular. "Amunet Khada," she boomed, "you stole from the Cirra Tribe. Now you must be bled."

I stared back from beneath my lashes, eyes unflinching. I just needed a few more moments. Strength was returning to my limbs. Just a few more—

The leader sliced.

Pain flashed through me as blood gushed out of my neck and into the waiting bowl in a scene hauntingly similar to what I'd just witnessed with my maid. I struggled, but the man holding my rope didn't falter. Keeping me firmly in place as the Cirra Tribe bled me out.

My heart was a deafening drum in my ear, slowing with each ounce of blood lost. Each blink lasted an eternity. I watched as the girl switched out one bowl for another. My blood glittered slightly—the remnants of the jinni's magic in my veins. Nothing like the shine from my decoy's qareen. Nowhere near as powerful as what that girl had stolen from me.

I laughed, blood bubbling out of my lips, dripping down my chin. Oh, that girl had made a very grave mistake. Did she really think she could steal from Shaya's daughter—from Shaya himself—and get away with it? She might have my power now, but it wouldn't stay that way for long.

"When I get my power," I wheezed, "I'm coming for your people first."

"You won't live that long," the girl replied.

I grinned. I didn't have to see myself to know that grin looked deranged, demonic, showcasing the darkness nestled inside me.

She blanched.

There was a distinct *thunk*, and then her eyes rolled back, and she collapsed.

For a moment, I didn't understand what had happened. But then the rope fell from my arms and familiar dark brown eyes were in front of me, and a cloth was pressed to my throat. "Hold this."

My tongue felt too big, words clumsy as I murmured, "Jasim?"

He grabbed my limp hand and forced it to my neck. "Keep pressure on it." Then he spun away, scimitar raised, as the leader snarled and lunged at him. Hyenas cackled, too, and pounced.

It was all happening too fast for my blurred vision to make sense of. Jasim's black curls fanned around him as he spun. Metal clanged. The smell of copper filled the clearing. People in face coverings hit the ground and didn't get back up.

The cloth under my fingers grew warm and sticky. I was still bleeding. It wasn't slowing. But my heart was expanding, relief and hope compounding on each other as I gazed at Jasim in blank shock. "You . . . came back?"

He grunted as he threw a hyena off him, sparing me a single glance. "You were right. My expectations of you weren't fair." He slashed again, blood spattered. "I don't want you to be anyone else. I'm sorry I made you think—" Jasim ducked before he caught a blade to the face. His foot shot out and knocked the tribesman into another, both of them crashing to the ground. "But I will never leave you. Be who you are, and I . . . I will be better. I love you, Amunet."

Dizzy with blood loss, adrenaline buzzing through my veins from terror, I smiled. He was here. He hadn't left me. Which meant . . .

It wasn't too late. I could be the girl he thought I was. I'd caught a glimpse of her in my qareen. It wouldn't be easy, but . . . but I'd try. And he would see the selfish side of me, the dark side aligned with the God of Death, and not shrink away. He'd already caught a glimpse of her, too. We would both get better. We'd grow, together. *Together.*

That light feeling in my chest grew and grew until I thought I would burst with the elation. "Jasim, I love—"

Shrieking filled the trees. Not a pained scream, not an animal's call, either. The Cirra Tribe whirled in its direction, alarmed.

And then an arrow shot out of the brush and burst through Jasim's throat.

The world went silent.

My ears closed up. My breaths echoed in my head.

I stared. At the protruding arrow, dripping red. At the wide-eyed shock on Jasim's face.

Then I screamed. My chest rattled with it, my throat strained. I watched helplessly as Jasim's knees buckled and hit the ground. Blood poured out of his throat, his mouth.

No, I thought, screeched, begged. *No!*

His eyes sought mine, those reassuring brown eyes that I'd turned to so many times, that had always been there when my mind got too loud, when I needed a lifeline to cling to, that had *just fucking come back.* Those eyes that even now, as he choked on a breath, bestowed me with *the look.* I scrambled toward him, sluggish and uncoordinated. My fingers clawed at the earth as I tried to drag myself closer, my nails broke, and dull pain pricked me. It was nothing compared to the agony welling up inside me.

Jasim's chest stuttered, that breath he fought so hard for trapped behind the arrow. And then his face went slack, and the light went out of his eyes.

My chest caved in. Tears branded my cheeks. An unholy shriek sliced up my throat.

Blood loss and shock threatened to rob me of my consciousness, but I hung on stubbornly. As if I could reverse the past few moments as long as I stayed awake.

Men surged into the clearing, tongues wagging with their battle cries, red-and-yellow sashes across their chests, many of them brandishing bows and arrows, like the one sticking out of Jasim's throat.

The man leading the charge came straight for me, gold-flecked brown eyes sparkling, lips pulled wide in a smile, his pointed ears poking through a mop of curly brown hair.

The khopesh in his hand swung wide, and then a tribesman blocking his path was choking. A line sliced clean through his throat, pouring out in a waterfall of red, coating his chest. Within seconds, his skin lost all color, and he fell, dead.

The man with pointed ears swung off his horse as the sound of a battle echoed around us. Feet tromped over Jasim's corpse. Hyenas howled and snapped their teeth, meeting blades. Spears locked with khopeshes. But it was as if he hadn't noticed any of it.

Prince Sen Almassi of the Dry Lands crouched in front of me, those gold-flecked eyes half mad. His bloodthirsty grin was the last thing I saw before I finally lost consciousness.

SIXTY-FOUR

AMUNET

I was in a cage. It rocked and jostled hard, creaking loudly, and with each lurch, my forehead smacked into the bars. But I was too weak to stop it.

A dull ache throbbed at the side of my neck. I reached up to feel it—

My hands pulled short. Wrists shackled. A glance down proved my ankles were, too.

Torches flared beside me, and I squinted to make out red and yellow sashes. I knew those colors.

The Dry Lands.

Immediately following that was *Jasim*.

He was dead. He'd come back for me. He hadn't abandoned me, even after all I'd said, all I'd done. He'd loved *me*. And now he was dead.

The sorrow was crippling. Heart shredding like paper. King Zaid had been right; Jasim was all I had. And Sen Almassi had taken him from me.

I turned my head to see through the bars at the rear of my cage.

The granite Lotus River dam stood out starkly against the tan, barren landscape. Behind me by a mile or two. Which meant I was already deep in the Dry Lands. To the left of the dam, on the horizon, the sun was setting, painting the sky in a deep bloodred.

The month was over. My birthday was ending.

A ripple flowed over me, stirring my clothes, brushing the top of my shaved head. I recognized it. It was out there, like a beacon in the distance.

My power.

Seeping away like a receding tide. Growing smaller and smaller.

Pulled away by that gods-damn servant. I could still feel it, but barely, like a single hair tickling the skin of my arm. When it should have been an explosion, an overwhelming surge.

Rage filled me, burning like venom in my veins. That bitch had stolen it from me. Power that Shaya needed, that was my birthright, that I had waited twenty fucking years for, that Jasim had *died* for.

Though my limbs felt heavy, I lifted my arm and banged on one of the bars with my manacle. It gave a resounding clang. "Hey," I croaked through dry lips. "Hey!"

A woman pulled up alongside me on a camel. She was dressed in a deep red breast wrap and skirt that didn't even reach her knees. A thin chain of silver was wrapped around her head, and a teardrop pendant rested against her forehead. She lifted an eyebrow.

"Release me," I ordered.

The woman's lips twitched in amusement, but she didn't respond.

My rage flared hotter. I wrapped my fingers around the bars, pressing my sweaty face to them, and bared my teeth. "Release me now. Or I will bring the might of Shaya down on you and your people."

The woman snorted. "Oh, Prince Sen's going to have fun with you." Then she dug her heels into the camel's side and cantered away.

"Get back here!" I yelled. "Let me go! *Hey!*" But no one looked my way. Utterly ignored my orders and banging.

The last of my energy filtered away, and I slumped back in my cage.

But my fury didn't abate. Jasim had been *good*. Loyal. Compassionate when no one else thought me deserving of it. And because of that, he'd died. All that goodness, and for what? A grisly death in a trickster's forest with no one to offer him a proper burial. Left to the insects and vultures to pick apart.

I squeezed my eyes shut against the onslaught of horrific images. That light feeling that had bloomed so freely just hours ago withered and died, rotted until not even a seed of it remained. If I weren't caged, I would've torn through Sen's forces with my teeth before going after the slave girl so I could drain every last drop of her blood.

No matter. I retreated into that quiet place inside myself that had allowed me to time my meals in Anwar's cell down to the second. I could be patient if I had to be. And when Sen made the mistake of opening my cage, he'd find me waiting for him like a coiled cobra. When I struck, not a single person would be left to call the Dry Lands home.

SIXTY-FIVE

ㅅㅅㅅㅅㅅㅅㅅ

SAMIRA

The pain was bright, but my surroundings were pitch-black. I was in so much agony that I could do nothing more than gape in a silent scream. It stole my voice, my breath. I collapsed to my knees on a ground that was both rough and pillowy. Almost like clouds but slightly off.

Out of the abyss of unending torment came a silky, sultry voice. "Well, well, well."

Every hair on my body stood straight up. I knew that voice. He'd only been a shadow before. An interloper in Zarqa's fortune. But when I lifted my head, he was no longer a mere shadow.

Slitted orange eyes emerged from the darkness. Sensual lips curled on an expertly chiseled face that was at once human and feline, beautiful and deadly. Hair black as the Shroud hung around his face. Despite the dark, his golden skin held a vibrant sheen. Thick muscles strained against silver armor, ancient carvings pressed into the metal.

"Shaya," I breathed. Terror blasted through me.

I dropped my head to the cushiony ground and lay myself prostrate, fighting the pain long enough to gasp out, "Forgive me, God of the Underworld."

Shaya's feet didn't make a sound, but I knew he'd come closer when his voice sounded directly beside me. "Forgive you?" he repeated.

"Yes, I—I took power that was not mine to take. I don't know why I— A moment of madness. I am so sorry. Please, take it back."

He laughed, the sound like boulders tumbling down a mountain. "Do you really believe you could steal from me?"

My brows furrowed. But I could only manage another "Forgive me."

He clucked his tongue. "Get your face off the floor, Samira."

My head jerked up at my name. But of course Shaya knew who I was. He was the God of the Underworld. There was no deception possible with him.

"Stand up."

Swallowing hard, I obeyed. My knees shook so terribly, I nearly fell right back down.

The god towered over me by at least a foot if not more. I'd seen his likeness all over Khada Palace and in the figurine in Rade's room. And yet my mind struggled to process it here and now. Right in front of me.

He'd come to punish me, to send me to the Trench. Every worst fear I'd ever had, everything I'd spent my whole life working against, was about to—

"Honestly, Daughter, get a hold of yourself. Your fear reeks."

I stared up at him, the world around me going quiet. "What . . . what did you call me?"

His slitted eyes gleamed. "You stole nothing from me, Samira Makara. The power was yours to take. Because you are my daughter."

I hadn't heard my surname in so long, I had forgotten it. But the moment he said it, it was like a bell ringing in my brain. That was my name. That was *my name*. Samira Makara. That was who I was.

But his daughter? That I most certainly was not.

"No. No, Amunet Khada is—"

"Amunet Khada is no one," Shaya interrupted. "A contingency plan. No longer needed, now that I have you back." He put a finger under my chin and tilted my head so that I was met with the full force of those feline eyes. "They tried to hide you from me, my daughter. But I never gave up my search. Now here you are."

My breaths came faster, power roiling in my veins. An alien feeling. All of this was alien.

Amunet Khada was Shaya's daughter, not me.

But my qareen had orange eyes. Not brown. Orange. Just like Shaya's. Now so did I. And I had green runes. Not black or even red. *Green*.

Rade had felt something when our runes touched. And Keir smelled something on them.

Out of fire were you born . . . Shaya commanded fire, ruled over an entire realm of it. *Out of water were you found* . . . I'd gone through a waterfall to find my qareen and take this power.

Oh gods.

"There is much you have forgotten about yourself, Samira. I want to help you remember. If you'll let me." He released my chin and said, "Let me show you the truth." He held out his hand. He'd said something similar before. *You do not know yourself. Let me show you.*

And just like then, I felt an irresistible urge to take his hand. What he said was impossible, unthinkable.

But.

If it was true . . .

Shaya's face softened. "Why did you kill your qareen, Samira?"

I blinked at the sudden change in subject. Part of me didn't want to answer, didn't want to think about the killing at all. "I don't know."

"Yes, you do."

"It was— The Merging required—"

"That's not why, Samira."

I shook my head as the pain inside me flared, and I found myself gasping, "She wouldn't stop crying. I wanted her to stop crying. To stop being so weak. Always so scared and so, *so* weak." Horrible guilt rose up inside me. What sort of monster was I to think such a thing?

"Because you saw your weakness reflected in her, and you hated it."

My eyes flew up to his.

Shaya's jaw was tense, anger making flames lick along the edges of his orange irises. But the anger was not directed at me. "You are the daughter of a god. Daughter of an Uncreated. You should *never* have had to feel weak." He spat the words with ferocity. "I lost you, my only daughter, and I failed you. But I vow to you, I will never allow you to feel that way again. All that I do will be to restore you to the mighty being that you are. Let me show you how strong you can be." He held his hand out more insistently.

I stared, heart beating too fast.

I was sick of being afraid and alone. I wanted to be strong, wanted it with a desperation that staggered me.

If I said yes now, maybe *I* would have the ability to save Kaldfold and Ashorah, save everyone, *and* never have to be scared again.

Greed destroys, greed burns.

It was easy for someone to condemn greed who had never known *nothing*. No money, no real home, no friends or family, no power or agency of any kind.

I didn't want that life anymore. I hadn't wanted it for quite some time.

I ignored the warning of Zarqa's fortune and took Shaya's hand.

It wasn't fire or pain that flooded me then. It was air. Like I had been starved of oxygen until that very moment, and with one gasp, I pulled in all of it. All the air that ever existed. Refreshing and electric and alive. It filled my lungs, spread to the very tips of my fingers and toes, and stoppered that void that had opened up in the Eye of Ketet.

Power. That was what it was. Strength and power. *My* power.

And as more of it flowed into me, I could feel my fear slipping away until the emotion was so foreign, I could hardly believe I'd spent so much of my life feeling it.

"Let us help each other, Daughter." Shaya's smile glinted with pride.

Keir was still fighting his qareen. Rade was still lost to the Mirror Realm. The Shroud was still a threat.

Yet when I looked up at Shaya, my lips curled into a smile identical to his. I gripped my father's hand tighter and let him lead me into the darkness.

ACKNOWLEDGMENTS

It is impossible to convey just how singularly incredible it is to be holding a physical collection of my words. Like most authors, I wrote quite a bit before making it to this point, and grew so accustomed to having my words remain intangible on my computer. But now they're here! You're holding them! I'm holding them! We're holding them! And I have so very many people to thank for that.

First and foremost, my warrior queen agent, Jenna Satterthwaite. In a world of nos, you are always my enthusiastic, supportive, and brilliant yes. Every single day, I am grateful that you decided to take a chance on me and my story about Ancient Egypt but also Vikings but also magic but also romance. You have made dipping my toes into the publishing world fun and seamless, which is not easy. You are a force of nature, a hard worker, and an all-around wonderful human being. Thank you for all you have done for me and *The Shrouded Queen*, and thank you to the entire Storm Literary Agency team, who have worked tirelessly with me!

Thank you to my acquiring editor, Abby Zidle. You went to bat for my novel, and without you, I would not be here. This book exists because of you, and I am so beyond grateful for that, as well as for your vision and feedback. Thank you to my editor, Ghjulia Romiti, and to my storytelling mastermind, Ali Chesnick. I never thought a three-hour video call about edits could be so fun until working with you, and I so appreciate your genius feedback and thoughtful approach to my book. You have helped make it so much stronger than I could have ever imagined. An enormous thank-you to everyone at

Gallery Books—who have blessed me with such a gorgeous cover, amazing communication, and outstanding work.

Thank you to Megan Plank, who gave the vomit draft of this book thoughtful page-by-page notes. You will forever be my first call for feedback. That's probably not what you signed up for when you decided to be my friend, but it's too late for you to back out now.

Thank you also to Sophie, Claire, Susan, and Micah, who all read different iterations and offered notes that strengthened it bit by bit.

Thank you to Bianca, Amshu, and Jade, who were there every step of the way, were constantly excited for me, and were given the unasked-for task of being my fresh set of eyes on my book. Sorry I made you wait, but I hope it was worth it! Thank you to Ashley, for being my bestie for over a decade and for nearly falling out of your chair when I told you I was *finally* getting published.

Thank you so, so much to my parents, who have lifted me up all my life and only ever encouraged me. Without you, I would never have thought this could be a real career. I love you!

To my Teta and Papa, who have instilled in me a love of reading and history: I know you asked for a great-grandchild, but I hope this placeholder suffices for now.

To the rest of my family, who have wished the best for me and been my cheerleaders, I love you so very much.

And lastly but most importantly, thank you to you, the reader. As a reader myself, whose brain is combusting at being on the other side of this page, I know how precious our books are, how much I value their escape and their heart, and I hope that I have managed to offer you a small bit of that with *The Shrouded Queen*. Whether you've followed me from my Wattpad years (I say with my full chest) or have just picked me up, I am humbled and truly grateful. Thank you, thank you, thank you!